About the author

Born and raised in San Francisco, Grant relocated to Southern California to pursue a career in television. He spent the next forty years writing and producing such shows as *MacGyver, Star Trek: The Next Generation, Lois & Clark, The Outer Limits, Eureka, Lost Girl and Bitten.*

Gideon is his debut novel.

Grant now lives in Central Oregon with his wife Marjorie and their yellow Lab, Buddy.

GIDEON

Grant Rosenberg

GIDEON

Pegasus

A CIP catalogue record for this title is
available from the British Library

ISBN-978 1 910903 50 6

*Pegasus is an imprint of
Pegasus Elliot MacKenzie Publishers Ltd.*
www.pegasuspublishers.com

First Published in 2020

**Pegasus
Sheraton House Castle Park
Cambridge CB3 0AX England**

Printed & Bound in Great Britain

Dedication

To my mother, who encouraged me to write at an early age.

To my wife, who encouraged me to write
at a much, much older age.

Acknowledgements

First and foremost, my eternal thanks to my wife Marjorie. Not only did she provide unflagging encouragement, moral and grammatical support and keen editorial suggestions, she also took over the never-ending chore of feeding, walking and housebreaking a rambunctious four-month-old puppy, allowing me time to write.

I owe a big thanks to my family: the Monaghan clan, for reading early drafts and giving me a collective thumbs-up; and to my three daughters, Laura-Lee, Elizabeth and Megan, who stuck with me through the tumultuous times and whose diverse personalities combined to inspire a complex and multi-faceted female protagonist.

To Dr James Guadagni, who helped me with the medical details, James Foley, who shed light on the intricasies of the California health system and to Jack Minkel and Wayne Svilar, whose help with police procedures and gang details were indispensable. Any errors in those areas are strictly mine.

To my many friends who read an early draft and believed in me: Jim Remensperger, Dave Richardson, Chris Condit, Clain Campagna, Cheryl Abel, Sue Edwards, Garner Simmons and David Cornue. Your contributions were much appreciated.

To two authors that I deeply respect and consider friends: Dean Koontz and Thomas Perry. After all these years, I can finally return the favor and send a novel to them.

To all of the amazing people at Pegasus Publishing who brought me into their family and worked diligently to produce what you're holding in your hands.

And, finally, to the memory of my parents. They raised, nurtured and loved me unconditionally… and gave me the great gift of being born and raised in San Francisco.

GIDEON
PROLOGUE

The house was an eyesore. It was the kind of house that kids passed by on Halloween. That is, if kids trick-or-treated in this neighborhood, which they didn't. Weather beaten paint peeled away from cracked stucco. Tarpaper showed through missing roof shingles, and the lawn was a desiccated memory. Surrounded by the obligatory chain link fence, the only things missing to complete the stereotype were a battle-scarred Pit Bull snarling at passers by and neglected piles of fly-infested feces. The eight-hundred-square-foot teardown was picked up in a foreclosure sale for just under $100,000, which, given the proximity to San Francisco, seemed like a steal.

Then again, the fact that it was located just off International Boulevard in one of the most dangerous neighborhoods in East Oakland, the price seemed a little on the high side. The residential block featured Chevys left to rust on front lawns, cramped houses where extended families took up all available floor space and spilled out into the yard with their hand-rolled smokes and 40s, and well-documented violence.

Oakland was carved up by at least a dozen offshoots of the Crips, but this area was property of the 38th Street Locos, a violent Hispanic gang that dealt drugs, ran prostitutes and occasionally killed rivals. Most of the cinderblock walls, storefronts and rotting billboards were treated like blank canvases for the Locos' ubiquitous tags. Oddly, one of the homes that had somehow escaped the gang's graffiti was the crappy little chain-linked eyesore.

The interior of the house was a depressing reflection of its outer shell. What marginally passed for a carpet was threadbare and stained with mysterious blots whose origins were too disgusting to dwell upon. It was a forensic fiesta of molds and carcinogenic spores. The once white walls were permanently coated a sickly yellow from years of smoke (tobacco and otherwise), and the furniture was a notch below the castoffs reclaimed from front yards of equally dilapidated homes. Liberal applications of duct tape were the only things keeping the furniture from disintegrating into heaps of rotted wood, frayed fabric and toxic cotton wadding.

The current tenant fit perfectly into this suburban nightmare; a glassy eyed, chain-smoking, two-time loser who bore a striking resemblance to an aged, road company version of Jeff Spicoli. He was known as 'Baby', a nickname he detested, which only prompted people to use it repeatedly.

When Baby was fifteen, he decided to get a tat "to show the world just how fucking cool" he was. After weeks of surfing the net for ideas and exotic designs, he came up with "Iceman". It was perfect. *He was chill. He was dangerous. He could hook you up.* The problem was, he was none of those things, so when he showed off the new ink (done in black 'Original Gangsta' font) that ran from his shoulder to his elbow, his schoolmates instantly started chanting, "Ice, Ice Baby" from the lamest *faux*-rap song ever. That quickly got shortened to "Baby", and the moniker stuck.

Baby was in his late twenties, but a steady diet of Marlboro Reds, bottom-shelf booze and myriad illegally obtained pharmaceuticals gave him the sallow appearance of a man in his forties. Like his house, he was weather-beaten and missing a few teeth, the result of his chronic crack habit. He lived day-to-day, hour-to-hour, taking life one score at a time.

Years ago, Baby had worked in the family business, but the only thing he could be counted on was his unreliability. That didn't sit well with his father, who oversaw a multi-faceted operation and had reluctantly taken his son in to keep peace with his wife. Baby desperately wanted to make his father proud, but there were two major impediments to that storybook fantasy: one, Baby was a fuck-up; and two, his father scared the crap out of him. Baby grew up believing theirs was a normal father/son relationship. When he found out that his friends didn't cower when their fathers came home from work, he just assumed their fathers were pussies.

Baby had a lot of issues, one of which was a proclivity toward sudden irrational violence. Whether this was due to his upbringing, his chronic ingestion of brain-cell-killing opiates, his total disdain for social mores, or just bad genetics, he was simply too unstable to be trusted with even the most mundane aspects of the job.

He exhausted the last ounce of familial tolerance the day he was sent to collect money from Johnny Simons, a long-time employee with gnarled, arthritic hands and a painfully curved spine. Johnny had worked for Baby's father for three decades, and even though he was a minor player, he was reliable as a Rolex. It just so happened that on this day, Johnny was a few hundred bucks short on a $4,500 payoff because he'd used the money to buy some medication for his diabetic wife. He swore to make up the rest the following week, with some juice, but Baby was terrified to go back to his father with a short envelope, so he did what any homicidal psycho would do. He snapped, and proceeded to beat Johnny with a tape-wrapped length of pipe, breaking Johnny's arm, shattering his orbital bone and splintering a couple ribs.

To keep the peace, the father paid Johnny's hospital bill (which ran into five figures), made a generous cash settlement to his wife and family, and informed all of his associates that his crazy-ass son would no longer be a problem.

Baby was cut out of the business until he could manage to get his shit together. He was dumbstruck. What the fuck did he do wrong? His father could only shake his head in wonderment; how could he possibly have spawned this idiot?

Baby had no choice but to accept the mandate. It was either banishment or a short ride out to the wetlands. He was exiled to the house in East Oakland and ordered to keep a low profile. Maybe one of these days he'd clean up his act and prove his worth to the family. It was an extremely unlikely prospect, but Baby lived in hope.

He vowed that he'd cut out the drugs (okay, cut down on the drugs) and eventually make his way back to the family. That was almost a year ago, and he had given up that pretense by day two. Baby got a monthly "allowance" from his cousin, who was the only friend he had. In return, Baby did occasional favors for his cousin, oftimes exercising his violent nature. As far as Baby was concerned, he'd proven himself over and over. He'd even killed for the family, and in his mind that meant he was a "made man". In reality, that only made him a bigger liability.

Baby's cousin was late with this month's cash. In fact, Baby hadn't heard from him for a few weeks, but Baby didn't worry. He'd show. He always did. In the meantime, Baby had his pizzo (glass meth pipe) and his 65-inch flat screen. With access to seven channels of ESPN, HBO and an extensive collection of porn, he'd get by.

Baby thumbed his disposable Bic, put the flame to the bowl of his pipe, and took a deep hit of smoke that had the aroma of burning plastic. His eyes lost focus and his brain swam in turgid waters. This was quality shit and gave him an immediate intense high. For a moment, Baby thought about calling Sherri to see if she wanted to party. Like all of "his women", Sherri was a crack whore who'd perform any perverse act in exchange for a few tokes of rock. But he was quickly coming down and the thought of having Sherri passed out on his sofa while he was trying to watch a football game turned him off the idea. Last time she was there, she puked all over his classic throwback Raiders' jersey.

He took a long pull from a lukewarm sixteen-ounce Bud and contemplated reloading his oil burner, when he heard a car pull to a stop outside.

Baby snapped his head around. Paranoia struck deep even when he wasn't blazed, but when he was riding the dragon his mind was a nest of insane rats running for shelter from the Orkin Man.

He lunged for the sofa and jammed his hand down between the sagging cushions, desperately searching, but all he came up with was a broken cigarette, a crumbled dollar bill and something that might have once been a French fry. A second wave of panic washed over him as he tried to remember what he did with his piece.

This sudden anxiety was due to him not fulfilling the arrangement that he had with Juan "Looney" Chavez, the 38th Street Locos boss. For a few 8-balls of coke each month, the gang left Baby alone as long as he didn't traffic in their 'hood. Unfortunately, Baby had binged and snorted the most recent payment. To compound the issue, Looney wasn't known for his benevolence when it came to extending credit. The irony of Baby's situation was glaringly obvious, which made it all the more inconceivable that it never crossed his feeble mind.

A car door slammed. Shit, shit, shit! Where the fuck was his goddamn gun?

The knock on the door literally made him jump, and a few drops of urine leaked from his shriveled penis, dotting his jeans. His thoughts were jumbled, his heart racing. Where the hell was…?

Behind the sofa! Last night he dropped it behind the sofa! The second knock on the door was more persistent. Baby frantically shoved the couch out of the way, and there it was: the Glock he bought off a homeless guy last month in the Home Depot parking lot. The moment Baby wrapped his nicotine-stained fingers around the well-worn grip, he was flush with a confidence he otherwise lacked. If they wanted to fuck with him, he'd kill the cocksuckers. Screw these bangers trying to strong-arm him. He'd had enough of their shit.

He was the *Iceman.*

Baby sidled over to the door and noticed his hand was shaking uncontrollably. Despite a desire to sound tough and in command, the noise from his throat came out like Barney Fife asking Thelma Lou to a barn dance.

"Who is it?"

From the other side of the door came the voice of a teenage boy going through puberty, "Delivery from the Golden Palace."

Food! Suddenly, Baby was starving. He was about to throw the door wide open when he stopped to think. Did he order food? Was this a trick? Could it be Looney? Cops? Feds? Anyone could be standing out there. Just then, a brilliant idea crept into his addled mind. "Leave it on the porch."

"You owe fourteen fifty-six."

Shit! What now? Maybe fire a few rounds through the door. He looked at the gun in his sweaty hand and had a flash of realization – he'd never even fired it. He didn't know if it worked. Fuck! Why was he having those lucid thoughts now? He liked it better when his mind was a smoke-filled cockpit with no one sitting at the controls.

He slunk over to the window and parted the grimy blinds. From this angle he couldn't see the porch, but he got a clear look at the dented Toyota Tercel parked at the curb. No self-respecting banger would drive a piece of shit like that, and it definitely wasn't wheels for a Fed.

Another knock was followed by the teen's chirpy voice, "Hey, mister. Do you want the food or not?" Baby caught a faint whiff of garlic and peppers and he began salivating like a Bernese Mountain Dog about to tear into a raw steak.

The hell with it. If someone out there wanted to kill him bad enough, he may as well face it head-on. That would be better than starving to death, right?

He opened the door a crack and was immediately relieved to see a skinny, pimply faced kid named Sherman Berger, wearing a Golden Palace tee-shirt and holding a greasy brown take-out bag.

"You okay, mister?"

As Baby dug into his pocket, Sherm caught a glimpse of the Glock in his other hand and the color drained from Sherm's face.

Baby held out a few crumbled bills. Sherm took the cash as Baby grabbed the bag and slammed the door.

Sherm attended College Prep High School in Oakland and had only recently started working as a delivery boy for the restaurant. Despite the fact his parents lived in Piedmont and were loaded, Sherm was doing this job at their urging to teach him about the "real world" and make his own money for college. This was his first trip into East Oakland, and if it was any indication of what the rest of the summer held in store for him, Sherm was willing to forego college altogether. Ten dollars an hour, plus mileage, wasn't worth getting shot.

He smoothed out the bills in his hand. Two fives. This wasted crack-head stiffed him almost five bucks, not to mention a tip. Sherm would have to make up the balance out of his own pocket. He had a fleeting thought of knocking on the door and demanding the rest of the cash, but his parents hadn't raised a fool.

As he turned and walked away, he muttered "asshole" under his breath. If he had any guts he would've screamed it aloud, but Sherm was blessed with an innate sense of self-preservation. So instead, he quickened his pace, leapt into his Tercel and angrily peeled away from the curb.

Crack generally leads to a loss of appetite, but when you forget to eat for a few days and the sticky aroma of garlic chicken fills your nostrils, your stomach takes charge and commands your brain to override the drug-dulled synapses and get some sustenance into your body.

Baby flopped back onto the sofa, ripped open the bag and pulled out the container of chicken. There was a superfluous set of chopsticks (who the fuck used chopsticks anyway?) in the bag, along with a plastic fork. He grabbed the fork and greedily shoveled a mouthful of steaming food into his meth-blemished maw.

The first taste was heaven. The combination of salty, garlicky, sweet and sour was unbeatable. Suddenly, the future seemed brighter. His cuz had given him assurances that things were looking up. In the last few months there'd been some reorganization within the family business, and Baby was confident that if he stayed in his cousin's good graces, he'd be welcomed back from this hellhole anytime now. Back to an unending supply of quality drugs, booze and babes. No more crack whores. No more scratching around for kibbles and bits. He'd get a new pad, a new ride, sharp threads. The *Iceman* returneth.

Baby had barely swallowed when he crammed another large forkful into his mouth. As he chewed, something suddenly felt wrong. He didn't understand what was happening as a wave of "oh, shit" washed over him.

He forced down the food in one mammoth, painful gulp and then a strange look crossed his face – an expression somewhere between awareness and panic.

Baby dropped the carton of chicken, grabbed his ever-present beer and chugged the warm brew, but he was having trouble swallowing. The beer sloshed down the front of his shirt.

He lurched to his feet, clutching at his throat. He stared wide-eyed at the chunks of chicken, red peppers and garlic that were strewn on the floor. What the fuck was going on? He'd eaten the same food from the same restaurant every week. What the hell was different? Why was his goddamned throat closing up?

Baby staggered into the kitchen on wobbly legs that were on the verge of collapse. A helpless marionette dancing on frayed wires.

A large window in the kitchen faced out to the street, and Baby shot a look in that direction to see if the delivery kid was still there. Maybe *he* could explain what the fuck was going on.

The street was deserted.

Baby's breath grew more jagged and more sporadic. He sucked hard at the stale air to no effect. His face grew increasingly red from lack of oxygen.

He lunged at a cupboard above the sink and ripped it open. He swept away cans of Chef Boyardee Ravioli and Dinty Moore Beef Stew that were long past their "use by" dates. There was nothing else in the cupboard, with the exception of some hardened mouse turds.

Baby spun around and made a desperate grab for the cabinet over the stove, tearing the door off its cheap hinges. His head was swimming and he was on the verge of collapse. He raked a stack of chipped Melmac dishes clattering to the floor and there, in the back of the cabinet, was the treasure he sought. His EpiPen.

He barely had enough coordination left to tear the EpiPen from its box. Summoning up every last ounce of strength in his pathetic body, Baby took in one last massive ragged wheezing breath, and jammed the needle into his thigh.

This would be a close call, but Baby had beaten death. He even managed a slight, pain-twisted smile, knowing that his windpipe would open in a few seconds and the sweet taste of oxygen would fill his lungs. But nothing happened. No rush of air. No relief.

What the fuck? He jabbed himself again, and again, to no avail.

Now in a full-on crisis, his only hope was to call 911. It meant cops or the fire department or paramedics arriving and finding his drugs, *and* his gun, but he had no choice. All that mattered was getting help fast. He needed was his phone. Where the hell was it?

Baby turned back to the living room to see the phone sitting on the coffee table right next to his pizzo. It was only twenty-five feet away, but to Baby it may as well have been on a distant shore.

His will to live even this shitty life was strong and it propelled him to his feet. He stumbled toward the coffee table, but only got as far as the window when his legs gave out.

He grabbed hold of the blinds to keep his balance, but his weight snapped the cheap mooring and the blinds ripped from the wall.

Baby slammed forward, his face flattened up against the window. He fought unsuccessfully to take in one more breath, and as he did, he saw the curtains in the house across the street close. Was there someone watching?

He mouthed the word "help". Did they see him?

He'd never know.

1

The San Francisco Mission District, known to locals as simply "The Mission", had a long, rich history. After James Marshall found that first gold nugget at Sutter's Mill in 1848, the west coast of California exploded and people poured in from every corner of the world. People looking to make a buck, steal a buck or simply have an excuse to get on a boat or covered wagon and head out to the shiny new Eden known as San Francisco. As if the attraction of becoming an overnight millionaire wasn't enough, enterprising hucksters offered bull and bear fighting, dueling, horse racing, round-the-clock prostitutes (complete with every STD known to man and some heretofore unknown) and all the cheap booze you could drink before going blind or insane.

Come for the gold, stay for the party. Start a new life or die trying.

During those years, the Mission was a landing place for working class Italians, Germans and Irish who flocked into the area en masse, establishing communities with their own churches, ethnic eateries and, of course, jingoistic bars catering to like-minded drinkers. In the 1940s, the Mission got a south-of-the-border makeover when a massive influx of Hispanics arrived. This set off a white flight, with most of the Europeans fleeing the city and establishing new ethnocentric communities in the surrounding suburbs.

The 1960s saw a new wave of immigrants, this time from Nicaragua, El Salvador and Guatemala. The roots of Central American/Latino culture took hold in the Mission and their influence was evident by the stores, restaurants and the abundance of colorful murals that adorned the buildings and alleyways. The artworks depicted everything from the Nicaraguan revolution and the Guatemalan civil war, to the celebration of Chicano traditions, music and everyday life.

In more recent times, the Mission underwent the inevitable beginning of gentrification that came with the burgeoning wealth created by the tech industry. While Pacific Heights and The Marina were already the established playgrounds of the uber wealthy, those neighborhoods of doctors, lawyers and titans of business were deemed too stodgy for the *nouveau riche*. Instead, the soul-patched hipsters gravitated to the trendier Mission because it was still "raw".

Most of these newcomers had no idea exactly how "raw" it was. Despite the influx of money, much of the Mission was a haven for undocumented immigrants and a melting pot of families from Mexico, South America and Asia. Plus, there was an unending stream of gang activity that showed no signs of slowing down in the foreseeable future. It was Norteños versus Soreños, Red versus Blue, forever clawing for territory and making inroads a half a block at a time, before triggering a firefight that made the streets of the Mission momentarily take on the fury of Fallujah.

The Mission Street Clinic was located in one of those pockets that hadn't yet been tapped by the magic wand of gentrification (or as some of the locals called it, "doucheification"). The clinic shared a block with Machu Picchu, a Peruvian restaurant that had been robbed twice at gunpoint, a Korean fluff and fold which had been vandalized half a dozen times, and Bobby's Quik Stop, a liquor store owned by the Juarez brothers from Oaxaca, Mexico. Bobby's was temporarily closed until the completion of the pending arson investigation and identification of the corpse of a twenty-three-year-old Asian man found in the ashes. Rumors abounded that the brothers Juarez were back in Oaxaca, their dreams of owning a business in the Los Estados Unidos a faded memory.

The clinic was one of the few buildings on the block that went without incident, despite the fact they kept an ample supply of medicinal opiates on hand. It's often said the safest place to live in New York is on the same block as the Columbus Citizens Foundation (aka the Guido Club). No one's going to mess with anyone in the middle of mob territory. The same general idea held true here – bangers from both the Norteños and the Sureños declared the clinic off limits because the caregivers who worked there selflessly served their community and never turned anyone away, regardless of gang affiliations.

The exterior of the building was graced with a stunning mural painted by Nico Barnes, a renowned local artist who owed his life to the folks inside. Nico had traveled to Haiti on a charity mission to teach art to young students (and to hook up with the hospitality hostess at the Abaka Bay Resort – charity missions can only fulfill so much of the soul). He returned stateside with a tan, a tattoo of a Caribbean enchantress stitched across his shoulders, and a severe case of leptospirosis.

When Nico stumbled into the clinic, his skin had yellowed and his kidneys were shutting down. The doctors quickly diagnosed the ailment and successfully stopped its spread. For the next two weeks, Nico was treated daily as an outpatient. Once his strength returned, he began painting the mural, which took him the better part of a month. It depicted a kindly gray-haired, white-coated doctor standing alongside a beautiful young blonde physician with jade green eyes and a stethoscope draped around her graceful neck. The two doctors appeared Christ-like as they watched over a long line of multi-ethnic patients who streamed in one door of the clinic on crutches or appendages in slings, and then miraculously strode out through another door in the pique of health. The mural wasn't quite New Testament, but it was a more positive recommendation than a Yelp review.

The Mission Street Clinic was not a typical urgent care operation. Open Monday-Saturday from 9am to 9pm, it was a hybrid facility that had the appearance of a small hospital emergency room. The well-worn waiting area featured plastic chairs (easier to sterilize at the end of the night), a few fake potted Ficus trees (the real ones hadn't lasted for more than a month), and the usual "No Smoking" and "Please Turn Off Cell Phones" signs, as well as an ironic "No Loitering" sign. This was one place where hanging out for up to an hour was not a form of loitering. And as diligently as the staff worked to move patients through, a long wait was frequently the unfortunate result of over-demand versus understaffing.

A counter of aging Formica was the line of demarcation between the waiting area and the treatment area that lay beyond a sickly green-colored wall. Over the years they'd tried different colors on that wall, but the traditional pale green seemed the least obtrusive and most soothing. The counter was the domain of a thickset woman named Ramona Vargas, a Dominican transplant who prided herself on her efficiency, intensity and peacekeeping abilities. The latter was a role she embraced with vigor and enthusiasm.

A story was still told in hushed tones; it was a tale about two rival gang members who were waiting to be treated for wounds. Heavily tatted thugs decked out in their reds and blues. Seething looks across the waiting room soon turned to verbal taunts that disparaged the legality of each other's parentage. Ramona could not, and would not, abide.

Before the taunts could escalate and one of these bangers did something incredibly anti-social, like yank a nine from his sock, Ramona vaulted (yes, vaulted) over the counter, grabbed both lads by their grimy napes and hauled their asses outside, leaving behind a waiting room full of stunned patients with "did that just happen?" looks on their faces.

A few moments later, Ramona marched these two back in. The bangers were clearly in more pain now than when they'd first arrived. With a cold glare that would've turned Ulysses to stone, she firmly planted them in seats next to each other, ordered them to "sit and stay". And they did, squirming in torturous silence until they were called to be treated.

As time went by, no one was really sure if the apocryphal event was fact or an urban myth that may have been started by Ramona herself. A lot of people claimed to have been there and seen it, while others called it bullshit, but the veracity of the story was a non-issue. No one had misbehaved in this waiting room for many years now. However, that wasn't to say that there weren't some notable characters. Two in particular stood out.

There was Moaning Myrtle. A waifish middle-aged woman with a pronounced Eastern European accent that only made her high-pitched whiney voice all the more grating. Moaning Myrtle (as she was dubbed due to her incessant complaining about phantom diseases) came in two or three times a week, recounting her most recent aches and pains. At first, the doctors didn't know if she was hypochondriacal or conniving. After a few visits, it became obvious.

Faking symptoms to acquire pharmaceuticals was a common occurrence in hospitals and clinics. Known as "frequent flyers" or "Oxy-Cons", doctors and nurses were savvy to these ruses, but had to be careful not to turn away someone who was genuinely in need of medical assistance. One ER doctor at SF General had refused treatment to a thirty-year-old man who he deemed to be nothing more than a "bad actor". The man died a short time later and his family sued the doctor and the hospital. It was easier to give these patients a cursory exam and prescribe some over-the-counter painkillers than to risk a lawsuit.

Myrtle had taken her ersatz afflictions to operatic heights and was well known throughout the city as a fraud. It wasn't long before the hospitals and clinics kept her on ice in the waiting room for hours. The downside of that tactic was she drove the real patients crazy. The upside was she eventually got the message and moved away, taking her one-woman show to another city.

And then there was The Hollow Man. A confused and wide-eyed homeless soul who wandered in, bringing with him a sense of sadness and desperation, as well as a stench that combined acute body odor with the fragrances of wet dog and spoiled milk. His hands were badly scarred from old burns, as was the side of his face. The waiting patients recoiled from his repugnant aura, but Ramona waved him up to the front desk and politely attempted to obtain some basic information. All the man would say, in a voice that sounded like a rusty gate hinge, was that Dr Harper had removed his heart and now he was hollow inside. He needed to see the doctor to make things right.

Ramona tried to calm him down, but the man became progressively more agitated. The situation quickly intensified as if a fire was suddenly ignited inside this troubled burnt man. Ramona played her wild card, threatening to call the police. The Hollow Man (as he was later christened) abruptly turned tail and fled.

He reappeared every day the following week and went through the same litany, and with each visit he got bolder. At first he requested to see Dr Harper. By Day Four, he demanded it. On his final visit, he was completely out of control, ranting about how hell's fury would rain down upon them all. When the doctors came charging into the waiting room to see what the commotion was all about, Ramona kicked into high gear. This was her domain and his behavior was not acceptable!

She stormed around the counter, steam rising off her head, and The Hollow Man's inherent desire to experience another sunrise kicked in. He bolted, wildly sprinting down the block, never to be seen again.

2

The central treatment area in the clinic was comprised of six curtained medical bays, and there was rarely a time when all of the bays weren't being used. The medical equipment was state-of-the-art back when Clinton was President. As was the case in most underfunded private clinics, the majority of the equipment was refurbished second- or third-hand and came from medical supply rental companies. The machinery got the job done, but was strictly designed for basic diagnosis and triage. Any sophisticated procedures were best done at a full-service hospital. Bottom line: you could get patched up at the Mission Street Clinic, but it wouldn't be your first choice for a kidney transplant or coronary bypass.

The clinic was currently staffed by four physicians, two nurses and a medical assistant, and they treated a wide variety of ailments, including: broken bones, lacerations, animal bites, allergic reactions, drug overdoses and gunshots. They prided themselves on forming personal relationships with the community, and as a result the care they provided was all-encompassing and administered with passion. The MSC wasn't exactly a throwback to simpler times when people came in to see the local doc and paid their bills with farm-fresh eggs and recently slaughtered chickens, but it was the closest thing the Mission had to doctors who cared more about their patients' wellbeing than how quickly Blue Cross would send them a check.

Doctor Kelly Rose Harper (whose face loomed on the outside of the building, much to her dismay) was a brilliant young physician. At the tender age of 33, she'd only been practicing as a licenced doctor for five years, but she'd fully immersed herself during her four years of Medical School at UC Davis and her three years of residency at Mass General (in conjunction with the Harvard Med Fellowship Program). During her stint in Boston she specialized in Emergency Room medicine, and by the time she came back to California, she operated like a seasoned pro.

Kelly had gotten an early start toward her medical education. Her father (the kindly gray-haired man in the mural) had been a renowned surgeon and she'd spent much of her childhood hanging out in hospitals, doing her homework in the break rooms and quietly (and contrary to hospital rules) standing in the shadows of the ORs, perched on her tiptoes to watch with fascination as the steadfast doctors and nurses worked tirelessly to patch up the stream of mangled masses who came through the swinging doors.

Slim, blonde and beautiful, Kelly turned heads when she walked down the street, but unlike most other women her age, she didn't work on it. If anything, she worked against it. Dr Harper was the epitome of function over style. When she was at the clinic, her hair was pulled back in a ponytail, she wore very little makeup, and dressed in comfortable non-revealing clothing. She adhered to a strictly professional credo and fully embraced the Hippocratic Oath to uphold ethical standards and preserve the traditions of her medical calling.

Kelly could've practiced medicine at any major hospital, but she chose to spend eighty hours a week at this cramped, cluttered clinic, sharing her gifts with the people in the Mission district. And every once in a while she'd have a patient who, for whatever reason, came rolling in from the more upscale parts of town.

Patients like Tara Epstein, the seventeen-year-old who lay prone on the exam table, slipping in and out of consciousness. Her $2,500 David Yurman necklace and $800 Valentino Rockstud leather cuffs ostentatiously set her apart from the locals.

As Kelly checked Ms Epstein's reactions to various stimuli, a nurse named Annie Egan made note of her vitals. Annie was a buxom fifty-year-old with flaming red hair who'd come over from Ireland when she was ten years old. The ex-wife of a San Francisco fireman, she spoke with an Irish lilt, had an unquenchable charm, and was well known for her propensity to party late into the night, preferably with men half her age.

The fourth person in the cramped med bay was Tara's friend Paris Papazian, who hadn't stopped sobbing since they'd arrived. Dressed in a Juicy Couture velvet hoodie, Rag and Bone skinny jeans and Yeezy ankle boots, her casual party wardrobe tipped the scale at over two grand, making her also look oh-so-stylish and ridiculously out of place in the inner-city clinic.

"Oh, my god... oh, my god... oh, my god... her mother's gonna shit when she finds out what happened," Paris prattled. "Is Tara gonna die?"

Kelly and Annie exchanged glances, exercising the utmost in tolerance. "Not tonight," Kelly responded. "Where have you two been?" One of the elemental components of diagnosing a patient was getting background information, but prying useable particulars out of teenagers who were high and afraid of parental repercussions was often a difficult proposition.

"Uh, you know. Some party."

"If you want to help your friend, I'm going to need a few more details."

"It was a house party in Cow Hollow. Some guys from USF. They had this sick DJ and one of our friends was cousins with..."

Kelly interrupted her, "If the party was in Cow Hollow, why'd you come all the way over here instead of going to the ER at Kaiser?"

"Someone at the party said that the doctors at Kaiser were kinda tightass and that this place was cool."

Kelly shook her head. "The doctors at Kaiser are extremely professional."

Somewhat chastised, Paris continued, "I didn't mean they were narcs. Just the guys who were having the party didn't want this coming back on them, you know?"

Even though Kelly wasn't that far removed from college parties herself, she was constantly amazed, and distressed, at how the minds of today's teenagers worked. "Were you with Tara the whole time?"

Paris stammered. "Kinda. I mean, not the *whole* time. She looked like she was gonna hook up with this hot guy on the soccer team so she, like, gave me the signal, you know?"

Kelly remained non-judgmental. "I assume there was alcohol and drugs."

She shrugged and nodded, as if to say, "It was a party."

"Darlin'," Annie interjected with a warm Irish smile, "we're not gonna call anyone's parents, but we need to know what Tara ingested if we're gonna help her. We really don't care what you did or who you did it with. We only care about what she put in her mouth."

"Like I said, I wasn't with her the whole time, but she was just having some cocktails. She used to be all into Mike's Hard Lemonade, but lately she's been drinking Jack Daniels Southern Peach."

"I'm not about to lecture you about underage drinking. Lord knows, I did a wee bit of that myself, but if you *are* gonna have a drink, it most definitely shouldn't be Jack Daniels Southern Peach."

Paris brightened up a little. "I know, right? It's like totally gross. I'm strictly Grey Goose and Sprite," she declared with a swell of sophisticated pride.

Kelly looked at the clueless little rich girl and didn't dare venture a guess as to what her SAT scores were. "It looks to me like Tara took some kind of sedative. Maybe a Valium or a Xanax."

Paris shook her head. "She totally wouldn't do that. Her sister is like a Valium freak and Tara rags on her all the time."

"It's possible she took it unintentionally," Kelly said. "Someone could've slipped Rohypnol into her drink."

Paris reacted. "Seriously? Roofies? Those fucking assholes!" Paris caught herself. "Oh, uh, sorry, but I thought those guys looked like D-bags."

Annie handed Kelly a syringe with clear liquid. "This is Flumazenil, which will counteract the sedative."

Kelly injected Tara, and after a few minutes the teen started to come around. Kelly turned to Paris with a penetrating look that conveyed importance. "Listen carefully. Tara needs rest, hydration and someone to stay with her tonight. I'd suggest you take her home and tell her parents everything, but that's up to you. Either way, you need to watch her. If she gets worse, get her to a hospital immediately. Can you handle that?"

Paris nodded gratefully. "For sure. I will. I promise."

Putting the fear of God into hapless teenagers was not an AMA-sanctioned tool, but it rarely failed. "Paris, don't let your friend down."

A look of panic crossed her otherwise vacant face. "I swear, I'll take care of her."

As Annie began filling out a release form, she asked, "How'd you get here? Dear Lord, please tell me you didn't drive."

Paris shook her head as if she'd never dream of doing something so irresponsible. "No way. I get pulled over for an underage DUI, my parents would take away my Beemer in, like, two seconds."

"I know everyone your age loves to party," Kelly said, "but don't put yourself, or your friends, in a position where someone can easily take advantage of you. Tara's lucky you were with her tonight, or else this could've ended in a really bad way. You've got to be more careful out there."

"We thought we were, but some random guy slips something into your drink. I mean, like, what can you do?"

"Keep clear of random guys."

"It's not so easy, doctor. All the guys we hang with are pretty random."

Just then there was a rising din from the admitting area. Never a good sign. Kelly whisked open the curtain surrounding the medical bay to see the tall, lean Doctor Viknesh Danabalan hurrying past, holding a handful of vinyl ice packs.

"Vik. What is it?" Kelly called after him.

Vik answered over his shoulder, "Gunshot victim. Alma Sanchez's son."

Kelly inwardly swore. She knew that one of these days the Sanchez boy would end up on the wrong side of a bullet.

She ran and caught up with Vik. "How bad is Oscar hit?"

"It's not Oscar. It's the younger one, Diego."

Kelly grabbed Vik by the sleeve and stopped him in his tracks. "Are you sure? Diego's only a kid."

Vik hailed from Singapore and spoke with an unaffected Oxford-educated accent. "The gangs indoctrinate them young." Kelly had known the Sanchez family for years and optimistically hoped that Diego wasn't going to follow in the footsteps of his older brothers, but unfortunately the allure of the gang was a powerful siren call for young Hispanics who wanted all the perks that went along with membership. They never thought about the downside, because going to jail or getting shot happened to other people, not to you.

Unless tonight your name was Diego Sanchez.

3

Diego lay on a padded table in the emergency operating area. This room was larger than the medical bays and reserved for patients who needed immediate triage.

Ten years old and reed-thin, he writhed in pain. Despite being taught at an early age to suck it up and never show emotions ("because emotions made you a *chavala*"), tears streamed down Diego's prepubescent face. An IV line had been inserted into his wrist and he was draped with a sheet from his groin to his neck. His pants were cut away, exposing his scrawny, bloody leg. Luckily for Diego, he was in good hands; those of Dr David Harper, the driving force of the clinic.

Dr Harper was just shy of his sixty-fifth birthday, had an enviable full head of steel gray hair and was in excellent health. His penetrating blue eyes were once compared to Paul Newman's, but David's had lost their twinkle almost two decades ago when his wife Mary was killed. Combine that life-altering event with years of treating the sick and dying, and even the most optimistic men grow hard.

Prior to establishing the clinic, David Harper had a distinguished career as the chief surgeon at St Francis Memorial Hospital in San Francisco. Every year he'd take a two-week sabbatical and donate his time to Doctors Without Borders, travelling to impoverished, quake-ravaged or war-torn areas. His well-thumbed passport included stamps from Rwanda, Liberia, Sierra Leone and Sri Lanka. It was David's way of giving back, and truth be told, dealing with real-life crises gave him a much-needed respite from the red tape and politics of a major metropolitan hospital. Despite the filth, the insects and deplorable living conditions, he always came back a stronger, wiser and more focused physician.

While David flew off to the far corners of the globe, his wife held down the fort and looked after the family. Mary Farnsworth-Harper was universally beloved and respected. She'd met David when he was doing his residency and she was clerking for the US District Court of Northern California. Her career in law was as promising as his in medicine, but once they decided to get married she took a leave from work to help support David. She'd always intended to return to the legal profession at a later date, but with the arrival of their first child, Jessica, that intention became progressively smaller and smaller in Mary's rearview mirror of life.

Instead, she threw herself headlong into community service. At one point, Mary was on six different volunteer committees and chaired the local chapters of both The Surfrider Foundation and the Children's Council of San Francisco. While David was on staff at St Francis, she spearheaded fundraising for the Coronary Care Unit renovation.

After Mary tragically died, David stayed on at St Francis, but bowed out of his yearly trek to stay close to home. He had two daughters who'd lost their mother, and David vowed to spend as much time with them as possible.

David's thirteen-year-old daughter Kelly was savvy beyond her years and could take care of herself, but the situation with sixteen-year-old Jessica was far more complicated. Jess was a spitting image of her father, from his cleft chin to his iridescent eyes. She was a gifted student, a superior athlete and had a dynamic personality. From the moment she could wrap her chubby toddler fingers around David's stethoscope, she wanted to be a doctor, "just like Daddy".

Few parents will ever admit they have a favorite child, but it was clear Jessica and her father had a special bond. It became a family joke, because it was equally evident that Kelly and Mary had a simpatico relationship. Fortunately, there was enough love to go around, so no one ever felt slighted.

One man undid that all in less than thirty minutes.

It was a lovely summer day in the city. Jessica had just gotten her driver's license and begged her mother to let her take the car so she and Kelly could go play tennis. Mary was reluctant because there was construction on almost every block in San Francisco, which meant congestion, closures and detours. But she was in the midst of getting the house ready for a fundraising event and was expecting deliveries from the florist and the caterer, so it was easier to relent than to waste time arguing with a headstrong teenager.

When the girls arrived at the court, Kelly realized she'd forgotten to bring the tennis balls. After a few minutes of Jessica questioning her little sister's memory and intelligence, Kelly indignantly offered to jog the two miles home to retrieve the missing balls. Jessica said that was ridiculous (which was the response Kelly was going for). Jess would drive back and Kelly would stay behind to stake their claim to the court.

When Jessica arrived home, she walked in to find a strange man spattered in blood, running down the stairs. She had no idea that this man had just killed her mother. She had no idea that a second later he'd savagely strike her in the head with a lead-filled, sawed-off baseball bat.

From that moment on, Jessica had no ideas at all.

Kelly blamed herself for what happened to Jessica. It was her fault that Jessica had to return to the house and come face-to-face with the demon that killed their mother. It was her fault that Jessica's life was shattered and ended up in a healthcare facility in a semi-vegetative state.

David did everything he could to make Kelly understand she had no hand in the horrible events of that day, but every once in a while she felt that he wished it had been Kelly lying in that bed instead of Jessica. She could see it in his eyes. Those penetrating blue eyes that he shared with her older sister. Kelly's feeling of guilt dissipated somewhat over the years, but hadn't gone completely.

It never would.

After Mary died, Kelly watched her father slip into an uncharacteristic funk and a dangerous routine. Despite his attempts to get closer to his daughter, he became more distant. David had never been more than a social drinker, but Kelly noticed that his scotch consumption increased. She also suspected he was taking valium to help him sleep, as well as some kind of stimulant to help him get through the day. If she didn't snap him out of this cycle, things weren't going to end well.

Kelly confronted him. She knew what her father needed; to get away from it all. The hospital, the police investigation, the ever-deepening hole. Doctors Without Borders needed him, and he needed them. She could fend for herself for a few weeks, and she'd look in on Jess every day. David unequivocally refused. Maybe next year he'd think about it, but not now. The wound was still too fresh, their family's future still too much in flux.

Kelly had inherited Mary's looks and her drive, but David underestimated how much she embraced her mother's stubborn streak. Kelly wouldn't let down, and finally, after much coercion, she convinced her father to take an extended sabbatical. He agreed on one condition: that she came with him.

So while Kelly's friends were spending their summer boating on Lake Tahoe and sunbathing in Maui, she, along with a team of international relief workers, was cooking meals and handing out clothing to people in Sumatra who'd been rocked by a major earthquake. David and a dozen doctors from around the globe worked eighteen-hour shifts doing triage on the sick and the broken. It was like an extended version of M*A*S*H without the punch lines.

After two exhausting, soul-scrubbing weeks, David and Kelly arrived home with new outlooks on life. Kelly had originally set her sights on fulfilling her mother's dream and becoming an attorney (she, at age thirteen, was "leaning toward family law"), but this recent experience made a massive impact upon her and she recalibrated her aspirations. After a long heart-to-heart with her father, where she explained she wasn't trying to tread in Jessica's footsteps, Kelly asked if it would be okay if she became a doctor. David's eyes brimmed with tears of pride and love. Nothing would make him happier.

Nothing except quitting his position at the hospital and opening a neighborhood clinic. His colleagues at St Francis were stunned that he'd throw away his seniority and years of practice as a surgeon. David was equally stunned at their reaction – he wasn't throwing anything away – he was starting something new and important.

Kelly and David mutually supported each other through the new challenges they faced, and along the way the most wonderful thing happened. They not only grew closer as father and daughter; they became friends.

Eighteen years later, David never regretted his decision. He called the shots, paid the bills and took incredible pride in the service they provided. Like his daughter, David was chagrined by the fifteen-foot-high visage of his face on the outside of the building, but the upside was everyone in the neighborhood knew him by sight. He never paid for a drink at any of the local watering holes. Not a one.

As David cleaned Diego's gunshot wound with alcohol, the boy let out a yelp like a puppy nipped by its mother. "Sorry, Diego. It's going to hurt, but we're giving you something for the pain." He turned to a short, dimpled Guatemalan nurse in her late twenties named Sonita. "Add 5ccs morphine to the drip, and he'll need a tetanus shot. And where is Dr Curtis?" he asked with a tinge of annoyance.

"He left about twenty minutes ago."

"Wasn't he scheduled to work tonight?"

"I'm not sure, doctor." Sonita was relatively new to the clinic, and the last thing she wanted was to get tangled up in personnel matters, especially between the doctors. On the other hand, Dr Harper signed her checks and she wasn't going to cover for a doctor who seemed to be on thin ice. Truth be told, Dr Curtis was kind of a *cabrón*.

David wouldn't allow his frustration to affect the work at hand. "Where are those…?"

On cue, Vik and Kelly arrived with the ice packs.

As Vik applied the packs around Diego's calf to slow down the bleeding, Kelly leaned over and watched as her father gently probed Diego's wound. "What've we got?"

"Small caliber through and through. Luckily it missed the arteries."

Kelly laid her hand on Diego's face. "How you doing, big man?"

Diego turned his face away, embarrassed by his tears. Kelly spoke soothingly, "I know it hurts, but it's going to be fine. Plus, you're going to have a wicked scar to show off."

Diego stopped sobbing for a moment. He hadn't thought about the fact that he was going through a rite of passage in the Mission. His first gunshot wound, and only ten years old. His brother Oscar didn't even have a knife wound. It *was* kinda cool.

Vik held Diego's leg as David wrapped it with a sterile dressing and a pressure bandage. Diego winced and drew in a sharp breath as they increased the tension on the wound.

Sonita returned with two hypodermic needles; one loaded with tetanus vaccine, and the other with morphine. Kelly took the tetanus hypo, while Sonita added the morphine to the IV bag.

Vik called out Diego's blood pressure. "BP is 90 over 52."

It was low, but tolerable. "We just gave you something that'll make you sleepy, okay?" David said in a warm, fatherly tone.

Diego nodded. "Okay."

"Doctor Kelly is going to give you a shot so you don't get an infection; understand?"

He nodded, but had obvious trepidation.

As she swabbed Diego's butt cheek, Kelly said, "Diego, this is going to sting a little bit."

"Why does *everything* have to hurt?" he asked pathetically. "This sucks."

Kelly and David shared a look. Out of the mouths of babes.

Without further hesitation, Kelly plunged the needle into Diego's quivering flesh and he let out an involuntary squeal. No one had told him this rite of passage was going be so damn painful.

Diego's howl was only partially muffled by the wall, and out in the waiting area his mother Alma sprang to her feet. "That's Diego! I need to be with him!"

Ramona shook her head. "Doctor Harper asked that you wait here until he called for you."

Alma Sanchez was an obstinate old bird, especially when it came to protecting her brood. She'd moved to the States from Sinaloa thirty years ago after her husband was killed by the Cartel. She'd made her way up the coast of California and settled in San Francisco, where she raised five sons. She never remarried and none of the fathers stuck around, so Alma was on her own. She held down three jobs, and it was only through sheer perseverance that she managed to be there for her kids.

Unfortunately, escaping the Sinaloa Cartel didn't mean her family had escaped "the life". Her oldest son, Rodrigo, was serving a ten-year stretch at Pleasant Valley State Prison in central California for possession with intent to sell, larceny and aggravated assault. Another son, Chavo, died during a weekend of gang violence where five young men were killed. The SFPD reacted by doubling their Gang Task Force and shutting down drug dealing in the neighborhoods for almost a month. Eventually, the furore of that weekend abated, and the police department reshuffled their manpower. Drug dealing resumed and the cops made it a lower priority, as long as violence was kept to "an acceptable minimum". Life on the streets reverted to its former *status quo*.

Of the remaining three Sanchez offspring, Oscar (known as "Spider") was an underboss with the Norteños, Tomas was in a youth correctional facility in Stockton, and then there was Diego. He was the youngest and held the most promise for the future. He was smart and had a kind heart. If Alma could keep him away from the gangs, he might have a chance, but that was a tall order.

Alma was half Ramona's size, but she could hold her own against anyone. "Diego's only a little boy. His mother should be back there with him. You know it."

Ramona puffed out her chest, as if she needed additional bulk to make herself more intimidating. "The Doctor knows how old Diego is, and he knows you're out here. He also knows what's best, so you'll wait."

Alma wasn't ready to back down. "What if that was your boy back there? What would you do?"

"I'd sing the praises of the Lord Almighty, because I've never been able to conceive children," which put an abrupt end to that argument. Ramona softened. "Alma, we need to fill out paperwork. Tell me exactly how this happened."

"I already told you! Diego was over at the Rec Center on 20th and someone drove by and fired guns. He wasn't doing nothing wrong."

"Why didn't you take him to the trauma center at St Francis? It's only a few blocks away from the Rec Center."

"Because you are my doctors."

"You know we have to file a report with the police, just like they do at St Francis."

Alma bristled at the comment. "Even though you disrespect me, I came here because you take care of my children."

Ramona smiled. "Alma, *por favor*. The doctors have great respect for you, but there are rules."

Alma backed down... a little. "Ramona, *por favor*. Tell the doctor I'm not going nowhere until I see Diego."

"Trust me. He knows."

It was ten o'clock when Ramona finally closed the front doors and turned out the lights in the waiting area; one hour later than usual. David liked to get his team out at a decent hour, but once in a while, especially on the weekends, the flow of patients was non-stop, and David had a difficult time turning people away.

As was their tradition, David and Kelly gathered in his small office to recount the day. Vik, Annie, Sonita and Ramona stopped by on their way out.

"Thank you all for staying late," David said gratefully. "I'm sorry we ended up short-handed tonight."

Vik shrugged. "No problem, Doctor. It comes with the job."

"It shouldn't, but I appreciate the sentiment." He turned to Ramona. "Do you think Alma will take Diego to St Francis? I called over and they agreed to see him as soon as he arrives." St Francis Hospital had much more sophisticated equipment and David wanted their team to give Diego a thorough examination before letting him go home.

"No way Alma's gonna take him. She's damn stubborn, that one."

David exhaled a weary sigh. "I can understand it from her point of view. The hospital system's not exactly designed to cater to undocumented immigrants."

A federal law required hospitals to administer emergency services to all patients, but due to these patients' immigration status, the hospitals were not generally reimbursed by Medicaid. As a result, most hospitals performed triage, then cut the patients loose. In recent years hospitals have been much stricter in determining if a patient actually qualifies for "emergency services" before he or she is admitted.

Since private clinics aren't legally bound to treat anyone, many "illegals" that need medical help are often left in the lurch. When David opened the MSC, he vowed not to turn anyone away, which was why the clinic was so popular, so crowded, and constantly on the brink of financial collapse.

"I'll swing by the Sanchez house and check on Diego," Vik said. "Nothing waiting for me at home except leftover chicken tikka."

David shook his head. "You've already put in a long day. Go enjoy your tikka."

"Good night, doctors," said Annie, a smile on her face.

"I know that smile," said Kelly. "Do you have plans tonight?"

"It's Saturday," she said, as if it should be obvious. "Got a Tinder date with a fine looking Jamaican man, and with any luck, it'll carry over to the morning."

Ramona asked the recurring question, "And how old is this one?"

Annie shrugged. "Age is a relative concept, darlin'."

Ramona nodded. "So he's under thirty." Annie responded with a smile. "Twenty-five?" asked Ramona.

"Have a lovely time," said Kelly. "And be careful."

"Ah, don't stay up worrying about me, Doctor. I can take care of myself."

Of that they had no doubt.

After the staff left, David slid open the bottom drawer of the oak desk he purchased secondhand when he opened the clinic. The desk had belonged to his favorite professor at UCSF medical school, and when the professor retired, David acquired it. He could think of no better way to honor his mentor and christen the new clinic.

The drawer still smelled slightly of the tobacco humidor the professor kept secreted there. David used the drawer for a different kind of stash and pulled out a bottle of single malt Clynelish and two glasses.

David cracked open the bottle. "I'll look in on Diego on the way home." He poured one glass and hovered the bottle over the other. "Care to join me?"

Kelly smiled and shook her head. "I should go. I'm meeting Pete in a little while."

"One advantage of dating a cop is you both keep insane hours." He raised the glass to his lips, then hesitated. "You know I hate drinking alone."

"Fine," Kelly gave in. "A small one."

As David poured, Kelly asked, "What are we going to do about Dr Curtis?"

Dr Nathan Curtis came from a very wealthy San Francisco family. Money can make life easier, but it often comes with a caveat. In Nathan's case, his family's fortune infused him with an inflated sense of self-entitlement.

In his late twenties, Nathan had already been dismissed from two medical residencies in the city. David saw something in Nathan and decided to give the young doctor another chance. However, this would be his third and probably final opportunity to prove himself worthy and establish a medical career in San Francisco.

"Nathan has the tools to become a good doctor some day, but he's his own worst enemy. We can't have someone working here who's unreliable. This isn't the first time he's left us short-handed."

Kelly shrugged. "He's got a lot of family issues."

"He's a spoiled rich kid with no sense of responsibility."

"You're being too harsh on him."

"Am I?"

"We both know how tough it is to become a doctor. I was lucky because I had you. From what I hear, Nathan's father is hardly the nurturing type."

"That may be, but we've got a clinic to run, and when he pulls stunts like leaving early, it puts patients' health in jeopardy. I told him last week if he did it again, I'd have to let him go."

"You gave him an ultimatum? How'd he react?"

"How do you think? He's not used to hearing the word 'no'."

"Do me a favor and talk to him to see what's going on before you cut him loose. If he lost this opportunity..." They both knew he'd likely be screwed.

"You were always a nicer person than me. I promise I'll hear him out before I show him the door." He raised his glass. "Enough about him. To Jess."

Kelly clinked his glass. "To Jess." She finished her drink in one swallow.

"Have you been to see her recently?" he asked.

"Last Sunday." Kelly didn't need to sugarcoat her statement and add how good her sister looked or how she was coming along. Things with Jessica never changed. "We're onto *The Prisoner Of Azkaban*."

David smiled. "I saw *The Goblet Of Fire* on her nightstand the last time I was there. Is this your second or third time through the series?"

"Third. She just can't get enough of Hogwarts," Kelly said with a sad smile, knowing that she could be reading *War And Peace* in its original Russian and it would have the same impact on her sister.

David finished his drink and poured another jigger into his glass. He leaned in to refill Kelly's glass and she covered it with her hand.

"We need to toast to your job offer," he said with a smile.

"The job I'm turning down?"

David reacted. "How can you turn it down? Director of Emergency Services is a very prestigious position."

"Complete with red tape, corporate politics and a bottom line mentality."

"You're just looking at the downsides. What about a great salary, wonderful benefits, actual vacation time…?"

"You mean all those things you left behind?"

"We're talking about you."

"Exactly, and you need me here. Especially if you're going around firing the rest of the staff."

David replied with a grin, "Don't flatter yourself. I can bring in another doctor."

"Why bother when you've got someone who's willing to work endless hours for minimal wages?"

"Speaking of which, I'll be able to cut you a check next week for your back pay."

Kelly cocked her head. "Where's the money coming from?"

"I'm liquidating one of my investments. It'll tide us over for a while."

Kelly reached for the bottle and poured herself another shot. She sipped the scotch, considering her father for a moment. "Dad, are you trying to ease me out the door?"

David was shocked. "You're not serious, right? I love having you here."

"Then what are we talking about? Once I decided to become a doctor, all I ever wanted to do was go into practice with you."

"And I'm the luckiest father alive. Sweetheart, what we do here is important, but it's a tiny pond. You were born for greater things, and you've been given a chance to push yourself, test your limits. Now's the time for you to make bold choices, take on new challenges. I don't want you to end up at age sixty-five, looking back on your life and having regrets."

"Do you?"

After a moment's thought, he nodded. "Some." Before Kelly could grill him, he continued, "My advice, for what it's worth as the man who brought you into this world, is accept the job and give it a few years. If you don't like it and want to come back, I'll try to find a spot for you."

"A few years…"

"That's what it takes to give it a fair shot. I'm not planning on retiring any time soon, so we'll have a lot of road ahead of us."

Kelly was still conflicted. "I'll give it some thought."

David drained his drink. "That's all this old man could ask for." He placed his hand atop hers. "I hope you never doubt how much you've meant to me and how much I appreciate you being in my life." He leaned back in his chair. "Now go on, and give my regards to Pete."

Kelly successfully fought back a tear. "I love you, too. Don't stay too late."

David smiled. "Don't worry about me. See you in the morning."

4

44 Degrees on Market Street was an upscale restaurant whose contemporary fusion menu attracted a well-heeled crowd. Walking distance from City Hall and the Opera House, the eatery drew a mix of white-collar locals, wealthy bohos and out-of-towners who wanted to experience the San Francisco foodie scene and had the foresight to make reservations a month in advance. During peak hours it was near impossible to get a table, and at 10:30pm the place still did a brisk bar business.

Kelly entered looking for Pete. He hadn't arrived yet, but sitting at the copper-topped bar was a stunning woman with shamelessly wavy auburn hair framing a Mediterranean face that recalled Ancient Greek images of Aphrodite. Many women would have spontaneously felt a rush of envy and instant dislike for someone who looked like they'd just come from a *Vogue* cover shoot, but Kelly's reaction was altogether different.

The woman was chatting with a younger man who resembled Brad Pitt circa *A River Runs Through It.* Kelly interrupted them with, "Buy a girl a drink?" and when the woman turned around, her face lit up.

Alexandra Russo was Kelly's oldest friend, and given the grueling schedules they kept, it was a joyous occasion when they got together. "Alexa" was gorgeous, but her beauty took a backseat to her intellect. A business powerhouse with an MBA from Columbia, she was Vice-President of a very successful hedge fund that had been first in the door at the outset of the tech boom. Alexa convinced the board that the silicon tsunami wasn't sustainable in the long run, so they put her in charge of diversifying the firm's holdings. When the dot-com bust took down most of the money managers in San Francisco, her company was there to buy up assets at a fraction of their value.

Alexa patted the stool next to her and signaled Philip, the white-shirted, black-vested bartender. "She'll have what I'm having."

As Philip poured a glass of chilled Chardonnay, Alexa introduced the man on her other side. "Kelly, this is Josh Friedman. He just joined our company."

Josh reached over and took Kelly's hand. "Nice to meet you." He had a magnetic smile that featured perfect white teeth. Josh held onto Kelly's hand until it became borderline awkward.

Alexa broke in, "Kelly's my oldest pal, and she's here to meet her boyfriend, who's late because he's probably in the midst of a murder investigation."

Josh's face reddened, and when he realized he was still clutching Kelly's hand, he went full-on turnip.

He released his grip. "It's late, and I've got an early morning meeting."

"Here's a little tip," said Alexa. "Get there fifteen minutes before it starts, otherwise you won't get a seat at the table, and huddling in the back row with the assistants would be a bad look."

He nodded. "Thanks. I will. Definitely." He bade the women a good night and executed a hasty exit.

As he left the café, Kelly sipped her wine. "Oh, my god."

"The wine or him?"

"Let's start with the wine. It's incredible."

"Marcassin. It's getting scarce, so Philip put away a case for me. Glad you like it."

"The upside of drinking with you is this." She held up her glass. "The downside is it makes the stuff I drink taste like urine."

"That's a pleasant thought. Whenever you need a wine fix, I can hook you up."

"You're my best friend, not my sugar momma, but… damn, this is good." She took another appreciative sip of the wine. "By the way, nice of you to put the fear of God into your new associate."

"He can handle it. Undergrad at Purdue, MBA from Harvard. Looks and brains. And if you can believe it, he's single and he's straight."

"That won't last long in this city, one way or the other."

"So true."

"Wait, you're not…"

Alexa actually snorted. "Me? First of all, I don't swim in the company pool. Secondly, I'm not a coug... at least, not yet."

Kelly smiled. Alexa could have any man she wanted. She'd never be classified as a cougar. "So, this was what? A little welcome-to-the-team cocktail?"

"It started that way, until he segued into his sad saga about the girl in Boston he left behind. It was a sordid tale of misguided ambition, unquenchable drug habits and perverse sexual appetites."

"That's what I interrupted? Sorry."

"Kel, I hear the same stories every day. If it's not aggressive junior executives who think that *Glengarry Glenross* is a training film, it's burnouts who've had early success then blew all their cash, stupidly assuming they'd continue to knock down seven figures every year. They wake up one morning to find themselves at the bottom of a financial well, wondering what the hell happened. Unfortunately, many of them turn to drugs, bleach blondes with fake boobs, or your everyday, run-of-the-mill embezzlement. Mine is a business that knows no mercy."

"So you're saying I should feel sorry for you?"

"Sorry for *her*?" They turned to see Pete Ericson. "Lemme guess. Your Jag got towed? Or, your personal trainer got deported back to Switzerland."

Alexa shook her head. "You're a shitty detective, and for your information, Franz is from Austria." Alexa leaned over and kissed Pete on the cheek. "Take care of my girl, okay?"

"I'm trying, but she can be difficult."

"Thanks for the wine, Lex," Kelly said, as she pulled Pete toward an empty table.

Moments later, they were sitting across from one another, casually holding hands. At thirty-seven, Pete was a few years older than Kelly and no less accomplished in his field, having made the grade of Homicide Inspector four years ago, seven years earlier than the department average. Blue collar, with only a public school education and two scant years of junior college under his belt, Pete impressively graduated third in his class at the Academy.

Six foot three, keen-eyed, square-jawed and broad-shouldered, Pete was the epitome of a "working man's cop". While a few of the flashier

Inspectors fancied themselves as media savvy and wore Versace and Ferragamo, Pete's suits were straight off the rack from Men's Warehouse, and his footwear came from Florsheim. He never understood why anyone would spend five hundred bucks on a pair of shoes to walk through an alley littered with needles, blood and piss… or worse.

Like Kelly, Pete grew up in his own family business, hearing fascinating and often morbid tales at the feet of his father and grandfather, both proud members of the force. Some of Pete's favorite memories were when his Dad and Grandpa had a warm buzz on and reminisced about the past. Their stories ranged from dealing with stoned, unbathed free-love Hippies in the Haight/Ashbury district, to trying to solve the riddle of the Zodiac killer, to shocking inside tales about Patty Hearst and the Symbionese Liberation Army.

Pete listened for hours on end; mesmerized by the firsthand accounts of how the SFPD dealt with the underbelly of the place they called The City. There was never a doubt he'd follow in the large footsteps of his family.

Growing up the son of a cop wasn't easy. His friends thought it was cool that if Pete ever got nailed for something like speeding, or maybe driving after having a few beers, his old man could just flash his badge and a get-outta-jail-free card would magically appear. When Pete went out with his buddies, they always tapped him to be the designated driver. He never argued and never touched a drop of alcohol, because the institutional penalty for stepping out of line would've been trivial compared to the punishment he'd face at home.

He loved his Dad, and in the Ericson household, love took the form of reverence and obedience. Being an only child, Pete didn't have the good fortune of an older sibling to test the boundaries of what he could and couldn't get away with. It was trial and error, and all it took was a few sharp smacks (that he never saw coming) and a few stern lectures (that he always saw coming) to guide him down the right path. Mrs Ericson never had to utter the words "wait till your father gets home".

As Pete grew older and stronger, the tacit threat of physical punishment faded away. Rather, it was the unspoken threat of letting his father down. The last thing he ever wanted to see was the look of disappointment in his father's face. And while Sergeant Ericson was never effusive with compliments or public shows of emotion, Pete knew he was loved. He only saw his father cry twice: once when the San Francisco Giants won the World Series in 2010 (after a fifty-six-year drought); and once when Pete graduated from the Academy. Seeing the pride welling up in his father's eyes at that moment was all the motivation Pete needed to work his ass off to be the best officer the SFPD had ever put on the street.

He knew he'd have success on the force. What he didn't know was if he'd have success in life, which to him meant finding a special woman with whom he could start a family. He already had one strike against him in the game of love. When Pete was twenty-two, he married Diane, a woman he'd met at City College. Their marriage was destined to derail before their vows were cold. When they impulsively tied the knot after two months of dating, they didn't realize how little they had in common.

Diane wanted the finer things in life. Pete wanted to be a cop. Those two streets rarely, if ever, merge. It wasn't long before Diane took to finding pleasure in the bottom of a bottle, and when that no longer did the trick, she stepped up to cocaine. At first she tried to hide it, but eventually got to the point where she didn't care if her policeman husband knew about her illicit habit.

It was no big mystery that Diane's wedding ring suddenly "went missing" a few days before Pete found her crashed out on the sofa, the remainder of an ounce of coke sitting on the Ikea coffee table. Pete knew their relationship was on rocky ground, but hadn't realized it was straddling a fault line.

After a quick, and yet surprisingly ugly divorce, Pete wondered how in the hell he'd gotten himself involved with her in the first place. The answer was glaring in its simplicity: Pete's father got married when he was twenty-two, so Pete's internal clock started ticking loudly when he turned twenty-one. It was completely irrational, but sometimes logic has no place at the table.

Just like his Dad, Pete got married at age twenty-two. The difference was, his father had found the right woman. Pete vowed that next time he'd wait until he was certain he had the right partner before stepping back into the batter's box.

When he met Kelly, his first reaction was she was out of his league. Like, *way* out of his league. Even though he was an Inspector, she was a *doctor*. Different colored collars altogether. Kelly came from the privileged class, complete with private schools, nannies and foreign vacations. Surely she was destined to marry a banker, a lawyer, or another doctor. Pete couldn't fathom her spending the rest of her life with a cop.

But life rarely takes a predictable path. Contrary to the song, life is not a highway. It's more of a winding country road, punctuated by the unexpected at almost every turn. Class distinctions, education, occupations… they mean nothing if there's an undeniable attraction, and the attraction between Pete and Kelly was palpable. He was quickly convinced she was the one; smart, independent, strong-willed and pure of heart. Also, he was pretty sure he wouldn't walk in one day to find her in a drug coma.

Kelly finished telling Pete why she was inclined to turn down the job at St Francis, but she wanted to get his input before making a final decision.

"I thought you'd already decided to take the job."

"I said I was leaning toward it, but a ten-year-old came into the clinic today with a gunshot wound. Ten years old! It brought back into focus how much our community needs the clinic, and how important it is that I'm a part of that."

"Think of the number of people you could help if you were at a large hospital," he said.

"Think of the bureaucracy."

"Think of the money." Pete smiled.

"I didn't get into medicine for the money, just like you didn't become a cop to get rich."

"That's why it would be nice to have a rich girlfriend. I even started a list of the places you could take me," he said with a straight face.

Kelly laughed. "Really?"

"I thought we could start small, like a week in Hawaii or something."

"A week in Hawaii. Any place in particular?"

"I heard that the Four Seasons in Maui was nice. I'm sure *you'd* like it there, and I'd go along if you twisted my arm."

"Good news, Inspector. Your arm's going to be just fine."

"Yeah, that's what I thought." Pete finished what was left of his scotch and signaled for another round. "What's your father say about this?"

"He agrees with you, but he's being a martyr. If I left the clinic, I don't know where he'd find the money to bring in another doctor, which means he'd put in even longer hours. At his age he should be taking a step back, not assuming more responsibility. As it stands, he's got no life whatsoever outside the clinic."

"Your father seems happy with a good book and a comfortable chair. He's not exactly the adventurous type."

"I worry about him. Ever since Mom died, he's filled the void with work. I'm afraid that one of these days he's going to realize life has passed him by and he'll be too old to do anything about it."

Pete placed his hand on Kelly's. "What about your life? You spend six days a week at the clinic, most of Sunday with Jessica, and barely have enough time to unwind at night before you start back up."

Kelly had heard it all before. She couldn't argue, because it was a fair assessment. And Pete never made it about him.

"I'm trying to find time for me... for us... but the clinic's going through a rough patch and my Dad needs me there."

"Sounds to me like there's more than one martyr in the Harper family," he said with a smile.

Kelly often wondered if the reason she was working at the clinic was because she felt she owed it to her father as a result of what happened to Jessica. Or was it because she was still trying to earn his favor? She'd never shared these feelings with anyone. They were too personal. Too painful. But maybe she should. Maybe it would be healthy to give some air to her thoughts. If nothing else, it might help her decide what to do about the job at St Francis.

"You could be right. Although, I never saw myself as Joan of Arc."

"You've got much better hair," he quipped. "All I'm saying is, you need to focus on yourself once in a while. Your father's gonna be just fine."

Kelly smiled. Maybe Pete was right. She'd spend some time focusing on herself.

Her father would be fine.

At that very moment, David *was* perfectly fine, happily walking down the street through the cool, moist San Francisco night. This weather always reminded him of his youth, going to Giants games at Candlestick Park with his best friend Jim and watching as the dense layer of coastal fog swirled in, sometimes making it impossible to see Mays in center or even McCovey at first. The stands were never more than half full and the temperatures plummeted in the later innings, but David and Jim always stuck it out to the end, cheering on the men in orange and black.

As he passed by Monaghan's Irish Bar, he stopped for a moment and looked in. The warm glow of the tavern was a siren song, beckoning him to enter and join the happy revelers inside. David momentarily considered ducking in for a Black and Tan, but then thought better of it. He still had a small glow from the scotch, which helped ward off the chill. That was his quota for the night.

He pulled up his collar and stepped off the curb. As he was halfway across the intersection, a dark grey SUV suddenly raced out of the murky shadows. It drunkenly weaved down the street and was headed directly toward him.

For the briefest moment David was frozen, transfixed by the rapidly advancing SUV. He watched as it grew larger, wondering if this was fate or something else.

Something more sinister.

David snapped back to reality and lunged to get out of the path of the hurtling vehicle, but his loafers weren't designed for traction and he lost his footing on the slick pavement, tumbling to his knees.

A massive rush of adrenaline surged through David's body, jolting him like a plunge in a frozen lake. He scrambled to his feet, and as he rose up, his eyes locked in on the man behind the wheel. David couldn't make out his features, but something about the driver seemed familiar. Before his brain could process that thought, David was hammered by four thousand pounds of steel and aluminum alloy.

His body tumbled through the air like a ragdoll flung by a petulant child, crashing back to Earth some twenty feet from the intersection in a crumpled pile of crushed bone and torn flesh.

The SUV never slowed down. Never the slightest hint of brake lights. The tires screeched and skidded as the car accelerated around the corner and vanished into the night.

5

As the waiter delivered their final round of drinks, Kelly still equivocated about whether to take the job at St Francis. She hated leaving things unresolved, so she wanted to make a decision, feel good about it and then move forward.

Pete read the situation and offered up some advice. "Kel, we're three drinks in. You should call it a night and weigh your options in the morning with a clear head."

She nodded and raised her glass. "An insightful suggestion from the intuitive Inspector." They clinked glasses.

Pete said, "Glad I could help."

Kelly smiled. "Talking about it with you *is* really helpful. Once I figure this thing out, let's head to the lake for a long weekend."

The thought of having Kelly to himself for three or four days was a rare opportunity. "Sounds great. I'll check on cabin rentals."

"Pump the brakes. I said once I figure this out."

"Which you'll need to do soon or your head's gonna explode. Plus, if I don't make reservations, you'll find some lame excuse to push this off, like that trip to San Diego last spring."

"I wouldn't classify having an emergency appendectomy as a lame excuse."

"Appendectomies are for wimps. You could've toughed it out if you really wanted to."

Kelly's laugh was music to Pete's ears. "So I've gone from martyr to wimp?"

Their banter was interrupted by the vibration of Kelly's cell phone. She glanced at the number and shrugged.

Pete said, "You gonna get that?"

Kelly shook her head. "I don't recognize the number."

"I do," Pete said somberly. "It's the 4th Precinct."

Suddenly concerned, Kelly answered the phone.

She had no idea that from that moment on, her life would never be the same.

6

The street outside Monaghan's was a flurry of police activity. Yellow police tape cordoned off wet asphalt awash with red lights from the police cruisers. Puddled blood looked shiny and black as fresh tar. The crowd of curious, morbid onlookers had quadrupled in size, and cell phones were held aloft, recording everything. David's pulverized body remained *in situ* until the crime scene investigators could photograph and document every detail. A thin plastic tarp had been draped over his corpse to provide a modicum of privacy, even though he was long past caring about such things.

Pete and Kelly had to park a block away and muscle their way through the outer rim of the rubbernecking crowd. One of the jostled onlookers took umbrage and squared off with Pete. "Hey, fuck off, man!"

Pete spontaneously transformed from caring boyfriend to hard-ass cop, whipping out his badge and getting in the man's face. "How'd you like your ass in jail for interfering with a crime scene?"

Just then, a slender, 5ft 8in middle-aged Asian man appeared, a gold shield hung around his neck on a lanyard. "Is this little prick causing problems, Inspector?" Without waiting for more prompting, the little prick disappeared into the crowd.

Pete turned to the Asian man, who happened to be his partner, Inspector Ronald Yee. Yee had just completed his twentieth year of service with the SFPD and was famous for his colorful language, his impeccable wardrobe, and one of the best clearance records on the force. When Pete was promoted to Inspector, he was extremely fortunate to have drawn Yee as his partner. "What do we know?" asked Pete.

"Just the baseline facts. I assume you're aware that the victim's been IDed as David Harper. He was hit by a dark grey SUV going west. Eyewitnesses stated that the vehicle was weaving down the street before it struck him."

"Is the Hit and Run Detail here?"

"Yeah, they're handling the scene. I just happened to be in the area when I heard the commotion," Ronald said. "Does Kelly know?"

"Kelly?" Pete looked around, and she was gone. "Oh, shit!"

Kelly had made her way through the throngs and ducked under the yellow tape. A uniformed cop tried to restrain her, and Kelly tried to push him away. "Leave me alone!"

Pete called out to Kelly as he bulled his way forward. "Kelly!"

In that moment of distraction, she broke away from the officer and ran toward the center of attraction… a body shrouded under a wet plastic tarp.

The cop intercepted Pete. "You know her, Inspector?"

"That's my girlfriend. The vic is her father."

"Damn. You don't want her to see that."

But it was too late. Kelly was already kneeling beside the shapeless form.

She looked under the tarp and the color drained from her face. Suddenly, her world stood still. Sounds faded away and seconds seemed like hours. Kelly heard a woeful keening fill the night.

She didn't realize the sounds of anguish were coming from her.

7

Colma, California, was founded in 1924 as a necropolis. Ten miles south of San Francisco, the city was comprised primarily of cemeteries (seventeen, to be exact) and boasted over one and a half million bodies interred, which outnumbered the living population by a thousand to one. Little wonder it was known as "The Town Where San Francisco's Dead Live". Colma was the final resting place of luminaries from all walks of life, which now included Dr David Harper.

Kelly wanted a modest, unpretentious funeral, but her father had touched too many lives and was revered by so many families that a small gathering was out of the question. Only two days had passed since David's death, and Kelly was overwhelmed by how quickly the arrangements had been made. The turnout was massive and the diverse makeup of the crowd was a reflection of David's widespread esteem. City Hall dignitaries, distinguished doctors, SFPD brass, and, of course, hundreds of locals from the Mission who owed their health and the health of their families to Dr Harper.

Kelly stood on wobbly legs, flanked by Pete and Alexandra, and watched through teary eyes as her father was heralded by the Mayor of San Francisco for his tireless service to the people of the city; as the head of the St Francis Memorial Hospital Board declared that their new surgical wing would be dedicated to Dr Harper; as the Captain of the SFPD expressed the deepest condolences on behalf of the entire department; and finally, as a soprano from the San Francisco Opera sang *Amazing Grace*.

By the time her song ended, the entire assemblage had joined Kelly in weeping for the newly departed.

Late that afternoon, an exhausted and emotionally drained Kelly arrived at the Peninsula Oaks Healthcare facility. Even on the best of days, a visit here was undeniably depressing. Peninsula Oaks was a private facility that specialized in traumatic brain injury and was home to Kelly's sister Jessica.

Kelly entered her room to find Jessica propped up in bed, her eyes closed and her breathing shallow. While Jessica resembled her father and Kelly her mother, there was no question that these two were sisters, this despite the toll that Jessica's condition had taken on her. In her mid thirties, Jessica appeared to be in her late fifties.

For the past twenty years, Jessica existed in what was termed a minimally conscious state; the result of the severe blow to her head that led to a brain hemorrhage. Like others with this condition, Jessica had extremely limited awareness of the world around her. She'd occasionally smile or cry in response to verbal or visual stimulation, and she'd sporadically utter the words "yes" or "no", but rarely in a logical context. The doctors had made it clear early on that making eye contact and attempting to grasp objects within her reach were positive signs, but not necessarily indications she was ever going to recover. The sad reality was, the longer Jessica remained in her minimally conscious state, the less her chances of ever recovering higher critical functions.

Like she'd done hundreds of times before, Kelly pulled up a chair and lightly touched Jessica's hand. Her eyes fluttered open and she turned to Kelly, but there was no sense of recognition. No focus to her gaze.

It took all of Kelly's remaining energy to force a smile. "Hey, Jess. How was your day?" There was no reaction. There rarely was. Kelly continued, "I'm sorry I haven't been here for a while, but…"

Kelly took a breath and steeled herself. Despite Jessica's lack of comprehension, breaking this news to her was much more difficult than Kelly had imagined. Because of Jess's special relationship with their father, his loss, under normal circumstances, would be devastating. At that moment, Kelly thought it fortunate that her sister lived in oblivion.

"Dad." Kelly's tears instantly welled up again. "Dad's gone. He was…" That was as far as she got before she was completely overwhelmed. She put her head down on her sister's lap, her body racked with sadness as she silently cried. Jessica remained blissfully deaf to the information, as well as to Kelly's grief.

Finally, Kelly raised her head, wiped her tears and pulled herself together. She had no choice but to be strong for the both of them.

"We buried him today. Hundreds of people came out to pay their respects. It was incredible to see how much he was loved. There was even a woman from the opera who sang *Amazing Grace*."

Kelly had done extensive research into her sister's condition, and while no one knew precisely what stimuli affected her, it was widely agreed that social interaction could be extremely valuable, and that whenever possible, she should personalize the conversation. "Remember when you sang *Amazing Grace* with the choir at the seventh grade recital?"

"Yes," Jessica said, her voice barely above a whisper.

Kelly smiled. She doubted Jessica's agreement was actually in response to the question, but it buoyed Kelly's spirits regardless.

"I wish you could've been there to see it all. It made me so proud to be his daughter." Kelly held back a sob and carried on, "He's with Mom now, and I'm sure they're looking down on us, knowing that pretty soon you're going to get better."

Jessica squeezed Kelly's hand.

Was that a muscular reflex or was Jessica acknowledging her sister? Whenever something like this happened, Kelly was reminded that inside this shell was a living person.

Kelly reached out and gently touched Jessica's face. "I promise I'll always be here for you, whatever it takes."

It was getting late and Kelly thought about foregoing *Harry Potter*, but she didn't want to fall into the habit of making excuses to shirk the obligation she had to her sister. Kelly still carried the overriding guilt that if she'd only remembered the tennis balls that day…

An hour later, Kelly was making her way out of the building when she was intercepted by Sylvia Spiro, the director of the facility. A thin, hawkish woman in her fifties, Ms Spiro exuded an air of forced sentimentality. She ran the non-medical side of this operation, and while it could be argued that she cared about the wellbeing of the patients, her main concern was the wellbeing of Peninsula Oaks' finances. "I heard you were here, Dr Harper. Have you got a moment?"

Despite a powerful urge to put off the officious director, Kelly was now completely responsible for her sister, and that meant dealing with all aspects of the facility, including Ms Spiro.

A few moments later, they were seated in a well-appointed office, tastefully done in warm tones and completely lacking in any personal touches. "Dr Harper, everyone here is heartbroken for your loss."

Kelly nodded, numb to the hollow condolences. "Thank you for the flowers."

"Of course." Ms Spiro paused for a moment, then launched in. "There's no good time to have this conversation, and now is probably the worst, but I was contacted yesterday by our head office in Dayton regarding your sister's account."

Kelly reacted like she'd been slapped across the face with something cold and odious. Her anguish was replaced with a sense of outrage and she felt her face bloom with anger. "You want to discuss finances *today*?"

Ms Spiro unsuccessfully attempted to defuse the moment. "No, not really. Like I said, I realize this isn't a good time, but…"

"But yet here you are, confronting me about money just hours after I buried my father." Kelly was spinning out of control, and at that point she didn't really care.

Ms Spiro knew she'd made a terrible situation even worse, but she had a job to do and a message to impart. "I'm afraid the financials are out of my hands. Your sister's account is three months overdue."

This revelation took Kelly entirely by surprise. For a moment she was speechless, trying to process this bombshell. "How's that possible? I thought her care was paid through the end of the year. My father…"

"Had every good intention. Because Jessica has been a patient here for so long, we agreed to extend a financial courtesy to your family; but there was recently a change in our corporate management structure and…"

Kelly had heard enough. After cycling through a full range of emotions since setting foot inside the facility a few hours ago, her attitude hardened. "I'll get you a check."

Ms Spiro nodded and smiled. "That would be excellent. We'd hate to have to take action. Corporations are not very compassionate when it comes to delinquent accounts."

Kelly stood, her demeanor frigid as a December morning in Siberia. "I said I'd take care of it."

Kelly strode out of the facility into the brisk night. Dizzy from fatigue, distracted by anger and fearful about the future, her mind was overloaded from everything that transpired in the past twenty-four hours. It was no wonder she didn't hear the SUV barreling toward her until the last minute.

Kelly recoiled backwards and just barely avoided being hit by the speeding vehicle. The SUV raced down the street without slowing down, as if nothing had ever happened.

Stunned and frightened, Kelly's heart was pounding.

Was she next on some killer's hit list?

8

Later that night, Kelly sat alone in her small condo. It was a cozy home, filled with comfortable furniture, high-end kitchen appliances (which didn't get much use) and hundreds of books. It was orderly and yet inviting. A reflection of the person who lived there, down to the alphabetization of the novels (by author, of course).

There were dozens of framed photos of family and friends. The frames were a potpourri of sizes and styles. At one point, Kelly considered redoing all of her photos in matching frames, but that proved to be too anal even for her.

Glowing embers in the fireplace cast a flickering, amber illumination into the darkened living room as Kelly nursed a tumbler of scotch and thought about everything that had occurred in the past few days.

The weight of recent events pressed down on her, making it difficult to breathe and virtually impossible to glimpse any sign of light or hope. Her glass was empty and she slowly reached for the bottle. To her surprise and dismay, it was empty as well. How full was the bottle when she sat down? How much had she drunk tonight? Did it even matter?

A photo album was on her lap, open to a picture taken when she and her father were in Sumatra with Doctors Without Borders. One tanned arm was draped across her father's shoulders, and the other laid across the back of Chandler, a mottled three-legged hound who'd adopted Kelly the moment she set foot in the village. She'd taken to the dog as readily as it took to her, and she'd named it after her favorite character from *Friends*. As Kelly stared at the photo, she wondered whatever happened to Chandler. It was far less painful than dwelling on what had happened to her father.

The knock at the door jarred her, sending an irrational jolt of fear and paranoia through her body. Even though she lived in a secure high-rise building, she was still extremely edgy after her near-death experience outside Peninsula Oaks. She looked at the clock on the mantle. It was after 11pm. Who would be...?

Another knock, this one more assertive. "Kelly? It's Pete."

Pete. Of course. Who else would it be? She'd called him, semi-hysterical, to tell him about the SUV that had nearly run her down. Kelly's heartbeat began to decelerate. She shook off her alcoholic haze and found her voice. "Hold on."

She heaved herself up from the chair, steadied her legs and made it to the door, opening it a crack, but leaving the chain secured. She wasn't sure why she did that. It was Pete standing in the hallway, not some stranger. Instinctively, at that moment, she needed to feel safe.

Pete's face was a mixture of concern, caring and confusion. "You didn't answer your phone."

"I'm fine. I just want to be alone."

"You sure?"

"No. I'm not sure of anything except that I'm angry and frightened and generally fucked up."

Pete rarely heard Kelly swear. "We could talk about it. Are you going to open the door?"

There was a long moment of silence as Kelly unsuccessfully attempted to work through the panoply of disjointed thoughts careening around her brain. Did she want someone to talk to or not? She didn't know. She didn't have the mental acuity to arrive at a decision, so she simply undid the security chain and left the door ajar, before she turned and walked back into the room.

Pete accepted the tacit invitation and slowly entered, turning on a lamp as he made his way to the sofa. She caught him glancing at the empty scotch bottle on the side table.

"Don't."

"I'm not here to judge. I'm here to help."

"How?"

"You tell me."

"You could start by finding the bastard that killed my father."

"Are you looking for closure or revenge?"

Kelly fixed Pete with a chilly glare. "How about justice?"

Pete reached out to touch her, but Kelly pulled away. "They might've found the car." He didn't know how much he should reveal at this point, since the news wasn't exactly promising.

Kelly impatiently flared, "Might've?"

Pete knew he'd made a mistake and now he was about to compound it. "A dark grey Jeep Cherokee with a dented front bumper and hood. It was reported stolen. Whoever abandoned it, wiped down the interior and drenched it with bleach. Forensics is trying to pull some usable prints."

"Bleach? That sounds like it was planned, which means it wasn't a random hit and run."

"Maybe. It could also mean that once the driver realized what happened, he tried to cover his tracks."

"What about the car that tried to run me down tonight?"

What could he say? With no license plate number and no witnesses, there wasn't much the police could do.

"We're checking the businesses in the area to see if any of them have security cams that might've caught something. Kelly, I doubt the two incidents are related."

Kelly's eyes blazed with burning intensity. "Really? My father was run down out of the blue and a few days later a car just happened to almost hit me, and the police department doesn't see a connection?"

"We're keeping an open mind, but at this point the answer's no."

Kelly was suddenly assaulted by a wave of physical and mental exhaustion. She exhaled and her head lolled forward. "I need to go to bed."

"Do you... want me to stay?" Pete asked.

"No." There was too long a beat before she realized how final that sounded. "I've got to meet with a lawyer in the morning and we're reopening the clinic in the afternoon. If I don't get some sleep, I'll be completely useless."

Pete thought about giving her a quick reassuring kiss, but Kelly's body language was unmistakable. He settled for an understanding smile and nod, and headed out the door.

He stopped in the hallway, wondering and worrying. He'd never seen this side of Kelly, and hoped that with some rejuvenating sleep and sufficient time, she'd bounce back. She'd been through a deeply traumatic experience and it could be months, maybe years, until she was able to come to terms with her father's murder and move ahead with her life. Pete had seen too many people… intelligent, gifted people, who were overwhelmed by tragedy and sorrow, which led to a downward spiral that ended with them losing all hope… and often their lives.

And so… Pete wondered, and worried

9

"The Law Shop" was a new concept in legal firms modeled after fast food franchises. "Shops" had sprung up in eight cities and consisted of a soulless collection of cubicles inhabited by recent law school grads or retired lawyers who wanted a part-time gig and an excuse to get out of the house. It was about a fifty/fifty split between newbies learning on the job and burnouts that had long résumés but were only moderately interested in the legal problems that faced their clients.

The consortium behind the legal chain was based in Los Angeles and had Hollywood sensibilities, which translated to mandating that every franchisee create the illusion of professional gravitas. Each "Shop" had one long wall lined with leather-bound law books, emulating the law libraries seen in every legal television series that ever aired. The fact that the books had such titles as "Wildlife And Fisheries Regulations for the State Of Georgia: 1954-55. Volumes I through XVI" didn't matter. These libraries were bought in bulk and were strictly for show.

The "Shop" that Kelly went to was housed inside a former bookstore nestled between Brookstone and TJ Maxx in the Tanforan Mall in San Bruno, a few miles south of San Francisco. She sat across from a young woman named Rhonda Jackson, who proudly displayed her diploma from the Thomas Jefferson School of Law in San Diego on a wall of her cubicle.

Kelly flipped through a meager stack of documents and shook her head. "I don't understand."

Rhonda tried to muster a modicum of empathy or even understanding, but failed. They didn't teach bedside manner at TJS. "Is there a problem with the will?"

"I don't know. Is this everything? All of my father's assets?"

"This is everything he disclosed. There may be other assets." She raised her hands and shoulders in a shrug. "Were you expecting more?"

"There's almost nothing here. The house is mortgaged to the hilt and the clinic is deep in the red. My father told me he had investments."

"Did he work with a brokerage firm? You could contact them and see if he had a portfolio."

"He never mentioned a broker to me."

Rhonda failed at a compassionate smile. "I've seen cases where people have multiple wills in order to hide money or property from their heirs. Not to be insensitive, but perhaps there was someone else in his life that…"

Kelly shook her head in bewilderment. "No. Definitely not."

Then again, maybe she didn't know her father as well as she thought. It was puzzling, but moreover, it was deeply disturbing to think he could've been keeping secrets from her.

Besides, what could he possibly have to hide?

10

Kelly entered the clinic through the back door, avoiding the throng of patients milling around the front of the building. She'd arrived an hour early to comb through her father's files, desperately hoping to find some clue about his mysterious "investments". The clinic was financially teetering, and Jessica's ongoing medical bills loomed large, casting an ominous shadow over Kelly's likelihood of staying afloat.

As the door was closing, a hand grabbed it and yanked it back open. Kelly spun around to find Dr Nathan Curtis staring back at her. His chubby face and thinning, slicked-back hair reminded her of a child molester in Iowa who'd been featured in a Netflix documentary. And like the child molester, Nathan sported a perpetual sheen of perspiration on his forehead and hands. He was the prototype of the "last kid picked" on the playground and an easy target for bullies. It wasn't until later in life that he'd inherited a sizeable trust fund from his maternal grandmother and learned the golden rule: the one who pays for the bats and balls doesn't get picked last.

"You startled me," said Kelly.

"Sorry," Nathan said, with a sheepish grin that was difficult for him to pull off. His voice had a nasal quality, the result of a deviated septum, and to make it worse, he had a slightly affected Ivy accent he'd honed at Princeton. "I wanted to catch you before everyone else arrived. Got a minute?"

Kelly was offended that Nathan hadn't attended her father's funeral, and her anger had compounded every day that he didn't have the courtesy to reach out to her with condolences. No flowers, no phone call, not even an email. Her father had given Nathan a huge break when it looked like his medical career might be over before it began, and Nathan's lack of appreciation was galling.

Kelly wasn't in any kind of mood to deal with him now, but knew that she'd have to face him sooner or later. May as well get it over with.

A short time later, Kelly was ensconced behind her father's desk, using it as a physical and psychological barrier. Being alone with Nathan was extremely awkward, since a tiny irrational part of Kelly harbored the notion that he somehow might've had a hand in her father's death. After all, David had made it clear that Nathan's job was on the line.

Nathan perched on the edge of his chair, profusely apologized for leaving early the previous week, and explained that he missed the funeral because he'd been out of town. He hadn't called or emailed because he felt it was only appropriate to express his deepest sympathies in person.

Nathan had an on-again-off-again relationship with the truth. Kelly had never known him to maliciously lie, but he'd earned a well-deserved reputation for obfuscating the facts.

A spoiled boy from a wealthy family with an overbearing father, Nathan always put Nathan first, which was not an admirable trait for a doctor. He should've gone the route of his father and become an investment banker instead of a doctor, but then any failure on his part would have been far too easy to quantify. Nathan was determined to become successful in his own right. However, there was one major problem with his career plan: he simply didn't care enough to put in the time or the energy it took to become a great doctor. He wanted success handed to him, like everything else in his life.

After Nathan finished his litany of excuses and his pandering effusive remarks regarding David, he finally got around to the purpose of his visit.

"What's going to happen to the clinic now?"

"It'll continue on as it did before," Kelly said with as little emotion as possible. She wanted this over and him out of the office.

"So you're retaining the entire staff?"

"Why wouldn't I?"

Nathan buried a smile. He'd dodge a major bullet if Kelly wasn't aware of her father's ultimatum. "With everything that's happened, I didn't know if you were planning on keeping things *status quo*. I really enjoy working here."

"But not enough to put in a full shift," Kelly retorted, trying to tamp down her growing ire.

"I screwed up. My father organized this big dinner with some important clients and I was obliged to attend. I should've told your dad earlier, but I forgot all about it until the last minute." He stopped to assess Kelly's reaction. Her stony demeanor made it clear she wasn't sympathetic to his excuses.

As much as Kelly found some small satisfaction in Nathan's discomfort, she was tired of his smarmy bullshit. She stood up, signaling the meeting was over. "I'm not going to make any changes right now. I'll continue to honor your position, but if I find I can't depend on you, I'll bring in someone else."

Nathan stood, now allowing the smile to come out. "You can count on me. I promise." He started to extend his hand, then thought better of it. No one liked a clammy handshake.

When Nathan got to the door, he turned back. "By the way, and this is none of my business, but if things get tight financially, I'd be happy to introduce you to my father. He runs a hedge fund called Vantage, and one of his clients is the Wallace Medical Group. They're rapidly expanding in the Bay Area and there might be some common ground."

Kelly was taken aback by Nathan's sheer brazenness. The dirt was still fresh on her father's grave and Nathan was making a play for the clinic? When she spoke, she didn't bother to hide her disdain. "Don't concern yourself about the finances of the clinic. Focus on putting in your hours."

Nathan was either too thick or too callous to take umbrage. He nodded. "Just thought I'd throw it out there. Can I get you anything from Starbucks?"

Kelly shook her head.

Nathan nodded, smiling. "Okay, boss. See you in an hour."

He closed the door behind him and Kelly sank back into the chair, wondering if she had the patience and fortitude to deal with the daily challenges of keeping the clinic afloat.

She also wondered what other hidden landmines she'd stumble across in the coming days.

When the clinic opened its doors, the flood of patients threatened to inundate the staff. Being one doctor short was bad enough, but the loss of David's medical expertise and ability to perform triage under the most intense pressure was glaring. There was an unspoken air of sadness and feeling of emptiness that permeated the clinic. The staff knew this sentiment was going to linger with them for a long, long time.

Given the workload and the frenetic pace of treating patients, time passed quickly. No one took a break. Kelly was invigorated by the work, and successfully compartmentalized thoughts of her father. She knew the pain would come crashing down once she had a moment to herself, so she kept busy, seeing one patient after another without a respite.

It had grown dark outside, the day was almost over and yet the waiting room was still filled to capacity. Kelly was in the midst of treating an overweight middle-aged man who'd sliced his foot on a broken beer bottle when Ramona ducked her head into the curtained medical bay. "Diego Sanchez is back. He's got a fever."

"Get him in now!"

"All the beds are full."

"Put him on a gurney and park him in the hallway. See if Annie can finish here with Mr Gattuso."

A few minutes later, Kelly rounded the corner to find Vik examining a flushed Diego as Alma Sanchez anxiously looked on. Kelly nodded to Vik. "How's the patient?"

"He's running hot and the wound is tender to the touch. There might be some foreign matter still in there. A bullet fragment we missed, maybe some threads from his pants."

"Let's reflush the wound and get a new set of pictures."

"Our x-ray machine's not working right now, Doctor," said Sonita, with a pained expression on her face. She hated to be the bearer of bad news.

Kelly snapped, "How long's it been down?"

"I don't know. It was working earlier today."

Kelly's face betrayed her rising frustration, but there was no time for that. Vik was speaking to her and she needed to calm down and refocus.

"Sorry, Doctor," she said to Vik. "What were you saying?"

"I'm worried about compartment syndrome."

Mrs Sanchez was alarmed by the doctor's level of concern. "What is that?"

Vik explained that pressure could be building up inside an enclosed space in Diego's leg. Kelly took Alma's hand in hers. "You've got to get Diego to the hospital. Now."

Diego protested, "No! You can fix me here."

Kelly turned to Diego, her compassion running high but her patience wearing thin. "Unfortunately we can't. You've got to get to a hospital."

Diego vehemently shook his head. He was only ten years old, but he already rivaled his mother's level of obstinacy. There was clearly something else at play here.

Kelly turned to Vik. "Dr Danabalan, escort Mrs Sanchez to the waiting room."

Vik moved toward Mrs Sanchez, who took a defensive posture. "I have to stay with him. He's only a child!"

Diego was embarrassed by his mother's outburst. *"Estoy bien, mama. Vete!"*

As Vik led Mrs Sanchez away, Kelly leaned over Diego. "Tell me the truth. Are you covering for someone?"

"No," he responded too quickly.

"Does this have anything to do with Oscar?"

"No, I told you already."

"Diego, do you want to lose your leg?"

Fear flashed across Diego's face. "You playing me?"

Kelly shook her head. "This is some serious shit."

Diego's eyes welled with tears. Kelly let him cry.

Back in her father's office, Kelly's frustration reached previously uncharted levels as she spoke to the medical equipment leasing company. She explained the obvious: they couldn't run a clinic without a working x-ray machine and needed someone out there immediately to repair it. That's when she was informed their service agreement had elapsed.

Kelly was dumbfounded. "How's that possible?"

The unsympathetic sales rep on the other end of the phone explained their bill was ninety days overdue. Did she want to talk to someone in billing?

"No," Kelly said, sounding like she was about to reach through the phone and strangle the rep on the other end of the line. "I want someone

71

out here to fix it or replace it! People are dying!" She hoped a little melodrama might prod him into a sense of urgency.

She was wrong.

Kelly was put on hold, and after five minutes of soft jazz that sounded like it was recorded on an eight-track tape that had been left in the sun, and a repeated sales pitch hyping the advantages of medical equipment leasing, Kelly was ready to take a sledgehammer to the x-ray machine. She finally got a human on the line, and after agreeing to have a cashier's check ready for the repairman in the morning, she slammed down the phone.

Kelly sat quietly for a moment, taking measured breaths, trying to control her temper. She couldn't make any sense of what her father had been going through before he died. Not paying the bills for Jessica's care; not keeping current on service agreements for the machines that were critical to the clinic. Were they in such dire financial straits that they couldn't afford to keep the place running effectively? If so, why wouldn't he tell her that? Or was the answer darker? Had her father somehow dug himself into a deep hole? Did he have a gambling problem? A drug problem?

First and foremost, Kelly had to figure out a way to pay the bills. Then there was the question of those landmines. What other secrets did her father have?

The enormity of the burden that he'd left behind suddenly overwhelmed her. She let out a roar and swept everything off his desk, sending it crashing to the floor.

She collapsed back in his chair and felt like having a good old-fashioned cleansing cry, but she knew there were patients out there who needed help. She'd cry later.

As Kelly rose, she surveyed the damage she'd done. She'd be here late tonight cleaning up the mess. On her way out of the office, she noticed a photo of her and her father, taken at her medical school graduation ceremony. His arm was around her shoulder, his face beaming with pride. She picked up the framed photo and noticed that the glass had cracked… one jagged line going right down the middle.

Kelly held back her tears as she gently set the photo back on the desk.

She'd definitely cry later.

Nine o'clock finally rolled around. The waiting room was empty and the onslaught was over. Nathan departed right at the stroke of nine without a shred of guilt. Just slipped out the back, Jack. He'd put in his hours and had places to go and people to see.

The rest of the medical staff gathered in the treatment area, where Kelly was thanking everyone for the amazing job they did under less than ideal conditions.

"If my father was here today, he'd be damn proud of you all. I can't thank you enough for the incredible…"

She was interrupted by someone rattling the front doors, followed by incessant banging. Ramona looked over at Kelly. Did she want to open the doors to another patient at this hour?

Kelly took a deep breath. "Go see what it is."

Moments later, Ramona hurried back in. "Looks like a teenage boy, bleeding. Someone propped him up against the door, then drove off."

Everyone was working on fumes, their eyes glazed over with fatigue, but Kelly wasn't the least bit surprised when Vik spoke up. "I'm good to keep going, Doctor."

The others chimed in. They'd stay as long as Kelly wanted them to.

A tear formed at the corner of her eye. This is why she needed to keep the clinic going. There were still questions of whether it was practical, or even possible. She'd deal with those questions tomorrow.

To Ramona, "Get him in here."

She later found out his name was Ruben "Joker" Garcia, aged 17. His tats revealed he was a member (or former member) of the 19th Street Sureños. He'd been shot three times in the stomach, and had been bleeding profusely when he was dropped off.

The doctors did everything possible to stem the bleeding, but Joker was too far gone. Had the Sureños delivered him to the clinic in hopes that the staff could perform a miracle, or did they dump him there to die?

The answer was inconsequential. Either way, Joker was just one more boy from the streets who met a violent end. There'd be one more grief-stricken family, and one more gallon of fuel tossed onto the growing pyre of hatred and revenge between the warring factions.

It would have been a tragic way to end the day, but unfortunately, the day wasn't over yet.

11

Nathan pulled his Porsche 911 Cabriolet into the circular driveway of his parents' magnificent home in the posh Pacific Heights area. Despite the late hour, the house was ablaze with light. Since turning sixty, Nathan's mother seemed to develop a new phobia every few months. She was already "suffering" from severe taphephobia (fear of being buried alive), pediculophobia (fear of lice) and Nathan's favorite, lyssophobia, the fear of going insane, which was one thing she *should* be concerned about.

In the past week, she'd suddenly come down with a case of severe scotophobia, the fear of darkness. The moment the sun started to disappear behind the horizon, ornate cut-crystal chandeliers throughout the house were fired up. Fortunately, Nathan's father could afford the exorbitant electric bills, but hoped that his wife's next phobia was something that didn't carry a greater financial impact; he was loath to spend money if it didn't result in a fiscal return.

The Curtis home (or "estate", as they preferred to call it) originally belonged to a distant heir of Charles Crocker, one of San Francisco's "Big Four" who made millions during the gold rush. The last Crocker to own the house was tragically addicted to opium (a habit acquired in the "pleasure dens" secreted in Chinatown backrooms) and sold off everything of value to slake his unquenchable thirst. This included artwork, furniture and even fixtures (a claw-foot bathtub, four pedestal sinks and six toilets). When he died seven years ago, the house was in a state of epic disrepair.

Randall Curtis had swooped in and purchased the home for well under market value. Unlike his son, Randall had the appearance of a wolf on the prowl, always looking for juicy prey, preferably something succulent that didn't put up much of a fight. He considered the purchase of the Crocker estate one of his greatest hunting trophies.

Two years and three million dollars later, the house had been transformed into an ostentatious mansion that quintessentially reflected its new owner. And because Randall never encountered a pretention he didn't embrace, he gave the home a name: "Golden View Manor" (you could see the Golden Gate in the distance on a clear day).

Everything about the house reeked of Randall's daily mantra: 'success at any cost'. In his world there were only two types of people: winners and losers. To be a winner you had to rise above the pack, even if it meant standing on the backs of the people you trampled to get there. There was no middle ground; you were either the top dog or a mongrel. Randall had no use for mongrels.

He suffered from "short man syndrome", an inferiority complex brought on by his below-average stature. Randall had maxxed out at five foot six ("and a half," he insisted) and every whispered leprechaun joke, every overheard Napoleon barb, every quietly muttered jockey comparison only served to exacerbate his drive to amass greater fortune at the expense of others.

He graduated at the top of his class at Stanford, and again at the Haas School of Business across the bay at Berkeley. Despite nagging accusations of scholastic improprieties and three claims of sexual assault, upon graduation Randall was heavily recruited by financial institutions. He joined a brokerage firm in San Francisco and it wasn't long before he was running his own division specializing in creative financing for start-ups, of which there were literally hundreds. While most died on the vine, a few developed into gold mines, and the bounty generated by the successful companies paid for the losers many, many times over.

Within a few years, the money was pouring in and Randall had a well-deserved (and heavily self-promoted) reputation as a corporate visionary. There were issues with him being untrustworthy, abusive and an all-round asshole, but his portfolio made him bulletproof. Or so he thought, until he drunkenly molested the seventeen-year-old daughter of the company's Chief Legal Counsel at the Christmas party. This triggered a closer look at his almost mythical funding formula and it turned out that Randall was running a Ponzi scheme. Shortly after the New Year, Randall was ousted, and one month later opened up his own firm.

Like his father, Nathan was a well-above-average student, but he lacked the drive and killer instinct to claw his way to the top. Even with

Randall's alumni connections, Nathan couldn't get into Stanford (nor did he want to), so Randall insisted he "at least" go to an Ivy to save face for the family. Nathan ended up at Princeton, which provided him with a three thousand-mile buffer from his family. Randall was happy because of all the schools in the Ivy League, Princeton was the least expensive.

Nathan never wanted to go into business with his father because he couldn't bear the thought of having to face Randall's tyrannical wrath on a professional basis. Nathan could see what others saw, that his father was a pompous prick who was intolerable if he didn't get his way. If Randall was to suddenly lose his money, San Francisco socialites would line up to buy tickets to see him drawn and quartered, and they'd giddily shell out extra for the souvenir t-shirts.

Nathan wanted to be a doctor. Specifically, a General Practitioner. It was a noble profession, he could make decent money and take pride in what he did.

When he told mother and father of his plans, Randall scoffed. If his son was going to be a doctor, then he should become a neurosurgeon. They made the most money and were held in the highest esteem in the medical pecking order. In Randall's mind, a GP was no better than a proctologist. "You might as well spend your days with your head shoved up someone's ass." Nathan didn't waste his breath setting his father straight on proctologic methodology.

Nathan had hoped to receive a modicum of support from his mother, but he wasn't at all surprised when that wasn't forthcoming. The once stunning and now matronly Catherine Curtis was a non-participant in this battle. Her days consisted of deciding on her next plastic surgery as she chased a youthful beauty that would forever tempt and elude her. In the meantime, she turned a blind eye to Randall's philandering and pretended she didn't hear the nasty murmuring of her catty acquaintances who all seemed to know about her husband's latest conquest.

The correlation between Randall's affairs and Catherine's deteriorating state of mind was obvious to Nathan, and there was no end in sight. The more his mother spiraled downward, the more his father cheated, perpetuating the cycle of familial destruction.

Nathan entered Randall's home office to find his father working the phones. It was 11pm on the West Coast, but there was always business to be done somewhere in the world. Randall snapped his fingers, signaling his son to take a seat while he wrapped up his call.

Nathan glanced around at the familiar surroundings. The walls were lined with photos of Randall with politicians. Senators, Governors and a few Presidents. There was a single photo of a thirty-two-year-old Catherine on Randall's desk, and Nathan knew it was there for show, not out of affection. The charade stopped with Catherine; there were no photos of Nathan to be found.

Randall hung up the phone with a smile. "Just closed a deal with the tech division of Wanda in Beijing to co-finance a new ride-share startup. If it works, we'll blow Uber out of the water in Asia." He lit his tenth cigar of the day, contentedly blowing the smoke toward the ceiling. "This thing with David Harper was a stroke of good luck, huh?"

Nathan was constantly surprised at how callous his father could be. After all these years, he thought he'd be immune to it by now, but Randall never ceased to amaze. "By 'this thing', you mean his death?"

"Of course I mean his death."

"It was tragic. Dr Harper was a good man."

"Well, it doesn't matter how 'good' he was, does it? He's dead, and we need to move fast to take advantage of that. You heard the other night at dinner that there's talk of a major gentrification project for that part of the Mission. If we can fold the clinic into the Wallace Group, it'll be a home run."

"Why that clinic? Why not just open another one in the same area? There are a lot of empty storefronts."

"Because the Wallace Group doesn't want competition. They have a pricing structure that only works if they have a geographic monopoly."

"What if the Mission Street Clinic were to close?" Nathan asked, instantly regretting the potential consequences of his suggestion.

Randall shrugged. "That's a fallback scenario. One of the reasons that clinic is so attractive is because it has an excellent reputation. Have you looked at the Yelp reviews?"

"It's gotten that rep because of the physicians, not because of the location."

Randall exhaled a blue cloud of Cuban smoke. "You really think the illegals who go there would care, or even notice, if the doctors were different? Not a fucking chance."

Nathan cocked his head slightly, like a dog hearing a high-pitched sound and racking its canine brain to make sense of it. How could his father be so clueless and yet so damn successful?

Randall continued, "Do you think the daughter's going to keep the clinic going?"

"She's idealistic enough, but it sounds like she's having money issues."

"Excellent!" Randall said with glee. "You're Mister Inside, my ace in the hole. For once in your life, I'm hoping you can come through for me and make something happen."

"I'm already working on it. In fact, we had a long and very productive conversation about it this afternoon." If Nathan learned one thing from his father, it was to embellish the truth. Despite the emotional and sentimental disconnect between father and son, Nathan was hard-wired to seek his father's approval. He knew theirs was a textbook dysfunctional relationship, but some things are genetically programmed.

"Great. I've already done my part, so I'm counting on you to do your part. Try not to fuck this up."

12

It was one in the morning when Kelly finally left the clinic. The police and coroner had come and gone, along with Ruben Garcia's body.

She was utterly exhausted. Even locking the back door on her way out felt like a complex task. Generally after a long shift she was mentally fatigued, but her body was adrenalized. It was a valuable mind-over-matter discipline that was drummed into young doctors in medical school. Regardless of how many hours you worked, it was critical to develop a reservoir of energy that could be tapped in the event that a major catastrophe occurred and medical help was needed. On most nights she dipped into that reserve just to get herself home.

Tonight that reserve was already sapped. The long day at the clinic, ending with losing a patient, culminated a miserably long week, and all she wanted was to get home, take a hot shower and collapse into her bed. Was that asking too much?

Evidently.

She heard a scuffling sound and turned to locate the source, but visibility in the heavily shadowed parking lot was extremely limited. The only illumination came from the low-wattage bulb that hung over the rear door of the clinic. The scuffling got louder, and Kelly could barely make out vague outlines of three people, slowly approaching.

Her paranoia ratcheted up several notches. After the events of the past few days, every sound and every shadow made her jumpy. She wondered if she'd be able to make it to her car before being assaulted.

As the trio got closer, Kelly could see they were young, and they were carrying weapons. Bangers! They had to be the Sureños, coming to see what happened to Ruben. Once they found out he'd died, there was no telling how they'd react, but Kelly guessed it wouldn't be a joyful outburst of appreciation.

She glanced over to her car. It was at least thirty yards away. One hundred feet. Could she get there in time?

She looked back at the gang, who had quickly closed the gap. As they stepped into the weak light, Kelly's paranoia gave way to confusion. They were in their late teens, all wearing long red t-shirts and red, flat-billed SF 49ers hats; red was the color of the Norteños, the dominant street gang in the city.

"Hey, Doctor," the leader said in a wispy, sing-song voice.

Kelly's heart raced. When she spoke, it was a soft, trembling sound that belied her fear. "What do you want?"

The alpha of this trio was Francisco Ramos. On the street they called him Gizmo. Whippet-thin, cold eyes and gold-capped front teeth, Gizmo had the mien of a hardened banger. There was something familiar about him, but Kelly had trouble finding his face in her fuzzy memory banks.

Gizmo's voice didn't fit the killer image he tried hard to project, but given his stature in the gang, it was almost certain that he'd taken a life or two. In a weird way, his melodic speech pattern made him scarier.

"What happened to the Scrap who was dropped off tonight?"

'Scrap' was just one of the derogatory terms Norteños used for the Sureños, their mortal enemies.

"I don't talk about my patients," Kelly said with an edge of irritation.

"Just want to know if the *puto* walked out or was rolled out."

Kelly hesitated. She knew word of Ruben Garcia's death would be old news throughout the Mission by breakfast. "He didn't make it. He was critically injured when he arrived."

Gizmo's posse traded high-fives, but their celebration was cut short by a scorching look from Kelly.

"A young man died tonight, and that's tragic."

Gizmo shrugged. "Shit happens, you know?"

Kelly finally placed Gizmo/Francisco. Years ago, when he was fourteen, he'd come into the clinic bleeding from a brutal slash across his abdomen. Kelly patched him up, and tried to impress upon him how fortunate he was. If the knife had penetrated his stomach a quarter inch deeper, Francisco would've spent the rest of his life with a colostomy bag... not a good look for an up-and-coming gangster.

She'd optimistically hoped the incident would convince him to find his way clear of the gang, but she knew he was destined to fall into the life like his brother, uncle and father before him. The life they knew; it gave them a larger sense of family and stature. More importantly, being in the gang was a source of income that they couldn't match elsewhere without an education and a lot of hard work… and, in reality, most of these kids didn't have any desire to break away from what they considered to be their destiny. The irony was that while joining a gang was the easy route, it resulted in the hardest life.

Gizmo's neck was inked with a large Roman numeral 14, which stood for the letter N (for Norteños). His left arm bore the words *"Nuestra Familia"* in heavily scrolled script, and his right arm featured the names of his *hermanos* who had been killed or put away for life.

"Francisco, right?" Kelly said.

"My homies call me Gizmo."

"How's your stomach, Gizmo?"

The duo behind Gizmo snickered at the sound of his name coming from this *guera*. Gizmo made a short chopping motion with his hand and they immediately went silent. There was no question who was in charge.

"My stomach?" He raised his shirt and showed his scar with pride. "The *chicas* love it," he said with a lascivious grin. "You did good, Doctor. We want you to do the same for Diego."

"Why are you concerned about Diego?"

"Because we take care of our own. The Sanchez blood runs deep with us, you know."

"I know. What I don't know is why ten-year-old kids are in the line of fire."

Gizmo shrugged. "Like I said, shit happens. Like when *pendejos* come across the line looking for trouble."

The Norteños were affiliated with *Nuestra Familia*, while their rivals, the Sureños, were an offshoot of the Mexican Mafia. The original factions were formed in a Fresno prison in the mid-1960s, and since then, the two sides engaged in a never-ending battle for power and territory. Too frequently, an innocent person was caught in the crossfire.

Case in point, Diego Sanchez.

Gizmo continued, "Norteños cruise up past 24th, they lookin' to start something. We gotta hold our line. They open up and Diego catches it. Spider tole us you gonna take care of him, but then we see him on the street and he lookin' ill."

81

"Diego needs to go to the hospital. I already explained that to him and to his mother."

Gizmo shook his head. "Diego is tough. He don't need no hospital. You can just give him some drugs and shit and make him okay." It wasn't a question. It was a command, tinged with a threat.

"'Drugs and shit' aren't going to make him okay," said Kelly. "I wish it was that easy, but it's not. You have to trust me on this."

Gizmo took a step forward and Kelly could smell the stale beer and cloying aroma of pot on his breath and clothing. "We do trust you. We don't trust the hospital. Too many times one of our own goes in and ends up dead or in jail. Diego's not going to any hospital, so you need to make him right." He punctuated this statement by lightly jabbing his finger into Kelly's chest.

"Hey! Who do you…?" Before she could finish her question, Gizmo shot out his hand and grabbed her face. "We like you, Doctor, but don't fuck this up. You take care of our little *hermano*. It's best for everyone, you know?"

The night's temperature dropped a few degrees when Gizmo smiled, his gold caps glinting. He released Kelly's face from his grasp, and then turned and strode away, his posse falling in behind him.

Kelly watched as the three of them disappeared back into the darkness from whence they came. She felt that her world was collapsing around her, and yet she had no idea what to do to put the pieces back together.

She desperately missed her father.

13

One of the most popular breakfast spots in the city was Mama's in North Beach, known for its French toast, warm family-owned atmosphere and long lines. Kelly and Alexa sat at a small table near the kitchen. The aromas of baked goods and fresh ground coffee had mystical properties, making them impossible to resist, and their table was littered with the remains of blueberry scones and orange-cranberry muffins.

Alexa was deeply worried about her friend. Kelly looked exhausted, her skin was pallid, and her face was puffy. Maybe from crying (which was understandable) and maybe from drinking (which was also understandable, but more problematic). Alexa was eager to do whatever it took to help Kelly get her life back on track.

Kelly had never asked Alexa for financial advice and was slightly embarrassed to do so now, but she didn't know where else to turn. After Kelly laid out the facts of the clinic's financial troubles, she sat back and waited for any sage guidance that her friend could impart.

"Do you have a full accounting of the clinic's assets versus debt?" Alexa asked.

Kelly shook her head. "I spoke to our CPA this morning. She's pulling together the financials and didn't have all the answers yet. She made it clear that the clinic was deep in the red and Dad put just enough in the business account each month to keep the wolves at bay. Barely."

"And that was money generated by the clinic?"

"I guess. According to his will, he didn't have any other assets. He mentioned some investments he had, but I have no idea what he was talking about. As far as I can tell, he didn't have a brokerage account or any hidden savings."

"How much do you need to keep the clinic afloat?"

Kelly shrugged. "All I know is we have a stack of bills, we're short one doctor, and I've got to make sure that Jess continues to get the best care possible."

Alexa leaned in. "I've got some money put away and..."

"Lex, I didn't come here to borrow money. I came for advice."

"My advice is you let me loan you money until you can get some financing in order. Seriously, it's not a big deal, and I'd feel so much better if you didn't have to agonize over this right now."

"That's extremely generous, and I love you for it, but it's a non-starter. My life is complicated enough. The last thing I need is to worry about paying you back." Kelly took a sip of her latte and asked, "Does your company do these kind of loans?"

Alexa shook her head. "Unfortunately, no. Our minimal investment is ten million."

"What do you know about Vantage or the Wallace Medical Group?"

Alexa's reaction was immediate and unmistakable. She spent the next ten minutes detailing how Vantage was the poster child of unscrupulous and exploitative business practices. There'd been an unending string of lawsuits over the years from clients who'd been mercilessly ripped off. Randall Curtis, the CEO of Vantage, employed more lawyers than financial analysts and had enough cash reserve to outwait and outmuscle every plaintiff. More than ninety percent of the suits ended in paltry settlements. Basically, Curtis was well known in the financial community as a bottom-feeding piece of shit.

"There are reputable companies out there who'll extend you a loan, but the interest rates may not be tenable for a small clinic. Kel, I know how much it means to you to keep the clinic open, but it may not be economically feasible."

"It was my father's dream. I have to find a way to keep it going. For him, for me, and for the community."

"I get it. Just promise me you won't make a deal with the devil."

Kelly hoped it wouldn't come to that, but she was running out of options. She managed a smile for Alexa's benefit. "Promise."

14

Kelly approached the clinic in an optimistic mood, comforted by the knowledge that if she had absolutely nowhere else to turn, she could take Alexa up on her offer. For now, she desperately hoped there'd be no more surprises.

It didn't take long for that hope to be obliterated.

The back door was ajar. Strange. The staff didn't arrive for another thirty minutes. Why would someone be there now, and why would they leave the door open?

She approached tentatively, before coming to an abrupt stop. The back door was normally secured with an electronic alarm, which had been prised off and tossed several feet away, along with fragments of the doorframe. What the hell was going on?

Kelly began to tremble. She didn't know if it was anger or fear or a combination of both. Did this have something to do with the car that tried to run her down? Was this the work of the Sureños because she couldn't save Ruben Garcia?

She took out her phone. Her hands were shaking so badly she had trouble hitting the speed dial for Pete. In a voice that was somewhere between panic and hysteria, Kelly explained what she was looking at. Pete responded in a soothing, controlled tone. He'd notify the Burglary Detail and they'd have a squad car there in a few minutes. In the meantime, under no circumstances was she to go inside. In fact, she should move away from the building and wait someplace safe for the police to arrive.

Kelly hung up and stared at the damaged door, trying and failing to wrap her head around what was happening. Just a week ago everything was going along fine, and now the fabric of her life was unraveling, a little more each day. If this continued, there'd soon be nothing left but a pile of mismatched threads.

Her thoughts turned dark. She fantasized about confronting whoever might be inside. A razor-sharp scalpel in each hand, she'd rain hell down upon the intruder, meting out justice and leaving behind a bloody mass of human carnage. Her father would be avenged.

Kelly's violent fantasy was cut short by the piercing sound of police sirens. She shook her head to help cleanse her mind. She'd never experienced anything resembling these murderous thoughts, and they scared the hell out of her.

A short time later, two uniformed officers emerged from the clinic, holstering their weapons. There were no intruders inside, but someone had definitely been there. Also, the power was out. Kelly took a moment to process this bit of news. Why was the power out? Did her father neglect to pay the electric bill as well?

One of the patrolmen suggested she wait until someone from Burglary arrived before she went inside. Kelly thanked him, but she didn't need an escort.

She stepped through the doorway and let out a horrified gasp. Beds were overturned, sheets and blankets shredded. Drawers of medical supplies were pulled out, their contents dumped with abandon, then stomped on. Bags of fluids were ripped open and watery glucose ran in tiny rivulets. The walls bore holes from chairs that were viciously hurled, and IV poles had been violently rammed into the plasterboard.

Kelly wandered from room to room in a state of shock. The damage varied, but her father's office was hit the worst; the desk had been ransacked and the file cabinets tipped on their sides. Her tears flowed unabated. So much time, effort and love had gone into building this clinic. It was the final testament to the memory of her father, and someone had savagely and maliciously vandalized that memory.

As she surveyed the senseless destruction, Pete arrived. "Damn. They really did a number in here."

Kelly was openly sobbing. "Why would someone do this?"

A moment later, a lanky middle-aged man with a prominent nose, pocked cheeks and sad eyes entered. He wore his badge on a lanyard around his neck.

"Hey, Pete," he said with a tired voice.

Pete shook the hand of Inspector Larry Poe from Burglary and introduced him to Kelly. She wiped her face on her sleeve and did her best to pull herself together.

The first question Larry asked was, "Have you checked the pharmaceuticals?"

They moved across the hall to the secured room that held the clinic's drugs. The door and the doorframe were made of steel, the locking mechanism had a double-action bolt that required the use of two keys. David Harper had foreseen the inherent danger in having a storeroom of opioids in a high crime area.

The door had clearly been kicked several times, and when that didn't work, it was struck with a chair. Fortunately, the door held fast.

Larry flipped a light switch a few times with no results. "Where's the electrical panel?"

"In the storeroom," Kelly responded.

A moment later, Larry had the panel open and easily identified the problem. "The breaker's off." He used a tissue to flip the breaker and the lights came back on. "I'm guessing they created an external power surge, which automatically shut off the electricity."

"What's the point of that?"

"Your security system operates via broadband monitoring. When the power's off, the internet goes down and the connection to the security company is cut. That's why the alarm didn't sound when they broke through the door. This wasn't a random break-in by a desperate junkie." Larry turned to Pete. "Probably gang-related."

Kelly slowly shook her head. "All we do here is help people. People in this community. Sureños, Norteños... none of that matters to me. And now this... I don't know what to do."

Pete wanted to reach out and take her in his arms, tell her everything would be all right, but he resisted the urge.

"Insurance should cover the damage," Larry said. "It looks a lot worse than it is. You'll be up and running again in a few days."

Kelly snapped her head around. "A few days?"

"It's a crime scene," Larry said, as if it were obvious. "We need to take prints."

Kelly's ire was rising. "If they were smart enough to cut the power, they were probably smart enough to wear gloves. I have to get this place cleaned up so we can be back in business."

Pete did his best to calm her down. "Kel, it's protocol. Plus, you're going to need a police report for your insurance claim, which means the crime-scene investigators have to come in and do their thing."

Kelly's frustration was growing by the second and threatening to blow.

Pete looked over to Larry, who got the message. "I'll see if they can make this a priority."

"Please," Kelly said a little too brusquely. "I have to go tell the people waiting outside they'll need to go somewhere else for treatment."

As she strode away, Larry turned to Pete. "She's the one whose father was killed in that hit and run?"

"Yeah. And now this."

Larry glanced around at the damage and shook his head. "That's some shitty week. Look, we'll go through the motions, but you know we're not gonna turn up anything, right?"

Pete nodded.

At the end of the day, they'd be left with more questions than answers.

15

The Vantage company was located on the thirty-fourth floor of 101 California Street in the heart of the financial district. This was the same floor where, in 1993, a man named Gian Ferri had walked into the law firm of Pettit and Martin and killed eight people and wounded six others before killing himself. Randall Curtis found that sordid piece of history a captivating factoid to share with prospective clients.

Randall's office was predictably ostentatious. Floor-to-ceiling windows were a visual gateway to the San Francisco Bay, the Bay Bridge and beyond. Bookcases were lined with leather-bound books that had never been cracked, and, of course, there was Randall's Wall Of Fame. Dozens of 8 x 10 photos, all framed in identical gold-leaf rectangles. Whereas his home office featured pics of him with politicians, this display was a testament to Randall's ego and was all about flash. Each photograph featured him with a famous athlete or Hollywood celebrity. All were signed with pithy tributes that read like they were coerced at gunpoint. The display was Randall's hackneyed way of saying to clients, "If you do business with Vantage, one day you'll be able to hang out with famous people, too!"

Randall paced as he spoke on the phone with the CEO of a copper mine in Ely, Nevada. Randall rarely sat down, and according to his gold Apple watch, he walked the equivalent of five miles a day while making deals. "We can turn Quadra into a huge player in the industry. I guarantee that with the new equipment we're talking about, you'll double your output to a hundred and twenty thousand metric tons per year. Once you sign the line of credit, I can have that equipment delivered within three days."

As he gave his spiel, Randall walked over to his beloved wall and squared up the slightly askew photo of him and Jimmy Garappolo. If Jimmy G didn't take the 49ers to another Superbowl next year, the picture would come down and join the collection of also-rans in the storeroom. "I'm telling you, Michael. Twenty-four months from now, Freeport-McMoRan will be making a play to acquire your company and you'll become a very, very wealthy man."

The door to his office opened. Standing immediately outside was a granite block of a man named Burr. A former college lineman who spent four years protecting his quarterback's blind side, Burr now spent his days protecting Randall's blind side. There were too many crazies out there with easy access to firearms that might hold a grudge against a ruthless bastard like Randall Curtis, who had no qualms about stepping all over "the little people".

The scent of Coco Mademoiselle wafted in a moment before a stunning blonde walked through the door. Randall held up one finger and finished his call, "Talk to your Board and get back to me soon." Randall smiled as he wound up to deliver his favorite lie, "The interest rates are fluctuating like crazy and I heard from my guy in DC that the Feds are planning another increase any day now, so don't wait on this."

Randall disconnected with a triumphant grin, then turned to face his shapely secretary. He famously lost his shit if he was interrupted while on a call, but Krista had only worked for him for a few days and wasn't aware of the correct protocol. Besides, Randall cut Krista a lot of slack because she was gorgeous, and because he planned to spend some serious long lunches with her at his suite at the Ritz. Instead of ranting, he smiled. "Yes?"

"Your son is here to see you, Mr Curtis."

"My son?" Randall was puzzled. "Nathan?"

Krista's face was blank. "He didn't say his name. Just that he was your son. I assumed he was. Should I ask him his name?"

"It's Nathan," a voice said a moment before he walked into the office. Nathan turned to Krista and motioned for her to leave. He watched her sashay out and then closed the door behind her.

Randall shifted gears from lascivious to caution. Nathan rarely visited the office, but Randall had a reasonable idea of why the prodigal son was standing there with a confrontational look on his face.

"I just came from the clinic."

Randall didn't take the bait. "And?"

Nathan approached his father, his round face reddening. "And it's closed today, but I think you know that."

Randall shrugged. "Why would I know that?"

"Because someone broke in and trashed the place."

"Really?" Randall was First Team All-Pro at feigning his emotions. "Your Doctor Harper is having a stretch of real bad luck."

Randall plucked a cigar from an ornately carved humidor and made an elaborate production out of clipping off the end with a sterling silver cutter engraved with his initials.

"Did your thug out there have something to do with this?" Nathan asked.

Randall took time to light his cigar, rolling it slowly to get a perfect ash started. The bootleg Cubans were fifty bucks a pop and were to be treated with respect. When he exhaled, he resisted the great temptation of blowing the smoke in the direction of the annoying scion standing before him. "That's absurd. I'm a businessman, not a mob boss. Next thing, you'll be accusing me of putting a hit on David Harper."

Despite his anger, Nathan's voice quavered. "I've heard the stories all my life about how Randall Curtis is cold-blooded when it comes to business. How he won't take 'no' for an answer. How he'll go to any lengths to close a deal, regardless of who gets hurt." Nathan took a step closer, and as he did, his tone grew bolder.

"You know who I heard those libelous stories from? You. So do I think you'd resort to heavy-handed tactics to drive Kelly Harper's clinic out of business? In a heartbeat."

"You can think whatever you want," Randall said in a snarky tone, "but don't go around spreading that rumor."

"Or what? You'll send your thugs after *me*?"

Randall shook his head and a smile creased his face. "I don't need hired muscle to deal with you, son. You know why? Because you're weak, and because you'll do exactly what you're told, which is to help me close this deal. Isn't that right?"

The air in the office suddenly felt thick and Nathan found it difficult to breathe. As a child, Nathan suffered from what the doctors called "psychological asthma"; his throat would close up when he became tense, nervous or afraid. In the Curtis household, those conditions occurred with regularity. Nathan reflexively reached for the inhaler he'd stopped carrying fifteen years ago.

"Are you feeling alright, son?" Randall asked without a shred of compassion.

Nathan stared at the man across from him and recalled a recurring childhood prayer… that someday Nathan would meet his *real* father.

16

Sergeant Miguel Urbina grew up in San Jose and joined the *Sureños Por Vida* at age twelve. A born overachiever, he rose from lookout to dealer in two years. By the time he was seventeen, he was point man for a half dozen pushers. Two years later, he was picked up during a routine drug sweep and landed at Ironwood Prison in Riverside County.

The *Emes* on the inside embraced him, and he gladly accepted their protection. It was only a matter of weeks before they invited him to take an active role in their prison rackets. While only nineteen, Miguel was whip smart and ambitious. Within six months, he'd opened up new distribution channels (muling in more drugs from the outside) and broadened their clientele base (the shit that came in was righteous and the guards became repeat customers). By his twentieth birthday, Miguel was a rising star… until life took a hard left turn.

Miguel's sixteen-year-old sister Rosa had gone to a friend's birthday party and had stepped outside for a smoke at the wrong time. It turned out that a classmate named Berto Mendez hadn't gotten an invite to the party and was beyond pissed. After fueling his courage and anger with a pint of cheap vodka and two black beauties, he grabbed his cousin's H&K MP5 and hopped into his brother's Taurus. He never meant to kill anyone, and yet fifteen minutes later, the party house was sprayed with bullets and Rosa was cut in half.

After realizing what he'd done, Berto turned the gun on himself. The final tally was two dead, four injured, and a neighborhood in mourning.

The shooting had nothing to do with gang warfare, but was clearly a result of the gang culture in South San Jo at the time. If a teenager a few miles up the freeway in Sunnyvale or Mountain View were to be excluded from a class party, he'd call up some friends to whine about the stuck-up bitch that was throwing the party and then post some regrettably dumb shit on her Facebook page. He wouldn't grab a semi-automatic rifle and go on a shooting spree.

Rosa's death hit Miguel hard. He pulled back from the *Emes* and kept to himself. They respected his decision and continued to watch his back, even when he decided to get an online diploma in Criminal Justice.

Miguel was released nine months early with an AA degree and a new outlook on his future. He spent two years as a gang counselor in San Jose, and helped extricate the Mayor's nephew from the *Varrio Sur Town*, which resulted in a blurb in the San Jose *Mercury News*. One thing led to another and Miguel was soon invited to take the test to join the SFPD academy.

Miguel Urbina was now forty-three, and had been running the SFPD Gang Task Force for the past six years. He knew the streets, the players and the plays. He got grudging respect from the Sureños. Even through he was 5-0, he'd walked the walk. He was much less popular with the Norteños, but that didn't stop him from getting the job done.

Miguel was heavy-set with broad shoulders and he took up more than his share of space in the cramped interview room. His presence was intimidating. The gangbanger sitting at the small wooden table tried to pretend otherwise, but his nervous tics and sweaty brow betrayed him.

Fernando "Nano" Rojas was second in command of the 19th Street Sureños. He could usually be found at the gang's crib on 19th and Lexington, but currently Nano was fidgeting in the stiff straight-back chair, facing not only Miguel, but Pete and Ron Yee as well. It was a full house and the air was ripe with body odor and testosterone.

"How many times I got to tell you, *ese*?" Nano asked, irritated as hell. Irritated to be sitting here instead of kicking with his homes, drinking Patron and relaxing with a blunt. "Joker was killed by those *chapetes* over on Mission."

Ron sat across from Nano while Pete paced, his features twisted into a bad-cop scowl. "Blaming the Norteños. That's original," Pete said. "You blame them when the fog rolls in. You blame them when the Niners have a shitty season."

"Hey, those *putos* wear the Niners' colors, the Niners deserve a shitty season, you know?"

"Get back to Joker. Did anyone actually see who shot him?" Ron asked.

"Shit, man. I don't know."

Miguel spoke up from the rear of the room, "I heard that Sad Boy saw it go down."

Nano shrugged. "Sad Boy ain't been around."

"Sad Boy. That's Ernesto Juarez, right?" Ron prodded, even though he knew the answer.

"If you say so."

Ron kept things positive. "And you have no idea where we can find Ernesto?"

Nano slumped down in his chair. "I told you, homes. He's gone. I'm not a fucking babysitter."

Ron sat back, letting the weight of the silence prompt Nano to keep talking. After a full minute, it worked.

"Maybe he's hanging with his cousin down in Merced or Turlock. One of those fucking dusty-ass towns in the Valley."

Pete leaned in. "So this Sad Boy sees Joker get shot by a Norteño, then runs someplace to hide. Sounds like a pussy to me."

"Sad Boy's no pussy," Nano replied. "Dude's only fourteen and already got made. He just someplace chillin'."

"Got a name for his cousin down in Turlock?" Miguel asked.

"*No lo se, Sargento,*" he said, spitting out the last word.

Miguel flexed his fingers and rolled his neck like he was about to get into the ring. He leaned in close, inches from Nano's face.

"Ask around, Nano. See what you can find out," Miguel said calmly with a not-so-subtle undercurrent of threat.

Nano tried to act tough, but his discomfort was showing. "I'll check with my boys."

Ron smiled. "That'd be really helpful, Nano. The sooner we can get some details, the sooner we can make an arrest and get the shooter off the street."

Nano was stone-faced. The Sureños had their own plans for the shooter.

As if reading his mind (which didn't take much), Pete leaned in and tapped his finger on the side of Nano's head. "Don't even think about retaliation. Any more blood spilled over this, and we'll come down on your ass like a fucking taco truck dropped from the sky."

Nano inherently knew when to shut the hell up and he responded with a dead-eyed stare.

"One more thing before you go," said Ron. "What do you know about the break-in at the Mission Street Clinic the other night?"

Nano shook his head, genuinely surprised at the news. "Someone broke into the clinic?"

Miguel nodded. "Word is, it might be your guys, acting all crazy after Joker died."

"Whose word? That's fucking bullshit, man," Nano said. "Some homies dropped him off, hoping the *blanca* there could work a miracle. No one really thought he was gonna make it. We ain't got nothing against the clinic."

Ron and Pete shared a glance. Pete had come to the same conclusion. It didn't make sense that members of either gang were responsible for the break-in. Which left the question... if not them, who?

Pete looked over at Nano one last time. "Get back to us about Sad Boy."

"I told you, *ese*. I'll ask around," Nano said, his ire rising.

"Today." Pete said.

"Or you'll drop a taco truck on me. I heard you. By the way, take a lesson from your partner how to dress, man. Dockers are for *pendejos*."

Ron and Miguel intercepted Pete before he could lay a beat-down on Nano's smirking face.

Ron was still laughing as he and Pete walked back to their cramped office in the two-story brick building that housed the Mission Station.

"Like a fucking taco truck dropped from the sky!" Ron broke into another fit of laughter.

"It was the best I could come up with at the time. I'm still working on this 'bad-cop' thing."

"Based upon my many years of experience, I've got an idea that would help in the future."

"Yeah?"

Ron stopped and faced his partner, dead serious. "Stop dressing like a *pendejo, ese*." Ron threw back his head and howled.

"First of all, these aren't Dockers. Secondly, who takes fashion tips from a punk whose wardrobe comes from the Dallas Cowboys' pro shop?"

"Good point, but it was still funny as hell."

"And I'll bet you can't wait to spread the joy with the rest of the squad."

"Me?" Ron said innocently, a moment before he broke into another bout of laughter.

They shared an office with six other Inspectors. On the infrequent occasions when everyone was on duty at the same time, oxygen became a rare commodity. The Inspectors were paired into four teams, and the desks of each team were pushed together face-to-face. It didn't afford much privacy, but it was an efficient use of space and led to better communication between partners.

The David Harper case was under the jurisdiction of the Hit and Run Detail, but due to the high profile nature of the victim, Homicide was looped in and asked to conduct a parallel investigation.

The story was still on the front page and the Mayor was adamant that he didn't want to be ambushed by the press due to his police department's failure to investigate every potential angle of this case. As such, Pete and Ron had been directed by their commanding officer to explore the possibility that David's death was intentional.

At this point, the case was stagnant. The two witnesses who'd seen the Jeep Cherokee couldn't provide a description of the driver because the windows had been blacked out. Forensics was still processing the vehicle, but was coming up empty. No prints. No hairs or fibers. No clues.

A thorough background check on David didn't turn up anything surprising or suspicious. He'd never been arrested, and there was no evidence of his involvement with drugs or gambling or sleeping with another man's wife... the three evils that could get a good man killed. He was a model citizen, and the more the facts lined up, the more it seemed highly unlikely that anyone had a reason to purposely crush him under two tons of automotive fury.

Pete and Ron also considered the incidents with Kelly. Were they somehow connected to David's death? Pete had already discounted

Kelly's close call with the SUV. She even admitted that she was distracted when she stepped off the curb. That left the break-in, which was much more ominous.

The preliminary report from Burglary confirmed that the perpetrators used something to create a power surge to knock out the electricity in the clinic, which led Ron to pose the question, "Do you really think that's the work of some random beaners looking for a score?"

Pete shook his head. "No. And I don't buy the fact that whoever did it was smart enough to knock out the power, but then didn't know about the steel door into the lockup. And, 'beaners'? Really?"

Ron leafed through the photos. "I think whoever broke in did exactly what they intended: to cause as much damage as possible. And, by the way, the term 'beaner' is not technically racist. The proud people of Mexico are known for their love of, and culinary dependence upon, the legume. Hence, referring to them as beaners is nothing more than a racially appropriate term."

"You, of all people…"

"Hold it right there!" Ron interjected. "Are you going to hit me with the fact that because I am of Chinese heritage, I can't use deprecatory adjectives when referring to people from other non-Caucasian races?"

"No. My point was that you, being one of the most decorated police officers in the SFPD, should be more vocally tolerant of the cultural mix we have in our city."

"When you put it that way…"

"Getting back to the clinic, why would someone run the risk of breaking in just to trash the place?"

"It always comes back to one question: who'd have something to gain from it?"

"Or, who had a massive grudge against the people who work there?"

Ron added, "Let's not completely dismiss the basic makeup of the criminal mind. The majority of the bad guys – white, black, brown, yellow or otherwise – are moronic dipshits. They think, 'Aha! We found a cool fucking way to break into this clinic! Let's do it!' And then once they're inside, they're like, 'Ah, shit! We can't get through this metal door!' And what do they do then? They take out their anger over the fact they were too fucking stupid to realize they had a stupid-ass plan to begin with."

"Sherlock Yee solves another one."

"When you've been at this as long as I have, and see the extraordinary depth of just how simpleminded the criminal element is, you, too, will be able to crack cases in a single bound."

As Pete looked through the crime-scene report, Ron got up and poured the remainder of a burnt pot of coffee into a chipped and stained coffee mug. "We're never going to find out who did this," Ron said, as he added an obscene amount of sugar to the coffee to cut the wretched flavor, "and the question is, does it really matter? Let's look at the chain of events in the light of realistic probability: David Harper was run over by a drunk driver; Kelly was distracted and stepped out into traffic, where she was almost hit by a guy driving home after a long day at the office; a couple of drug dealers figured the clinic was an easy score, but didn't figure on a steel door. Period. If you look at all of the events separately, they're easy to explain. If you try to tie them all together, you only end up tying yourself in knots."

Pete held his partner in high esteem, and had to admit this made sense. A lot of sense. "So, where do we go from here?"

"If you strongly believe these incidents have some connection to David Harper's death, add them to the murder book and we'll work them into the case. Otherwise, the clinic break-in becomes the sole purview of those dumb shits in Burglary and we move on. Your call."

Pete wanted to stay involved with anything that impacted Kelly, but he couldn't connect the dots between David Harper's death and someone breaking into the clinic. He knew they had to let this one go and stay focused on what mattered: determining if David Harper was the victim of involuntary manslaughter or premeditated murder.

17

St Francis Memorial Hospital was built atop Nob Hill more than a hundred years ago. Thirty years later, the spectacular Grace Cathedral was constructed a few blocks away. Both institutions were renowned for their excellence and both attracted either patients or parishioners from all over the Bay Area.

Kelly stood on the periphery of the St Francis Emergency Services area and watched as the doctors and nurses performed an intricate dance in perfect harmony, handling patients expediently and with utmost care. The ER was stocked with cutting-edge medical equipment: CT scanners, digital radiography, a portable x-ray machine and numerous six-channel patient monitors that were linked to the nurses' stations. It was worlds away from the clinic.

An attractive middle-aged woman with perfectly coifed hair and dressed in a subdued business suit informed Kelly that Dr Knudsen could see her now. As they made their way down a freshly scrubbed hallway, the woman asked if Kelly would like something to drink. Kelly's tank was dangerously close to empty and she gratefully accepted the offer of coffee. The stronger the better. The woman smiled and said they had an espresso machine in the lounge.

Minutes later, Kelly sat in the office of Dr Donald Knudsen, the Chief of Emergency Services. He was perched behind a large mahogany desk that was spotless, save for a few neatly stacked file folders and a framed photo of a multigenerational family posing outside a beautiful beach house on some exotic island.

At age sixty-eight, Knudsen had a runner's physique and still took part in the annual Bay-To-Breakers race that wove seven and a half miles through the hills of San Francisco and ended up at the shore. Tightly trimmed silver hair circled a bald crown, and designer glasses helped round out a thin face. Knudsen's most distinguishing features were his rich baritone voice and disarming smile. Combined with a charming sense of humor, Donald Knudsen was a hospital fundraiser's dream.

"I was devastated to hear about your father. He was an incredible physician and a wonderful man."

"Thank you. I'm still trying to come to grips with the fact he's gone."

"It's a process. Everyone handles it differently. My mother and I were very close and she died when I was in college. For years I'd instinctively reach for the phone to call her."

"I smell my father's aftershave every time I walk into his office. I can hear his voice calling out instructions in the clinic." Kelly sighed. "He was such a huge part of my life. When does the pain of missing him go away?"

Knudsen leaned back in his chair, a sad smile crossing his face. "There's no timetable. I thought about my mother every day for a few months, and then one day I realized it had been a week since she'd crossed my mind. I felt an overwhelming guilt." He shook his head. "I didn't miss her any less, I'd simply compartmentalized my memories and got on with living my life. It's been almost fifty years and I still miss her, but now when I think of her there's no sadness. I focus on the good times, and there were many."

He leaned forward in his chair. "You'll get there, but don't try to rush it. It's important to mourn." He leaned back in his chair. "I hope you're here to tell me that you've decided to join us."

"Not quite yet."

Knudsen nodded. "I realize how difficult it can be to make important life choices in the midst of all that's happened. Did you have more questions about the position?"

Kelly wasn't there with questions. She explained that she desperately wanted to keep the clinic open, but lacked the necessary cashflow (the insurance company was balking at covering the damage due to the fact that the security system wasn't functioning). She'd come to ask Dr Knudsen if he'd give her a little more time to decide about the job. If the clinic failed, she'd put that phase of her life behind her and would gladly join the staff at St Francis.

Knudsen tented his long fingers. "Since we're losing Dr Remensperger at the end of the month, I need to fill the Director of Emergency Services position rather quickly."

Kelly nodded. "I understand if you can't..."

"However," he interrupted, "given your excellent credentials, the extraordinary circumstances and my deep respect for your father, I'll keep the offer on the table for two more weeks."

Kelly felt the first wave of relief she'd had in several days. "Dr Knudsen, I truly appreciate it."

Knudsen stood. "I wish you the very best of luck with the clinic, but on the other hand, I hope you'll be part of the St Francis family. I know you'd thrive here and we'd be lucky to have another Dr Harper on staff."

As Kelly shook his hand, her sense of relief turned to self-doubt. Having this job as a fallback was a wonderful option, but in her heart she knew she'd never be happy here.

18

Kelly slid onto a stool at 44 Degrees and Philip approached with a bar rag and a smile, pulling a wine glass out of the overhead rack. He placed it in front of her and reached for a bottle of chilled Chardonnay.

"Am I that predictable, Philip?"

"I'm sure you're mysterious in real life, Doc, but your drinking habits are kinda one-note... not that there's anything wrong with that."

"I'm actually not that mysterious, but let's change it up tonight. Bourbon. Something off the top shelf."

"See? I would've never taken you for a bourbon drinker. There's definitely mystery lurking under the surface."

Philip grabbed a bottle and presented it to her. She nodded absent-mindedly. Not being a bourbon connoisseur, she didn't know the difference between Wild Turkey and Michter's Limited Edition, so when he showed her the bottle of Buffalo Trace Eagle Rare, she had no reaction.

"You said top shelf, right?"

"Is this the good stuff?"

Philip opened the bottle, poured a small amount into a glass, added a drop of water and slid it over. "You tell me. The first one's free."

"Ahh. Gently setting the hook." She raised the glass and sipped the amber liquid. A smooth warmth worked its way down her body and slowly transported her to a happier place. "Where's this been all my life?"

"Right up there, waiting for you to discover it. Two things you need to know. It's strictly for sipping and it's not cheap."

"I'm buying," said a warm voice from behind Kelly.

She turned to see a distinguished-looking man in his late fifties. He was impeccably dressed in an expertly tailored Brioni suit, topped with a Canali overcoat. Kelly pegged him as a broker, a lawyer, or God forbid, a hedge fund manager. For one frightening moment it occurred to her that this might be Randall Curtis, having tracked her down to talk to her about the clinic.

"Thank you," she finally managed, "but I'm waiting for my boyfriend."

"I apologize. I didn't mean to give the wrong impression, although I have to admit I'm flattered. My name is Matthew Benedetto," he said, as he handed her a business card. "I'm an old friend of your father."

"My father passed away," she said, the pain evident in her voice.

"I was at his memorial. A very deserved and extremely moving tribute. I should've said I *was* a friend, but I still feel a deep kinship with him. I hope that doesn't sound callous."

"Not at all."

Kelly looked at the card in her hand and a quizzical look crossed her face.

"A lawyer. I'm sorry, but my father never mentioned you."

"I'd be surprised if he had." Benedetto pulled an envelope out of his coat pocket and placed it on the bar. "He wanted you to have this, if and when."

For the first time in days, Kelly felt a sense of hope. Could this have something to do with the investments her father talked about?

Benedetto dropped a large denomination bill into Philip's tip jar. Philip glanced at it and nodded gratefully. It would easily cover Kelly's drink, and the next one after that.

Kelly weighed the sealed envelope in her hand as Benedetto bade her a good evening and left her with, "Call me if you have any questions."

He turned and headed out the door into another chilly San Francisco evening.

Kelly carefully opened the envelope and poured the contents out onto the bar. There wasn't much inside: a key to a safe deposit box and a power of attorney letter giving her access to the box. What the hell was this all about?

Before she could ponder the question further, Pete came striding into the restaurant. He didn't know what kind of mood Kelly was in, given everything that had gone down in the past few days, but he put on a smile and hoped for the best.

Kelly stuffed the key and letter into her purse as he arrived at the bar.

"You started without me," he said, as he leaned over and kissed her on the cheek.

"It's been one of those days."

"I can see." He nodded at the bourbon in front of her. "Going with high octane tonight?"

She nodded. "Anything new on Ruben Garcia?" Kelly had lost very few patients, and when she did, she not only felt an unwarranted guilt, but also a kinship and a desire for justice.

Philip slid Pete a Cutty and rocks, and moved on down the bar. Pete took a drink and responded, "The Sureños claim the shooter was a Norteño. Rumor is, there's an eyewitness but conveniently he's nowhere to be found."

Kelly slowly shook her head from side to side. She knew what would happen next. What always happened from time immemorial. "And now the Sureños take out one of the Norteños and call it even?"

"The Gang Task Force is clamping down on both sides, hoping to avoid a war."

"So many wasted lives," she said, taking another sip of her bourbon. "Any update on my father's case?"

Pete had hoped to avoid that question, but he wasn't surprised when it arose. "We still have people canvassing the area, talking to anyone who might've seen something."

"So the answer is 'nothing new'."

Pete nodded. "For now." Then he quickly changed gears. "What's new with you?"

"I met with Dr Knudsen at St Francis."

Pete's face lit up. "You took the job?"

"Not exactly. He agreed to keep the position open for two more weeks while I try to sort out things with the clinic."

"That's good news, isn't it?" he said cautiously.

Kelly nodded. "It gives me a viable option if the clinic's forced to shut down."

Pete smiled for the first time in a while. "Options are good. Feel like celebrating?"

"I feel like getting drunk," she said, as she downed the rest of her bourbon and slammed the glass down on the bar.

19

The next morning, Kelly nervously entered Wells Fargo Bank, her stomach in knots. While she was optimistic the safe deposit box held something of value, she couldn't get over feeling she was doing something illicit. Why would her father stash something in a safe deposit box? And how come he never mentioned it, or Matthew Benedetto? She'd played the possible reasons over and over in her mind, but couldn't arrive at a logical answer.

In a few minutes, the mystery would be solved... or would it just be starting?

She headed toward the bank manager's area. As was the norm these days, local branch executives were either under-achieving lifers on the downside of their careers or fresh-faced college grads that worked on commission and were hell-bent on leveraging customers into home loans.

Elliot Weems was the former. A robust man in his mid sixties with a bad comb-over and a suit jacket that was shiny with wear at the elbows. He brightened as Kelly approached, and rose up from behind a slightly nicked desk, extending a hand with chubby, ink-stained fingers.

"Elliot Weems. What can I help you with, Ms...?" He'd left the end of the sentence dangling in anticipation that she'd supply her name.

Kelly reluctantly shook his meaty hand, and surreptitiously wiped her palm on her skirt as she sat. She introduced herself as she slid the key and the power of attorney over to Elliot.

He picked up the letter and perused it, his lips partially moving and his large head bobbing as he read the legal document. "This looks fine, but I've gotta get my manager to sign off. Can I offer you some coffee or water while you wait?"

The longer this took, the more eager she was to open the box. She felt like a child on Christmas morning, being told that she couldn't have her presents until her parents were showered, dressed and had polished off a proper breakfast. "I'm pressed for time," she said. "How long will this take?"

"Just a couple of minutes. In the meanwhile, you can take a look at this." He handed her a brochure detailing all of the wonderful benefits of banking with Wells Fargo. He flashed her his "closer" smile that he'd perfected over the years. It was particularly effective with young women. At least it was in Elliot's fantasy world.

Her eagerness to see the contents of her father's mysterious safe deposit box grew exponentially as she waited. Elliot would take his time getting approval so that this potential customer could look over the brochure. It was a tired tactic and most of the time the colorful leaflet would be tossed back on his desk unread. But if one or two customers a day had their interest piqued by the latest bank come-ons, Elliot would turn on his self-imagined charm and reel in the fish.

After ten grueling minutes, Elliot returned, confirmed everything was in order, and led Kelly back to the boxes. Along the way, his pathetic attempts at small talk were met with brief cold smiles and one-word answers.

The box was the largest model available, and when Kelly slipped it out of the wall, she was taken aback by its weight. Elliot offered to carry it into a curtained-off area, but Kelly didn't want his hands anywhere near the box or her.

She set the metal box onto a table with a loud thud as Elliot slid a red privacy curtain closed behind her.

As the anticipation grew, her heart pounded like it was trying to burst from her chest. She had no idea what awaited her, and her eagerness was somewhat tempered by her fear of discovery. She took a calming breath, then opened the box and peered inside.

"Holy shit!" she gasped, unable to contain her stunned reaction.

20

Kelly stood in front of Matthew Benedetto's building, located on Marina Boulevard across from the small craft harbor. After the Loma Prieta earthquake in 1989 (better known to sports fans as the "World Series Earthquake"), most of the homes along the Marina were either flattened or damaged beyond repair. Wealthy investors flocked to the area with bags of money (many in foreign denominations) to buy up lots belonging to homeowners who either couldn't afford to rebuild or had no desire to spend the next few years fighting with their insurance company and/or the city zoning commission.

One of those investors was Benedetto, who was able to acquire a prime corner lot with an unabated vista of the San Francisco Bay. His friends said he was lucky to be so fortunate, but luck had nothing to do with it. The fifty-year-old house that stood on the land prior to being shaken off its foundation belonged to one of Benedetto's former clients who had moved back to Croatia after Benedetto successfully secured a hung jury non-verdict on charges of counterfeiting and tax evasion. His client owed Benedetto his freedom, and several hundred thousand dollars in unpaid legal fees. The lot and the rubble covered the debt.

Benedetto commissioned a Mediterranean side-by-side duplex. One half housed his legal practice and the other served as his residence. The irony of constructing a law office upon the very location where many laws had been transgressed wasn't lost on him.

The leather satchel Kelly carried felt heavier with every step that propelled her closer to answers. A small, tasteful brass plaque above the doorbell read "Benedetto and Associates". Kelly wondered how large the firm was and what kind of law they practiced. Based upon what she found in the safe deposit box, she had no idea how Benedetto fit into her father's life, and she was anxious to find out.

She pushed the doorbell, but didn't hear a buzzer, chime or bell from inside. Either the office was incredibly well insulated, or…

The door swung open and an attractive, stately woman with short gray hair stood before her. She looked vaguely like Judi Dench and exuded a grace and strength to match. Kelly expected the woman to have a British accent, but when she spoke it was with soft Southern tones. She extended her hand and introduced herself as Mrs Mathews. Period. No title was necessary. She invited Kelly into the large waiting area and quietly closed the door behind her.

Kelly accepted an offer of water, and when Mrs Mathews left for the kitchen, Kelly used the opportunity to check out the surroundings. The spacious area was tastefully decorated with what Kelly imagined were very expensive antique pieces. Beautiful landscape paintings gave the room a comforting, tranquil feeling.

She rose to examine the paintings up close. One appeared to be the rugged coastline of Carmel. Another was a majestic windswept pine that brought to mind the iconic lone cypress in Monterey. The last was unmistakably the view of the San Francisco Bay from a perch high above the famous inlet, well before the eastern and western shores were connected by bridges. All three works were painted by Guy Rose. Kelly was unaware that Rose was one of the founders of the early California art scene and had studied under Claude Monet. She was also unaware that she was looking at well over a million dollars worth of oil, canvas and God-given talent.

When Mrs Mathews returned with the water, Kelly commented on the serenity of the paintings. Mrs Mathews nodded in agreement, and left it at that. She was the paragon of understatement.

In the awkward silence that followed, Kelly ventured a question. "How many associates does Mr Benedetto have working here?"

"Presently, it's only the two of us and a few paralegals. Occasionally, he will hire additional staff if the need arises, but Mr Benedetto likes to handle things personally."

"How long have you worked with him?"

"Going on twenty years," she said without any hint of emotion. She was stating a simple fact that required no further elaboration.

"Did you know my father?" Kelly asked.

Mrs Mathews shook her head. "I never had the pleasure of meeting Dr Harper."

Kelly was confused. "Wasn't he a client here?"

Mrs Mathews' smile was as inscrutable as a Tibetan monk. "You can discuss that with Mr Benedetto. He'll be with you in just a few minutes. Is there anything else I can get for you?"

Kelly shook her head. "I'm fine, thanks."

Mrs Mathews nodded, then turned her attention to her computer screen and began typing at breakneck speed.

Kelly glanced down at her hands and realized she had a death grip on the satchel straps. Her knuckles were white and her fingers were cramping. As she slowly opened her fingers to get the blood flowing again, Mrs Mathews intoned, "Mr Benedetto is ready for you."

Kelly got up and crossed the polished oak floor that glistened in the soft morning light. She awkwardly waited at the door for a moment, then raised a tentative fist to knock. "Go right in," said Mrs Mathews.

The brass doorknob felt cold to the touch. She had a moment of hesitation. Perhaps deep down she didn't really want to know the truth, but she'd come too far to turn back.

She opened the door and entered.

Benedetto was standing, and greeted Kelly with a warm, welcoming smile as she crossed the spacious office. This was clearly the lair of a very successful person. Dark woods, soft leathers and thick Oriental rugs. Benedetto motioned for Kelly to join him at the large windows that overlooked the bay.

She hadn't gotten a close look at Benedetto the other night at the restaurant. He was a few inches taller than she was, which put him around five ten. He appeared to be in good shape and was attractive without being handsome. His hair was an unremarkable shade of brown streaked with gray. There was nothing physically extraordinary about Benedetto, except the manner in which he carried himself. He was self-confident, charming and approachable. She had no idea of his professional relationship with her father, but felt that whatever it was, her father had been in good hands.

She'd soon come to seriously question that evaluation.

Kelly took in the view, which was extraordinary on a day like this when the fog lifted and the skies were a shade of blue that defied definition. The Golden Gate rose up majestically from the rippling bay waters, its art deco orange towers reaching up to the heavens. Off to the right, a red and white tourist boat cut a wake as it powered out to Alcatraz with a load of curiosity seekers who wanted to experience firsthand the one-time home of The Birdman, Machine Gun Kelly and Al Capone.

"Incredible," Kelly said.

Benedetto nodded. "I never get tired of it."

"This must be what they had in mind when they coined the phrase 'a million dollar view'."

Benedetto smiled. It was more like a six million dollar view, but he wasn't about to correct her. "I've been very fortunate in business."

Kelly upended her satchel and a dozen bundles of twenties and fifties tumbled out onto a low teak coffee table. "Did your business involve my father?"

"Occasionally."

"There's a little more than five thousand dollars here. Where did it come from?"

"Why don't we sit down?"

Kelly was in no mood to sit. Suggesting you "take a seat" was akin to "we need to talk".

Nothing good ever followed.

Benedetto gently pushed on. "You asked me a question. A very important question that has deeply personal implications for you. I'll do my best to explain everything, but it's going to take some time." Benedetto motioned to a plush club chair. "Please."

Kelly relented, settling into the chair and steeling herself as Benedetto began his story.

"It all started with the murder of your mother."

Kelly thought she was ready for anything, but she wasn't ready for that. How could this money have anything to do with her mother's death? A voice inside her head strongly urged her to stop Benedetto right there, but this train had already left the station and was picking up steam. Kelly knew she had to ride it to the end of the line.

Benedetto continued his narrative. "The man arrested for the crime was Clarence Musselwhite, a drug mule from Miami and small-time coke dealer. When his money ran low, which was often, Clarence would break into houses and steal whatever he could fence."

Kelly's voice was laced with venom when she picked up the story. "I know all about Musselwhite, how my mother and sister happened to be home that day, and what he did to them. What's that have to do with my father... and this?" She indicated the cash on the table.

"What you don't know is Musselwhite possessed highly incriminating evidence against a West Coast syndicate boss named Dominic Bruno. For obvious reasons, that was never made public. Nor was the fact that Musselwhite cut a deal with federal agents. In return for his testimony against Bruno, the murder and assault charges were brushed under the carpet and Musselwhite was placed into the Department of Justice WITSEC program."

Kelly felt like someone punched her in the stomach. She experienced a sharp physical pain and needed a moment to catch her breath.

Her mother had been brutally raped and murdered, her sister permanently hospitalized, and now she was being told that the man responsible had been allowed to go free? It had to be a mistake. "We were told Musselwhite died," she said in a voice barely above a whisper.

Benedetto nodded. "That he had a heart attack while being transferred from county jail to a more secure location. That was the government's cover story."

Kelly was in a state of stunned disbelief. "This doesn't make any sense. You're telling me the San Francisco Police Department agreed to this?"

"Not the department *per se*, but someone high up in the administration signed off. I don't think they were given much choice in the matter."

"This can't be true. The man murdered my mother! How could the authorities just let him go?"

"Somebody in Washington felt that taking out Bruno was critical to the 'war on drugs', which in their opinion outweighed homicide and assault. Plus, a federal conviction against a mob boss was great PR in an election year."

This last piece of information hit Kelly like a sledgehammer. "You are fucking kidding me." She surprised herself... did she just say that aloud?

Benedetto took no enjoyment in being the bearer of this news, and unfortunately he was only getting warmed up. "I'm sorry, but you wanted the truth."

Kelly sat silent as the pain of her mother's death, so long dormant, washed over her like it happened yesterday, unleashing a torrent of emotions. Tears welled up in her eyes and she violently shook her head. This wasn't the time to mourn anew.

"Are you all right?" Benedetto asked with genuine concern.

She wondered if she'd ever really be all right again, but she managed to nod and bade him to continue.

"A year later, Clarence Musselwhite was spotted in Scottsdale. He'd dyed his hair, shaved his beard and took to wearing glasses, but that wasn't enough. Dom Bruno, who was incarcerated at Pelican Bay, got word of the sighting. He'd known that Musselwhite had flipped on him and had entered WITSEC, but until that point, had no clue where the Federal Marshals had stashed him.

"I was Dominic's attorney and he requested to see me. Dom told me about Musselwhite and then made a highly unusual request: to relay that information to your father."

Kelly recoiled. "Why?"

"In Dominic's mind, there were two people whose lives were destroyed by Musselwhite: his and your father's. He felt it was only right for your father to know the truth. We argued back and forth. My feeling was your father, and you, had mourned and it was best not to reopen that wound."

"But you told my father anyway."

"Dominic made it clear that if I didn't tell him, one of his people would. Given the alternative, I thought it would be better coming from me."

Kelly felt like she was in the middle of a boxing ring, getting pummeled with sharp jabs; each blow landing harder and doing more damage. "How did he take it?"

"He reacted to the news much as you did. He was shocked, but moreover, he was incensed."

Kelly tried to speak, but no words came. This man Benedetto had come into her father's life, and now hers, and turned it upside down. What do you say to that?

Benedetto let her sit quietly, giving her time to digest this information. Finally, Kelly broke the silence. "What happened next?"

"I have to caution you that the story gets darker from this point on."

"Do I want to hear it?"

"That's up to you. Personally, I think not knowing the truth is worse than facing it."

Kelly walked to the window and stared out at the bay.

After a few moments, she turned back and nodded.

21

"Your father spent two agonizing weeks dealing with the reality that the justice system completely failed your family."

"Musselwhite was a murderer! I don't care what information he had. He should be rotting in jail."

"David shared that sentiment almost word-for-word. The more he thought about it, the angrier he became. He showed up here one day and said he was contemplating taking justice into his own hands."

"His own hands? What do you mean?"

"Your father lived by a strong moral code, but in the end he couldn't ignore his primal urge to avenge your mother's death. One week after our meeting, Musselwhite was found dead of an apparent heart attack. No foul play was ever suspected."

This was an uppercut that Kelly never saw coming. She was staggered by this information.

"No. What you're suggesting is impossible. As much as my father loved my mother and my sister, he would never *kill* a person."

"I know it sounds far-fetched..."

Kelly responded with vitriol, suddenly hating the man who was weaving this absurd story. "You didn't know my father like I did!"

"You're right. I knew him in a completely different light."

Kelly paced, shaking her head. She knew it wasn't true, but she couldn't figure out why Benedetto would be making this up. What was his game?

She turned from the window. "When my mother died, my father went into a deep depression. I'd never seen him like that. I was frightened. Frightened for him, for me and for my sister. He drank more and used pills to help him sleep. After a while, he found his way out of the darkness. When he did, we vowed to always be open with each other. There were no secrets between us, so this tale you're spinning is utter bullshit. Now, what I want to know is, *why* are you doing this to me?"

"Kelly, I have no agenda. No ulterior motive. This isn't something I chose to do. It's something I promised your father, because *he* wanted you to know the truth."

Despite Kelly's contemptuous glare, Benedetto pressed on. "After Musselwhite died, your father underwent a long and painful metamorphosis. He struggled for months with what he'd done. Not only was he living with a horrible secret, he was breaking his solemn promise to you. Throughout it all, he kept coming back to the same conclusion: Musselwhite deserved to die and his death undoubtedly saved the lives of other potential victims."

Kelly was lightheaded and her legs were leaden. She eased herself back into the chair. "About a year and a half after my mother died, my father started acting strangely. I was afraid he was going into another tailspin."

"That timetable coincides with what I've told you."

For the first time, she began to consider that maybe, just maybe, all of this was *true*; that her father actually killed the man who murdered her mother. But, her father... a *killer*? It was unimaginable. Wasn't it?

Benedetto was speaking again, but Kelly couldn't understand what he was saying. It sounded like she was underwater. He paused, then asked if she was all right. Kelly could make out the words, but they were just words. They had no meaning.

Nothing made sense.

She had no idea how long she sat there, her mind trying and failing to deal with the information that Benedetto had imparted. It was like the first time she'd tried marijuana. Ideas and thoughts had floated through her mind like wisps of smoke. Disconnected, without substance or definition. Amusing notions had flitted around her head, teasing her with their brilliance, but flaming out as quickly as they materialized. That was then, and this was now. She forced herself to come back to the present.

Kelly refocused, looked at Benedetto like he was a complete stranger, then glanced down at the pile of cash on the table.

"Did he steal this money from Musselwhite?"

Benedetto reacted as if he were offended on behalf of David Harper. "Absolutely not. You father was no thief."

"You just told me he killed a man. Stealing a few thousand dollars would be like jaywalking in comparison."

Benedetto cautiously continued, knowing that what came next would further shatter Kelly's world. "After Musselwhite's death, rumors began. A rippling of underground hearsay, things posted on dark web message boards. Wild, totally unsubstantiated theories about how Dominic Bruno had somehow arranged for Musselwhite's death. The stories coalesced into an urban myth that there was a shadowy person who'd made it happen without leaving a trace."

Kelly was dumbstruck with this information. "That's why Bruno insisted on telling my father about Musselwhite? Because he hoped my father would carry out revenge?"

"No one pushed your father to take action against Musselwhite, just like no one pushed him toward the choices he made afterwards."

"Afterwards?" Kelly was already devastated by what she'd been told, and she correctly sensed she wasn't going to be too thrilled with what came next.

"People began believing the myth was true. That there *was* someone who could provide a discrete and valuable service."

"Okay, stop right there! Even if I believed that my father was capable of killing Musselwhite, which I don't, you'd never convince me that he, what, became a contract killer?"

Benedetto didn't react. No nod. No shake of the head. He just looked at Kelly with sympathetic eyes.

"Answer me!"

"I think you know the answer."

"I think it's all bullshit! I'm not going to sit here and listen to these lies!"

"No one's forcing you. You can leave whenever you'd like. I'm only carrying out your father's wishes."

"To inform his daughter that he killed people for a living."

"You're trivializing the facts."

Kelly was exhausted and felt a pounding headache coming on. The voice in her head came back, this time screaming for her to get far away from this man and pretend none of this ever happened. But an infinitesimal seed of doubt had been planted, and that was enough to keep her captive to hear the rest of the story. She took a deep breath and slowly exhaled, wishing she'd stuck with that meditation class and mastered how to center her chi.

"All right. I'll play along. No more interruptions. Just fulfill my father's dying wish and lay it all out for me and I'll be gone."

Benedetto nodded. "Once I told him about the whispers in the ether, he did what any sane person would do. He walked away. In the meantime, I had a highly skilled and discrete computer expert run a string search on some of the most obscure and heavily encoded message boards. This resulted in an extensive list of individuals who were eager to get in touch with the mythical hit man.

"About two months later, your father called me. He'd finally found some degree of peace with what he'd done, and was considering helping others in similar situations to find the same level of closure."

Despite her promise of no interruptions, Kelly couldn't help herself. "My father was a gifted doctor. He took an oath to *save* lives."

"Which is precisely what he felt he was doing. He only took assignments where he was absolutely convinced the world would be better off if the target was eradicated."

"And you acted as the middleman, providing him with these 'assignments'?"

"I screened the requests, the majority of which were either completely absurd or thoroughly unwarranted, and then reviewed the remaining ones with your father."

Kelly drew upon every ounce of patience she had to continue with this insane conversation. "And these people who were making inquiries; did they have any idea who the mystery assassin was?"

Benedetto shook his head. "Shortly after Musselwhite died, Dominic Bruno was killed in prison. Your father's identity remained a secret. It wasn't long before the legend began to grow. There was a man out there who was not an ordinary mechanic. A man who was a brilliant maestro and made each hit look like an accident or natural causes. His *modus operandi* was that he had none. The mystery man needed a name and the moniker of Gideon, 'the biblical Destroyer', stuck."

"Gideon, sure. Why not?" As Benedetto's narrative grew more elaborate, Kelly's disbelief was compounded. "You make him sound like some kind of comic-book superhero." She picked up one of the cash bundles. "What's this, then? Blood money?"

"Operating money. Expenses come with the job and leaving a credit card trail is obviously unwise. The remuneration for your father's services was funneled into a brokerage firm after passing through a complex layer of companies. Payouts were done over an extended period of time to keep the amounts under the government's radar."

"You not only lined up hits, you also laundered the money?"

"I did what was necessary. I have no illusions as to the illegality of my role in this."

"So why do it?"

"That, I'm afraid, is personal. There's still some money in the holding account, in addition to what you have in front of you. The proceeds were used to keep the clinic open, as well as provide care for your sister. That was another significant reason your father took the jobs. He believed the benefits of helping others outweighed the moral and ethical lines he crossed."

"I said I'd hear you out. I can't begin to imagine what con you think you're working, but I'm not biting."

"I understand, and so would your father, which is why he wanted me to give you this." Benedetto opened the drawer of a side table and pulled out a well-worn, thick leather journal. "He kept copious notes."

He offered the journal to Kelly, who instinctively pulled away. If this really was her father's journal, then everything she just heard was true. She couldn't let that be the case. She didn't want to touch it. She didn't want anything to do with it. Benedetto placed the journal atop the packets of cash on the table.

Kelly asked the obvious question, "Why would any intelligent person keep a journal detailing how or why he murdered people?"

"David needed an outlet to express his thoughts, so he wrote them down. Also, he knew that what he was doing was so utterly out of character and impossible for you to believe, he wanted you to have a record of it in his own hand. You father made a vow not to keep secrets from you, and this was his way of fulfilling that promise." Benedetto tapped his finger on the journal's cover. "He kept it hidden at his house, and per his wishes, I retrieved it upon his death."

119

As Kelly's doubt slowly began to erode, she was assaulted with the ramifications of the story Benedetto had told her. "If, for the sake of argument, all of this *is* true, do you think my father's death was intentional? That he was murdered as some kind of payback?"

Benedetto's face remained passive, thoughtful. "It's certainly possible. Hit-and-run accidents occur with great frequency, but given your father's involvement with the illicit side of life, it wouldn't surprise me to find out that he was targeted."

"But if his identity was a tightly held secret…?"

"I'm hoping it's remained a secret. If his identity has been compromised, you and your sister may be in danger. My associate is continuing to monitor the dark web and any mentions of Gideon are automatically flagged. If there *is* any link to your father, I'll contact you immediately."

Kelly stared at the journal on the table and shied away from it like it was a hissing snake about to strike. "What am I supposed to do with that?"

"It's up to you. You can burn it, hand it over to the police, or put it in a safe deposit box and forget about it."

"After what you've told me, how could I possibly forget about it?"

"There is another option. Embrace it."

"You mean accept what my father had become?"

"Or carry on his legacy."

Kelly couldn't believe this man; this intelligent, successful attorney had just suggested that she become an assassin. She didn't dignify it with a response.

"Before you make any decisions about what to do with the journal, take it home and read it. And I'd urge you to do it soon."

22
(David's Journal)

The world as I knew it ceased to exist the day Mary was murdered. Prior to her death, I saw every day as a celebration of life; every challenge as a hill to conquer; every tick of the clock as a moment to be savored. I'd experienced my share of death in the hospital and I was aware of how precious, and yet how tenuous life could be, but when Mary's life was stolen from her, the lens through which I viewed the world shattered and my outlook became skewed.

Mary wasn't the only casualty that day. My precious daughter Jessica had a future that promised nothing but joy and success. Every room she walked into was lit up by her exuberance and her buoyant personality. Now she spends her days lying in a hospital bed, oblivious to the past, unaware of the present and having no concept of the future.

For forty-seven years I lived a blessed life, brimming with happiness, prosperity, a loving and beautiful wife and two remarkable daughters. I never once imagined that someone would come along and destroy all of that. I never imagined a heartless, savage animal like Clarence Musselwhite.

Once Mary and Jess were taken from us, I knew life would never be the same, but had no idea that <u>this</u> is where I'd end up. Mary's death left me devastated. Not only because she was gone, but because of the way in which she died. The post-mortem exam revealed she'd been raped and strangled. Musselwhite then beat her with a blunt implement – the coroner surmised a baseball bat – fracturing her skull, breaking her jaw and splintering three ribs. My precious Mary was monstrously violated, then her body brutally destroyed.

After the killer finished with Mary, he turned on Jessica and continued his onslaught, crushing her temporal lobe and leaving her to die at the bottom of the staircase. Death didn't take her that day, but perhaps that would have been a kinder outcome.

I pleaded with the police to see the crime-scene photos. The inspector tried to reason with me, but I convinced him I could handle it. After all, I'd seen thousands of anatomical photos and read dozens of autopsy reports. The inspector warned me that seeing clinical photos of patients couldn't compare to seeing brutal photos of loved ones. I knew that intuitively, but I insisted, explaining it would give me the closure I desperately needed. I was a fool. I should have listened to him. The images, which will forever haunt me, drove me to the precipice where I now stand.

The subsequent darkness that enveloped me couldn't be eased with drugs or alcohol, but if Kelly and Jessica weren't in my life, I'm convinced I would have kept trying, using more opiates until I achieved my goal of making the pain finally go away. Poor sweet Jessica lies in a bed, blissfully unaware of her mother's death. I had to stay strong for her. And Kelly, my vibrant beacon of light, gives me a reason every day to fight the demons that whisper in my ear at night.

In Kelly, I see so much of Mary. At first it was somewhat off-putting. I'd catch a glimpse of my daughter and for a brief moment I'd think my wife was in the room and that everything that had happened was merely a horrific lucid nightmare. But then reality would kick in and I'd know that the events of the past were real, and that the angel in the room was my daughter. I began to cherish those moments and savored the memories they evoked. Kelly was always special, but after that unspeakable day, she became so much more so.

There's one other powerful thing that carried me through the day. Revenge. The police assured me the case against Clarence Musselwhite was a lock. The District Attorney said he'd seek the death penalty. Even though I took an oath to save lives, I knew I wouldn't be satisfied until Musselwhite was strapped to a chair and administered a lethal injection.

But Musselwhite never went to court. He died of a heart attack, or so the story went. It was an egregious turn of events. I needed him to suffer. He got off much too easily. I craved for him to experience intense pain and fear, and I never felt an ounce of remorse for harboring those emotions.

For months afterward, I lived with the anguish of losing Mary and Jessica, and the bitterness of wanting their attacker to have faced a more violent and painful ending... but I had to get on with my life. I managed to compartmentalize my memories and emotions and focus again on living in the present. I vowed to make the most out of each day. And then, two weeks ago, I got a phone call... a call that changed everything.

Musselwhite was alive. His "heart attack" was a story concocted by federal agents. He had information that was critical in putting a mob boss behind bars, and in exchange Musselwhite was placed into witness protection. He got a new identity, an apartment in Flagstaff and a monthly stipend paid for by US taxpayers. This monster who'd ruthlessly killed my wife and destroyed my daughter's life was playing golf in the Arizona sunshine, drinking beer and getting a tan, while he should've been rotting away on death row.

The man who presented me with these details was a lawyer named Benedetto. After hearing my enraged reaction, Benedetto did something extraordinary and shocking: he offered to give me Musselwhite's current address. It took me several moments to understand the implication; he was providing me with the opportunity to seek vengeance.

At first I thought this was someone playing a bizarrely cruel joke, but I couldn't fathom who might go to such lengths to concoct a story like this, and to what end? If it was some kind of barbaric scam, what would possibly be the payoff? I suspended my disbelief long enough to hear what else Benedetto had to say.

As he elaborated on the behind-the-scenes machinations that went into Musselwhite's release, it became more apparent that Benedetto was laying the groundwork that could result in Musselwhite's death... at my hand. It was a ludicrous notion. I was a doctor, for God's sake, not a hit man. Despite Mary's death and my violent outburst at hearing this story of the government faking Musselwhite's death and arranging his release, I'd never intentionally take another person's life.

As the days dragged on, the idea of actually killing this despicable criminal started to gnaw at me like a hungry rat nibbling on cheese. The notion that had been planted with Benedetto's disclosure had begun to take root. I knew, of course, that this was a sick but satisfying fantasy. It's a popular theme of movies, but Liam Neeson doesn't have to deal with the reality of committing murder and then facing the consequences. However, that didn't stop me from contemplating the infamous perfect *murder. If I <u>was</u> morally bankrupt and could bring myself to kill another person, how would I do it?*

There are three basic considerations: 1) Musselwhite's death would have to look like an accident; 2) there could be no trail leading back to me; and 3) he needed to suffer an excruciating death.

I've now spent a torturous week filled with emotional and moral turmoil. I've been sleeping less and drinking more. A bad combination, given that I must be clear-headed. I told Kelly I was attending a medical conference in Arizona over the weekend. It's the first time I've lied to her since I assured her that Santa was real, contrary to what her know-it-all friends in first grade told her.

Rightly or wrongly (I suspect it's the latter), I've made up my mind. I know it won't bring Mary back and that Jessica won't magically regain consciousness, but tomorrow I leave here with the intent of killing Clarence Musselwhite. I've formulated a plan that fulfills my 'basic considerations', and now it's a question of whether or not I'll go through with it. I've convinced myself that the world will be a better place without Musselwhite in it. At least, that's the justification I'm using in what may be a futile attempt to assuage my guilt.

I honestly don't believe I'll have the nerve to go through with this. Many years ago I took skydiving lessons, and once I got up in the plane and it was my time to leap out into the endless blue sky, I froze. I yearned to experience soaring through the air, but an overwhelming sense of self-preservation washed over me. My lizard brain took control of my body, and despite my extreme embarrassment, I backed away from the open door and clutched the straps that hung from the side of the fuselage until my hands were numb.

The question is, once I see Musselwhite, will I take the leap or not? I honestly have no idea, but I intend to find out.

23

Kelly sat motionless, staggered by what she'd read. She was eager to continue, but was filled with apprehension. This journal written in her father's concise hand was stupefying. She felt like she was tumbling down a steep endless hill, catching only fleeting glimpses of earth and sky.

Kelly bowed her head between her legs and took long, slow breaths until she regained her equilibrium. Once her world stopped spinning, she began to critically analyze what she'd read. Was her father a killer? It was *impossible*, and yet, not. In a matter of hours, everything she thought she knew about the man that raised her was in question. She'd patterned her life after him. He'd been her role model, her shoulder to cry on, her...

The knock on the door resounded like a gunshot and shattered Kelly's concentration. Her mind was in a muddled haze when the second knock jarred her back into harsh reality.

Kelly rose and tentatively crossed to the door. She was wracked with a fear that had no rational basis, but gripped her just the same. "Yes?" she said, her voice wavering.

"It's Pete."

She was suddenly paranoid. Why was he here? Had he come across the truth while he was investigating her father's death? Did he know about 'Gideon'?

From the other side of the door, "Kelly? You okay?"

She took a long moment to center herself, then opened the door wide to allow her boyfriend entry.

Pete's face was etched with concern. "Is everything all right?"

"It's just been a hell of a day."

"I'd say a hell of a week. I don't mean to push it, but do you feel like company?"

Kelly pasted on a weak smile and opened her arms, allowing Pete to engulf her in a warm embrace. Kelly looked over Pete's shoulder and spied the journal sitting on the coffee table, open for all the world to see.

"The bedroom," she cooed into his ear.

Pete swept Kelly off her feet and carried her across the room, breezing past the journal whose secrets, for the moment, remained hidden from outsiders' eyes.

Some time later, Pete propped himself up on one elbow and lightly brushed a stray hair from Kelly's forehead. Her face had a sheen of sweat from a lovemaking session that was far more intense than usual.

"I'm going to be sore tomorrow," he said with a grin.

"That's reassuring. I'd hate to think you could contort into those positions without pulling a muscle."

She sat up, pulling the sheet with her to cover her breasts. The intimacy was over.

"Any news about my father?" she asked.

Pete was about to comment on the time and place of this line of questioning, but thought better of it. He knew Kelly was desperate for information.

"Not yet."

Kelly's face flushed. "So whoever did this is going to get away with it?"

"Your father's death is a priority for the department."

"Are you still looking into the possibility it could've been deliberate?"

"We're exploring every angle, but we haven't found anything that leads us to believe your father was intentionally run down. There's nothing in his past to indicate someone would want to murder him. Can you think of anything we're missing?"

Kelly betrayed no emotion. There was plenty she could think of, but nothing she could share. However, she wanted to get out ahead of any information the police may find elsewhere.

"Not really. My father had threatened to fire one of our doctors, Nathan Curtis, but there's no way Nathan would..." She didn't bother to finish that absurd thought.

"Were there any patients in the past few months who were angry at him, or who made threats?"

Kelly shrugged. "A few pill seekers who got turned away. There was a homeless man who made some empty, incoherent threats. I don't know his name. We called him 'The Hollow Man'. He quit coming around a few weeks ago." It was a fool's errand for Pete to consider any of their patients, but she didn't want him to think she was hiding anything.

Pete said he'd follow up on Nathan and the street people in the neighborhood. You never knew where an investigation would take you. "Had there ever been a break-in at the clinic before the other day?" he asked.

"No. I'm sure my father would've mentioned it. Why?"

"The timing was too coincidental."

"Do you think it could be related?"

"Probably not, but I'm not a big believer in coincidence."

Pete's phone buzzed. He didn't have to apologize. Kelly knew that a homicide cop was always on call.

"Yeah?" As he listened, his eyes grew larger. "No shit. I'll be there in ten." He disconnected. "I'm sorry, but I've gotta roll on this."

Pete got out of bed and as he slipped into his pants, he looked back at Kelly, "I promise to keep digging until I have all the answers."

She forced a smile. "I know." Unfortunately, that could be a very big problem.

The fact was, she wanted answers, too, and the only way she was going to get them was to dive deeper into the journal, which she intended to do the moment Pete left.

24
(David's Journal)

I never imagined I'd intentionally take another person's life. In medical school they try to prepare you for that rare Sophie's choice when two lives hang in the balance and you can only save one. I was put in that position once, early on in my career, and prayed I'd never have to make that decision again.

And yet just days ago I willingly put myself in a much greater morally tenuous situation. The decision whether or not to become a murderer.

Clarence Musselwhite had been living under the pseudonym Dave Richardson in an apartment complex on Camelback Road. Indoor and outdoor pools, a shiny fitness center and a putting green. His two-bedroom apartment was setting the federal government back $2,500 a month. The more I learned about him, the more incensed I became.

I spent two hours at the pool, propped up on a chaise, a book on my lap and a Diamondbacks cap shadowing my face. I observed Musselwhite as he shamelessly, and unsuccessfully, hit on women twenty years his junior. He was in his mid forties, his skin leathery brown and his thinning hair bleached by the Arizona sunshine. I caught a glimpse of the crook of his left arm, which featured a fresh needle mark to go along with the dozen others that had scarred over. Musselwhite was defiantly abusing his freedom. He was a rapist and murderer who was openly injecting illegal drugs into his veins, and yet he didn't have a care in the world.

At least that's what he believed.

I watched as he downed three beers, chasing the last one with a double whiskey sour. This detestable excuse for a human being was living the high life without a scintilla of remorse for his past actions. Any indecision on my part was evaporating with each passing minute.

Between the sun, the alcohol and the drugs, Musselwhite began to nod off. Fortunately, he eschewed a mid-day nap in the scorching heat poolside and headed up to his apartment.

While I'd conceived a detailed plan, I knew it had to remain flexible, since I had no way of anticipating all the variables in play. My hope was that an opportunity would present itself and I'd figure out how to proceed as I went along. I waited for thirty minutes, slid my novel into my backpack, then casually headed toward the apartment building.

I climbed the stairs to the third floor, and made my way down to 303 without seeing another person. I listened at the door for a full five minutes before I slipped on a pair of surgical gloves and took out an electric lock-pick. Moments later, the tumblers fell into line and the door opened. I quietly slid inside and gently closed the door behind me.

My heart was pounding so hard I was certain the sound was audible throughout the apartment. What if he was awake? What if someone else was in the apartment with him? What if he wasn't there at all? What the hell was I doing there? The moment of truth was upon me.

The next decision I made would shape the rest of my life.

It came back to one very basic emotion. Revenge. Bad for the spirit, but good for motivation. I could've left the apartment, gotten back in my car and put this insanity behind me, but my rage toward this man was all-consuming. I'd come to do a job and I was determined to see it through.

I silently set my backpack down on a chair and withdrew a hypodermic needle. I contemplated the needle for maybe thirty seconds, which felt like an eternity.

As I approached the bedroom, I heard snoring. Luck was on my side. The door stood open and I looked in to see Musselwhite asleep atop the bed, a can of beer and an ashtray with a half-smoked joint on the side table. In the corner of the room, propped up against the wall, was a sawed-off baseball bat. The bat that destroyed my family. It took superhuman restraint not to grab the bat and smash Musselwhite into a pulpy mass of blood and bone shards. However, that would've made it damn impossible for investigators to conclude his death was an accident. Better to stick with the plan.

Thick pile carpet absorbed my footsteps and Musselwhite didn't know he had company until I slid the syringe precisely into his latest puncture mark. As the needle went in, I depressed the plunger and injected him with a lethal dose of curare, a rare poison I'd picked up years ago during one of my Doctors Without Borders trips to South America.

Musselwhite bolted up into a sitting position, completely disoriented. He barely had time to spew out "who the fuck are you?" before paralysis began to take hold. His eyes grew wide as his diaphragm started to shut down. I explained to him in vivid detail what was happening to his body. As I wrote earlier, one of my main objectives was to make Musselwhite suffer a slow and painful death. Curare poisoning is particularly cruel because the victim is awake and aware of what's happening as his body functions slowly cease.

As his life ebbed from his body, Musselwhite formed a word with his lips. It was either "who?" or "why?". He only needed my name to fill in both blanks. There was a flash of recognition in his eyes, followed by a pathetic and extremely unsuccessful silent plea for help. I stood by and watched, forcing myself to take in every second of his death throes. I owed it to Mary and Jessica.

Finally, it was over. I'd avenged my wife and daughter.

I wondered what they'd think if they knew I'd become a murderer.

25
(David's Journal)

It's been a month since my trip to Arizona and I've lived with constant anxiety that any minute there'd be a knock at the door and I'd open it to find myself face-to-face with the police. I was confident I'd covered my tracks and left no clues at Musselwhite's apartment. I hadn't taken a plane or a rental car, hadn't stayed in a hotel, and I hadn't made any cell phone calls (I'd left my phone at home in the off-chance that I could be tracked through the internal GPS – I read online that's possible). The Scottsdale PD determined Musselwhite's death was a heart attack (it was technically asphyxiation due to paralysis of the diaphragm, but I wasn't about to correct them).

Despite the police department labeling the death as "natural causes", I felt little relief. Like the narrator in Poe's "The Telltale Heart", I was racked with guilt and feared that if confronted by the police, I'd sing like a canary.

For the first week after my trip to Arizona, I felt ill. I was ailing both mentally and physically as I tied myself into Gordian knots trying to justify my actions. I couldn't keep food down and sleep was futile. I've always been an active dreamer, and in the days following my return home, my nocturnal film festival featured images of extreme violence and death. In my nightmares, Musselwhite was alive, taunting me about how he killed Mary and threatening to do the same to Kelly and Jessica.

As the weeks dragged on, the graphic memory of the traumatic event slowly started to loosen its claws on my psyche and become less of a dominant thought in my day-to-day life. I slowly grew more confident that my arrest wasn't imminent and that I'd gotten away with the crime.

My association with Benedetto was over. Since he'd been the conduit to my "interaction" with Musselwhite and that chapter in my life was now closed, there was no reason for any future contact. Or so I thought.

And then the letter arrived.

It came to the clinic via courier and I found it amidst a stack of bills, some of which were past due. The letter was addressed "Personal" to my attention. There was no return address. I assumed it was another solicitation for a random charity, a credit card application or one of my favorites, an invitation to hear the virtues of the Neptune Society.

I nearly fed the envelope unopened into the shredder behind my desk, but my curiosity got the better of me. In retrospect, I should've trusted my initial instinct and converted the unopened envelope into confetti.

Inside was a bank draft for $9,500 from a company I'd never heard of, and a handwritten note on a post-it. It said, "For services rendered. Will explain tonight. My office, 8pm." There was no doubt as to who sent the check, but "services rendered"? The combination of the note and the check were baffling and more than a little foreboding, but I had to admit, Benedetto knew how to pique my interest.

I had a difficult time focusing for the rest of the day. Fortunately, our patient load was lighter than usual and I was able to make it to the Marina with a few minutes to spare.

Benedetto had a banquet of appetizers brought in from Acquerello, one of the most exclusive Italian restaurants in the city. I hadn't come to eat dinner; I had serious questions that needed answers. But when I was confronted with the aroma of garlic, lobster, truffle butter and shaved Parmigiano Reggiano, I was immensely appreciative of his thoughtfulness.

We shared the incredible food, along with a rich Barolo from the Piedmont area. I don't know much about Italian wines and have no idea how much this one cost, but it was exceptional. If the aim was to impress me, Benedetto was succeeding.

As we ate, we discussed the contents of the letter. What services had I provided and to whom? Benedetto relayed to me the portion of the Musselwhite story he'd previously left out: the identity of the crime boss who Musselwhite flipped on. A sweetheart named Dominic Bruno, who, thanks to Musselwhite, had been sentenced to spend the remainder of his years behind bars. Bruno was returning the favor, giving sensitive information about Musselwhite to Benedetto to pass along to me.

I'd been used. My first reaction was anger, followed by indignity. But before I did something foolish, like toss the rest of my extraordinary wine in Benedetto's face, I checked myself. I had no one to blame. Yes, I'd been fed information and led down a path that ended in Musselwhite's death, but it had been wholly my choice. No one put a gun to my head to put a figurative gun to Musselwhite's.

Benedetto went on to explain that nobody beside Dominic Bruno knew that I was involved, and that yesterday Bruno was killed by a fellow inmate. The entire scenario had me reeling. How did I come to be caught up in the middle of this bizarre chain of events? And where did the money come from? And was there any more wine?

Fortunately, the answer to the last question was yes. As Benedetto opened another bottle, he told me Bruno had been extremely grateful and wanted to show his appreciation to me in the only way he knew how… cash. The money had been passed along to Benedetto, who then put it "into the system". After it went through a legitimate brokerage account, it was as clean as a check from the US Government. Taxes had even been paid.

Blood money. I wanted nothing to do with it. It sullied the reason for my actions. I killed Musselwhite to avenge what he'd done to my wife and daughter, not because of what he'd done to a mobster. Accepting money was a personal and ethical affront.

But was it? Second doubts swept over me. I had exacted revenge for Mary and Jessica. I'd watched with grim satisfaction as Musselwhite suffered. Would accepting money for that be an insult, or would it be icing on the cake? The clinic was in desperate need of an infusion of funds. And there were Jessica's hospital bills. Wouldn't it be sweet irony if Musselwhite's death kept the clinic afloat and saved the lives of deserving people?

Midway through the second bottle, we agreed that Benedetto would set up an account to funnel the rest of Bruno's $25,000 "endowment" into the clinic.

By the time the bottle was empty, he had proposed another business venture.

26

Pete pulled into a gravel lot at the northern tip of Hunter's Point that extended into India Basin. Hunter's Point Shipyard opened in 1870, and after several permutations, finally closed in 1994, leaving behind a large chunk of uninhabited land bordering the bay. It was an ideal place to dump a body.

The remains of Ernesto "Sad Boy" Juarez had been found earlier in the evening by a few twelve-year-olds who'd come out to the docks to chill (and smoke some tree). One of them took a picture of the body and posted it on his Facebook page. It went viral in less than an hour and the Bayview Station dispatched two uniforms to the scene, where they found the stoned preteens and the corpse. The cops sealed off the area and took detailed photos of the deceased, which were sent out to the neighboring stations, hoping for an ID.

Miguel Urbina knew who it was the moment he saw Ernesto's face.

Ron was examining the body when Pete ducked under the police tape. Two 7000-lumen lights on tripods turned the darkness into a harsh, bright tableau.

"That's definitely Juarez?" Pete asked.

Miguel nodded. "It seems Sad Boy never made it down to Turlock."

"This poor little fucker took three to the chest and one to the nether regions. That's just spiteful," Ron said.

Pete crouched down to get a closer look. "Any idea how long he's been here?"

Ron shook his head. "I'd say a day or two. Forensics is en route."

"Looks like me and the boys will be putting in some overtime," Miguel said.

"You think this'll spark a fire in the Mission?" Pete asked.

Miguel's face hardened. "First Joker and now this? This could spark Armageddon."

27

Kelly rose later than usual. After reading her father's second and third journal entries, she had to force herself to stop or she would've been up all night. As it was, the only way she got any sleep was to take two Temazepam. Six hours later, the alarm on her phone roused her from a fitful slumber. On the way into work, she stopped for a double latte.

Techs from the security company were finishing installation of a new alarm pad for the back door. Kelly entered the building, her stomach in knots, hoping she could reopen the clinic later that day. She was relieved to see that Inspector Poe made good on his promise, and the crime-scene investigators had finished their work sometime in the wee hours of the morning.

The rest of the staff arrived a short time later and rolled up their sleeves. They spent a few hours cleaning up the destruction caused by the vandals and wiping up the fingerprint powder from the police. By noon they were ready to serve the community.

Once the doors opened, the flow of patients was non-stop. It was as if the people in the Mission had put their ailments on hold until the clinic was up and running. The staff treated a multitude of injuries, ranging from a woman with a fractured wrist caused by tripping over her miniature Labradoodle, to three second-graders who shared a case of conjunctivitis, to a middle-aged man who "accidently fell" on the Ken doll that was lodged in his anus.

Basically, it was business as usual.

Late in the day things slowed down a little and Kelly was able to take a fifteen-minute break in her father's office (she'd always consider it her father's office). Five minutes later the door opened and Nathan stuck his head in. Despite her growing discomfort with Nathan, she couldn't turn away any of the staff who were busting their butts to treat the patients. She waved him in.

Nathan perched on the arm of the chair opposite the desk and while he tried his best to be casual, his tone was annoying. Lately, everything about him annoyed the hell out of Kelly.

"Did the police find out who trashed the place?"

Kelly tried to remain neutral, but when she spoke, her voice betrayed her annoyance. "Not yet, why? Have you heard anything?"

Nathan overreacted. "Me? No. Just curious."

"I appreciate your concern. I'll let everyone know if I get any information that I feel is appropriate to pass along."

Most people would have picked up on that slight, but Nathan was impervious to insult. "I don't know how long it takes for insurance companies to pay for damages, but I wanted to remind you that my father has a potential buyer who'd be very interested in discussing some kind of arrangement with you. In fact, he'd be happy to set up a meeting," Nathan said with a smile, "with no obligation, of course."

"The clinic's not for sale, Nathan."

Not yet, he thought.

A little while later, Kelly told the staff she needed time to reorder supplies and equipment that were damaged in the break-in. She didn't want to be disturbed unless there was an emergency.

She went back to the office, closed the door and did something she'd never done before… she locked it. David had always wanted the staff to feel like family and have unfettered access to him at all times. Kelly felt the same way, but given everything that had recently transpired, she needed privacy.

She intended to do some reading.

28
(David's Journal)

To say I was appalled at Benedetto's suggested "business venture" would be a massive understatement. In the very short time I spent with him, it was obvious that Benedetto was far more than he appeared. He was clearly wealthy and successful, and definitely intelligent, but while he was extremely erudite, he had an undeniable dark side. What I found incredibly off-putting was the ease and confidence he exuded in dealing with, and in, criminal activities. It was like sitting across from Tom Hagen, graciously offering me a deal I couldn't refuse.

Benedetto's question was simple enough: would I be interested in taking on an assignment to dispatch someone the same way I did Musselwhite?

He wanted to know if I'd <u>kill</u> another person.

How does someone even react to that?

Before I could sputter out my response, Benedetto calmly explained how this came about. Without going into much detail here, rumors had circulated that Musselwhite's death wasn't natural... that he'd been taken out by order of Dominic Bruno. No one knew the specifics, so they did what people do; they made things up.

The story went that there was a man out there who moved in the shadows and could take lives without the mess of a drive-by, a garrote or a car bomb. Before long, half a dozen deaths were wrongfully attributed to this mystery man, and his reputation grew, fueled by reckless speculation and fabricated conspiracy theories.

The fact was, Bruno's crew was in the dark, as was the entire underworld. However, it was common knowledge that Matthew Benedetto was Bruno's lawyer, and some desperate intermediaries reached out to him with inquiries. If he knew of someone who could, you know, do a favor for an influential friend, that friend would definitely show his appreciation. In other words, name your price.

All of which led to the question on the table; did I want to kill someone for money? If not, Benedetto would never mention it again and we'd go our separate ways. If so, he'd take care of the details, as he did with Musselwhite, and handle all of the finances, including laundering the money and putting up a secure firewall so no one would ever know my identity.

Benedetto finished his pitch and my response was quick and definitive. I was not a hit man (I may have said "fucking hit man"; I honestly don't recall). Killing Musselwhite was a unique and singular situation and didn't mean I was going to turn to a life of murder-for-hire.

Benedetto nodded. He hadn't expected me to accept the offer, but nevertheless felt compelled to pass it along. After all, he knew the clinic was desperate for money and that Jess's treatments were expensive.

He said if I had second thoughts or questions, he'd be happy to have another conversation, and that next time he'd bring in food from the restaurant of my choice (he said this last bit with a smile). And with that, we bade each other good night.

I don't plan to ever dine with Benedetto again.

29

Three quick knocks on the office door startled Kelly out of her chair. She opened it for Annie, who informed her that Diego Sanchez was back again and looked much worse than before.

He was lying on a bed as Vik cleaned his leg. The wound was red and festering, swollen and tender to the touch. When Kelly got there, Vik gave her a quick rundown; Diego's vitals showed clear indications of a rampant infection.

Kelly held her frustration in check and gently asked Diego, "Did you go to the hospital?"

Diego's face was flushed with fever and a ten-year-old's guilt. "I did, I swear, Doctor Kelly, but they made me wait for, like, an hour. It was bullshit. They didn't care nothing about me, so I left."

Kelly mopped Diego's face with a cool washcloth. "Where's your mother?"

"She's at work. I'm telling the truth."

"I believe you, Diego. Do you believe the things I tell you?"

"I guess so."

"Then listen to me. Do you know what a prosthetic leg is?"

Diego scrunched up his face. "Maybe. I'm not sure."

Kelly pressed her tough love. "It's a leg made out of plastic and metal. It straps on right about here." She gently touched Diego's thigh. Tears were already forming in his eyes as the thought of losing his leg took shape in his mind.

"It goes all the way down to a plastic foot."

The tears were now flowing freely down Diego's cherubic face. "I don't want a fake leg."

"Then we've got to get you to the hospital now."

Diego vehemently shook his head. "No! I can't."

"Diego. *Escuchame*! I know about the Sureños, and Joker. I don't care what you were doing when you got shot. You think you're protecting the Norteños by keeping your mouth shut, but there's no one to protect except yourself! Oscar and the others in the gang want you to live. I want you to live, but you need surgery. We can't do that here. If you're bleeding internally, you're not only going to lose that leg, it'll probably kill you."

The pain in Diego's eyes was heartbreaking. Kelly wanted to take him in her arms and tell him everything would be all right, but that's not what he needed right now. Instead, she pushed him harder. "I know you're trying to be a good brother, but is it worth your life? Think about your mother. She's already lost one son. Isn't that enough?"

Alma Sanchez burst through the doors of the emergency room at St Francis Hospital, frantically looking for the admitting desk. She loved all of her children, but Diego was her youngest and the closest to her heart. He was a sweet little boy, and Alma was intent on saving him from the streets. The thought of losing him altogether sent her into a frenzy.

Alma grabbed the first person she found with a name badge, a plump white-haired woman who worked in medical billing.

"My son Diego Sanchez is here," Alma blurted. "He's only ten years old and…"

Before the dazed administrator could respond, a voice called out from across the waiting area, "Alma! He's still in surgery."

Alma turned to see Kelly striding in her direction and rushed to her, grabbing Kelly by her shoulders. "Surgery? No, no, no! How bad is it?"

Kelly guided Alma to a molded plastic seat, then sat down beside her, taking the older woman's hands in hers. "I'm not going to lie. His wound was full of infection. The doctors are treating it and doing everything they can to save his leg."

"Save his leg?" Alma broke down. "He's such a good boy. The best in the family. He works hard in school. Diego has a future."

"The doctors here are excellent. He'll get the best treatment possible."

"Doctor Kelly," she beseeched, "don't let my son die."

30

Pete, Ron and Miguel arrived at Franklin Square at 9pm to find Nano sitting on a swing, smoking a joint. Next to him was Ricardo *"Payaso"* De La Cruz, the 19th Street Big Homie. De La Cruz had picked up the nickname Payaso (which meant 'clown') when he was in first grade, and it stuck, despite the fact that there was nothing funny or buffoonish about him. Payaso walked with a cane and had a noticeable limp as a result of what he termed a "hunting accident" a few years ago. The 'accident' that left him partially crippled also left two mothers to bury their sons.

A dozen blue-clad bangers hung around in the park. They unsuccessfully tried to look nonchalant. The bosses didn't regularly meet with cops, especially not in public, and everyone was on edge. Things could go sideways in a hurry.

Payaso wanted to meet in the open to demonstrate his authority. Franklin Square was in his 'hood. In his mind, he could do whatever he wanted, with whomever he wanted, while he was on his home turf.

Miguel made the introductions, but they weren't necessary. Pete and Ron didn't work the gang detail, but they were well aware of Payaso. His name came up whenever a Norteño went down.

Nano blew out a cloud of noxious marijuana smoke and smiled. Miguel's hand was so fast and unexpected, it seemed like a magic trick when the blunt suddenly flew from Nano's fingers.

"Respeto, cabrón." Miguel didn't need to raise his voice to get his point across.

Nano jumped off the swing and was ready to do something stupid, when Payaso's cane smacked him in the ass. "You heard the man. Chill the fuck out, Nano."

His manhood stripped, Nano glared at Miguel, then muttered, "Fuck this shit," as he slunk over to one of the steel chairs that lined the playground.

Payaso gave his head a small shake, as if to say, "It's hard to get good help these days," then addressed Pete and Ron. "You looking into who killed my boys?"

Ron nodded. "I know you're pointing at the Norteños, but without a witness that's no help."

Nano couldn't restrain himself. "There was a witness, but they fucking killed him!"

"We might've protected Sad Boy if you gave us the information we asked for," Pete said with an icy edge to his voice.

Payaso responded in kind. "You're the police." He pronounced it 'Po-Leese'. "Instead of coming down here, why don't you head up to 25th and shake up those *Norputos*? They know who pulled the trigger."

"We wanted to give you the courtesy of hearing your side first," said Ron.

Payaso smiled, showing off a set of teeth that looked like the keys on a piano that had sat outside in the rain. "Courtesy. I like that. We're always happy to help out 5-0 and *El Sargento* when we can."

"Appreciate it, Payaso," said Miguel. "We're also here to tell you that the police are going to handle this. We don't want any more shooting."

"My boys aren't causing the fireworks, *ese*. Just payin' the price."

"Word is, Joker was the one who shot Diego Sanchez," said Pete. "You know anything about that?"

Payaso shrugged. "Never heard of no one named Diego Sanchez."

Pete stepped closer. "Ten-year-old kid. His brother Spider is with the Norteños."

"Ah," Payaso nodded. "*Bichito*." The gang members behind him cracked up when he referred to Spider as a "little insect". "Small man with big plans."

"What do you mean?" Ron asked.

"He's like number three or four over there. His little brother catches a slug, next thing you know, one of my homies catches one, too. Could be *Bichito* had something to do with it, or could be he just playing like he did, make him look a little taller. Only one way to find out for sure."

"How's that?" asked Pete.

"Get all those Mission Street *putos* together for a big meet, and then drop a fuckin' taco truck on their heads," Payaso said with a clownish grin.

This got a big laugh from the boys. Pete had a different reaction, lashing out with a vicious sidekick that caught Payaso in the chest, violently propelling him off the swing. Twelve Sureños reached for their pieces, as did Miguel and Ron. It would've gotten real ugly real fast if Payaso hadn't raised his arms to signify he was fine.

He slowly got to his feet with the help of his cane and hobbled over to Pete. The air was heavy with tension. Payaso's next move would decide if blood was spilled tonight on the playground. "It takes *huevos* to attack me in front of my homies," Payaso said.

Pete replied, "It takes stupidity to call out a Homicide Inspector."

Payaso slowly nodded, then leaned in, speaking in a voice that only Pete could hear, "You get a pass tonight, Inspector. But try that again and someone could get hurt. Might be you… might be someone you hang with. You know?"

Enraged, Pete grabbed Payaso by his blue hoodie and was about to 'try that again' when Miguel's hand came down hard on Pete's shoulder. "We're done here, Inspector."

Pete held tight for another few seconds, then opened his fingers and backed away. The last thing he wanted to do was instigate a firefight in the middle of the city.

Payaso flashed Pete a final fuck-you smile, then motioned to his gang, who followed him out of Franklin Square.

Pete watched until they disappeared into the darkness, and his thoughts immediately turned to Kelly, wondering where she was.

31

As Diego's primary care physician, Kelly had access to him throughout his stay. Her presence gave the boy a comforting familiar face and helped to encourage him as the doctors worked tirelessly to save his leg.

By ten o'clock that night, Kelly was ready to collapse. She toyed with the idea of grabbing a thirty-minute nap in the doctors' lounge, but there was no reason for her to stay at the hospital. Diego had been moved into the ICU. He was out of danger and now only time would tell if Diego would walk out of there on two legs or hobble out on one.

Since Annie had driven Kelly and Diego to the hospital, Kelly's car was back at the clinic. She called for a Lyft and stepped outside to wait. The cool air was preferable to breathing the stuffy, antiseptic oxygen inside the hospital. The area outside the main doors was congested with a large, chatty Asian family waiting for one of their relatives to be discharged, so Kelly walked down the block for some quietude. The Lyft app said her driver would be there in ten minutes. She used the time to clear her head and think about the myriad tasks she had in front of her.

Top of the list for tomorrow would be exploring financing options for the clinic. Second would be to start the interview process for a doctor to replace her father. Of course, she couldn't hire anyone without an infusion of funds, so maybe she should hold off on looking for additional staff for now.

She didn't need to add "read journal" to her mental checklist. The journal was safely nestled in her oversized shoulder bag. She knew, because she'd checked every few minutes to make sure it was there.

Kelly had only read a handful of entries and the revelations therein unnerved the hell out of her. Once again she pondered the question of whether she was better off knowing the gruesome details of her father's secret life or if she should quit reading now, before she waded too far out into the water and couldn't find a safe way back. She could ponder all she wanted... she already knew the answer.

Her thoughts were interrupted by the sound of someone walking down the street in her direction. She didn't hear any voices, but could make out the heavy breathing of a thickset dog and the tapping of a cane.

Kelly immediately assumed the worst. This could be trouble. Was she being paranoid or sensible? It didn't matter. Her ride would come along any minute, but in that minute bad things could happen.

Very bad things.

Tightly clutching her shoulder bag, she quickly turned back toward the hospital, and right into a 'no parking' signpost that stood between her and safe harbor. She hit the post hard with her left wrist and forearm, jarring loose her shoulder bag, which tumbled to the ground.

Ignoring the pain, Kelly lunged for her bag. As she did, she heard a loud growl as a pugnacious dog bore down on her.

She turned in terror, expecting any moment to be in a life-and-death struggle with a Pit Bull whose sole intent was to rip out her throat. Instead, she was staring down a hundred pounds of piebald, slobbering bulldog.

"Henry!" The voice coming out of the dark belonged to an elderly woman. She emerged a moment later, moving as quickly as her knobbly geriatric legs could carry her. "Henry! Stop right there!"

The bulldog halted its advance a foot from Kelly. Henry barked a friendly greeting as his stubby tail kicked into high gear and saliva dripped from his jowls. A bright red nylon leash trailed behind him.

"He's friendly," said an aged man as he made his way forward with the use of a highly polished, twisted walnut walking stick.

"Are you all right, dear?" asked the woman. Without waiting for an answer, she forged on, "We're so sorry. Henry belongs to our daughter and we're taking care of him tonight."

"He's a little much for us," said the man, "but this is the first time he's pulled away."

Kelly had gotten to her feet and slung her bag back over her shoulder. "I'm fine. I just stumbled."

The woman got a closer look at Kelly and smiled. "You're Dr Harper's daughter, right?"

Kelly returned the smile. "Yes."

The woman's smile stayed on her face, but turned sad. "He was a wonderful man. He operated on both of us. Saved our lives."

"I'm glad," Kelly said warmly.

"We were so sorry when we heard what happened," offered up the man. "We lit a candle for him and made a contribution to the homeless shelter in his name."

Kelly teared up. It was just one more story of how her father touched the lives of so many people in the city. "That's very kind of you."

The woman reached out and gently stroked Kelly's cheek. "He's with the Lord, looking down at you now."

Kelly's unspoken thought was, "I wouldn't be too sure about that." Fortunately, her Lyft driver pulled up at that moment and provided her with a graceful escape.

Kelly arrived home thirty minutes later. Her plan was simple: wash her face, brush her teeth, and fall into bed. But as she set down her shoulder bag, she felt the pull of her father's journal.

Sleep could wait.

32
(David's Journal)

Two months have passed since Benedetto dangled a repugnant offer of employment in front of me like tainted meat before a malnourished wolf. I've documented my initial reaction to becoming a hired killer. Nothing could change my mind about flushing all sense of morality (and legality) down the drain. I've spent my entire career helping others. I swore to embrace the Hippocratic Oath to uphold ethical standards. In any definition of the word, assassination falls well outside the bounds of ethical standards.

But the reality of life has once again come knocking. It's the reality of the clinic being on the verge of defaulting on a score of overdue bills, and Jessica's ongoing treatments being threatened by my inability to cover her expenses. Medical insurance covers the basic minimum, but Jess needs, and deserves the best treatment possible, regardless of cost.

I've looked at my options: try to get another loan (I've already taken a second and third against my house and don't have any other collateral); sell the house and use the proceeds to keep things afloat (once I paid off the loans, the proceeds would be negligible); leave the clinic and go into private practice or try to get a job as a surgeon at a major hospital (I assume I could find a job, but competition in San Francisco is fierce and hospitals are turning toward younger/more affordable doctors, which would mean relocating out of town). Last and certainly least is revisiting Benedetto's obscene offer.

Is my need for financial support sufficient reason to forego my basic beliefs? It's a ludicrous consideration... or is it?

The more I think about it, the more I see how hypocritical I'm being. I voluntarily killed a man, albeit a man who truly didn't deserve to be walking the same streets as the rest of humanity, and if left unchecked, he'd have undoubtedly committed more heinous crimes in the future. To me this was the definition of a person who unquestionably got what he deserved.

There are thousands of people just like Musselwhite who are committing terrible offenses against innocent people. Murder, kidnapping, exploiting children... the list goes on. Do those miscreants deserve to die as well?

I've never been a political activist. Like most of my associates, I could be classified as a liberal Democrat. I'm pro-choice, a staunch believer in human rights across the board, and a vocal advocate of stricter gun control laws (treating gunshot wounds on a weekly basis tends to make doctors biased). When it comes to capital punishment, I've never leaned too far in either direction.

I guess my stance on that has now been established.

Which brings me back to the question: do evil people like Musselwhite deserve to die? If the answer is yes, who should be the one to mete out the punishment? Certainly not me. Why risk everything to bring an unknown criminal to justice, regardless of how reprehensible his or her actions are? I'm not a superhero. It's neither my responsibility nor my desire to act like one.

It's terribly naïve to think that stopping one drug dealer is going to stem the opioid epidemic, or that neutralizing a serial rapist is going to put an end to the rampant violation of women in our society. However, taking some of the most vicious violators "off the board" does have a certain appeal.

Starting from the premise that I'd never consider such an outlandish offer to coming around to where I'm now considering it is a tectonic shift in my entire outlook on life. I still have grave reservations, but at the very least, I want more information.

While the following is a huge rationalization, there's a line in the Hippocratic Oath that states, "I will remember that I remain a member of society, with special obligation to all my fellow beings."

Like I said above, it's been two months since my meeting with Benedetto. Moments ago I contacted him and said I'd like to stop by.

His only question was if I liked Indian food.

33
(David's Journal)

This isn't a diary and I don't sit down every evening to record my experiences and emotions. By and large, nothing too interesting happens in the life of a physician who runs a neighborhood clinic, unless you consider things like the middle-aged woman who was knocked unconscious in a car accident. That wasn't the interesting fact in this case; it was the cause of the accident... the woman was driving while being pleasured by a remote-controlled vibrator being operated by her twenty-eight-year-old boyfriend sitting in the passenger seat. He got a little too playful and when he turned up the speed, the woman had a massive orgasm. Her pleasure was short-lived, as she lost control of the car and slammed it into a street lamp. She was one of the more talked-about patients for weeks.

My reason for keeping a journal is to have someplace to record my feelings about my "other job" and to leave a written record for my daughter Kelly (and hopefully, one day, Jessica).

After my last meeting with Benedetto, I came away convinced that I could make a difference. As outlandish as it seemed, I decided to take on an assignment. The target met my first requirement: in the eyes of anyone (with the possible exception of his mother), he was deserving of eradication. I don't know (nor do I want to know) who was offering the bounty on this individual, but I didn't pass judgment on them. Benedetto assured me that the target was not a business rival of the individual requesting the job, so I assumed it was personal. I could relate.

His name was Charles Crane. He went by "Chazz", which should tell you just about all you need to know. Chazz was a thirty-one-year-old bodybuilder and wannabe stuntman/actor who had a condo in Santa Monica, a few blocks from the Pacific Ocean. He lived off a trust fund and spent his days pumping iron, shooting up hormones and going out on auditions. He spent his nights raping young women.

The dossier on him was thin but complete. Chazz wasn't a complicated guy. He was a defective human being who destroyed the lives of helpless females without giving it a second thought. The obvious question was, why hadn't he been arrested? Because, while Chazz was detestable, he wasn't stupid. His MO was to break into the apartments of single women in the dead of night and use chloroform to knock them out. He left behind no DNA. His body was completely hairless, with the exception of faint eyebrows. He didn't suffer from alopecia; he suffered from the vanity that comes along with bodybuilding. All photos of him showed a bald man who worshipped his bulging and oiled physique.

After Chazz brutally raped the women, he'd disappear into the night. To date, none of the dozen victims could identify their assailant, but all suffered the physical pain of forceful entry, and the mental trauma that came along with that. Police departments across three cities (Venice, Santa Monica and West LA) were working together to find the culprit the Los Angeles Times *had dubbed the 'Midnight Rambler'.*

In the case of one victim, the damage was more than traumatic. She was a young actress named Natalie. Her film credits were meager: "Woman On The Phone", "Young Mother In The Library" and "Head Cheerleader". Natalie lived the typical Hollywood life: auditions, waiting tables, and the occasional 'short film' shot by a friend. One night, Natalie got a visit from Chazz, and awoke to discover she'd been repeatedly raped and sodomized.

She was raised a good Catholic and was a strict Straight Edger. The physical pain of her injuries, combined with the shame of being violated, overwhelmed her. Natalie's body was found three days later when the massage therapist in the next apartment complained of a terrible smell. Natalie's death was attributed to a drug overdose, but her injuries were attributed to the Midnight Rambler, who now officially had blood on his hands.

If Chazz rendered his victims unconscious and left no DNA, how did anyone know that he was the rapist who terrorized the Southern California beach communities? Because Chazz frequented dance clubs and liked to party. His drug of choice was GHB, also called Liquid X. It renders a person less inhibited, which is not a good thing if you're hiding dirty secrets. Chazz got talkative one night and regaled a Bro with details of his sexual exploits, emphasizing that he liked it rough and he didn't take 'no' for an answer. The Bro had witnessed Chazz's pathetic moves at the club, which never resulted in a hook-up, so either Chazz was lying, buying or crossing the line.

The Bro suspected it was the latter.

It happened that the Bro was acquainted with one of the Midnight Rambler's victims, and some of the salacious details that Chazz lustfully provided were in sync with the injuries she had suffered. Calls were made and options were weighed. Because Chazz had money and connections, the victim's parents came to the conclusion that turning over this partial information to the authorities wouldn't result in an arrest or long-term incarceration. And worse case, he may attack their daughter again out of spite.

Which left one option, dealing with Chazz in a more personal way.

And so began a succession of queries through a complicated web of nameless and faceless contacts, eventually coming to the attention of a sympathetic individual who was "connected".

When the request came to Benedetto, he made a few calls of his own. It didn't take long for him to be convinced that Charles Crane and the Midnight Rambler were one and the same. He compiled the dossier and then made one final call.

To me.

The more I read, the more I put myself in the shoes of the families whose lives were torn by the brutality forced upon their daughters, and the more enraged I became. Chazz was a scourge that needed to be stamped out. I knew if I took the assignment I'd be crossing into a dark territory from which there was no turning back. But hadn't I already crossed that borderline?

I took the job.

The dossier on Chazz provided me with all I needed to formulate the ideal plan. He injected himself daily with human growth hormones. HGH was a favorite among bodybuilders as it stimulates the growth, reproduction and regeneration of cells. Basically, it helps build muscle… the primary goal of iron pumpers who spend hours looking at themselves in gym mirrors.

Chazz got his illegal supply of HGH from a company in China. Each morning he had his breakfast of four egg whites, chased with sixteen ounces of Muscle Milk and finished by shooting a dose of HGH into his butt cheek. Over the years I learned that illegal drugs, especially those being produced in places like China or Russia, are often tainted with impurities, some of which can be fatal.

Chazz lived in a bottom floor condo in a six-unit building. Since it was winter and I was close to the ocean, the weather was chilly, which meant I didn't stand out in a dark, non-descript coat and baseball cap. I waited in the shadows until Chazz pulled away in his black Mustang Cobra. I checked my watch; it was 10pm. Every Tuesday night he played poker with C-list actors and junior talent agents. Chazz knew that the way to break into 'the business' was through connections, and this minor league crew was the best he could manage at this stage of his career. The last hand of the night was always dealt at 1am, getting Chazz home thirty minutes later. It was ample time.

The condo was new construction, which meant the locks were cheap and easy to pick. I slipped inside without incident and glanced around. The décor was chrome, glass and black leather. I'd seen operating rooms that were less antiseptic. The only personal touches were framed photos of Chazz, body oiled and veins popping, holding trophies he'd won in various local competitions. My disdain for this man continued to grow.

The kitchen was equally sterile. Chazz had no sense of style, unless 'meticulous' was a style choice. Not a utensil out of place or a smudge on the glassware. I quickly found his stash of HGH in a cupboard, between a box of hypodermic needles and an industrial-sized tub of whey protein.

I closely examined his HGH vials one by one, to make certain that my replacement vials were identical. I'd erased all doubts about this assignment prior to driving south, so I had no qualms about switching out the vials of HGH for vials I'd prepared which were laced with a cleaning solvent called carbon tetrachloride. I chose carbon tet for a few reasons: it was a trace chemical that was commonly found in illegally produced drugs (it was often utilized to wash out steel vats used to make the drug); it was extremely toxic; and it was a chemical cousin of chloroform. The poetic justice was too symbolic to pass up.

Once Chazz injected himself with the tainted HGH, he'd rapidly develop severe nausea and abdominal pain, followed by dizziness and an irregular heartbeat. In a short time he'd lapse into a coma and within a few hours die of either liver or kidney failure.

I'd made the switch and was headed for the door when I heard the growl of a powerful engine and caught sight through the window of Chazz's Cobra pulling back into the underground garage. What happened? Was the surveillance information wrong? Was he suddenly sick? The reason didn't matter. All that mattered was getting the hell out of there fast.

My gloved hand was turning the doorknob when I looked back to the kitchen one last time and remembered that one of the authentic vials had rolled off the counter and was lying under the breakfast table. I'd meant to retrieve it when I was finished, but in my hurry to leave, it slipped my mind. If Chazz found the vial he'd know someone had been in his condo and all bets were off.

I dashed into the kitchen and grabbed the errant vial. I shoved it into my pocket and was moving toward the front door when I heard his keys sliding into the lock. I was trapped.

My brain kicked into overdrive, searching for a plan, but I drew a blank. The intense stress of the situation short-circuited any ability to problem-solve. In that moment, it appeared that my career as a hit man would be over before it began. Suddenly, my feet took command of my body and silently carried me back into the kitchen. The only place to hide was the walk-in pantry. I quietly slipped into the cramped space and gently shut the door. The pantry latch-bolt clicked into place at the same moment Chazz opened the front door. If I was lucky, he'd only returned home because he'd forgotten something and would be heading right back out. It turned out luck wasn't on my side. I knew I was either going to be exposed, and probably beaten to death by the muscular behemoth, or I'd be spending a few hours in his pantry, holding my breath and praying he didn't want a late-night snack.

As Chazz moved around the kitchen, I did my best to calm my breathing and remain perfectly quiet. I wished I'd planned better, or that I'd been more careful in the plan's execution, but I never once questioned my decision to take on this job. In fact, as I uncomfortably stood there with a case of creatine powder jammed into my lower back, my resolve to successfully carry out this assignment grew exponentially. The only thing that separated me from a man who had viciously raped a dozen young women was a two-inch hollow panel door. And yet I wasn't the least bit afraid. My overriding emotion was the disappointment I'd feel if he didn't shoot himself up with poison and pay the price for his actions.

Chazz eventually turned off the lights and headed upstairs. I waited for ten minutes before I risked cracking open the pantry door. I half expected him to be standing there, a butcher knife in hand, a triumphant grin on his face for luring me out into the open. But my luck had returned. Not only was he nowhere in sight, but I heard the shower running and Chazz singing 'We Are The Champions' in an off-key falsetto as the water pounded down on his chemically inflated torso.

I quickly made my way out of the condo, relocked his deadbolt, and got the hell out of Dodge.

Two days later, I received a message from Benedetto. The body of Charles Crane had been found on the floor of his kitchen. He'd been dead for at least twelve hours. A nearby hypodermic needle and empty vial of HGH had been tested and found to contain very high levels of carbon tetrachloride. According to one of Benedetto's sources, the Santa Monica Police were testing the other vials and had come to the obvious conclusion that Mr Crane had gotten a bad batch of HGH from China. Another example of how illegal drugs can kill.

One week later, $9,500 was deposited into my "brokerage account", with additional equal deposits to be made each month for the next five months.

I'll be able to pay Jess's bills and keep the clinic afloat... at least for a while.

34

While Kelly had been en route home to read about her father's first foray into murder-for-hire, Benedetto was finishing up a long day's work. He was seated at the window, sipping a glass of fifteen-year-old single malt and gazing out at the lights on the bridge. This was his favorite part of the day. The wind down. He was soon to discover that this day wasn't yet over.

Mrs Mathews entered carrying a distinctive navy blue file folder. Benedetto saw her reflection in the window and bade her join him.

She complied, first stopping at the bar. A moment later, she lowered herself into the matching club chair and laid the folder on the table between them. Benedetto raised her glass. "To Natalie," he said.

This was part of the evening's ritual. Closing the day with a drink and a toast to Mrs Mathews' daughter, who tragically took her own life many years ago.

Cora Mathews came to work for Benedetto just before the turn of the century. Born and raised twenty miles outside of Mobile, she displayed a genius level proclivity for numbers at a very young age. A professor of applied mathematics and statistics at the University of Alabama heard tales of a twelve-year-old named Cora who could solve complicated quadratic equations in her head. What was more impressive was the fact that Cora was a normal, well-adjusted little girl; she just happened to have the mind of an advanced math scholar.

By the time she was in her early twenties, Cora was working at the RAND Corporation, consulting on the design and viability of future weapon systems. It wasn't long before she was recruited by the NSA to work in-house. It was during those years that computers rapidly changed the way intelligence was gathered and analyzed, and Cora was at the forefront, writing programs that were far more advanced than anything coming out of Microsoft.

While in DC, she married a career diplomat, gave birth to a beautiful daughter, discovered her husband was cheating on her and got a divorce. By that time, she was burnt out on the NSA and the dark direction the government was heading with invasive surveillance, so she moved west, looking to make a new start.

The moment she walked into Benedetto's office, he knew she was a keeper. He hired her on the spot, and every day after that he thanked his good fortune that she'd entered into his life.

It had been a Tuesday morning when Mrs Mathews called in to say she had to take care of a family matter and would need a few days off. She'd already arranged for a temp to take her place and hoped Mr Benedetto wouldn't mind. In the two years she'd been working there, Mrs Mathews had never requested any time off. Benedetto asked if there was anything she needed from him. Her response, "I honestly don't know yet. Perhaps."

She returned to work the following Monday. Stoic as always. When Benedetto arrived, she followed him into his office and handed him a file folder. She didn't know what to do with the information she'd collected on a man named Charles Crane, but requested that Benedetto read the file.

That was how Cora Mathews broke the news to Benedetto that her daughter had died.

Benedetto did some judicious editing to the file before he gave the dossier to David Harper. That set the wheels in motion and became the genesis of Gideon, The Biblical Destroyer.

Mrs Mathews, her glass still aloft, smiled a weary smile. "To Natalie." She took a sip, then tapped a perfectly manicured finger on the file folder. "You need to see this."

35

Kelly put down the journal and rubbed her jaw. She hadn't realized she'd been clenching her teeth while she was reading, riveted to every word. The entry detailing her father's first "hit" left her reeling. The loving man that raised her had a cold, calculating and very dangerous alter ego.

Surgeons generally have well-deserved reputations for their arrogance and belief that they're infallible. Those character flaws threaten to outweigh their talent. One of the things she'd always admired about her father was that he was never arrogant and could be quite self-effacing. In her mind, he didn't have any flaws.

Now she'd come to find out that his flaws were in a league all their own.

Her mind was still abuzz like a hive of frantic bees when her cell phone vibrated. It could only be Pete at this hour, and she couldn't deal with him tonight. After what she'd learned about her father, she wasn't sure she'd be able to deal with Pete ever again. How could she possibly have an open and *honest* relationship with anyone... especially a policeman?

Kelly was about to let the call go to voicemail when she saw it wasn't from Pete. It was a 415 area code, but she didn't recognize the number. Given the tumult in her life, she decided it was best to answer it. She was surprised when she heard Benedetto's voice.

He apologized for the late call, but he had some information that was extremely important. Kelly asked if it could wait until tomorrow. She was in for the night and frankly didn't have the energy to come across town. Benedetto said he was outside her building, and the sooner they talked, the better.

Ten minutes later, Benedetto was seated next to Kelly, the blue file folder opened to a candid photo of a handsome young thirty-year-old man with thick black hair. He was getting out of a Maserati Gran Turismo.

"His name is Tommy Moretti. Do you recognize him?"

Kelly took the photo and after a moment shook her head. "Should I?"

"No. I'm relieved you haven't seen him around."

Benedetto went on to explain that from the moment Gideon 'went into business' there were people looking to take him down. "My tech came across information a few hours ago that indicates your father's death *may* have been a result of someone discovering his identity."

Kelly looked at the photo again, this time with the knowledge that she could be staring at the face of the man who killed her father. "Is he the one?"

"It's a strong possibility. His bio's in here, but I'll give you the gist of it. Moretti's mother died in childbirth and his father took off. Tommy was raised by his Uncle Arthur. Arthur ran the family business, which consisted of drugs, extortion and human trafficking. Arthur had two sons of his own. One joined the Army and was killed in Afghanistan, and the other put more product up his nose than on the street. On Tommy's twenty-first birthday, Uncle Arthur gave him the ultimate present: oversight of the drug operation, which left Arthur free to focus on trafficking and providing entertainment for people who sought the darker levels of human depravity."

"How does my father fit into this?"

"Your father killed Arthur Moretti."

Kelly slowly shook her head. Even after reading the last journal entry, she had a hard time believing any of this was true.

"If my father killed almost two dozen people like you say, what specifically points to this Tommy Moretti?"

"Someone took credit for Gideon's murder in one of the 4chan chat rooms. The posting stated the date and time, which coincided with your father's death. Messages on the dark web are routinely routed through multiple servers to protect the identity and location of the user, but my tech developed a program that unravels the spider web."

"And he determined where the message was sent from?"

Benedetto nodded. "A business registered to Atlas Manufacturing… a shell company belonging to Arthur Moretti. Tommy is Arthur's only

158

relative involved in the day-to-day operation. He has a reputation for being impulsive and violent."

Benedetto placed the file folder on Kelly's coffee table. "This is everything I have on Tommy Moretti. Businesses, places he frequents, that kind of thing."

Kelly closed her eyes. Between her fatigue, her father's journal and now this information about Moretti, her body and mind simultaneously hit the wall. Her whole being had been on overdrive for so long, she didn't know when she was simply going to flame out like a sputtering candle deprived of oxygen.

When she opened her eyes, she saw Benedetto's look of concern. "I apologize," he said. "I should've waited until morning."

"No, I'm glad you came," Kelly said, finding a reserve of energy she didn't know she had. "Do the police know about Tommy Moretti?"

"They've known about the drugs and have been compiling a case on him for years, but have been unable to gather sufficient evidence to put him away."

"But they aren't looking at him as a possible suspect in my father's death?"

"Not that I know of."

"I'll tell Pete about him tomorrow."

"The police will want to know where you got this information. If they start examining your father's past, it would destroy his reputation."

Kelly shook her head in frustration. "So, I have the name of the man who probably killed my father, but I can't tell anyone. What's the good of knowing if I can't do anything about it?"

"For now, just be extremely cautious. As I said before, if Moretti killed your father, he may be targeting you and Jessica as well. We'll talk again in a day or two, as soon as I find out more."

Every time Benedetto delivered more information, Kelly's life got exponentially more complicated.

It's said that ignorance is bliss. Kelly longed for her blissful past, and held little hope she'd ever recapture that feeling moving forward.

36
(David's Journal)

Arthur Moretti runs a family business. It's not a typical family business like a small grocery store or plumbing repair or a neighborhood clinic. Moretti deals in drugs, extortion and human trafficking. It's the human trafficking that I find especially abhorrent. His associates kidnap young girls, predominantly runaways or foreign students taking a year abroad, then sell them into bondage to some of the most debauched people on earth.

There's not a doubt in my mind that Moretti is a scourge on humanity. Eliminating one man won't put an end to this slave trade, but it may staunch the flow for a while, and if only one young girl is saved, it'll be worth it.

I'm clearly not alone in my assessment that Moretti is evil personified. Someone with substantial means wants Moretti gone, and like the other requests that flow my way, that someone wants his death to look accidental. Hence, Gideon was asked for 'by name'. Like all of the assignments I've undertaken, I have no idea who's making this request, nor do I want to know. Two-way anonymity is crucial in this line of business.

Despite the fact that I've now been at this for a while (Moretti is my eighteenth assignment), I don't take what I do lightly. Killing another man (or in one case, a woman) is a monstrous act. Each time I carry out an assignment, it weighs heavily on my mind and eats away at my conscience. While I wonder if my soul is eventually destined for heaven or hell, I've decided that prior to my demise I'm determined to bring about the early demise of others if it makes the world a little safer.

I began my preparations for Arthur Moretti by acquiring his medical history. It's easy to get hold of records when you have access to medical databases. Due to HIPAA privacy rules, it's neither ethical nor legal to obtain someone's information without their consent, but given that I eventually plan to murder him, taking a look at Moretti's records is a violation that hardly troubles me.

I took perverse satisfaction in discovering that Arthur had a history of cardiomyopathy and arrhythmia. It was only a matter of time before his heart gave out on its own, but the individual who wanted him gone wasn't willing to wait for that eventuality. Most people who hire Gideon are rather impatient when it comes to their requests being fulfilled.

I took some time off from the clinic (I told Kelly I was attending a conference in Santa Barbara) and spent a few days observing Arthur Moretti. While he ran a dangerous and violent business, Moretti himself was a frail man in his mid-seventies. Like many people his age, he had developed some set routines.

Every night he sat in the same chair, turned on the same lamp and read the San Francisco Chronicle. *Over the course of ninety minutes, he chain-smoked half a pack of Winstons, drank a glass of warm milk laced with Old Crow, then creakily made his way to his bedroom.*

It's become clear to me that the most effective plans were the least complicated. The more complex the scenario, the more things can go wrong. In the case of Arthur, the best method for achieving the desired result was extremely unsophisticated, but required a degree of risk. I had to get inside his house.

I thought a man of Arthur's criminal stature would have elaborate security, but that wasn't the case. When he was home, one of his no-neck soldiers stood guard. Since Moretti kept no cash or valuables in the house, the only protection he needed was personal. Hence, his armed companion. When Moretti left for the day, the house was locked but vulnerable.

At the advice of Benedetto, I've mastered several break-in techniques (the internet, especially the dark corners of the web, is a trove of information, some of it quite frightening). The tools I need, like the electric lock-pick, have been supplied by Benedetto.

Once I let myself into Moretti's home via the back door (which was screened from the neighbors by a tall hedge), I made a few simple adjustments to the electrical cord and light switch of his table lamp. I was inside the house for less than five minutes and left behind no traces of ever being there.

That night I positioned myself next to a commercial dumpster in the alley next to Moretti's house and settled in. The rank odor of decaying food burned my nose and made my eyes water, but my discomfort was minimal compared to what I had in store for Moretti.

I watched through my pocket binoculars as he sat down, placed his Winstons on the table, and pulled out the day's Chronicle. Moretti took a sip of his dairy-diluted bourbon, lit up a smoke, and then reached for the lamp switch.

As he twisted the black knob to turn on the lamp, his body was jolted by a massive surge of electrical current. He looked like a man doing the St Vitus dance.

After his erratic and violent twitching, Arthur's blackened hand slipped off the switch. He slumped back into his chair, steam rising off his balding pate.

I can't say I was happy to watch him die. I don't get joy from other people's misery, regardless of how despicable (the one exception was Musselwhite). Nor did I feel remorse. The job was done, a horrible person was eradicated, and my compensation would keep the clinic running for another few months. Some people would look at this as a "win-win".

I look at it as karma.

The next day, the Chronicle ran the story of Moretti's demise on page four. His death was being investigated, but the police were already saying it appeared to be an accident due to a faulty electrical connection. Rather than detailing Arthur Moretti's sordid life, the Chronicle opted instead to flesh out the story with family-friendly statistics about how many people died each year as a result of defective wiring.

That marked the end of Arthur Moretti. I understand from Benedetto that Moretti's business will take a serious hit, and may be inherited by his nephew or perhaps taken over by a rival family. Unfortunately, drug dealing and trafficking will continue, but at least one person has paid his dues.

37

After Benedetto left, Kelly was too amped up to sleep. Instead, she'd gone back into her father's journal and read about him carrying out his "assignment" on Arthur Moretti. She could no longer pretend that the things Benedetto had told her were fabrications. She'd read enough of the journal (all that she could stomach so far) and accepted the reality that her father moonlighted as an anonymous assassin. Now, in addition to dealing with the void created by his death, she had to come to terms with his secrets.

She'd finally climbed into bed, but her mind kept taking her to places where sleep was not an option. Her thoughts turned to Jessica, who was now her responsibility. Kelly loved her sister dearly and would do whatever was necessary to take care of her, but every once in a while her subliminal thoughts toward Jess took a harsh turn. Kelly couldn't help but have selfish flashes where she considered her sister as an emotional and financial burden... and then she remembered that it was her fault Jessica had been put in harm's way, and that made her feel even worse.

Tomorrow was visiting day.

Kelly was accustomed to the smell of hospitals, but she never got used to the cloying aroma in the hallways of the Peninsula Oaks Healthcare facility. The parent company in Dayton had done extensive consumer research regarding every aspect of the facility's décor, including the fragrance of the freshener they used. They concluded that the smell of ylang-ylang was the most soothing, but Kelly always associated it with this place, and in turn with her sister's bleak condition. To her, ylang-ylang was annoying as hell.

It was Sunday; the day when family members came to visit out of love, guilt or a combination of both. Most of the visitors chose to come after lunch, since the mornings were busy with physicians doing their rounds and patients being readied to be put on display. Kelly came early so she could spend some quiet time with Jess, and because she had an appointment in the afternoon that she couldn't be late for.

As Kelly grabbed hold of the door handle to her sister's room, she took a moment to brace herself. It was never easy to see Jessica in her condition, but Kelly made it a point to always greet her with a reassuring smile. When she entered the room, her smile quickly faded and turned to alarm. Jessica's bed was empty.

Kelly ducked out of the room and looked down the hallway to see a man with dark, slick-backed hair pushing her sister in a wheelchair. It took her a moment to realize that the man was Tommy Moretti!

She yelled for him to stop, but the man paid no attention. If anything, he seemed to speed up, heading directly for the exit door at the end of the hall.

"STOP!" Kelly raced down the hallway. Benedetto had been right. Moretti had targeted her helpless sister. Kelly's worst nightmare was playing out right in front of her eyes.

She caught up to him just before he could roll Jessica outside. Kelly roughly grabbed his shoulder and spun him around.

It wasn't Moretti, and the woman in the wheelchair wasn't Jessica.

The man pulled out his ear buds and loud rap music blared forth. "What's the matter?" he asked.

An embarrassed flush crept across Kelly's face. "I'm sorry," she stammered. "I thought you were someone else."

Ms Spiro had come around the corner in time to witness the incident. "Is there a problem here?"

Kelly sputtered, "No... I... uh..."

Ms Spiro pasted on her patented meaningless smile. "Dr Harper, this is Frank Pace, our new physical therapist. He specializes in neurological PT. Frank, this is..."

"Jessica's sister. I can see the resemblance. Nice to meet you, doctor."

Kelly apologized again and asked Ms Spiro the whereabouts of her sister. As if in response, a freshly bathed Jessica was wheeled around the corner by a buxom, jovial Filipino nurse named Cookie.

Kelly reentered Jessica's room as Cookie was propping her up in bed. "Her hair looks nice," Kelly said. Even though Jessica was only thirty-six-years-old, she had streaks of dull gray in her otherwise brown hair, which was common among bedridden patients.

Cookie smiled at the compliment. "I wash it every Sunday morning after her physical therapy," she said with her usual enthusiasm. "I'm thinking of bringing in a coloring kit and getting rid of that gray."

Kelly shook her head. "We'll wait until she gets out and then go to a salon. It'll give us both something to look forward to." She turned to her sister. "Won't it? Hair color, cut, a mani/pedi. It'll be a whole new you."

Jessica stared at a point on the far wall, completely oblivious.

Cookie told Kelly to buzz her if she needed anything and then departed, closing the door behind her.

Kelly waited a moment, then went to the door and cracked it open. She peeked out to make sure no one was lurking and then crossed back to the chair beside Jessica's bed.

"How you doing today, Jess? It looks like you've been spending time outside. You've got some color in your cheeks." Kelly gently stroked her sister's face.

"Remember I told you that I got a job offer at St Francis? I spoke to the head of Emergency Services and explained how I needed more time to consider the position. He said they'd hold the job open for two weeks, which was very kind of him. You remember St Francis Hospital, right? It's where Daddy used to work." Kelly smiled with the recollection of an old, happy memory. "We used to sneak into the break room and blow up the surgical gloves, then draw faces on them." A tear formed at the corner of Kelly's eye.

A strand of Jessica's hair came free and gently bisected her broad forehead. Kelly reached out and tucked the tress back into place.

"I met a man the other day that was a friend of Daddy's," she said in low tones. "He told me some stories... some incredible stories."

She looked over at the closed door, then glanced around the room. For the first time in all of the years she'd been coming here, she wondered if there were hidden surveillance cameras. It was possible that the facility installed audio/video to monitor the patients and/or the nursing staff. Kelly knew she was being paranoid, but she needed to be constantly aware not to say anything that could accidently expose her father's past.

Despite Kelly's desire to share her recent revelations with someone, now wasn't the time and this wasn't the place. "You know what? I'll save the stories for next time."

The same strand of hair had worked itself loose and again lay across Jessica's face. Kelly reached behind her sister's head and undid the loose bun, allowing her wavy locks to flow freely.

Jessica's lips curved up slightly. Whenever her sister's physical actions coincided with appropriate emotional responses, it reinvigorated Kelly's hope.

She flashed back to childhood images of Jessica before she fell ill: a seven-year-old Jessica dressing up a four-year-old Kelly like she was a living doll; ten-year-old Jessica and seven-year-old Kelly leaning over the pier at Lake Tahoe, using kite string and bacon to catch crawdads; teenagers sitting around a campfire with their parents, young and innocent enough to be enthralled by their father as he spun scary stories about ghosts and goblins. The sweet memories triggered a flow of tears.

At that moment, Kelly knew she'd do anything to protect her sister. Her beautiful, defenseless sister was not going to fall victim to a killer… even if it meant Kelly taking matters into her own hands.

Just like her father.

38

For the past few years Kelly routinely did an early morning run that started on the Embarcadero and took her along Fisherman's Wharf, past the barking sea lions at Pier 39, then transitioned onto Jefferson, turned left at the Argonaut Hotel, past the Buena Vista, then around Ghirardelli Square, where the finest domestic chocolate was still being made. After passing these tourist landmarks, she'd loop back toward her condo. The run was two and a half miles and Kelly averaged it in about twenty minutes.

As a result of everything that had recently happened, she'd forgone the run and opted for additional sleep... that was, when sleep came. After seven days of feeling mentally and physically out of sorts, she decided to reinstate her jogging regimen, if for no other reason than to have some time to clear her head.

When she returned from her visit with Jessica, Kelly slipped out of her jeans and sweater and slipped into her sweats and road-scuffed teal and orange New Balance runners.

She put in her ear buds, dialed in her "morning mix" and hit the streets. Two blocks later, she passed a black Suburban, the engine idling. The windows were tinted, but she could make out two people inside. She didn't think much about it at the time. San Francisco was constantly packed with humans, residents and visitors, and a couple of folks sitting in a car, probably trying to figure out how to maneuver the clogged traffic in the city, didn't raise alarms.

In fact, she forgot all about it... until she swung past Ghirardelli and saw the same SUV again. This time it was slowly moving down the street. Either looking for a place to park, or following her.

Kelly's pace picked up, along with her heartbeat, and she suddenly veered down an alley, cut through a parking lot, and reemerged two streets over. The Suburban was nowhere in sight. She slowed her pace back to normal, hoping her pulse would follow. Was she being overly suspicious? Yes. Did she have every right to be? Hell, yes.

She completed her loop and started her cool down, a brisk quarter-mile walk around the block. As she strode past the beautiful old Victorians, she kept her eyes peeled for the Suburban, but her mind was totally consumed with thoughts about Tommy Moretti. One moment she was convinced it would be best to tell Pete everything and let him take it from there. But, and it was a significant "but", how could Pete ignore the fact that David Harper had been a hit man with eighteen notches on his belt?

She considered a different scenario with equal weight. Putting the events of the last ten days, including her father's death, in the past and simply getting on with her life. Tying everything up with a neat bow and attempt to expunge her recent memory. This option presented myriad issues. Unless she underwent hypnosis or deep psychotherapy, she'd never be able to forget the things she'd learned in the past few days. Plus, there was the issue of her and Jess's lives being in jeopardy. If that threat *was* real, she couldn't ignore it. And to top it off, she hated leaving things undone. She lived for closure.

Which meant option three… confirming whether or not Tommy Moretti had killed her father. If he had, well then… what? Eliminate him? Who was she kidding? Killing Moretti was a pipedream. A violent, self-gratifying fantasy. Maybe her father could justify murder, but not Kelly. She was a life-long, dyed-in-the-wool pacifist.

Which brought her back to the original conundrum: what could she do with the information she had?

Kelly rounded the corner and saw a shiny new Mediterranean Blue BMW 540i parked in front of her condo. She assumed it belonged to one of the freshly minted tech millionaires that flooded the city. She was headed toward the front door of her building when she heard someone call her name. She turned to see Alexa getting out of the car, holding two bags from La Boulangerie.

Kelly glanced at her watch as she crossed to meet Alexa. "Nice car."

Alexa shrugged. "The lease on the old one was up."

"By 'old one' you mean the green Jag that had, what, three thousand miles on it?"

"The company sets the rules. What's a girl to do?" Alexa raised up the butter-stained bags. "I brought brunch. Can I interest you in an almond croissant? Maybe a Kouign-amann?" she asked. "I had Jamie make a lowfat latte with a pinch of cinnamon. He knew exactly who it was for and he said to give you his best."

Kelly took the coffee with a smile and nod of thanks, but didn't have time for her best friend and favorite baked goods. Not today. "Lex, you know I love you, almost as much as I love the Boulangerie, but I've got to be somewhere at one."

"Pete can wait."

"It's not Pete."

Alexa flashed a sly grin. "Really? Something you're not telling me?"

"No," Kelly lied. There was a world of things she wasn't telling Alexa. "I know it's hard for you to understand, but sometimes people get together in non-sexual ways," she said with a smile.

"I deserved that." Alexa dropped her smile and turned serious. "I'm worried about you, Kel. Between your Dad and the clinic and the job offer at St Francis, you've got way too much on your plate."

Kelly wondered how Alexa would react if she knew what was actually piled on that plate. "I'm trying to sort things out."

"Promise me you'll call. We can grab a bottle of wine and have a slumber party, like old times."

Regardless of what happened in the next week or two, Kelly's life had taken an irrevocable turn, and the "old times" may be a thing of the past. Still, she managed a smile. "Sounds good. Talk later."

After a quick exchange of cheek kisses, Kelly peeled off and headed inside. Alexa knew something was eating away at her friend. Something deeper than the death of her father and the money problems at the clinic. There was something just under the surface that Kelly was struggling with, and Alexa worried that whatever it was could send her childhood friend hurtling down a dark and potentially dangerous path.

An hour later, Kelly sat on a bench in Golden Gate park and watched the carousel rotate to the strains of Oom-Pah music from the German band organ nestled in the middle of the glossy herd of lions, tigers, camels and dragons. She wistfully thought back on the lowfat cinnamon latte as she nursed a cup of harsh coffee from the park refreshment stand.

Two little girls with pigtails merrily squealed as they rode atop twin giraffes. They looked to be about three years apart. Kelly smiled, filled with the memory of her and Jessica riding this same carousel many years ago. Happier times.

Matthew Benedetto arrived at precisely one o'clock and sat down beside her.

"Odd place to meet," Kelly said, watching the little girls slide off the giraffes and climb aboard two colorful unicorns with flowing fiberglass manes.

"I find the music strangely soothing, and the clamor of children provides excellent sound cover."

"My father used to bring me and Jess here."

"I know."

She turned to face him. "You don't miss a trick, do you?"

"Over the years your father and I became quite close. He desperately needed someone to talk to after his assignments; someone with whom he could share his feelings and his many misgivings. The emotional impact of the job was too overwhelming to keep bottled up. For obvious reasons, I was the only person he could confide in."

Kelly shook her head. "It makes me sad that he couldn't confide in me."

"He felt terrible about keeping secrets from you. But there are secrets, and then there are secrets. He would've loved to talk to you about it, but it was too much of a burden to lay on someone else... especially his daughter."

The two little girls let out joyous shrieks as they clambered down their horned steeds and got atop a pair of roaring tigers.

"Have you decided what you're going to do?" Benedetto asked.

"The police have no leads, so they won't get onto Moretti without a push, but I have no idea how to go about that. I have no idea how to go about any of this."

"As you consider the options, keep this in mind," Benedetto said, sounding every bit the experienced lawyer. "If Moretti's arrested, he'd most likely try to plea bargain by giving them information about your father."

"Does he have any proof?"

"I don't know, but in this day of rushing to judgment, your father's reputation would suffer irreparable harm, which would also taint you and Jessica."

Kelly glanced over to the merry-go-round. The sisters were done with the carousel and made a dash for the swings, their laughing mother not far behind. The image of a happy, loving family. It was her life, pre-Musselwhite. Kelly wondered why she'd been dealt a crappy hand from a stacked deck and feared if she stayed at the table, she'd be playing a game she had no chance of winning.

She looked back at Benedetto. "You're saying the only way out of this is to…"

He stopped her from completing the sentence. "Don't misconstrue my comments. The only thing I'm saying is, through no fault of your own, you've found yourself in an untenable situation. If you want my opinion, destroy the journal and forget everything we've talked about."

"What about the threat of more violence from Moretti?"

"That's purely conjecture on my part. If Moretti was responsible for your father's death, he's already gotten his revenge. He'd be taking a huge risk to kill two more people."

"But he might."

Benedetto nodded. "Growing up in a crime family makes him unpredictable." Benedetto pulled a thick envelope from inside his coat and handed it to Kelly. "It's a surveillance report on Tommy Moretti. It will give you additional insight into who you're dealing with."

Kelly's stomach churned. Was it the stale coffee or nerves? "If I did decide to… to take matters into my own hands, is there some kind of procedure to follow? Some kind of protocol?"

Benedetto felt terrible for this young woman who was faced with a no-win situation, and he was well aware that he was responsible for getting this ball rolling many years ago.

"There are no procedures, no organization, no one who comes in after you and cleans things up. Everything you do needs to be meticulously planned before you move forward. This isn't something you can enter into lightly on any level, since it would require tremendous effort; physically, mentally and emotionally.

"Let me be clear," he continued, "if you're considering taking another person's life and you're caught, there's no safety net. If you succeed…"

Kelly completed Benedetto's dire thought, "My life will be forever changed."

39

It was 7pm, and Pete was at his desk, digging through incident reports. Sunday nights were usually quiet in homicide, as most fatal incidents took place on Friday or Saturday. One homicide team was on the street and the other two didn't punch in until tomorrow morning, so Pete was able to focus on reviewing the reports in the Harper murder book, hoping to find something he'd overlooked. The case was growing colder by the day, but he was taught to never give in to defeat, regardless of how slim the odds of success.

He hoped for an epiphany… that "aha" moment when the facts of the case suddenly lined up and pointed at the killer with a flashing neon arrow. Unfortunately, police work almost never panned out like that and most cases were solved by hard work, luck, and, as his partner often told him, the sheer stupidity of the perpetrators.

Pete was ready to take a break when Ron entered, carrying two bags of Vietnamese food. The smell of ginger, mint and chilies filled the office, setting Pete's salivary glands into overdrive… until he saw the name of the restaurant on the bags.

"You went to Saigon Kitchen?"

Ron was already clearing off his desk. "Best Vietnamese food in the city."

"I heard the health department closed them down because they found rat shit in the kitchen."

"Nope. Just issued a warning."

"Meaning the restaurant still has a rat problem?"

"Every restaurant in the city has rats. It just so happens the rats that frequent Saigon Kitchen have more refined taste buds."

"Why don't we go with Chinese food like everyone else in the department? We're only a few miles away from a dozen excellent restaurants in Chinatown."

Ron knew Chinatown inside out. He'd spent five years in that precinct and was part of the team that helped bring down Raymond "Shrimp Boy" Chow, the powerful leader of the Hop Sing Boys.

"Because it's a pain in the ass to get there, there's never any parking, and, by the way, that's racial profiling."

"Me suggesting we eat Chinese food makes me racist? You grew up in Millbrae, for fuck's sake. If you suggested we try Scandinavian food because my great grandparents came from Norway, I wouldn't be offended."

Ron pulled the food out of the bags. "You won't have to worry about it. The last thing I want to eat is pickled herring and boiled potatoes. Are you eating or not?"

"I'll just grab a burrito out of the vending machines."

"You're fucking kidding me. You'd rather eat a microwaved burrito that's loaded with preservatives and so-called meat – which, by the way, is probably ground rat – instead of a truly delicious, fresh meal from one of the most authentic restaurants in the city? And what about the sanitation level of the factory where those ass rockets were made?"

"You've got a point."

"Of course I do. I'm the senior partner. Think how miserable you'd be if you scarfed down a green chili burrito and then we had to roll on a call. You'd be like, 'Excuse me, Ma'am, I'm really sorry about your husband lying dead on the carpet, but could I use your bathroom?'"

"Okay, okay," Pete gave in. "Did you get me shredded pork banh mi?"

"Don't I always take care of my partner?"

As they dug into their food, Ron informed Pete that he spoke to Urbina, who'd told him there were shots fired not far from the BART station at Mission and 24th. "Couple of kids on the corner saw the car. Fortunately, no one was hit."

"24th and Mission is Norteño territory, right?"

Ron nodded. "This thing's heating up. Miguel's working his contacts to try to get a bead on Spider, but no one's talking. I know Kelly's been taking care of his little brother. Maybe you could ask her to have a chat with Mamacita."

"I could ask, but I'm doing my best to keep her out of the middle of this."

"Yeah. I get that. Besides, I doubt Spider's mom would give up her kid." He nodded toward the three-ring binder labeled with David Harper's name. "Find any hidden gems in there?"

"Not really. There's a consensus that the driver was the only person in the vehicle, but that's about it."

"Nothing new from Forensics?"

Pete shook his head. "They're still waiting for some test results to come back."

Ron spoke between mouthfuls of grilled lemongrass pork shoulder. "What about the names you got from Kelly?"

Pete and Ron had agreed that Pete would take the lead on the David Harper investigation while Ron helmed the other cases that they caught. "Both non-starters. Nathan Curtis comes from Pacific Heights money. Never been in trouble before. And the transient they call The Hollow Man is in the wind. Some of the uniforms remember seeing him around the Mission encampments, and the folks there all said he was crazy."

"Pot kettle."

"Now *that's* profiling. Anyway, no one knew his name or anything about him, except that he had bad burn scars on his face and hands. He's either moved on or lying in a stupor in the basement of some tenement. Not worth our time."

"So we're nowhere. It's been over a week and we've got three other homicides on our plate that need to be cleared."

Pete was waiting for Ron to drop this on him. The murder of David Harper was big news, but it was last week's big news. The Mayor and Chief would love to ride the wave of some positive headlines, but as every day passed, the case got less attention and the leads became increasingly stale.

"I'm giving a hundred percent on our active cases, but that doesn't mean I'm going to stop grinding on David's death."

"Your star's on the rise here, but don't spread yourself so thin that your work suffers." Ron had finished his pork and was picking at a carton of noodles. "I've seen it happen before. An Inspector thinks he can keep all the plates spinning, but at some point there are just too many fucking plates, and then they all come crashing down."

"I can handle the load, Ron," Pete said with a little too much edge.

Ron nodded, not in agreement but as a precursor to a story. "Did I ever tell you about the first partner I had when I worked out of Bayview?"

"Jim Foley? He was the one who ate his gun, right?"

"Right."

"You told me that story the first day we teamed up. You said it was a 'cautionary tale' about a cop getting so personally involved in a case that he didn't realize he was sinking under the workload. One day he was so far underwater he only saw one way out."

"I'm glad you paid attention."

"An Inspector who shoots himself in the head is the kind of story that leaves an impression, but if you're worried that's the road I'm heading down, you can relax. Like I said, I can handle it."

"Those are the exact words Foley spoke the last time I saw him alive."

"Point made." A moment later the desk phone rang. Pete answered, "Homicide. Ericson." As he listened, a look of amazement came over his face. "Yeah, that's great. Thanks for calling. I owe you Giants' tickets. Let me know as soon as you get the results." Pete looked at the receiver as if he'd never seen a telephone before, and slowly put it back into the cradle.

"Well?"

"I don't believe in kismet, but that was Victoria in Forensics. They found some hair fibers embedded in the driver's seat backrest. They're going to run DNA on them and see if they match the owner of the car. If not, they could belong to our guy."

Pete pulled out his cell phone and was about to make a call when…

"Don't do it," Ron said.

"Do what?"

"Call Kelly."

"She's in a tailspin. She needs to hear some good news."

Ron shook his head. "A few hair fibers that probably won't lead anywhere is not good news. It's a crapshoot. The worst thing you can do is build up false expectations. Besides, you won't get the results for at least a few days."

Pete looked at his partner, then at the phone. "You're right," he said, as he slipped the phone back into his pocket. "I'm worried about her."

"You're underestimating her. She's strong. She'll pull through."

Pete wished he shared his partner's conviction, but he wondered if Kelly had the strength to come out the other side.

Across town, Kelly wondered the same thing as she sat at the window counter of a coffee shop, doing something she never dreamed she'd be doing.

40

Kelly had been at the coffee shop for just over an hour and was nursing a double cappuccino. It had grown cold long ago, but that didn't matter. She neither tasted nor enjoyed it.

The file on Moretti was open on her lap under the counter and she glanced down at his photo for what had to be the tenth time. His face was burned into her memory banks, and soon she'd see him in the flesh.

At least, that was the plan.

The building directly across the street was home to The Battery, a swanky private club that Moretti had joined a few months ago. He dined there every Sunday night. He either loved the cuisine or he was working hard to impress the law-abiding members. Kelly assumed it was the latter.

The club took its name from its location on Battery Street in the financial district, and was the latest hangout for young wealthy dealmakers in the Bay Area. They came from the tech industry, the financial sector, and in the lone case of Moretti, organized crime (although he was invited into the club based upon his "legit" businesses, which were essentially shells for laundering cash).

Moretti joined The Battery because, in his mind, it put him on the same level as the latest wave of moneyed entrepreneurs who currently dominated the business and social scenes in San Francisco. He longed to be part of that crowd and not some punk who got rich because he was born into a crime family.

Hushed stories circulated around The Battery about Moretti, and the members thought it was cool to have one of their own potentially be part of the mob. Of course no one ever talked about it in Moretti's company. They were much too chill for that. And much too afraid. While the techies designed killer apps and the hedge funders made killer deals, word was that Tommy took the term to a whole other level.

Moretti was friendly, generous to a fault and a wonderful conversationalist. In a room full of computer nerds and business school grads, he was a breath of fresh air. He had connections that ran deep, and he happily doled out Warriors and 49ers tickers to his fellow Battery bros. They didn't know how he came by the tickets, and they made a point to never ask.

While Moretti ate his dinner, Kelly wondered what in the hell she was doing. Like her father before his "first time", she was profoundly conflicted. She knew she was in way over her head to even consider taking lethal action against Tommy Moretti, but what could she do to protect herself and her sister? Her options were few, and they ranged from dreadful to horrendous.

Up to this point, Moretti was nothing more to her than a photograph. A color image of a man she despised and wished terrible things upon. She wanted to see Moretti in person to get a visceral reaction.

As the minutes slowly crawled by, her apprehension swelled. The acid from the coffee was eating a hole in her stomach lining and the non-fat milk foam that laced the drink seemed to be curdling. She tried a breathing trick she'd learned in her beginning yoga class, but that only resulted in her feeling lightheaded. When her phone buzzed, Kelly flinched and knocked her coffee cup over. Fortunately, it was empty.

She pulled out her phone and saw the number. It was Pete. She couldn't remember if they'd made plans for tonight. Was she supposed to be meeting him someplace for dinner? Or was he calling to check up on her? Either way, it didn't matter. She wasn't leaving her perch until...

Just then, the door to the club swung open and Tommy Moretti stepped out with two other men. All were young, handsome and dressed in expensive hipster gear that was designed to look casual but exude wealth. All three had an aura of success.

As Pete's call went to voicemail, Kelly focused on Moretti, who was finishing up a story that the others found hilarious. They slapped him on the back in a display of camaraderie, and exchanged fist bumps in a show of appreciation for his amazing wit.

When Moretti's Maserati pulled up and the attendant hopped out, Tommy bade his friends a good evening, which was met with a round of smiles. They loved this guy. Tommy slipped the attendant a twenty, which brought a smile to his face as well. If Kelly hadn't known any better, Tommy Moretti appeared to be quite a catch. Good looking, rich, well liked and generous.

Before he slid into his car, Moretti looked across the street. His eyes seemed to focus directly on Kelly. His expression was ice cold and it sent chills through her body. Did he just happen to look in that direction, or was he actually staring at her? Kelly froze, not wanting to create any movement that would attract attention. She held her breath and forced herself not to look away, or even blink.

The whole incident lasted maybe five seconds and the moment was finally broken when Tommy slipped into the driver's seat and glided into the night.

Kelly was unnerved, but she was glad she'd made the decision to see him in the flesh. Despite the persona that Moretti worked so hard to cultivate, there was something vile about him.

Something that exuded evil.

41
(David's Journal)

Several months have gone by without an assignment. For this I'm thankful, and yet, I have to admit I miss it. Not because of the money, although finances are getting tight. I miss the incomparable adrenaline rush. As I write that, I feel guilty and unclean. To experience an emotional kick from taking another's life is clearly a depravity. Does it make it any less deviant or perverse because the victims are cankers on society who prey on the innocent? Perhaps. At least that's the mental salve I apply to justify my actions and the adrenal surge that stimulates my senses.

I don't equate my experience as a contract killer with the emotional and physical rush felt by a cliff diver, or a bullfighter or a Formula One driver. Dangerous occupations and thrill-seeking hobbies are like drugs to action junkies who thrive on the cascading endorphins.

The difference is, my end game is murder. I'm not trying to compare apples to elephants here, but risking your life to terminate another's raises the bar to astronomical heights.

While I may miss that feeling, I'm not looking forward to another assignment. I'll undoubtedly accept it (if the target meets my criteria), but I truly don't enjoy ending another person's life. I do it for what I believe are the right reasons, which is a far cry from taking pleasure in the act. If it sounds like I'm conflicted, that's because I am. Extremely conflicted.

I relish the simplicity and calm of just being a doctor and a father. I'm constantly worrying about the dangers of being exposed as Gideon, but I've learned to push that dread to the rear of my mind, where it's become a persistent low-thumping angst.

Taking on the role of Gideon has provided me with a clear and unique perspective on life. I've learned what's important and necessary to be productive and truly happy. It doesn't take a lot, just appreciation *for those you love and caring for those who need. There will always be a huge hole in my life left by the death of Mary, but her death has set me on a path that <u>might</u> be making me a better person (if becoming a killer can possibly make you a better person).*

I've become a better father, a better doctor and a better friend. I've rid civilization of more than a dozen people who were an affliction on the world. Some were husbands, some were fathers and three were grandfathers. One was a wife and mother. They all left behind families that mourned; but, moreover, they left behind legacies of pain, misery and suffering. Legacies of debauchery, corruption and malevolence. I'll go to my grave convinced the world is a better place for their absence.

Dying is not a fate I dwell upon, but given my unusual and dangerous pastime, my odds of going prematurely have greatly increased. Because of that, I do everything I can to protect myself when I'm in Gideon mode, from my methodology to covering my tracks.

The most important aspect of my modus operandi *is that I don't have one. There can be no patterns. I take great care (and pride) in devising murders to appear to be accidents or natural causes. To date, none of my hits have been investigated as homicides. The "perfect murder" is not one that goes unsolved. It's one that's never suspected.*

One of the things in my favor is that urban police departments are loath to take on murder investigations unless they strongly suspect a homicide has taken place. Their caseload is too heavy to bother with deaths that appear to be accidents or suicides (just last year, 35,000 people died from unintentional falls, 58,000 from unintentional poisoning and 47,000 from suicide).

I've learned that almost all forensic labs across the country are ill-equipped, understaffed and underfunded. They have huge backlogs of evidence to be tested, so they're forced to prioritize their workload to support prosecution as opposed to investigation.

I'm not an assassin by trade. Every job I take puts me into foreign and dangerous waters. The only way for me to survive those waters is to use the skills and knowledge I've acquired over the years.

For example, having done extensive charity work in South America and Africa, I'm familiar with a long list of little-known and highly toxic substances that can bring on death and not leave an easily identifiable trace. Poisons are only one of the arrows in my quiver, and I haven't used the same one twice. No repeatable patterns.

Another critical element in remaining anonymous is to leave no trail. I never use credit cards and I avoid locations that have security cameras (which is getting increasingly difficult since they've popped up everywhere). If I have to travel by air, the reservations are made through one of Benedetto's companies under fictitious names, and he provides me with the appropriate identification to go along with the tickets. I don't ask where he gets these documents, or exactly how deeply he's entrenched in the shadows. I don't want to know. I've never taken an assignment overseas, nor do I intend to. There's a bottomless swamp of deplorable people right here in the good old US of A.

I've never donned a full disguise, but do whatever I can to mask my appearance. A simple change of hair color and wearing different (but not distinctive) glasses go a long way toward hiding in plain sight. Glasses have worked for Superman all these years, so there must be something to their particular cloaking power. The most important thing is to blend in, or better yet, not be seen at all.

Recording my feelings and thoughts in this journal sounds like a "How To Be A Hit Man For Dummies" handbook. Nothing could be further from my intent. Perhaps one day in the future (hopefully long into the future), this will be read by Kelly. I've instructed Benedetto that in the event of my death the journal is to be given to her, and her only.

Kelly... if you're reading this, it means I'm dead. It also means you've now discovered my dark secret. I hope you can understand the events that brought me to this precipice and why I took the path I did. I'm not proud of what I've become, but nor am I ashamed. I haven't gotten to this place easily and I don't underestimate the consequences of my actions. I've unsuccessfully attempted to put aside the moral ambiguity of "right vs wrong".

I've become a murderer. It's not my proudest accomplishment as your father, or as a member of the human race. I never wanted to lie to you or keep secrets from you, but my actions aren't something I could ever discuss. To do so would've put you and Jess in danger, and risked shattering our family. I couldn't allow that to happen. You've been my anchor, Kelly. Without your love and your friendship, I'd be adrift.

In a twisted way, and please don't take this wrong, it's the strength of our father/daughter bond that's given me the wherewithal to do the things I do. The things in the light... and especially the things in the dark. I can only hope that one day you'll forgive me.

42

Kelly went back to work on Monday morning and tried to keep her focus on her patients, but her mind kept leap-frogging between her father's journal and Tommy Moretti's frigid glare.

At one point in the day, she found herself at the pharmaceutical lockup, mentally cataloging the drugs they had on hand. She was taking stock of what she could easily obtain in the event she decided to move ahead with her as yet unformed plan.

She was lost in thought when she heard Nathan behind her. "Dr Harper?"

Kelly spun around, hoping her face didn't belie her sense of 'getting caught'. "Doctor Curtis."

"I wanted to let you know that I spoke to my father last night and he'd love to sit down with you to talk about financial support for the clinic. He suggested the three of us have drinks tonight at the Olympic Club."

"I thought the Wallace Group wanted to buy the clinic outright."

"That's still an option, but there are several different financing scenarios he'd be happy to lay out for you. I've explained how important the clinic is to you, and to the neighborhood, and he'd be honored to help you find a favorable solution that will work for everyone."

"I didn't know your father was so altruistic. I've heard that he's a very shrewd and tough businessman."

This caught Nathan off-guard. He'd been instructed to tell Kelly whatever was necessary to get her to the table. Randall would take it from there and close the deal. However, based upon Kelly's attitude and body language, this wasn't going to be the slam-dunk that his father imagined.

"He's smart, and can be tough, but he sees this as his opportunity to give back to the community. I'm sure he'll figure out a way to make a buck and take advantage of the good press, but his heart's in the right place on this one." Nathan surprised himself that this bullshit flowed so easily out of his mouth. Maybe the apple didn't fall far from the tree after all.

Kelly wasn't buying it. "Let me be clear. This clinic's financial wellbeing is not your or your father's concern. We're not going to talk about this again, all right?"

Nathan looked like a scolded child. "I was only trying to help."

Kelly's smile was so fake it couldn't pass an audition for a bit part in a local theatre company. "I appreciate it. Now, we've got work to do."

Nathan turned and headed out the door. He was totally humiliated. Kelly was right for chastising him… he was pushing too hard for something he knew was wrong.

Once again his father made him feel like an ass.

Kelly turned back to the drug cabinet, selected a small bottle of pills, two vials filled with clear liquid and a few syringes, all of which she slipped into her pocket. When she looked up, Vik was standing there. Had he seen her?

Kelly pulled herself together and greeted Vik with warmth. "Dr Danabalan. Is everything okay out there?"

"Yes, but I spoke to one of the ICU nurses at St Francis and she told me that Diego's infection is winning the battle. He's out of immediate danger, but they don't know if they'll be able to save his leg."

"I was going to drop by there this morning on my way in, but got hung up. I'll swing by later."

Vik stood there, awkwardly trying to find a way to broach the real reason he came to see her. Kelly picked up on the obvious cue.

"Was there something else?"

The last thing Kelly needed today was dealing with personnel issues, but Vik was a rarity – tireless, brilliant and charming with patients. He was worth taking care of, even if it meant listening to him bitch a little from time to time.

Vik was clearly nervous, but he took the leap. "This may be inappropriate, but I've heard Dr Curtis talking about the clinic being sold to the Wallace Group."

"Dr Curtis likes to talk. I've told him repeatedly that the clinic isn't for sale, but he has a hard time accepting that as the truth."

Vik smiled. "That is good news. I've had experience with the Wallace Group, and they are a medical disaster. A few years ago I worked at a clinic in San Diego in a low-income area that was on the verge of gentrifying. The original clinic was struggling and eventually bowed to the financial pressure of selling to the Wallace Group. They came in, painted the walls, refurnished with new chairs and sofas, and replaced the entire staff with doctors they had under contract. And then raised their rates by thirty percent. They churn patients as quickly as possible to generate maximum fees."

"You just summarized the sad future of medicine. I'm not selling, so it won't be an issue, but I appreciate your concern. I really do. By the way, I need to leave here in about an hour, so I'd appreciate if you could take charge for the rest of the day and lock up this evening."

Vik beamed. He'd been asked to do this a few times in the past, and each time it made him feel that he truly belonged and was appreciated. "I would be most happy to, Doctor." He hesitated for a moment, then continued, "There is one other thing."

Kelly leapt to the assumption that Vik may ask for additional pay for taking on more responsibility.

"It is none of my business, but if the clinic is having financial problems, I'd be willing to defer my salary for a while."

Kelly's face reddened. She was embarrassed to have so drastically misjudged Vik's character. "That's incredibly nice of you…"

"Also, my brother Krishan, who recently moved in with me, graduated from the Duke-National University of Singapore medical school and completed his internship at Kaiser in Oakland. He would gladly offer his services to you at a very nominal fee while he explores local opportunities for a residency position."

"Vik, I don't know what to say. I'm touched, and I'm sure my father is looking down on us right now with a tear of gratitude in his eye." Kelly had no problem promoting the notion that her father's soul was in heaven, despite her serious doubts.

Vik smiled. "When I came here from Singapore, this community embraced me. Since then, I've been invited into their homes, shared their food, and made to feel like family. It is my obligation and honor to repay

187

them with the best care I can provide, and that means keeping this clinic open."

Kelly dabbed at a tiny drop of salty water that formed at the corner of her eye. "You are truly special, Doctor, and all I can say is I appreciate your warm support and your dedication. We're going to be okay."

"I know we will."

When Vik left, Kelly reached into her pocket and pulled out the bottle of pills. The label read Zolpidem (better known as Ambien). She still wasn't certain how she was going to deal with the Moretti situation, but a plan was slowly starting to take shape.

43

It was coming on four o'clock when Kelly arrived at Peninsula Oaks. The sky was free of clouds and sunshine filled the late afternoon with cozy warmth. It was a perfect day for a stroll in the woods, or in the case of the patients ensconced at the facility, a wheelchair ride through the extensive and impeccably groomed grounds. Towering oaks were surrounded by vibrant green lawns and colorful beds of seasonal flowers.

Kelly brought Jessica out to their favorite spot under the canopy of a tree that stood on the outskirts of the property, away from any well meaning or curious healthcare workers who could accidently drift into earshot of the sisters' heart-to-heart.

Birds overhead sang never-ending songs and unseen insects buzzed nearby. It was a lovely setting, but not one that engendered great joy. Jessica was comfortably secured in her chair with padded straps, and she stared off into the distance, unaware that Kelly was sitting on the wrought iron bench facing her.

Kelly hadn't come to inform Jessica what she intended to do. Rather, she'd hoped that by verbalizing her plans, even to someone who had no cognitive ability to understand them, it would help her decide how to proceed.

This may have been a ridiculous idea, but Kelly desperately needed someone to talk to, or in this case, someone to talk at. She understood why her father couldn't share his secrets, just as she couldn't talk to Alexa (and definitely not Pete) about what she was considering. Using Jessica as her own "journal" gave Kelly an outlet that she otherwise lacked.

After making sure they were alone, Kelly leaned over and spoke in hushed tones. "Jess, we could be in danger. There's a man, I'm pretty sure he's the person who killed Dad, and he might try to hurt us, too. I'm not going to let that happen."

Kelly went on to tell her sister about the terrible people who shouldn't be walking around free. People who were a threat to society. As she spoke, she had a growing reaffirmation of how strongly she felt about her family and the evils that had befallen them. Dealing with Moretti wouldn't be about revenge; it would be proactive, and perhaps to a lesser degree, perform a public service.

Kelly's mind was racing; had she just adopted her father's attitude about making the world a better place by stamping out some of humanity's worse cancers? Had she crossed over? Was she willing to pull the proverbial trigger if and when the time came? She knew one thing for certain... she was ready to take the next step in her plan.

She glanced around the gardens again before she continued, "His name is Tommy Moretti. I'm going to find out if he's the one responsible, and if he is, I'm going to stop him."

Kelly wondered if she would've confided in Jessica if her sister was healthy and had all her faculties. Should Jess ever become fully functional again, Kelly vowed to trust her with all of the family secrets.

She desperately hoped that the darkest Harper secrets were in the past.

44

Kelly found street parking on Waller, one block south of her destination on Haight. Scoring a metered space in that area was akin to winning Power Ball, and she took it as a good omen. She was going to need all the good juju the universe chose to shower upon her.

The days of peace and love in the Haight were long since passed, but the commercialization of them still lived on in this neighborhood, which boasted the most famous cross streets of the hippie movement. Tourists flocked to the corner of Haight and Ashbury, cruising the boulevard to buy up *faux*-vintage t-shirts emblazoned with the names of rock bands from the sixties, exotic bongs and hash pipes (mostly made in China) and used vinyl.

Haight appeared to have a lock on vintage clothing stores, and Kelly walked past several: Wasteland, Relic Vintage and The Love Of Ganesha. She headed into Buffalo Exchange, a trendy chain that also had a store in the Mission. Kelly knew the two women who ran the shop in the Mission; a lovely couple from Portland who were raising a beautiful six-year-old girl named Tina. Tina was an orphan from Santiago and suffered from Osteogenesis Imperfecta, also known as "brittle bone disease". Fortunately, Tina's case was classified as Type 1, or mild. Even so, Kelly had treated her for a broken tibia, a fractured ulna and two broken fingers over the course of just two years. Her mothers showed their appreciation by giving Kelly massive discounts on whatever she wanted from their shop.

Despite the fact that Kelly was on a budget, especially since she discovered the clinic was deeply in debt, she wanted to keep the evening's plans under the radar, which is why she drove three miles in congested traffic to pay full price for an outfit she'd only wear once.

An hour later and $300 lighter, Kelly exited with a side slit black dress, a pair of leather ankle boots and a red purse with a shallow false bottom. The latter would definitely come in handy. Her next stop was

Piedmont Boutique, which was readily identified by the oversized plastic legs in fishnet stockings and pumps that protruded from the second-story window. The boutique was well known for outfitting drag queens and had everything necessary to complete a full transformation.

Kelly spent thirty minutes trying on different wigs. From a sedate brown wavy cut to a blue pixie style to a ginger Afro. Each wig gave her a completely different look, but not the look she was going for. She finally settled on a black Pageboy, which made a simple but bold statement. It was sexy and flirtatious without being vapid.

The young woman who helped Kelly wholly embraced the Goth look, complete with deep red eyeliner, black lips and multiple piercings. Kelly used her as inspiration and bought the appropriate makeup.

She headed home with her purchases to begin the metamorphosis.

45

The line outside The Patch was thirty deep. Since the nightclub's opening six months ago, business had been thriving, which was the norm for a newly crowned hot spot. The question was, could it stand the test of time and still be packing them in a year from now?

The club was located in Dogpatch. Once a shipbuilding hub, the area was in mid-transition from an artists' enclave to an arts-and-design neighborhood. Adjacent to Pier 70 and a stone's throw from the bay, Dogpatch was home to fashion-forward stores and eateries, as well as the headquarters for the San Francisco chapter of the Hells Angels.

When Kelly's Lyft driver pulled up to the club, he explained that as a single (and hot) female, she wouldn't have to wait in line. Solo women were like neodymium magnets, drawing in overconfident men with unrealistic expectations. Men who couldn't wait to drop a few hundred dollars on ridiculously overpriced cocktails with locale-inspired names like The Currfew (Courvoisier, Triple Sec and lime juice), The K9 (Ketel One and eight fruit-based ingredients) and the douche-bros favorite – The Doggie Style (a pint of Thirsty Dog Brewing's Labrador Lager with a shot of Fighting Cock bourbon).

As Kelly stepped out of the car, she drew several appreciative glances as well as a few stalker-like ogles. The black dress clung to her like a kidskin leather glove and had the desired effect of showing off her lithe figure. She'd been judicious with her makeup, opting for black eye shadow with blood red hints nearest her tear ducts, and deep red lipstick. Kelly's natural milky complexion was the perfect canvas and the overall look was striking and yet approachable.

Her long blonde locks were woven tightly under the black wig, which was secured with a dozen bobby pins. Kelly had to fight the constant urge to make sure the synthetic hair was on straight.

Everything about this moment felt awkward. Her clothing, her makeup, her hair, the club. None of it was remotely familiar or the least bit comfortable. Kelly was not a clubber. In fact, she'd been to a grand total of two, both with groups of women who were celebrating upcoming nuptials. She hated the noise, the crowds and the whole vibe. She was certain she'd be instantly pegged as a pretender. An upper-middle class prig who had no business trying to get on with this crowd.

Kelly paused, working up the confidence to take the plunge. If she couldn't muster the courage to go inside, she'd never be able to follow through on her plan. Actually, "plan" suggested a well-thought-out course of action, which didn't exactly define Kelly's strategy.

Her intent was simple enough. Get Moretti alone, seductively encourage him to drink, slip him some Ambien to loosen him up and see if she could get some answers. Even though Ambien wasn't a "truth serum", when mixed with alcohol the result was disorientation and lack of concentration, which in turn made lying more difficult. If things proceeded accordingly, Kelly would leave the club knowing whether or not Moretti killed her father. If the answer was affirmative, she'd regroup and consider her next move.

What next move? This was insanity! It wasn't too late to turn back, to forget this crazy idea. Once again, she considered dropping this whole thing in Pete's lap. He'd figure how to deal with Moretti and, at the same time, somehow keep her father's reputation clean. Pete was smart and he loved her. He'd move heaven and earth to make this all work.

As Kelly dug her phone out of her purse, she heard someone yell, "Yo, T!" She turned to see Moretti give the doorman a fist bump, slip him some cash, and glide into the club. Her blood instantly ran cold. A tremor rippled through her body and her hands began to shake. She'd been fooling herself thinking she could go through with this.

She was about to call Pete, but was momentarily distracted by the photo on her home screen. A twelve-year-old Kelly with her arm around her sister Jess, mugging for the camera. It was her favorite picture of the two of them. Less than a year later, their mother would be raped and bludgeoned and Jess would be bashed into a vegetative state.

The memory steeled Kelly's resolve. Moretti didn't commit those acts of violence, but if guilty, his crime was equally heinous… the death of her father.

She slipped her phone back into her purse.

Every journey, even one as insane as this, began with a single step.

Kelly took hers.

46

The Patch ticked every box of the things Kelly hated about dance clubs: the aggressive darkness split by blinding shafts of ever-moving colored beams of light; the blasting, mega-amped pounding bass notes that made her physically nauseous; and the tightly packed bodies that triggered an intense feeling of claustrophobia, or worse, being buried alive. The legal capacity of The Patch was four hundred, but like most clubs, they squeezed in twenty percent more customers. The owners were happy to roll the dice that the City Fire Marshal wasn't going to cruise in on a Monday night and do a head count.

The air was thick with the smell of alcohol, weed (even though smoking was strictly prohibited) and pheromones. Of the five hundred people in the club, four hundred and fifty of them were hoping to get laid that night. It was like being in a warehouse teeming with over-sexed, salivating male dogs and flirtatious bitches in heat, all doing a ritualistic mating dance that involved watered-down cocktails and inane conversation shouted over thunderous music.

Kelly was unsuccessfully attempting to navigate her way though an undulating throng of bodies moving en masse to mind-numbing House Music. She had something called a Spaniel Spritzer in her hand. One taste of the bitter concoction was all she could stomach, but she carried it as a prop.

She hadn't known what to expect once she was inside, but with the passing of each second she felt more out of her depth. How was she going to find Moretti? Between the cacophony, the noxious smell of Paco Rabanne, and the sweaty horde, Kelly became disoriented.

As she shuffled forward, she felt a hand on her shoulder. She spun around, imagining Tommy Moretti at the other end of the hand, but instead she was face to face with Josh Friedman, the man she'd met at the restaurant with Alexa. Damn it! If Josh were to tell Alexa that he'd spotted Kelly at The Patch, it would raise a plethora of questions, none of which Kelly was ready to answer. Questions she'd never be ready to answer.

Josh wore a broad sloppy smile and was doing a yeoman's job keeping his shit together, even though he was clearly loaded. "You look really familiar," he slurred.

It suddenly dawned on Kelly that she was in disguise. She'd only met Josh the one time and she'd looked completely different. Plus, Josh's mind was currently blanketed by a layer of dense fog that showed no indications of lifting any time soon. With a little luck, she'd be able to pull this off without any collateral damage.

Kelly lowered her voice an octave or two and drew upon her time in Boston to speak in a semi-believable Massachusetts accent. "I don't think so. Anyway, I'm here with somebody." As she spoke, she wondered if her voice sounded as ridiculous to Josh as it did to her.

Josh bobbed his head up and down. "That's cool. So am I." He nodded toward the bar and Kelly caught sight of a woman with wavy brown hair that contravened the rules of science by lustrously shining in the dim light. The woman was facing away from them, but Kelly didn't need to see her face to know it was Alexa. Things had just gotten much more complicated. While Josh wouldn't equate this dark-haired Goth chick to the blonde doctor he met a week ago, Alexa would see through her makeup in less time than it took to say, "what the hell are you doing here?"

At that very moment, Alexa turned toward her. Kelly immediately reversed direction, swimming against the stream of clubbers who were herding toward the bar like a slice of suicidal lemmings marching for the cliff's edge.

As she struggled to put some distance between herself and Alexa, Kelly thought she heard her name being called. It couldn't be. It was impossible to hear anything above the music, but there it was again. A woman calling out "Kelly?"

Curiosity got the better of her. She had to know if she'd been made. Kelly kept moving, but risked a single glance over her shoulder to see if her oldest friend was knifing through the legion of revelers like an icebreaker in the Antarctic. If so, she'd have to call the whole thing off.

Kelly was angry at herself for not anticipating this scenario. Why hadn't she done more preparation? Why hadn't she devised a smarter plan? Fortunately, Alexa wasn't heading in her direction. In fact, Kelly couldn't see her at all. She sighed her relief. Maybe she *could* pull this off. Maybe her plan wasn't…

And that's when she slammed directly into Tommy Moretti.

47

Kelly froze.

All of her carefully rehearsed lines instantly vanished into thin air. Her mind and body were overcome with a boiling rage that stultified her.

She snapped out of her stupor and realized that Moretti was saying something to her; leaning in close to speak into her ear over the music. "Are you okay?"

Kelly nodded. She felt his breath on her neck. He smelled of cigarettes and patchouli oil. "I haven't seen you in here before."

"First time," Kelly said. There was no reason to disguise her real voice, but she still hid behind her quasi-Boston accent like it was an extra layer of protection.

"You here by yourself?"

Kelly managed a smile. Normally a simple task that she now struggled to perform. "I was supposed to meet a friend here, but I don't think she made it."

Moretti grinned, brimming with confidence. He was handsome and he knew it. He used it. Kelly saw past the charming façade to the lascivious wolf behind the mask and wondered how many women fell for his act.

He looked at the glass in her hand and shook his head. "That shit is nasty. You like Dom?"

Kelly shrugged, pointed to her ear. She didn't understand what he was talking about. Who was Dom?

Moretti raised his voice. "Dom Perignon." He mimed drinking a glass of champagne, then raised his brows expectantly.

"Oh. Sure. I mean, I guess. Never had it."

Moretti laughed. "Tonight's your lucky night!"

Would it be, she wondered?

He took Kelly's hand in his. The moment was electric, but not in a sexual way. It was like grabbing hold of a live eel. She fought the urge to rip her hand out of his grasp, but the die was cast. She'd leapt into the turgid water, and now it was time to swim.

The crowd magically parted, creating a narrow alley for the two of them to make their way upstream toward Moretti's reserved table.

A few minutes later, they were seated side by side at a table for six that was nestled in a claret-colored leather booth. The booth was one of two dozen that lined three walls of the VIP room. The fourth wall was three inches thick, floor-to-ceiling glass that looked into the club's main room. The observation wall was designed to bring the vibe of the club into the exclusive lounge, and to show the riff-raff on the other side what they were missing by not being a "VIP".

A "Patch VIP" was anyone who shelled out $250 for the privilege of buying premium alcohol at double mark-up and having it delivered to the table by a scantily dressed waitress. The fact that all of the tables were full on a Monday night spoke volumes about the disposable wealth among the Bay Area millennials.

The music from the dance club was muted inside this sanctuary, allowing conversation to be conducted at a reasonable level.

"This is sweet," said Kelly, doing her best to sound impressed.

Moretti filled two flutes of champagne and replaced the bottle into the nearby ice bucket. Kelly couldn't have hoped for a better drink selection: carbonation opened the pyloric valve, allowing alcohol to enter the blood stream faster; the bubbles would dissolve the Ambien quicker; and the pale color would hide any residue.

Moretti raised his glass to Kelly and she responded in kind. "To new friends," he said, with a look that some might interpret as heartfelt. Not Kelly.

They clinked and sipped. She wasn't a champagne drinker, but she knew quality when she tasted it, so she was sincere when she remarked, "It's really good."

"It'll do."

"Where are your friends?" she asked.

Moretti was puzzled. "What friends?"

"You have a table for six. Are you meeting some people here?"

"I met you."

"So, what… you come in every night and reserve a table and then cruise the club, hoping to get lucky?"

Anger transmogrified Moretti's face into something ugly for an instant. A moment later he flawlessly shifted gears and got himself under control and back to his normal charming self. It was frightening and fascinating to watch and happened so quickly that if you weren't looking for it you'd have missed it.

Tommy smiled with a self-assurance reserved for people who were firmly rooted in a position of power. "This table is permanently reserved for me. Has been since they opened. And I only come a few times a week to take in the scene. I know the people here who are worth knowing, so there's never a shortage of friends stopping by. When I see a beautiful woman who's clearly out of her element, I like to courteously extend a hometown welcome. Where's the problem with that?"

Kelly shrugged. "Nothing, if that's the way you roll in Frisco."

Moretti held up his hand and stopped her.

Kelly reacted, worrying that she'd already somehow screwed this up. "Did I say something wrong?"

"Tragically wrong. Never, ever say 'Frisco'. That's a place in Texas. You can call it San Francisco, SF or The City… capital T… capital C."

"I didn't know you people were so touchy."

"Only about that. Anything else goes around here. *Anything*. So, how do you 'roll' at clubs in Beantown?"

"Beantown. Touché. It depends where you go. If you hit the blue-collar clubs like the Whiskey, guys are looking to spend as little as possible and get laid. The uptown clubs, like The Grand, are thick with Harvard grads and BU trust-funders that throw around cash but bore the fuck out of you with stories about their summers in the Hamptons. And at the end of the night, hope to get laid."

"Not everyone is looking to get laid."

Kelly gave him a look that clearly translated to "gimme a fucking break".

"No longshoremen, no corporate attorneys. I get it. What *are* you into?"

She shrugged. "Having a good time. No strings."

Moretti refilled their glasses. "You came to the right place. I'm Tommy, by the way. I promise no stories about the Hamptons."

Kelly didn't realize she'd almost finished the first glass of champagne. She had to be careful to limit her intake. It was critical she kept her senses sharp. "I'm Sofie." She raised her glass and they toasted. "Nice to meet you, Tommy."

Moretti tipped back his glass and effortlessly drained its contents. He was clearly well practiced. As he refilled his flute, he looked over to Kelly, who put her hand atop her glass. "Still working on it."

"We're not going to run out. I've got an open tab."

"I'm not surprised, but I've got a big day tomorrow and I can't stagger in with a hangover."

"Top-shelf champagne doesn't give you a hangover."

"Bullshit. Too much of anything with ethanol leads to dehydration and a decrease of glucose in your system. Then bam! You feel like shit."

"What are you? A doctor?"

"A doctor?" Kelly had given considerable thought to her cover story and knew that the best lies were those that cleaved closest to the truth. Talk about what you know, but give it a spin. "I teach high school bio."

"You're a high school science teacher?"

She nodded. "I'm here for a science teachers' convention that starts tomorrow morning. There are about two hundred of us from all around the country."

"I never had a teacher that looked like you."

Kelly shrugged. "Different times; and I don't look like this in class. What do *you* do for a living?"

"I'm self-employed."

"That tells me nothing. A total cop out."

"You said no strings, so what's it matter?"

Kelly shrugged. "I guess it doesn't. It's just that you remind me a lot of this guy I use to hang with."

"Yeah? What did 'this guy' do for a living?"

"He was a fixer. If you had a problem, he made it go away. For a price. Always had a lotta flash cash."

Moretti finished his champagne and no sooner had he plunged it upside down into the ice bucket, than a cute waitress with a skirt that was too short and breasts that were too large appeared with a new bottle, a fresh ice bucket, and two sparkling glasses. She smiled at Moretti, flashing a mouthful of porcelain veneers that looked like they'd been applied by a first year dental student.

He slipped the waitress a ten, and she silently retreated back from whence she came. Kelly sipped her drink as Moretti peeled away the foil on bottle number two, then worked out the cork with the efficiency of a seasoned pro.

"That's what you think I am? A fixer?"

"Just saying you remind me of him. Same good looks, same smooth moves."

"Looks and moves. Nice. What happened to him?"

"No one knows. One day he was around and the next day, gone. Rumor was he was overdue on payments to some people who had a low tolerance for excuses."

"Gotta pay to play. How long were you with him?"

"About a year."

"You didn't mind that he was hooked up?"

She shrugged. "It was never boring. Besides, everyone's got their dirty little secrets. I'm sure you do."

"Can't make it in this town by following all the rules. You just have to be creative as to which ones to bend and which ones to break."

She took a sip. "This is finally starting to get interesting."

As he leaned closer, he put his hand on Kelly's thigh. It took every ounce of willpower she had not to rip it away.

"Bad boys turn you on," he whispered into her ear with a hot, boozy breath.

She gently removed his hand, a teasing smile on her face. "It depends."

"On what?"

"On how bad they are."

The hook was in the water… now to get him to bite.

Just then, a hoarse voice asked, "Tommy?"

A short, stocky man in his late twenties stood in front of their table. He wore black jeans and a semi-sheer black T that was two sizes too small for his broad, muscular frame. His shaved head was almost a perfect circle. Kelly thought he looked like Charlie Brown on steroids.

Moretti was not at all pleased with the interruption, and if looks could kill, Charlie Brown would've been sent out of the club in a body bag, which was still a realistic possibility.

"Do I know you?" Moretti asked, his voice ripe with disdain.

At that moment, Charlie Brown realized that maybe, just maybe, he shouldn't have crashed this party. But desperate times called for desperate measures, and he was desperate.

"Sorry to bother you, Bro, but…"

"Then why the fuck are you?"

A single bead of sweat formed on Charlie's shiny dome. Kelly watched in fascination, waiting for the droplet to succumb to gravity and begin its slide down his face.

"I'm a friend of Rasheem Pine. He said you could hook me up."

Kelly couldn't believe her luck. She knew about Moretti's drug dealings, but now that the lid to Pandora's box was publicly cracked open, it would make her segue into his darker secrets that much easier.

For his part, Moretti was doing what he could to nail the lid shut again. "I don't know anyone named Rasheem Pine. Leave us the fuck alone."

The sweat bead finally found its way down Charlie's face, and was joined by others. He was either jonesing, nervous, or scared shitless. Probably all three, which is why he had the temerity to shoot out a beefy hand and grab Moretti's arm.

Moretti was stunned into silence. He couldn't believe that this roided piece of shit would dare touch him, let alone in the middle of the club, and while he was working a woman.

"Come on, Bro. I promised these guys I'd deliver and you gotta help me, or they're gonna fuck me up bad. I got money and…"

Moretti grabbed two of Charlie's fingers that were wrapped around his arm and viciously snapped them backwards. While the sound of the bones breaking couldn't be heard over the music, Charlie's howl of pain loudly resonated throughout the VIP room. All heads turned in his direction.

As Charlie grabbed his mangled fingers and backed away, Moretti was on his feet. His face was mottled with blooms of rage. He grabbed Charlie by his shirt and shouted in his face, spittle flying from his mouth. "You cocksucker! Who the fuck do you think you are?"

Charlie lashed out with his good hand and caught Moretti with a tight jab to the solar plexus, momentarily knocking the wind out of him. Charlie looked around in panic. How quickly could he get the hell out of there? He'd come to score drugs and was now in a fistfight with one of the biggest dealers in the city. How did this go so wrong so fast?

As these questions ran through his dense skull, Moretti let out a roar and attacked with an adrenaline-fueled rage, launching an all-out assault that turned Charlie into a human punching bag.

Kelly was appalled and frightened by how quickly things had escalated, but recognized she wouldn't get a better opportunity.

As she opened her purse, she felt dizzy. She'd only drunk one glass of champagne and she'd never had a problem holding her alcohol. She chalked it up to her surroundings, the dull, muted thud of the music and the overwhelming stress.

Kelly managed to slip a tiny vial out of her purse. It held the granules from two Zolpidem capsules. She'd planned to use only half of it, but figured that a double dose would work better, faster and not have deleterious effects. She dumped the entire contents into Moretti's champagne. The miniscule grains fizzled and immediately dissolved. Perfect.

This was going to work!

Two husky bouncers made their way toward the melee, but the VIP crowd was on their feet, surrounding the gladiators and shouting encouragement to their boy Moretti.

Charlie was reeling and fell back against a table, sending drinks flying. He managed to grab hold of a bottle of Grey Goose Cherry Noir by the neck and wildly swung it at Moretti's head.

Moretti stepped back, the bottle barely missing his face, then shot out a fierce kick to Charlie's right knee. Charlie collapsed like a house of cards in a gusty wind, writhing in pain. The bouncers finally made it through and got to Charlie before Moretti could inflict more damage.

As they dragged away a hobbling Charlie Brown, Moretti smoothed back his hair and turned back to Kelly at the table.

"Is that bad enough for you?"

"Tell me that wasn't for my benefit."

"If I said yes, would you be impressed?"

Kelly shook her head and truthfully responded, "I'd be terrified."

"Sorry that happened. People don't usually come up to me and start a fight."

"I'm going to have a great story to tell the other teachers tomorrow."

He smiled. "I'm glad I could make your trip memorable."

Kelly was hit with a more powerful wave of dizziness and nausea.

"Are you alright?"

She nodded and forced a smile, then patted the seat next to her. "Why don't you sit down?"

Moretti shook his head. "I don't like attracting attention. Let's get out of here."

"Don't you want to finish your drink? We just opened a new bottle."

"We can get Dom anywhere. I know a place that's quiet."

Kelly's mind was becoming increasingly muddled and her thoughts disjointed. A dozen tiny voices were whispering through the haze, but she couldn't make them out. Despite a gnawing sense of foreboding, she felt completely helpless to do anything about it.

"Sofie? You coming?" Moretti smiled, the picture of innocence. But, there was something behind the smile.

Something unsettling.

48

Kelly didn't know where she was or how she got there. She was wrapped in a cloud of confusion and had only vague recollections of Moretti half-guiding, half-carrying her out of the club. Her head reverberated with convoluted echoes of a conversation in Moretti's car about where they were going, but she couldn't coalesce that muddle into a coherent thought.

She was reclining on a U-shaped leather sectional that took up one corner of a tastefully decorated living room. Paintings of the Tuscan countryside hung on the wall. Bookcases on either side of a massive flat screen were lined with Roman urns and water jugs.

Kelly sat up and was instantly hit with a rush of vertigo. She felt like she was aboard a rowboat in the middle of a violently turbulent ocean, and had to physically brace herself so she wouldn't tumble onto the floor. Something was drastically wrong and Kelly instinctively knew she was in danger. She closed her eyes and forced herself to concentrate, to fight through the swirling fog, and then she suddenly remembered. She was in the lion's den.

Moretti had brought her to his home.

That definitely wasn't part of the plan.

How long had she been there? Why did her brain feel like it had been put through a blender? Her confusion led to anxiety, which in turn elevated her fear. She needed to get out of there. Now!

Where was her purse? Her eyes desperately darted around the room, but her bag was nowhere to be found.

Just then, Moretti entered the room from the kitchen, holding a bottle of Cristal and two flutes in one hand, and a large bottle of Fuji water in the other.

"Ah, back to the land of the living," he said.

He crossed the room and set the bottles and glasses on a sleek coffee table in front of the sofa. "This is the good stuff," he said, as he began uncorking the champagne.

"How long have I been here?" Kelly was alarmed to hear herself slurring the words.

"About a half hour. You were totally out of it. When we got here you said you needed to lie down for a minute, then collapsed on the couch." Moretti wiggled the cork loose, then let it dramatically explode from the bottle like it was shot from a tiny cannon. Cristal bubbled forth in a display of opulent waste.

He filled the flutes and slid one over to Kelly, who shook her head. "I've had enough."

Moretti grabbed the bottle of water, unscrewed the top and handed it to Kelly, who accepted it gratefully.

She took a swig. It tasted fine. In fact, it tasted great. Kelly chugged down half of the bottle before she stopped to catch her breath. She was still groggy and slipping in and out of lucidity.

Kelly turned to Moretti. "What did you do to me?"

"What? I didn't do anything," he said with what appeared to be genuine innocence and concern.

Kelly shook her head, trying to clean out the cobwebs and achieve a burst of clarity. It worked, at least long enough for her to realize... "Rohypnol! You gave me a roofie!"

In retrospect, it was blatantly obvious. Her cognitive facilities were still too murky for her to understand that she'd gone from the hunter to the hunted, but she was clearheaded enough to be outraged.

"Do I look like the kind of guy who needs to roofie a woman? That's a total punk-ass move." He took a sip of the Cristal and smiled his approval.

Moretti was handsome and successful. He *wasn't* the type to roofie a woman; or was he? At this point, Kelly had absolutely no idea.

Moretti saw the confusion on her face and offered up an answer. "I've heard a few of the bartenders at The Patch have been known to spike drinks of women who are there alone. When bartenders get off their shift, they go for the kill. I wouldn't be surprised if there was something in that spritzer you were drinking."

Kelly took a pause. Maybe he wasn't the one who drugged her. Maybe she'd misjudged him.

"Listen," Moretti said, "you were in bad shape at the club, so I brought you back here so you could sleep it off. I would've taken you to your hotel, but I don't know where you're staying."

Kelly drank more water, hoping it would dilute the drugs in her system, but in her current state of mind she couldn't recall if Rohypnol reacted like that. In her current state of mind, she couldn't spell Rohypnol.

She put the bottle on the table. "I have to go. Where's my purse?"

Moretti shrugged. "No idea. Maybe you left it at the club."

Panic set in. "I need my phone. My wallet."

"You can use my phone and I'll give you cash if you need it." Moretti smiled. "I'm happy to take you to the hotel, but I seem to remember you wanting to know about my dirty secrets. Still interested?"

So there it was. The lid to Pandora's box being lifted once again, its wicked mysteries huddled in a dark corner, making vague promises about creeping into the light. Unfortunately, Kelly was in the dark as well. She had enough self-awareness to know that she lacked the mental dexterity it took to lead Moretti to admit he'd committed vehicular manslaughter... but you never knew where the conversation might go.

Another crossroad, another decision.

Kelly finished the remainder of her water and nodded. "Okay. Talk."

49

Moretti downed his Cristal and slowly refilled his glass, letting the anticipation build. He was used to being in control, and he was clearly in the driver's seat. He took a sip of champagne and smiled appreciatively, before he finally broke the silence.

"I inherited a business from my uncle," said Moretti. "He died of a heart attack not long ago and left behind a large diverse portfolio."

Kelly struggled to process what Moretti was saying. Her mind was in hyper-drive, aching to be an active participant in a dialogue that was unquestionably the most important of her life. "Portfolio? Like stocks and bonds?"

He shook his head. "He had a hand in a lot of businesses. He was good at making money for himself and his partners. And he knew how to deal with the competition."

She was aware that Arthur Moretti was a criminal and that Tommy had followed in his footsteps. Getting Tommy to admit it was important. Or was it? Damn it! She had no idea. If only she could think clearly.

"Deal with the competition?" she asked, hoping this would lead somewhere useful.

Moretti took another sip, and nodded. "My uncle was very persuasive in laying out alternate business models. After a little coaxing, his new partners always agreed to terms."

Click. Even with a small percentage of her brain cells firing, that statement left no doubts.

"It sounds like your uncle was a mobster or something."

Moretti smiled. "He was a businessman and entrepreneur."

Kelly felt another wave of fatigue, and once the wave crested it crashed hard, battering her with pounding ferocity.

Moretti saw the confusion in Kelly's eyes and he casually checked his watch. "I was waiting for that second hit to give you a little tune up," he said with a satisfied grin.

Kelly shook her head. It was becoming more and more difficult to stay awake. "In the water…?"

Moretti's smug look gave her the answer.

Damn it! She was losing consciousness too fast. Still so much to learn.

"Why?"

"Isn't it obvious, Kelly?"

The mention of her name sent a sudden jolt of adrenaline through her entire being. Enough to push her consciousness to the surface for a few moments.

Moretti saw it in her eyes and savored her moment of revelation. "I've known about you for months. You and poor Jessica. Once I found out about your father's side-job, it wasn't hard to gather info on his lovely daughters."

He smiled, downed his drink, and continued, "I've spent many nights thinking about what I was going to do with you, and now here we finally are."

He saw her panic, smelled her fear and despair. This was even better than he'd hoped for. Kelly tried to move, but the drug was coursing through her body and rendered her physically incapacitated.

Moretti placed his hands on her shoulders, gently caressing her skin through the thin fabric. Kelly could barely muster a faint murmur of revulsion and was completely helpless to do anything to stop him.

"I didn't know you were going to dress up sexy for me. It makes this whole situation so much more… provocative."

Moretti dug his fingers deeply into Kelly's shoulder. Pain rippled through her body, but she remained powerless to resist. "I hope you like it rough, although I don't think you're gonna remember much, except the agony." He ripped her dress down the middle, exposing her breasts.

"The night your father died was one of the best nights of my life," he whispered huskily in her ear, "but this is gonna be a close second."

Kelly screamed. At least she thought she did, but no sound came from her mouth. She watched through heavy lids as Moretti hurriedly unbuckled his pants.

She knew that she was going to die here tonight at the hand of the beast who killed her father. Her final thought before she blacked out was if she'd only confided in Pete, this nightmare wouldn't be unfolding.

A tear rolled down her face, followed by darkness.

50

The shrill ring of the phone shattered the silence. Pete bolted up in bed and grabbed his cell, checking the Caller ID. He hoped it was Kelly. He'd been trying to reach her all night with no luck. His fortunes hadn't turned. The call was from work. Why would someone from the department be calling him at this hour? His thoughts went in a dozen different directions, all bad. No good news ever came in the middle of the night.

Well, hardly ever.

The voice on the other end of the line belonged to Victoria from the Forensics lab, and no voice ever sounded sweeter, especially when she informed Pete that the DNA results were back and the hairs from the headrest didn't belong to the man who owned the stolen car. Now that the follicle analysis was coded, they could run the results through the FBI's Combined DNA Index System. This usually took weeks, but Victoria had gone to school with a tech at CODIS and was optimistic she could get her request bumped up to the front of the very long line.

Pete thanked her profusely and assured her that those Giants' tickets would be in a luxury box. He knew the VP of Marketing at the ballpark, and while he didn't make a habit of abusing that friendship, every once in a while he cashed in a chip.

Victoria, now extremely motivated, said she'd call her friend in DC and roust his ass out of bed.

Pete tried to go back to sleep, but knew it wouldn't come. He was too jacked up with the hope that the next call would give him the name of the man who killed David Harper.

Maybe *this* would be the "aha" moment where things suddenly fell into place. He fought the urge to call Kelly and wake her up in the middle of the night. He smiled as he pictured her curled up in her blankets, her hair splayed across the pillow and her face the model of serenity.

51

Kelly slowly opened her eyes. The lids were heavy and the lashes gummy. She ached all over, especially between her legs. Despite the fact her mind was still shrouded by the drugs, she knew she'd been raped. Maybe repeatedly. She could smell Moretti's scent on her body, feel bruising on her neck and breasts where he'd savagely grabbed her, and the sharp outline of teeth where he'd bitten her.

The Rohypnol effectively erased any memory of what had happened in the past few hours. She was thankful she couldn't recall whatever heinous acts he'd committed and hoped those memories were permanently wiped clean. She'd clearly been violated, but the mental outrage and physical pain wouldn't truly hit her until later.

The last thing she remembered was Moretti ripping her dress, and then being awash with a sense of helplessness. However, he'd said something about her father. About his side-job. About his death. She wanted more information, some specific details, but at this point she was certain of two things: Moretti was guilty, and she was in imminent danger.

Kelly struggled to sit up, which immediately set her head spinning. The Rohypnol urged her to lie back down and retreat into a shell of oblivion, but her survival instincts were stronger and pushed her to find some degree of lucidity. Kelly bit down hard on her lip, drawing blood, hoping that the pain would provide a jolt. It did, for at least a few moments.

And then she realized she was alone. How had that simple fact evaded her until now? Feeling a blossom of hope, all she needed to do was make it to the door and disappear into the night. But first, she needed what was in her purse. Without it, she'd never get far.

Kelly sluggishly surveyed the room, her eyes rolling in and out of focus. The purse was nowhere in sight. Had she left it at the club? Did Moretti stash it somewhere?

It took all of her concentration and strength to lift herself off the couch. She could only manage one step before she collapsed to the carpet with a dull thud. Kelly struggled to raise her head a few inches so she could look underneath the couch, and her effort was rewarded with the discovery of her purse.

As she reached out her hand, she heard a door open down the hall. If Moretti walked back in now, she was ripe for more abuse, or worse. She closed her eyes tight, childishly hoping that if she couldn't see him, he couldn't see her either. The next sound she heard was another door opening, then closing, followed by running water. He'd gone into the bathroom.

There was still hope!

She dragged out her purse and opened it to see that it was empty. No phone, no keys, no cash. But that didn't matter right now. What Kelly needed was tucked in the false bottom. She managed to pry up the stiff leather divider and reached into the one-inch recess to find what she was looking for: a syringe pre-loaded with Flumazenil.

She slid the needle into her arm and depressed the plunger, shooting the antidote into her veins. She'd brought it along in case she needed to bring Moretti out of his haze, but since the night had taken a sharply different turn, the drug could end up saving her life.

The Flumazenil worked quickly and Kelly could already feel the haze begin to dissipate. The first message that came through was loud and clear.

Run!

Kelly got to her feet and managed to stay upright. So far, so good. The room was large and the door seemed miles away across a vast expanse of Berber carpet. She took an experimental step toward the door.

Maybe she wasn't going to die here tonight.

She advanced another step and her outlook seemed brighter than at any time in the past several hours. As she inched closer to freedom, she heard a toilet flush. Panic set in, and at the same time her adrenals kicked into overdrive. She felt a surge of strength. The question was, could she make it all the way across the room to the front door before he came back in? If he caught her trying to run out, she was finished.

And then another thought occurred to her.

A few moments later, Tommy Moretti strode back into the living room, a grin on his face and an erection in his pants. He was ready to party again.

What he wasn't ready for was getting bashed in the back of his head with a heavy clay Greek funerary urn.

Moretti collapsed, face planting into the thick carpet.

She hoped she hadn't killed him.

They had unfinished business.

52

Kelly slowly and awkwardly made her way down the street, her steps teetering. While the Flumazenil worked to clear her head, she was still unstable on her feet and appeared either over-medicated or over-served. She'd put on one of Moretti's sport coats to cover her torn dress, and while she detested the feel of it against her skin, she'd had no other option.

The night was cold and damp, chilling Kelly to her core. She had no money and no phone, but she had an idea. It wasn't a great idea, but an idea nonetheless. She staggered forward, impelled by a desperate sense of urgency. She hurried her pace, but lacked the mind/body coordination to pull it off and she stumbled, crashing to the pavement with bone-jarring intensity.

Kelly laid there on a sidewalk filthy with city grit and canine waste. The world seemed to turn on its axis, sending her tumbling down a dark well into mental oblivion.

She had no concept of how long she'd been stretched out on the pavement before being propped up to a sitting position, her back against a wall. When her vision came into focus, she was staring straight into the eyes of Gizmo.

"You okay, lady?"

Kelly looked around, straining to figure out if this was a dream or if she was actually face to face with Francisco Ramos. Her sense of normalcy had been turned upside down. She was Alice, aimlessly staggering through Wonderland, and she'd somehow ended up at a tea party with a gangbanger.

"Where... where am I?"

"Dolores Park. What happened to you?"

"I need to talk to Oscar."

"Oscar who?" Gizmo asked cautiously.

Kelly reached deep to come up with his street name. "Spider. I mean Spider."

"Spider? How you know Spider?"

"You… you're Gizmo, right?"

Gizmo had no clue how this drunken *guera* knew his name. Maybe they partied together some night when he was already baked. He smiled at the notion of making time with someone so fine.

Suddenly, Gizmo's face went slack. The short black hair, the Goth makeup, the bruises on her neck. She looked nothing like the blonde doctor that was taking care of Diego Sanchez. The same doctor that took care of him many years ago. It was her jade green eyes that gave her away. Those were eyes a young boy never forgot.

"Doctor Kelly?"

She nodded.

Gizmo's demeanor quickly shifted. This woman had the blessing and protection of the Mission Street Norteños. Mess with her, you mess with the gang. "Who did this to you? We'll fuck him up bad."

Kelly shook her head. "I need Spider."

"Spider's not around. I can take care of it for you. Just gimme a name."

She grimaced as she struggled to stand up. *"Necessito Spider, por favor. Es muy importante."*

Gizmo didn't want to be waking up his man at three in the morning. It would be a show of weakness if he couldn't handle this situation. He'd be labeled a *chavala*.

"You can trust me. I swear," he said.

"I know… but tonight… I need to speak to Spider. Please."

Her desperation was so intense, Gizmo could almost feel its cold tentacles. He pulled out his cell, made the call, and then handed the phone to Kelly.

A short time later, Kelly was slouched against the back door of the clinic. Gizmo stood some twenty yards behind her in the shadows. He'd been instructed to bring her here, watch her back and make sure no one tried to mess with her. He was curious what was going on, but had learned early on that you don't ask questions. They could get you hurt, or worse.

Kelly spent several minutes blankly staring at the electronic lock on the back door. It took a four-digit code, but recalling that code required a degree of mental keenness that she currently lacked. She tried running number combinations in her head, but nothing was remotely familiar. Damn it! She'd punched the code into the keypad a few thousand times in the past couple of years.

She let her hand hover over the keypad for a moment, hoping that pure muscle memory would kick in and do the work for her. She didn't need to know the actual numbers if her fingers remembered the pattern. She focused all of her attention on her hand, willing it to perform its magic, but it just hung in the air as if waiting for inspiration of its own.

After a grueling minute that felt like an hour, her fingers finally settled on the keypad and slowly punched in four numbers. A moment later the entry pad light switched from red to green.

Kelly got the pharmaceutical keys from a box tucked away in her father's desk and entered the tiny room where the meds were locked up. She feverishly sorted through the various drugs until she found more Flumazenil. It was the last dose they had.

Her hands were shaking as she tried to draw the liquid drug into a syringe. Suddenly, the ampoule slipped from her grasp and fell toward the tile floor. There was a split second where time slowed down and she watched in horror as the glass capsule tumbled in the air, then hit the tile floor... and bounced. Real time resumed and Kelly scooped up the ampoule to complete filling the hypo.

Sitting on the floor, she plunged the needle into her arm and injected the fluid into her system for the second time tonight, praying for the strength to finish what she'd started.

Ten minutes later, Kelly got back to her feet, already feeling more alert. She was cautiously optimistic that adrenaline would keep her going for the rest of the night. She still had much to do.

Kelly returned to the office with a handful of items: two ampoules containing a clear, viscous liquid; three syringes, surgical gloves and a length of rubber tubing. She stuffed everything into a bag, along with five banded rolls of her father's "operating cash" that she'd stored in a small safe in the corner of the office. Once she connected with Spider, she'd have everything she needed.

At least, that was her hope.

She looked around the office, letting the warm memories of her father wash over her. Her father, who she dearly loved, dearly missed, and who had set all of this in motion so many years ago.

Kelly wondered what he'd think if he knew what she was planning.

53

Kelly stood in the dark outside Moretti's door. She'd played out a dozen different scenarios in her head how to handle the situation. As the Rohypnol had abated, her sense of violation had snowballed. Not only that, but the knowledge that Moretti had killed her father fueled her outrage and desire for revenge. It wasn't too late to turn Moretti over to Pete and let things take their due course, but she couldn't bear the idea of sitting across from Moretti in court, watching his smug-faced grin. And there was always the possibility of him going free.

It had happened before.

Not this time.

Kelly opened the door to find Moretti where she'd left him; tied to a heavy chair with extension cords. She'd wrapped dishtowels around his hands to prevent ligature marks. A sock was stuffed in his mouth and held in place with a sheet she'd torn into strips.

Moretti fiercely struggled against his bindings when he saw her. His face was red with intense strain and seething anger. The avalanche of obscenities that would've spewed from his mouth silently died inside him.

Kelly set her bag down and pulled on a pair of surgical gloves. Moretti watched with rapt interest as she proceeded to take items out of her bag and line them up on the table. A large silver spoon, a disposable lighter, a hypodermic needle. Moretti's interest turned to alarm when Kelly pulled out a baggie of white powder. His eyes grew large and he violently shook his head from side to side.

"It's uncut. Not the usual smack you get on the street that's been stepped on four or five times with flour or talc. They call this 'Caballo', because it's strong as a horse."

Kelly dipped the spoon into the baggie and scooped up a hefty dose, making sure to not spill any on the floor. She fired up the lighter and began to cook. "You're going to tell me how you found out about my father."

Moretti shook his head defiantly. He wasn't going to tell this bitch anything. He knew this was only a scare tactic and he wasn't falling for her bluff.

"I don't want to do this, but trust me, I will."

Her hand was shaking as she drew the liquid heroin into the syringe. Could she actually go through with this? At this point, what other choices did she have? If she walked away, he'd hunt her down and kill her. If she called the police, her whole world would come tumbling down.

She could do this. She had to do this.

Kelly laid the needle down on the table and a wave of relief came over Moretti's face. He knew she wouldn't do it. Unfortunately, he'd misread her objective. She needed both hands to tie off his arm with some rubber tubing that seemed to magically appear.

Moretti renewed his futile attempt to break free, violently straining against the cords, but there was no escape.

As Kelly knotted the tube around Moretti's exposed bicep, she whispered in his ear, "Tell me what I want to know or this won't end well."

She thumped his forearm and watched as a large vein came to the surface. She plucked up the syringe and held it in front of Moretti's face. "Your choice. Talk or…?"

Moretti slumped his head forward in defeat. He stopped his rebellion and slowly looked up, nodding.

"Good," Kelly said. She carefully undid his gag and pulled the sock out of his mouth. The moment she did…

"You fucking cunt!" he screamed.

"Who told you about my father?" she asked, struggling to remain calm.

"Fuck you!"

Kelly roughly grabbed Moretti's face in her free hand. "Does anyone else know about him?" she asked with a growl.

"This bullshit is weak," Moretti said combatively. "We both know you're not going to do this."

Kelly's face hardened with resolve. "Try me."

Her intensity suddenly made Moretti realize he might actually be in danger. He'd gone too far, and now he had to play by Kelly's rules.

"Look, I'm sorry about what happened tonight," he said, doing his best to sound genuine. "I was completely out of line and I apologize. Between the drugs and the alcohol… well, you know. Anyway, you're right to be pissed off, but I didn't kill your father. Now, untie me and…"

She shook her head in disbelief. "Untie you? You drug me and rape me, and now you, what… want to be friends? Maybe hang out together?"

"I'm telling you the truth. I didn't kill your father."

"Fuck you. I gave you a chance, which is more than you gave him."

Kelly jammed the needle into Moretti's vein and hit the plunger. His eyes flew open in disbelief. He'd been sure she was bluffing. In fact, he'd bet his life on it. For a moment, he felt nothing. She *was* bluffing! The powder wasn't heroin! It must be sugar or…

Suddenly, Moretti's train of thought derailed. His brain was cranking out dopamine, flooding his body with sheer bliss.

Kelly watched as he went through the phases of a heroin injection. Euphoria, followed by drowsiness. Moretti's head began to dip, and his breathing became erratic.

She reached out her gloved hand and felt the vein in his neck. His pulse was slowing down to match his shallow breaths.

Moretti had no idea that he was dying, and Kelly had no intention of letting him off that easy.

She had a second hypo ready, this one with Naloxone, better known as Narcan. She slipped that needle into the same vein, as close to the original hole as possible, and gave him the injection.

Moretti was abruptly yanked out of a peaceful, happy dream and into a violent nightmare. He gasped for air as he clutched his spasming stomach. His face grew flush and his head spun like he'd just stepped off the Tilt-A-Whirl.

"What… what did you do to me?" he sputtered weakly.

"Narcan. It blocks the effect of the heroin, and flips the switch on all of those tiny pleasure receptors, so all you feel is the pain. In a few minutes, you'll even out and we can continue our conversation."

54

Pete was dressed and finishing his second cup of coffee. He'd tried to temper his expectations, but he wanted to be ready when the call came. Besides, sleep was a faded notion this morning. Ever since Victoria's call, his mind was racing and his blood was pumping. He had David Harper's murder book open on the kitchen table and he flipped through the pages, even though he knew every report in the binder by heart. This simply gave him something to do while he waited.

It was just after 4am when his cell rang. Victoria had come through with flying colors. CODIS identified the hairs as belonging to a Thomas Moretti. She gave Pete his last known address, which was a house in Noe Valley. Pete wasn't familiar with the name, but if Moretti was in the FBI files, it meant he had a record, and chances were good that he was in the SFPD system as well.

He thanked Victoria profusely and fired up his computer.

The hunt was on.

55

The Narcan left Moretti with a pounding headache, abdominal contractions and a dry, scratchy throat. He tried to call out, but all he could manage was a faint rasping noise.

"Ah, you're back," said Kelly, as she came in from the kitchen, holding two bottles of water. "How does it feel to be on the other end? I found a broom in the closet and considered the irony of sodomizing you, but then remembered I'm not a psychopath. I'm just an ordinary person who's been drugged, raped and had her father murdered by a brutal, despicable excuse for a human being."

Moretti was a dead man unless he could convince her to let him go. He'd underestimated her once and wouldn't make that mistake again. He'd tell her whatever she wanted to know. Whatever it took to get free, and then when the time was right, he'd show her the meaning of brutality.

Kelly took a long drink from her bottle and held out the other one. "Thirsty?"

Moretti nodded. Kelly set the bottle down on the table. "Let's see how the next few minutes go. You answer my questions and you can have all the water you want. If not," she held up another hypodermic needle; this one was already loaded with heroin. "And just so you know, I only had one dose of Narcan." She looked at the syringe and then back at him. "You don't want to piss me off again."

Moretti took a few deep breaths, slowly blowing out through his mouth. "Water?" he croaked.

Kelly limited him to a small sip, just to lubricate his throat, but not enough to slake his thirst.

"I didn't kill your father," he said with all the sincerity he could muster.

"Did you not understand the rules here, or do you still think I'm bluffing?"

"It's true! I wasn't driving that car. Turn me over to the police. I can prove I didn't do it. You've gotta believe me!"

Kelly knew he was trying to sow seeds of doubt, buy time, or both. She wasn't going to fall for it. "What you *said* earlier was that the night my father died was one of the best nights of your life," she hissed. "Of course, that's when I was tied up and you were about to rape me. Now that the roles are reversed, the story's conveniently changed." She leaned back. "You can see why I'm confused, Tommy. I don't know which story to believe."

He shook his head. "I was happy about your father's death because he murdered my uncle, but I wasn't driving that car. I swear!"

Kelly shook her head in disbelief as she picked up the syringe.

"No, no, no! Listen, you wanted to know how I found out about your father. Gimme a chance to explain."

She stared at him in silence, the syringe poised.

Moretti continued, "After six or seven people mysteriously died, there were whispers that they were victims of some kind of phantom assassin. They called him Gideon."

"Who was doing the whispering?"

"People who share similar interests."

"You mean criminals."

"Fine. Criminals, dealers, mobsters, whatever you want to call them. Anyway, as the body count continued to grow, members from surviving families formed a group called 'The Committee' and offered a bounty. Five million dollars to anyone who could uncover Gideon's real identity."

"And then kill him," Kelly said, completing the thought.

"No! Just ID him. The people who put up the money wanted the satisfaction of dealing with Gideon on their own terms."

Kelly felt a flush of anger and her hand gripped the syringe tighter.

Moretti noticed this and spoke faster. "There are people on the message boards who compile all the information they can find on Gideon, and then provide it to subscribers for a few thou a month. Of course, no one's certain which deaths are attributable to Gideon, since a lot of people on the fringe die of accidents or natural causes, so the data's filled with holes, but these guys came up with a list of, like, twenty-five or thirty potential candidates. Your father was one of them."

Moretti stopped, sweat dripping down his face. "Can I get some more water?"

"Finish your story."

"When I saw the name David Harper, it rang a bell, so I did some research and found out everything I could about the murder of your mother and what happened to your sister. Then I dug around and read some rumors that Musselwhite didn't die in that police van, but was in witness protection and died of an overdose, like, a year later. Since your dad was a doctor, the pieces of the puzzle started to fall into place. So I kept close tabs on him."

"You were spying on my father? On both of us?"

He nodded. "I figured I might be close to finding out Gideon's identity, so yeah. I paid a guy to tail your father for a month, including a trip he took to Seattle. He was gone for two days, and during that time a woman who lived out on Mercer Island died from poison. Turned out the poison came from a plant she'd brought back from a trip to Hawaii and her death was ruled accidental."

"What's that have to do with my father?"

"It was classic Gideon. A hit that doesn't look like a hit. Plus, the victim fit the profile. She was suspected of poisoning her last three husbands... all of them had shit-loads of money. She was also suspected of killing two of her stepchildren. Word was, one of the families hired Gideon to even the score."

"So you assumed my father was this mysterious killer," Kelly said, doing her best to keep her voice calm. "Who did you tell?"

"No one! I needed to be absolutely positive before I went to 'The Committee'. Other people had gone to them with "proof" of Gideon's identity, but each time they were wrong, and each time they were made to regret it."

"You're saying no one else knows about this?"

He nodded, and tried to sound upbeat. "Your father's name was low on the list of possibles, so I doubt he's on anyone else's radar."

Moretti thought he actually had a chance of getting out of this alive. He'd told the truth, or at least as much as he could, given his current situation. If Kelly knew he'd shared this information with someone else, he'd be finished.

"If you were the only person who knew, then it stands to reason that you were the one who killed him," Kelly said in a voice just above a whisper.

"No! I mean, someone else *could've* figured it out on their own, like I did. When I said no one else knew, I meant that I didn't tell anyone. Why would I? I wanted the bounty for myself."

"The bounty," she said with unbridled disdain. "Setting my father up to be murdered."

Moretti had no response to that. He didn't realize it at first, but by telling the truth, he'd backed himself into a corner. "Okay, yes. I was hoping to cash in, but don't forget, he killed my uncle. Your father was an assassin. Who knows how many he killed."

"Eighteen," she said calmly. "Eighteen loathsome creatures who all deserved what they got. *Especially* your uncle."

Despite his attempt to remain calm and temper his anger, Moretti's rage was growing. "I loved my uncle," he spat out. "He took me in, raised me like his own son."

"That explains a lot. Your uncle dealt in human trafficking, which is abhorrent." She didn't realize it, but she was quoting her father's journal almost word for word. "The world is a better place without him."

"Fuck you!" Moretti shouted. "Fuck your holier than thou bullshit! Your father was a fucking murderer!"

"My father was a hero!" Kelly was surprised as the words tripped out. "He was a brilliant doctor, a loving father and a great man. He was revered as a saint by the people he treated. And in his spare time he risked his life to exterminate vermin."

Moretti erupted in a frenzy, wildly thrashing from side to side, trying to break free of his bonds. As he opened his mouth to scream more profanity, Kelly shoved the sock down into his throat.

In the abrupt silence that followed, she heard the faint sound of musical chimes. It was the text alert on her phone. Moretti's eyes darted to the left, and there it was again.

Kelly followed the sound to her cell phone, which Moretti had tucked under the throw pillows on the couch. Having the phone in her hand immediately gave her a sense of security.

She tapped the screen and the message came on. She read it straight-faced without a scintilla of emotion. She read it a second time, then set the phone down next to her. She turned back to Moretti. "Now that I know the whole story, the question is, what to do with you? If I let you go, you'll come for me, and maybe even my sister."

Moretti vigorously shook his head from side-to-side.

"You expect me to believe you? You peddle narcotics, you strong-arm local businesses to pay for protection and you sell women into slavery. You're not a man to be trusted, Tommy."

Moretti's eyes grew large, beseeching Kelly to spare him.

"And let's not forget, you're a rapist. The lowest form of human trash. Most women, and probably most men, would find that to be an offense worthy of extreme punishment. At the very least, castration." The blood rushed from Moretti's face. "I saw a large, extremely sharp knife in the kitchen."

Moretti lost it and started shaking uncontrollably.

She let him stew in the juices of terror for a moment, before adding, "No, too messy."

She raised up the hypodermic needle, "I'll *stick* with this."

Kelly looked at the syringe with admiration, mesmerized by the sheer power it held.

Moretti made muffled feral sounds, trying to spit out the sock. He needed to reason with Kelly, to assure her that if she let him live he'd move far away. She'd never hear from him or see him again. Plus, he had money. Lots of money that she could use to keep her clinic going. Whatever she wanted. Goddamn it! Why did he drug her? Why did he rape her?

Everyone has a defining moment in his or her life.

Kelly believed that hers came when her mother was murdered and her sister was attacked. Later on, she believed that her true defining moment was when she traveled to Sumatra with her father, saw the sickness and poverty, and made the decision to become a doctor.

When her father was killed, Kelly's life took a sharp turn. That had to be her defining moment.

But now, with her thumb on the plunger of a syringe loaded with liquid death, ready to thrust into the vein of the man who was responsible for the murder of her father... it was *this* moment that would define her life going forward. Would she embrace her humanity and do the right thing, regardless of the complicated consequences that would follow, or would she embrace her fear, anger and twisted sense of vengeance?

It all came back to her father.

Should she follow his teaching or follow his example?

Kelly turned to Moretti, a look of serenity on her face. "I'm going to ask you one question. If you tell the truth, I'll let you go." Moretti fervently nodded. Kelly leaned in close, her lips brushing his ear. "Did you kill my father?"

Moretti shook his head from side to side. "Are you sure?" she asked. Moretti solemnly nodded. Kelly stared him in the eye. "Final answer?" Moretti nodded again, this time with total conviction.

Kelly raised her phone so Moretti could see the text message. It was from Pete and it read, "Kel – I know you're asleep, but wanted to let you know we got a DNA hit on hairs found in the car. A man named Tommy Moretti. He lives here in the city, he's got a long record and there's a strong possibility he's the killer. We're going to take him down."

Moretti's eyes bulged out in disbelief. No! How could they...?

... And then he felt the rush of drugs coursing through his system. He looked down to see the needle sticking into his arm. As he looked back up, he was staring into the face of Kelly. She looked surprised, as if shooting him with the lethal dose of heroin wasn't a conscious act.

He tried to recall the events that led to this moment, but his mind ceased to function coherently. This was Moretti's defining moment; it was also his last.

Kelly stared in disbelief and horror. She was witnessing a human being go into death throes. A death that she'd caused! Her immediate instinct was to help him. To save his life. But instead, she stood by, watching, letting the guilt flow over her.

She deserved to share in his ordeal.

She pulled the sock from his mouth and Moretti gasped for air as his organs started shutting down. With his life dwindling away, his lids opened and he looked at Kelly one last time. His eyes reflected a man resigned to his fate. Hers reflected a woman who was tinged with doubt and a tiny, involuntary degree of sympathy.

A few moments later, Moretti's head slumped forward. Kelly checked the vein in his neck for a pulse, which was non-existent.

It was over.

Kelly was overwhelmed with the reality of what she'd done. She stared at the dead body in front of her and was hit with the cold, harsh realization that she had crossed over.

She was a murderer.

A murderer who needed to act now! The police knew about Moretti. She had to get out of there… but first she had to erase any evidence that she'd been there. How? She had no idea what she'd touched. What about loose hair strands? And her saliva on the water bottle. What else? What else??

She looked over at Moretti. She couldn't leave him tied up. He'd clearly been murdered, unless…

She'd have to move fast. The police could be there any moment.

Her heart was racing and her breath grew jagged as her eyes frenetically darted around the room. Where to begin?

Just then, she felt her stomach lurch. Kelly bolted for the bathroom and barely made it to the toilet before she violently heaved.

As she wiped her mouth, she glanced at herself in the mirror. She didn't recognize the person staring back at her. The pallid face. The hollow eyes.

Kelly thought that the death of Moretti meant this nightmare was over, but she was wrong.

It was just beginning.

56

Pete was parked down the block from Moretti's house, waiting. A car pulled up behind him and flashed his lights. Pete checked his watch. 6:15am. A moment later, Ron Yee tapped on the window, holding two cups from Starbucks. Nothing like a caffeine jolt for an early-morning takedown.

They approached the house cautiously. They'd done their homework on Moretti and assumed he'd have weapons in the house. They weren't anticipating a shoot-out, but both were wearing vests and held their firearms at their side, just in case he decided to do something desperate or stupid.

When there was no response to their persistent knocking, Pete pulled out his phone. "We'll throw out the net. I want to pick him up before he finds out we're onto him."

Ron had moved to the window and was peering in through a thin partition between heavy curtains. "Don't bother with the APB. Looks like our boy decided to call in sick this morning."

Ron went to work on the front door locks. Five minutes later, they walked into the living room to find Moretti lying face up on the floor, shards of pottery near his head, and a syringe sticking out of his arm.

As Pete slipped on a pair of thin latex gloves, Ron conducted a sweep of the house. Pete gently pressed Moretti's neck and found no pulse. There was a fine line between preserving evidence and making a definitive determination of the status of a victim, so Pete carefully raised Moretti's eyelids and shone a light into the pupils. They were fixed and dilated.

The eyes of a corpse.

Ron walked back into the room. "All clear. Checked his bathroom and closet and it appears he lives alone. His bed hadn't been slept in, which leads me to believe this piece of shit partied solo last night." Ron looked down at Moretti and gave him a half-hearted salute. "You saved the city a lot of time and money, asshole. On behalf of the entire legal system, we appreciate you embracing your civic duty." He turned to Pete. "Seems obvious to me what happened. What's your read?"

"The needle sticking out of his arm kinda tells the story. Either he took the wrong dose or he got a hot load. Lost his balance, fell backwards into the bookcase and crashed into one of those clay pots. The crime-scene guys can fill in the blanks, but on first impression, I'm with you. Self-inflicted overdose."

Pete looked down at the body and was filled with a sense of satisfaction. More so than any other case he'd worked in a long, long time. This one was personal, and now the file on David Harper's death was finally closed. He couldn't wait to tell Kelly.

She'd be ecstatic when she heard the news.

57

Less than five miles away, Kelly sat at her kitchen table, staring into space. She'd arrived home some time after 5:30am and had no illusions that she'd be able to fall asleep without meds. The problem was, if she took enough Ambien to quell her intense anxiety, she'd be laid out for an entire day, and she needed to be at the clinic by 8:30. So she'd opted for the alternate path and popped a couple Dexedrine. Kelly hated the harsh buzz of speed, but knew it was the only way she was going to make it through the next eighteen hours.

She'd showered and dressed, covering the bruises on her neck with a seldom-worn turtleneck sweater. The only things holding her back from walking out the door were a throbbing headache and an overwhelming sense of guilt. She reached for her "World's Greatest Daughter" mug and tears formed in her eyes. Flashes of her father brought a lump to her throat, making it difficult to swallow. Would her memories of him grow fonder over the years, or would she become increasingly resentful of the path he'd forged?

Kelly wiped her eyes and took a sip of cold, bitter coffee. She wished the day was already over and she was crawling back into bed, seeking refuge from reality.

The events of last night would haunt her for the rest of her life. The question was, how would they impact her immediate future?

She was about to find out.

The knock at the door rattled her. She looked at the kitchen clock and saw it was a few minutes before eight. Who'd be knocking at this hour? And then she realized she was late for work. She should've already been on the road.

A second knock was followed by a familiar voice, "Kelly?"

It was Pete. Oh, shit. Pete! Why was he there? Did he know that she'd been at Moretti's? That she was the one who killed him? Was he coming to arrest her?

"Kelly? You home?"

What was she going to do? Run? Where? She had nowhere to go. If she was going to be arrested, she may as well face the consequences. It *was* self-defense, wasn't it? She held out hope, however slim, that she wouldn't be spending the rest of her life behind bars.

She finally opened the door to find Pete, his face a stoic mask. "It's over," he said. "We found Moretti this morning. Dead."

Kelly was filled with dread as she waited for the other shoe to drop. "Dead?" she croaked. "How?"

"He overdosed. Still had the needle in his arm."

"What happens now?"

"The crime-scene investigators are there. They'll send whatever they find to the lab for the standard tests and we'll see what comes back. It was pretty clear that Moretti's death was self-inflicted." Pete showed the slightest glimmer of a smile. "Sometimes, karma's a real bitch." His smile grew larger. "Not only was Moretti a major dealer, but we're convinced he was driving the car that killed your father. A piece of shit's been taken off the street, your father's been avenged and you won't have to look over your shoulder any more."

Pete slowly opened his arms and Kelly broke into tears and fell into his embrace. She flinched when he hugged her. The reaction was as much psychological as physical. Pete released her, and gently stroked her hair.

"It's over, Kel. You can get back to your life now."

Kelly doubted if that would ever be possible.

58

She found parking a block from Benedetto's office. After her conversation with Pete, Kelly knew she wouldn't be worth a damn at the clinic today. Not until she took care of a few things that weighed heavily on her mind. She'd spoken to Vik, who happily agreed to go in early, along with his brother Krishan.

As Kelly rang the buzzer at Benedetto's office, she realized it had only been three days earlier that she stood there, oblivious to the facts about her father.

Three days.

It felt like a lifetime.

Benedetto opened the door and led Kelly back into his office. She gladly accepted his offer of coffee, hoping the caffeine would dampen her headache. Once they were comfortably situated, Benedetto wanted to hear what had happened last night. "Leave nothing out."

Kelly was totally blindsided. She'd called him and asked for this meeting, but hadn't mentioned a word about Moretti, or Pete coming to see her. Nothing.

"How did…?" she started.

"If I hadn't made it clear, I'm well connected in this city. If there are places where I don't have an insider, I know people who do, as well as a tech expert who's constantly monitoring the electronic landscape. Do you want to tell me what happened, or should I tell you what I've heard?"

"I came here to discuss how to distance myself from this situation, not to be debriefed," she said with slight indignation.

"I can't help you move forward until I know exactly how much exposure we're talking about."

"Exposure?"

"Kelly," he began in a softer tone, "you did what you thought was best for you and your sister. I understand that completely. Believe me, I do. But you took a monumental risk and the only way I can hope to protect you against any blowback is if I'm up to speed on every detail."

"By blowback, you mean arrest?"

"And possible retribution. Nothing this significant happens in a vacuum. You know that better than anyone. Your father was killed and you reacted. Now Moretti is dead, and there could be a countermove. It's like a continuous game of chess, but played by people who often make decisions based upon emotion instead of intellect. Some consider it biblical, 'an eye for an eye', while others think it's the only way to retain respect. Whatever the motivation, when a person's killed, you have to be prepared for other dominoes to fall. The trick is to anticipate them and avoid getting crushed under them. Do you understand?"

"I understand that you were the one who started me on this path in the first place."

"I believe that distinction belongs to your father, but let's not quibble. I'm here to help."

His words struck a chord. She clearly understood the severity of her situation. "Where do I start?"

"Start with staking out The Battery."

She reacted. "How did you know about *that*?"

Benedetto shook his head. "Don't worry about how I know. I want to find out about the things I don't know."

Over the next two hours, Kelly told her story in as much detail as she could recall. Benedetto dutifully listened and occasionally prompted her with a question or asked for a clarification while he made copious notes on a legal pad. During her narration he didn't comment upon her actions or question her judgment.

Kelly wrapped up her story and was exhausted. The Dexedrine had worn off and she was on the verge of crashing.

As if on cue, Mrs Mathews arrived with a tray of fruit, pastries and bottles of 5 Hour Energy. The kitchen was well stocked with an array of fresh, healthy foods, as well as cases of "energy boosters", which were the go-to source of caffeine for the paralegals who frequently toiled in the back rooms.

Benedetto excused himself to make some calls and Kelly used the time to refuel and check in with the clinic. Vik assured her they had everything under control, and they were managing fine. She needn't worry... but, of course, she did.

Benedetto returned, settled in behind his desk and asked Kelly if she was feeling better. She thanked him for the food and the drink and said she was almost back to normal.

"Good, because I want to make sure you understand what I'm about to tell you." Gone was the friendly tone, replaced by the demeanor of a stern professor or a disapproving father.

Kelly bristled. "I'm not stupid."

"No one's questioning your intelligence. It's your judgment that's highly suspect."

"I know I was in over my head and probably made a few mistakes..."

Benedetto shook his head.

"What?" Kelly asked.

"'A few' is being dangerously naïve. You're incredibly lucky to be alive *and* not the target of a police investigation. At least, not yet."

"I know, but..."

"You have no idea. If there's any hope of you surviving this next time..."

Kelly was shocked. "Next time! There won't be a 'next time'!"

"That's exactly what your father said."

"I already told you, I'm not picking up where my father left off. What happened with Moretti was a one-time situation. As it is, I doubt I'll ever be able to come to terms with it."

"Time has a way of softening even the sharpest edges."

Kelly stood up. "Not these."

Benedetto raised his hands in surrender. "I didn't mean to suggest you follow in your father's footsteps. But, there are other exigencies we need to discuss."

"Like?"

He motioned for her to sit. "Hear me out, then you can walk away and never have to look back."

Kelly had no choice. Benedetto possessed information, and the only way to get it was to play by his rules.

She sat back down and he gently but firmly began his appraisal. "I'd like to review your actions leading up to this morning. Not to scold you or to prepare you for another outing, but rather so you're forewarned in the event Mr Moretti's death turns out to be something other than a simple open-and-shut case."

Kelly flinched. "Have you heard something about the investigation?"

"A few things. At this point, the police are considering it self-inflicted. The good news is, if they were to find your prints or DNA at his house, they aren't in any law enforcement databases, so they wouldn't get a hit. The other positive factor is that the SFPD, like all departments these days, have an impossible time keeping up with their caseloads, so when a case like Moretti's presents itself, everyone up and down the chain is eager to stamp it 'closed' and not waste time or assets digging beneath the surface."

"Okay. Now comes the part where you tell me how I screwed up?"

Benedetto looked down at his notes and started in. "When you were across the street from The Battery, you said Moretti looked at you. Do you think he recognized you?"

"I didn't think so at the time. I wasn't sure he even saw me." She shrugged. "I don't know. Maybe he did."

"Never place yourself in a situation where you can be seen, or worse, recognized by your target. It puts them on alert, which is the last thing you want."

"I told you, there aren't going to be any more 'targets'," she insisted.

"Moving on; when you purchased your costume, you exposed yourself to many people, particularly the sales help. Plus, you were clearly out of your element, which potentially made you stand out."

Kelly nodded. She didn't like where this was going. "In retrospect, I can think of a dozen ways I was sloppy, but I wasn't thinking in those terms."

"Which can get you killed, or at the very least embroiled in a murder investigation. The choice of picking up Moretti at The Patch was your second biggest mistake. Even though you were in disguise, you put yourself at tremendous risk by engaging him in public."

"There were a few hundred people there," she said defensively.

"Doesn't matter. Any detective worth his salt, like Inspector Ericson, could get a composite drawing of the dark-haired woman who spent time with Tommy Moretti in the VIP lounge. On top of that, the club has at least two dozen security cameras, and I'd wager your face was caught on several of them."

Kelly was deflated. She thought she was being clever, but she'd left a trail of breadcrumbs that Inspector Clouseau could follow.

"However, your most critical lack of judgment was going home with him."

"I explained that. It wasn't my choice. I was drugged."

"You put yourself in that position. And, what was your plan again? To drug him and get him to confess to killing your father?"

Kelly felt her face redden. She was humbled and embarrassed.

"I'm not here to second guess you, but your 'plan' was riddled with holes," he said in a softer tone.

"I thought if I could get him to drop his defenses and then get him talking…" The rest of the plan was left unsaid.

"You can't go into something like this and wing it. Every step should've been thought through with excruciating detail."

"Are you done? Is it my turn to ask you a few questions?"

"As many as you'd like."

"Why didn't you know about the $5 million bounty on Gideon?"

"I'm fully aware of it."

Kelly flared with anger. "Don't you think it would've been important to tell me about it?"

"As far as I'm concerned, it was a non-issue. We've been feeding disinformation to their so-called computer experts for years. Your father's name was only on a list because of the death of Musselwhite. The fact that Moretti stumbled upon your father's true identity was sheer happenstance."

"Did my father know there was a price on his head?"

"I never mentioned it to him."

"Why not?" Kelly was stunned, and yet not at all surprised. Benedetto was extremely stingy with the information he doled out.

"Because it would have been an unnecessary distraction. Your father already knew he was putting himself at risk."

"Well, now that I know there's a bounty, and that my father's name is on a list, what can we do about it? Even though he's gone, it's obvious that if other people were to 'stumble upon' his identity, my sister and I could be in jeopardy."

"True, unless Gideon were to carry out another assignment."

Kelly violently shook her head. "Haven't you been listening to what I've said?"

"Every word." Benedetto paused for a drink of water and to give Kelly a moment to calm down, then continued, "Arthur Moretti has a son named Angelo, who's a small-time dealer that lives in Oakland. He's a screw-up and was banished from the family business a few years ago. He and Tommy were very tight growing up. Like brothers. Tommy was angry when Arthur forced Angelo out, but he didn't want to rock the boat. Instead, Tommy gave Angelo a monthly cut that kept him afloat.

"I have it on good authority that Angelo's not in touch with anyone in the family and spends most of his time in a drug-induced haze, so he's probably not aware that his cousin is dead. However, once he finds out, he'll no doubt make a play to reclaim a share of the family business."

"What's all of that got to do with me?"

"Maybe nothing, maybe everything. You said that Moretti swore he hadn't told anyone else about your father. What if he did? What if he used his surrogate brother as a sounding board? After all, Angelo's father was supposedly murdered by Gideon. The best way for Angelo to get some much-needed cred and prove himself worthy would be to take revenge against Gideon's family."

"You're proposing that I kill a man because he *might* know my father's identity?"

Benedetto shook his head. "I'm not proposing anything. I'm merely giving you information that you may find" – he shrugged his shoulders – "useful. There are a few other things to keep in mind."

Kelly sighed. "Of course there are."

"If Angelo was to suffer a fatal accident, I could plant the information that his death was attributed to Gideon, signifying Gideon's still out there, which would put to rest any suspicions regarding your father. Also, there's a person who's highly motivated to see Angelo Moretti taken off the boards and is willing to pay to make that happen.

In fact, your father had already committed to the assignment. Have you read his entire journal?"

"No, I find it too painful. As to your subtle suggestion, I'm having a really difficult time dealing with what I've just been through. There's no way in hell, for any amount of money, that I'm going to put myself in that position again. Besides, as you pointed out, I screwed up everything! I'm not cut out for this. Why don't you find someone who is? Let him or her inherit the Gideon mantle. They can take Angelo 'off the boards', and it'll be a win-win all the way around."

"It's much too risky. Your father was a unique man with specialized skills and driving motivation. There are innumerable people out there who will kill for money, but no one who could take the place of Gideon. No one but you."

"I don't know whether to thank you or curse the day I met you. Either way, I plan to go home and burn the journal. Don't take this wrong, Mr Benedetto, but I pray our paths never again cross."

59

After leaving the Marina, Kelly felt a powerful urge to see her sister, so she headed south on the Bayshore. Along the way she replayed her conversation with Benedetto in her head. She was seething, but wasn't exactly sure why. Was it his ridiculous suggestion that she should consider killing *another* human being? Or was it because he made her feel like a complete idiot?

Neither. Deep inside, she knew the reason. She was angry at herself for getting entangled in this morass. Even though she could rationalize the fact that Moretti had intended to kill her and Jessica, she should've gone to the police and let them handle it. Maybe her father's name would've been dragged through the mud, but then again, how could Moretti, or anyone for that matter, prove that David Harper was a hitman known as Gideon? It was such an absurd notion that no one would've believed it.

Damn it! It was so obvious in hindsight. And now, because of her reckless decision, she could be the target of this Angelo Moretti. To make things worse, the police were no longer an option; not without implicating herself in Tommy's murder.

She heard Benedetto's voice like he was sitting in the passenger seat. *'If Angelo was to suffer a fatal accident, I could plant the information that his death was attributed to Gideon, signifying Gideon's still out there, which would put to rest any suspicions regarding your father... There's a person who's highly motivated to see Angelo Moretti taken off the boards and is willing to pay to make that happen... Your father had already committed to the assignment.'*

Kelly was so inside her head, she missed the turnoff to the facility. Swearing, she got off at the next exit and doubled back, hitting construction on the side streets, which only served to worsen her already foul mood.

When she pulled into the parking lot, she turned off the ignition and remained in the car. Suddenly, she wondered why she came.

Kelly felt the pressure building up inside of her. Her secret was burning a hole in her conscience and she needed to share it with someone. Someone who wouldn't be judgmental. Kelly again pondered whether she'd be as willing to share with her sister if she weren't lying in a bed in a waking coma. The answer was yes. That's why Kelly was here.

She'd come for confession.

They were back at the idyllic spot under the majestic oak tree on the edge of the facility's grounds. The day was blustery and Cookie recommended that they remain inside. Surely there was a nice warm spot in the "day room" where Kelly and her sister could visit. Kelly replied that Jessica always loved the cool San Francisco weather and thought the crisp, clean air would be a welcome change, so she bundled Jessica up in a thick sweater and wheeled her out. The air was less "crisp" and bordered on "cold", but the upside was they were alone in the garden, and Jessica didn't seem to mind.

Kelly gently caressed her sister's cheek, then sat down across from her so they were face-to-face. "Jess," she said in a low voice, "I killed him." There was no reason to dance around the facts.

Once she uttered the statement aloud, she felt a twinge of relief, followed by a heavier dose of guilt and remorse. Kelly knew if she didn't continue with the rest of what she came to say, she'd resent it later.

"He was the one who killed Dad, and he would've killed us as well." Kelly searched her sister's eyes for a reaction, but there was nothing. Not a hint of emotion. No miniscule nod, not the tiniest crease of a smile or even a fleeting blink. Jessica's head was slightly cocked to the side, and her eyes were fixed on the motionless hands in her lap.

Kelly hadn't expected acknowledgement, but she'd hoped that somewhere in the husk of what used to be Jessica there was a scintilla of understanding.

Undaunted, Kelly continued, "He was evil and deserved what he got. I'm positive of that. If I had to do it again, I would." Did she honestly believe what she was saying, or was she simply trying to give herself absolution? It didn't matter. It felt good to vocalize her actions. Confess her sins. Wasn't that the purpose of confession? It wasn't about being judged by a faceless priest, but rather to give air to your wrongs. To hear them aloud and wallow in the guilt. And then, miracle of miracles, to be forgiven.

Kelly wouldn't find forgiveness. Not here. Not ever. But that's not why she came. She had something else on her mind.

"Jess, there's another man. Someone who might be a threat to us. The problem is, I can't go through this again. I'm hoping there's another way." Kelly stopped. She didn't know what to say. Could she really sit here and tell her sister that they could be in mortal danger and that she had no idea how to protect them?

It was a lie.

"You understand, right? I killed one man and I can't kill another. I promised to look after you, but…"

Jessica slowly raised her eyes skyward as if searching for answers somewhere deep in the infinite universe, then lowered her head and stared into Kelly's eyes. Kelly broke out in goose bumps and felt a lump in her throat. "Jess?" she whispered.

Jessica kept her stare, boring into Kelly's very soul.

Kelly knew her sister's reactions were involuntary, but nevertheless wondered if this was sign. A sign that Jessica was counting on her to follow through on her promises. To do whatever was necessary. To quit her whining and her excuses, and take care of business.

Wasn't that what family was for?

60

After reading aloud another chapter of the wizarding adventures of Harry, Ron and Hermione, Kelly left Jessica safe and warm in her room and headed back to the freeway. It was going on three o'clock, and city traffic was a bitch. It would take her an hour to make it back to the clinic, which meant the day would be more than half over. On top of that, she was on the verge of collapse. She called Vik to see if they could handle things without her for the rest of the day. He reported it was unusually light today and that everyone had already committed to stay on until closing. "Even Nathan?" Kelly asked. Vik confirmed that Nathan had happily agreed to do whatever was needed.

Kelly was impressed. Maybe Vik could take a more active hand in running the clinic and give her some time off to deal with… whatever. Before Vik hung up, he reminded Kelly that it was the 15th of the month, and the payroll checks were sitting on her desk waiting to be signed. He thought everyone would be okay getting paid tomorrow, but Kelly wouldn't hear of it. She knew that Ramona, for one, lived paycheck to paycheck.

She told Vik she'd swing by on her way home.

There was a three-car accident just south of Brisbane and traffic was backed up for miles. Kelly got off at Hillside Blvd and wound her way north. Hillside took her directly through Colma and past the myriad graveyards, including Cypress Lawn, where her father had been interred just a week earlier. She thought about stopping and putting fresh flowers on his grave, but the memories were still too raw.

She wasn't ready to visit.

It was after five when Kelly entered the rear door of the clinic. Vik was tending to an elderly man with a cut on his forehead and Sonita was wrapping the ankle of a grass-stained high school soccer player with a bad sprain. He was clearly in pain, but that didn't stop him from awkwardly trying to hit on Sonita.

Nathan was busy treating Olivia, an eight-year-old wailing girl who'd been bitten by a Mastiff. Fortunately, the dog was a puppy and had only nipped the girl's calf. The standard treatment in cases like this was to administer antibiotics and tetanus shots, which were a nightmare for a terrified second grader. The good news was they could forgo expensive and painful rabies shots since there was no reported outbreak of rabies in the area. That news failed to leaven the mood of Olivia's mother, who was hysterically ranting about "finding that dog's owner and suing his Mexican ass off!" (which everyone within earshot knew was both ludicrous and wildly offensive).

Kelly leapt into the fray, taking the mother aside and calming her down by explaining that her ravings were creating a frenzied situation that only made her daughter more frightened. Kelly firmly and compassionately made it clear that the mother needed to wait in the reception area so the doctors could give their undivided attention to her daughter.

As the mother was begrudgingly led away by Ramona, Kelly wheeled a stool next to the bed and soothed the terrified little girl, stroking her hair and speaking in tranquil tones. "Olivia, I'm Dr Kelly. We're going to make you better, okay?"

Olivia's tears ran down her reddened cheeks. Kelly gently wiped them away with some tissues and then removed the stethoscope from around her neck.

"Do you want to hear your heartbeat?"

Olivia stopped crying long enough to manage a nod. Her breathing was jagged as her sobs weakened to a snivel. Kelly gently put the eartips of the stethoscope into Olivia's tiny ears and placed the bell on her chest.

While Olivia was distracted and calm, Nathan and Kelly exchanged glances, then he carefully slid a syringe of antibiotics into her rump. Olivia winced, but Kelly kept her pacified with the stethoscope.

"Can you hear that sound? It goes like 'thumpity-thump'." Olivia meekly nodded. "That's your heart. Isn't that cool?"

Kelly removed the eartips and put them into her own ears, then listened. "Wow. That's the strongest heartbeat I've heard all day! You're in very good shape. Do you play soccer?" Olivia nodded, the faintest crinkle of a smile beginning to form.

"I'd bet you're really good."

"I scored two goals last week!"

"Two? That's amazing. What are the names of kids on your team?"

"Emma, she's my best friend, Lily, Natalie, Addison, but everyone calls her Addie, Brooklyn, Isab... OW!"

Nathan finished up the tetanus shot and covered the spot with a Peppa Pig bandage.

"You're very brave," said Kelly. "Doctor Nathan just gave you two shots and you made it through without a single tear. I'm pretty sure we've got a candy bar that you can take home with you."

"My mother doesn't let me eat candy. She says it'll make me fat."

Kelly hid her disdain for Olivia's helicopter mom behind a smile. "Okay. I'm going to tell your mother what a great patient you were and that you deserve a treat. Would that be alright?"

Olivia nodded. "Maybe we could stop for Froyo on the way home?"

Kelly nodded sagely. "Frozen yogurt is an excellent idea. I'll suggest it to your mom."

Olivia beamed. "Thanks, Doctor Kelly. And thanks Doctor Nathan for making me better."

Nathan grinned. This was the best part of being a doctor.

A short time later, Kelly was in her office, signing the last of the checks, when Nathan entered. She smiled. "Dr Curtis. I wanted to thank you for working an extra shift today."

Nathan motioned toward the chair. "Can I...?"

Kelly nodded. "Nice job with Olivia."

"If you hadn't defused the mom and calmed down the daughter, I don't know what I would've done."

"I'm sure you would've handled it fine."

"I'm not so sure. You may not have noticed, but I don't deal with people very well," he said with a half smile. "Maybe my father was right. Maybe I should be a surgeon. They wear their lack of compassion as a badge of honor."

"Some do. I think once you have more experience, you'll have a better idea of where you want to specialize. Maybe pediatrics."

"Maybe. I wanted to talk to you about the clinic..."

Kelly wearily shook her head. "Nathan, please don't..."

Nathan raised his hands in surrender. "That's not where I'm going with this. I've done a lot of thinking, about my father, about this place. He wants to broker a deal to buy you out. Don't do it."

Kelly raised her eyebrows, wondering where this was going. Nathan rushed on, "This clinic is special because you make it that way. The way you treat the patients, the way you embrace this neighborhood, the way you care. The Mission needs you, not some faceless corporation that would turn this into a factory."

Kelly was impressed. "Where'd that come from?"

"The heart. What I really wanted to say was, if you need some money to keep this place going for a while, I have a trust fund I can borrow against."

Kelly smiled warmly. "That's very kind of you, Nathan, but I can't accept that. Somehow, we'll manage. And for the record, don't ever let anyone say you lack compassion."

Nathan paced in the parking lot, his cell phone pressed against his ear as he listened to his father rail at him for screwing up this deal. Randall pulled no punches in his assault against Nathan's intelligence, backbone and even questioned his parentage. Nathan took the punches in stride, giving his father all the time he needed to vent his anger and frustration over the fact that he had guaranteed his client he could deliver. Not only was Randall going to look like a fool, but losing this client could potentially cost him millions down the line. As usual, Nathan fucked up. And as usual, Randall would need to do the job himself.

When the call was finished, Nathan calmly slid the phone into his pocket with a satisfied smile. He doubted his father would ever get over this "grand betrayal of trust", and frankly, didn't care. He knew his father's rep; whoever had dealings with Randall Curtis thought he was an abrasive and abusive prick. Nathan, on the other hand, had always been the faithful son, straining to find rationalizations to explain away his father's heavy-handed dealings.

Those days were over.

61

Less than twenty-four hours ago, Kelly had stood outside The Patch, debating whether or not she should go through with her so-called plan. Between then and now she'd come face-to-face with her father's killer, been drugged, raped, and committed murder. As if that wasn't enough, she'd also discovered there was another person out there who might be gunning for her and Jessica. The capper was the suggestion that she should consider donning the mysterious mantle of Gideon and become a crusading assassin.

Kelly knew she'd been drinking too much since her father died, but now was not the time to stagger aboard the wagon. She poured herself two fingers of the Clynelish she'd brought home from the clinic, and nestled into her reading chair with her scotch and her father's journal. She flipped to the end, interested in only reading the final entry.

(David's Journal)

I've been offered an assignment that I find intriguing, primarily because it's the first time I've been approached to take out a family member of someone I previously killed. The target is Angelo Moretti, the son of Arthur Moretti. As always, I don't question who wants him off the board and why. Benedetto handles those details and I trust him. However, I'm extremely interested in the crimes (or more biblically, the sins) this person has committed to determine for myself if he or she warrants the attention of Gideon.

Benedetto provided me with a dossier on Angelo's violent and perverse appetites. Simply put, this piece of filth is a serial pedophile/murderer. A destroyer of young lives; in his case, the younger the better. He'd been accused of two counts of statutory rape/assault (twin sisters), but the cases were dropped when the girls' parents changed their story. Without their testimony and cooperation, there was nothing to pursue. It seemed obvious to all that the parents had either been bought off or scared off.

After that, Angelo conveniently took a yearlong vacation to Southeast Asia, where a man with enough money could play out just about any sexual fantasy that suited him. Evidently, Angelo did just that. During his spree in Thailand, two underage prostitutes were strangled to death. The Thai authorities, who had a reputation for leniency toward wealthy foreigners, refused to look the other way and they arrested Angelo. His father paid double the government's usual bail/ransom and they in turn happily shipped his son back to the States.

When he returned home, Angelo was given an insignificant job in Arthur's organization, but only lasted a few months before he was cut out of the family business. The details were foggy, but Benedetto heard it had something to do with Angelo's inability to control his anger.

The last piece of information on Angelo is unsubstantiated (but one that Benedetto is trying to confirm), and if it turns out to be true, my decision to take this contract will be made much easier.

A few months back, a fourteen-year-old girl in Oakland was raped and strangled. Her body was discovered behind Carmen Flores Rec Center. No prints were found and there were no witnesses, so the case was never solved, but word on the street was Angelo had been bragging about how he'd gotten away with murder... again.

As I read the report, my blood was pumping. My heart was filled with rage. Was it because I have two daughters? Was it because of what happened to Mary? Or was it because this man was clearly a menace to society and shouldn't be allowed to be walking around where he could inflict pain and misery on others?

I'm awaiting an update from Benedetto, but my gut tells me that Angelo will be Gideon's next mark. In anticipation of that, I'm starting the process of gathering personal information and will then begin to formulate a plan.

So there it was. Angelo Moretti had been destined to be Gideon's latest victim, and ironically, it was his cousin Tommy who'd saved his life without even knowing it.

Kelly reread her father's entry and imagined herself as a would-be executioner. Did Angelo Moretti's unsubstantiated crimes warrant the death sentence? She remembered being outraged when she'd read about the teenager who was found in East Oakland. At the time, Kelly had felt a sense of indignation and hoped the guilty bastard would be caught and hung by his balls. Could this be her opportunity to carry out that sentence?

Her train of thought was derailed by a knock on the door. Pete had left a message on her phone suggesting they get together for a drink or dinner, but she was in no condition to see him.

She had a lot of issues to unpack first.

After closing the David Harper case, Pete's life was back to normal. Kelly's was anything but. In fact, her life seemed to get more complex and dysfunctional with every passing hour.

A second knock prompted her to get up and quietly cross to the door. Kelly peered out the peephole, then broke into a smile. She swung the door open for Alexa, who was holding a bottle of Marcassin Chardonnay in each hand.

"I seem to recall that you liked this," she said with a grin. "Would you happen to have any wine glasses?"

"If you're not too fussy, I think I have some plastic cups."

"Plastic, paper or a wooden chalice. I'm not precious about my stemware."

A short time later, they clinked their Riedel glasses and repeated their usual toast to friendship, health and finding true love. It was silly, but heartfelt.

"Where've you been?" Alexa asked. "I left you a few messages."

"It's been a crazy day," said Kelly without a hint of understatement. "I meant to get back to you, but…"

"It's okay. Running the clinic by yourself, not to mention all of the other things going on in your life. Speaking of which, anything new on the finance side?"

Kelly shook her head. "I'm looking into a few options. So far, we're still managing to keep the doors open."

"You've got a standing offer from me if you find you need some gap financing."

"I know. You're the best. So, what've you been up to?" Kelly asked, changing the subject. She adored Alexa, but had no desire to get into a heavy conversation about life. Not now.

"Same old. Long hours, unrealistic clients all looking to make a fast buck with no risk."

"Sounds as boring as my life."

"There was a little excitement today. Have you ever heard of a local drug dealer named Tommy Moretti?"

A shiver ran through Kelly's body. "No. I get all of my drugs legally," she said, as she downed the rest of her wine and refilled her glass. "What about him?"

"I was at a club in Dogpatch last night and Moretti was there. I heard he got into a fight in the VIP lounge, then split with some woman."

Kelly feigned disinterest, but was anxious to hear the word on the street. "And?"

"They found Moretti this morning, dead. He ODed on heroin."

"What happened to the woman?"

Alexa shrugged. "No idea. Pete probably has the details. All I know is, the club scene's getting dangerous. You're lucky you're not out there trolling."

"There's something to be said for living a predictable, monochromatic life."

Alexa sipped her wine and fixed Kelly with a look that only close friends could get away with. "How *is* your life going?"

"What do you mean?"

"I know you're dealing with your father's death, *and* the clinic, *and* Jess. Any one of those would be a hell of a lot to take on, but the mental and physical strain of handling all of that is immense."

"Then you know how my life's going."

"But I don't. There's something I'm missing. I've seen you deal with horrific situations, and I was always amazed at how you could compartmentalize your emotions and tackle every challenge methodically and intelligently. And now there seems to be… something. I'm not being helpful because I can't verbalize what it is that I don't understand, but just know I'm here. Talk to me."

Kelly didn't immediately respond. Alexa raised her glass and drank, keeping her eyes on Kelly the whole time, gauging her reaction. There was none.

Alexa broke the awkward silence. "Is everything okay with Pete?"

Kelly couldn't reveal that dating a cop right now was extremely awkward. She reached over and laid her hand atop Alexa's, giving it a loving squeeze.

"I'm sad, I'm exhausted and I'm frightened about the future. It's as simple as that. I don't know how the blend of those thoroughly depressing states of mind manifest into what I'm projecting to the outside world, but there you have it." She sipped her wine and smiled. "Don't worry about me, Lex. Time heals all, right?"

"Time, sex and expensive liquor. I can only provide one of the three, but if you want, we can make this a weekly treatment session."

"Deal. I'll check my insurance plan and see if this type of procedure is covered."

"If not, you need to switch carriers." She split the remainder of the bottle between their two glasses and they turned their conversation to Alexa's love life, which was always a fanciful distraction that took them long into the night.

Tonight, however, Kelly couldn't focus on Alexa's tales of the impossibly handsome wealthy men who wanted to take her away to exotic locales. Tonight, all Kelly could think about was Angelo Moretti; his intentions and his potentially limited life expectancy.

62

Pete was slipping on his sport coat when Miguel Urbina entered the homicide bullpen.

"You heading out for the night?" Miguel asked.

Pete nodded. "Shift's over. Ron took off a little early to read a bedtime story to his grandson."

"Really. It's almost eleven. What time's this kid go to sleep?"

Pete settled back into his chair. "I don't ask. I got a feeling this 'grandson' is a thirty-eight-year-old named Monique who works the back bar at Slattery's, but you didn't hear that from me."

Miguel spun Ron's chair around and straddled it. "Things are heating up in the Mission. Someone sprayed the Sureños' clubhouse with an automatic. Aimed high and tattooed the roofline. Sending a not-so-subtle message."

"Why can't these fuckers just text each other instead?"

"'Cause then I'd be out of a job," Miguel said without a smile.

"Anyone seen Spider? I got a feeling he's at the heart of this."

Miguel shook his head. "Spider hasn't shown his face, but I've got a CI inside the Sureños. He called earlier to say he was onto something that could defuse the tensions, but he needed a little more time."

"And that was it? No indication of what he was talking about?"

Miguel shook his head. "He's playing it close until he's sure. I got the idea it was a game changer."

"Let's hope the game changes fast, before these assholes start aiming lower."

Oscar "Spider" Sanchez was holed up in the cramped back room of a small taqueria owned by the uncle of one of the Norteños. He was perched on a sagging sofa, playing 'Gears Of War' on Xbox. His thin arms and small hands moved with lightning speed as he slaughtered aliens using an AR15 with a built-in chainsaw. The violence on the television screen was a throwback to old-fashioned gore, and despite the dismemberment of bodies and the flowing lakes of blood, Spider's face showed no signs of any voyeuristic enjoyment. He was all business. Staying sharp.

The door opened and Gizmo entered, along with two of his boys, all carrying heavy duffels. Spider paused the game on a still-frame of a four-armed alien who had just been brutally decapitated. "You got the stuff?" he asked.

The duffels were unzipped to reveal hardware. Lots of hardware, ranging from handguns to assault rifles. "My cousin came through, big time," said Gizmo, a buzzed grin spreading over his face.

Spider took a 9mm Luger out of the bag and ran his hand over it with admiration, knowing what it could do. "*Toro* know about this?"

Luis "*Toro*" Echavarria was *el jefe*. As per his name, he was a bull of a man in his mid-thirties. Had done time, made his bones (or earned his tears, as they said) and came out of prison with a pipeline to suppliers around the state. You didn't fuck with Toro, but sometimes the underbosses had to take care of business of their own. As long as you didn't steal from *la familia* and didn't do anything stupid to bring down heat, Toro was cool. He just wanted his taste.

Spider had plans of his own. He'd loop in Toro when the time was right.

Gizmo shook his head and swallowed hard. "Nobody knows shit about this. I swear."

Spider glanced over at the two younger bangers. They nervously shook their heads. He casually pointed the nine at them. They swore on the lives of their mothers' that they didn't say a word to anyone.

He pulled the trigger. A dry click. The bangers exhaled.

Spider smiled. He had work to do.

63

While Spider and his boys were inspecting their firepower, Nathan Curtis was sitting in his car in the parking lot behind the clinic. A thick cloud cover obscured the waning moon, blanketing the lot in a cloak of darkness. The area was empty, save for a kid dressed in a red sweatshirt who was passing by, smoking a cigarette. Nathan watched as the kid disappeared into the night.

The dim light above the clinic's rear door provided the only illumination, so when two hulking figures sidled up, Nathan wasn't sure if they were who he was expecting. Once they started splashing the door with gasoline, his suspicions were confirmed.

"What are you doing?" Nathan asked, as he got out of his car.

One of the men stepped into the light. It was Burr, Randall's head of security. He was holding a gas can, as was his little brother Junior, who tipped the scales at three hundred pounds, much of it former muscle that had long ago lost its tone and turned to fat.

"I thought my father would try something like this," Nathan said.

"You don't want to be here, Nathan."

Junior reacted. "Wait. Is this the guy you were telling me about? Your boss's punkass son?"

Nathan boldly approached them. "I'm not going to let you do this."

Burr smiled and dismissively shook his head. "Let us? Get the fuck out of here before you get hurt."

Junior emptied his twenty-gallon can around the base of the clinic door. As Burr joined in, Nathan leapt at him, trying to rip the can away. Burr swatted Nathan with a backhand that felt like a hammer blow. The sickening crunch that accompanied it was the sound of Nathan's nose being relocated.

"I told you to get the fuck away!" Burr bellowed.

"Dude," Junior loudly whispered, "keep it down."

Undaunted, Nathan scrambled to his feet and wildly attacked Burr, punching him in the kidney. Burr grunted, then whipped around and brought the heavy can down in a wide, overhead arc. When the can connected with Nathan's forearm, the bone snapped like a dry tree branch.

Nathan roared in pain, his arm jutting in an obscenely unnatural angle.

"Bro!" Junior growled. "Your boss is gonna be pissed!"

Burr shook his head. "Nah. He hates this little fucker."

Burr raised his size 14 Doc Martin, ready to deliver a rib-crushing stomp, when the voice of an eighteen-year-old cut through the night.

"*Pendejo!*"

Burr and Junior turned to see a skinny Hispanic banger decked out in a white T-shirt underneath a red hoodie. "Leave him alone."

Burr and Junior exchanged looks and broke into a laugh. "Seriously? After we fuck him up, you're next, spic," Junior said. He held out a fist and Burr dapped him.

Spider, the skinny banger, calmly pulled a black matte Glock out of his belt. "This clinic and the doctors are protected by the Mission Street Norteños, motherfuckers."

Nathan was completely taken by surprise at this sudden turn of events. Never was there a time when he was so happy to see a banger brandishing a weapon in his general direction.

Burr snatched a Sig Sauer P229 from a rear holster and aimed it at Oscar. "Yeah, well, you might want to get back to your clubhouse, Jose, before I drill a hole in your sorry Norteño ass."

Junior had a shit-eating grin spread across his otherwise vacant face. He loved hanging with his older brother, especially when they got a chance to kick some immigrant tail. The grin slowly faded when Junior saw a red wave ripple through the parking lot.

What the fuck?

Burr's gun hand began to tremble when he realized that Spider hadn't come alone.

"What's wrong, *ojete*?" said Spider. "How many shots you got in that thing? Enough for all of us?"

There were twenty Norteños behind him, all packing weapons, and all eager to find any excuse to use them.

Burr laid his gun on the ground, and slowly raised his hands above his head. Junior followed suit.

Spider looked over at Nathan. "You okay?"

Nathan slowly got to his feet. Blood was cascading from his nose and he was cradling his arm in severe pain. Despite that, he nodded. "Okay."

Spider signaled to one of his guys. "Take him to the hospital. Ahora!"

Nathan began to protest, but Spider shook his head. "We got this."

The red wave began to close in.

Burr and Junior shared a look.

They were so fucked.

64

The Spreckles Temple of Music (better known as "the bandstand") at Golden Gate Park was built in 1900 and still featured concerts every Sunday. The rest of the week it was a mecca for tourists, the homeless, and seagulls.

When Kelly arrived at 7am, Benedetto was already there, amiably chatting with a woman who had the face of a dried apple doll. As Kelly approached, he gave the woman a few dollars, which engendered a warm, toothless grin. The woman cheerfully tottered off and Kelly took a seat next to Benedetto on one of the long green benches. The rest of the benches were devoid of human life.

"How are you feeling today?" he asked.

It had only been one day since she'd murdered Tommy Moretti.

"Still wondering if things will ever get back to normal."

"Your father wondered the same thing."

"If that's supposed to make me feel better, it doesn't. I've read a lot of his journal and his life was anything but normal."

Benedetto was well aware of David's constant internal struggle, from the moment he killed Musselwhite. He didn't expect Kelly's life would be any easier, regardless of whether she crossed the line again.

"Did he make mention of Angelo?" Benedetto asked.

"It was his final entry. If the 'rumors on the street' are true, Angelo is even worse than his cousin. *Are* they true?"

"Since the time your father would've written that, more details have come to light. There was an eyewitness who reportedly saw Angelo near the rec center with the young girl on the night she died."

"Then why haven't the police arrested him?"

"The eyewitness was an elderly man and he died last week. The police could make an arrest, but until they have more concrete evidence, they have no case."

"So, based upon the account of one old man, you think Moretti's guilty?"

"I think he's guilty based upon everything I've heard from my sources. He was out of his mind on drugs when he committed this heinous act, and because he suffers from an inferiority complex, he boasted about it. The fact that an eighty-three-year-old man with a bad heart picked him out of a six-pack of police photos was the icing on the cake for me."

Kelly still wasn't convinced of Angelo's guilt. The reality was, she didn't know anything about Benedetto's supposed "sources", and, for that matter, didn't know much about Benedetto himself, except what he'd told her and what she'd read. Over the years he'd represented a number of high-profile criminals, but that didn't mean he had reliable contacts. And there was still the possibility that Benedetto was using her. To what end, she didn't know, but the information he came up with felt rather convenient.

"If Angelo killed that little girl, he deserves to suffer the consequences, but that's not my responsibility."

"I completely agree," Benedetto said. "You can walk away any time and let justice run its own course. That's not your concern or mine. I only worry about how Angelo will react once he finds out his cousin is dead."

"You already laid out the worst-case scenario and it's only conjecture. Angelo may not have any idea about Gideon's identity."

"True, but forewarned is forearmed. I'm simply trying to do everything I can to protect you and your sister."

"Why? Why's our wellbeing so important to you?"

"Because," he said, with a look of compassion, "I bear the guilt of setting everything in motion. If I hadn't brought your father into this morass years ago, none of this would be happening. He'd still be alive and you wouldn't be in any jeopardy. This is my doing and the least I can do is try to make it right."

"I'll tell you what you can do to 'make it right'. Kill Angelo yourself."

"I'm not a killer," he responded calmly, like they were having a perfectly normal conversation about the weather.

"Neither was I until yesterday. Why not join the club? In fact, *you* could take over my father's legacy."

Benedetto shook his head with a mirthless smile. "I'm not cut out for it. I lack the expertise, the training and the drive. All of which you have, whether you believe that or not."

Kelly was about to refute his statement, when she realized he was right. Her medical expertise and training gave her a skillset. And there was no debating her drive to take out Tommy Moretti, and potentially his cousin.

"If I *were* to kill Angelo Moretti, where does it end?"

"Hopefully right there."

"Hopefully? No more Morettis are going to emerge from the shadows?"

Benedetto shook his head. "Not that I'm aware of."

"But? I know there's a but."

"No one can predict what the future holds."

"Thanks for the fortune cookie wisdom."

Benedetto shrugged. "It's the best I can do under the circumstances. If you opt to explore the situation with Angelo further, I brought you this." He held out a thumb drive. She looked at it like it was radioactive. "It's virus-free, not encoded and can't be tracked. It's just a four-gig memory stick from Office Depot with some basic information."

Kelly surprised herself by taking it and shoving it into her pocket.

"Oh, and one…"

"Don't say one more thing. Please, I can't take 'one more thing'."

He smiled. "We all have verbal tics. I wanted you to know that some time today $9,500 will show up in the clinic's bank account."

Kelly's eyes flew wide open. "What are you talking about? Don't tell me this is because Tommy…"

"No. It's the final payment for a job your father did last year."

"How do I explain that income to the accountants?"

"When the dust settles, I'll walk you through the mechanism we set up years ago. It's never raised a flag at the government level, and since the money is used to support a clinic that's running in the red, I highly doubt you'll ever be audited."

Kelly was barely functioning on minimal sleep and could hardly pull her thoughts together. All she knew was the sun rose this morning and would probably set tonight.

Past that, her future was murky as hell.

65

It was highly unusual for a cop to introduce his confidential informant to anyone else on the force, especially if that CI was embedded in an Hispanic gang. *Nuestra Familia* and the Mexican Mafia were both steeped in family and honor. You weren't recruited into these gangs, you were born into them. As such, it was rare to find a member who was willing to flip on his *hermanos*, and when you did have one in your pocket, the last thing you'd do is risk burning him by exposing his identity to anyone else.

The story that Eddy Romero had to tell was explosive, and Miguel Urbina knew it would carry substantially more weight if Romero recounted it directly to the Inspectors who were handling the Garcia and Juarez murder cases. It was a risk, but police work was all about managing risks, so Miguel made the decision to trust Ron and Pete with Eddy Romero's life.

Miguel laid the groundwork with Pete and Ron beforehand, giving them Romero's backstory and vouching for his veracity. Eddy was a Sureño who did time in the Arizona prison system (he spent four hard years in Winslow, a town two hundred miles northwest of Phoenix with two distinguishing features: a state prison and a street corner made famous by The Eagles). One day, a fight broke out in the yard between a few Sureño inmates. Chuy Lopez died when a nine-inch shiv was buried in his ear. The inmate who wielded the shiv was Eddy.

Romero was looking at stacking another fifteen to twenty on his sentence, but then a strange thing happened: the prison officials became "uncertain" about which inmates were actually involved in the brawl. With no eyewitnesses willing to step forward, the murder charge against Romero disappeared. Four months later, Eddy was released, at which time he migrated to San Francisco, where he was embraced by the 19th Street Sureños.

The gang had no idea that Romero's release was arranged by authorities who needed someone on the inside to help them make a case. Two months later, the head of the 19th Street Sureños was brought up on three charges of murder and racketeering.

So Miguel trusted Romero. Pete and Ron could judge for themselves.

The SFPD had a few off-the-books apartments around the city that they used for a variety of purposes, from housing high-risk witnesses, to serving as crash pads for management-level officers who were having marital problems (or in one case, an extramarital affair, which didn't go over well with the top brass). The apartments were particularly handy for meetings such as this.

Pete and Ron entered to find Miguel sharing beers with a small, muscular man in his mid-thirties. He was covered in the usual gang ink, including, but not limited to, some prison tats that were done by someone lacking any artistic talent.

Eddy rose and shook their hands. His grip was strong, his eyes were bright and he exuded confidence. He gave the impression that if he hadn't run afoul of the law early in life, he could've done well in whatever field he chose.

This initial impression was challenged when Eddy spoke. His speech pattern was slow and slightly slurred. Miguel had prepped them for this, explaining that while in prison, Eddy's diaphragm was injured in a fight, which resulted in a case of dysarthria. It took a while for Pete and Ron to adjust to Eddy's cadence, but it didn't detract from the information he laid out.

According to Eddy, Fernando "Nano" Rojas had been tired of playing second fiddle in the Sureño symphonic and decided to make a play against Payaso. He'd kept his plans under wraps, but somehow Joker (Ruben Garcia) got wind of Nano's intentions. Joker happened to be Payaso's cousin, so his loyalties were obvious. Or at least, that's what everyone thought.

Instead of going to Payaso with the news, Joker decided to leverage his way into getting a little something for himself. His intelligence and skills were limited, and he was destined to never be more than a foot

265

soldier under Payaso, but if he played his cards right he could end up an underboss to Nano.

Unfortunately, Joker was a shitty card player.

The meeting between Nano and Joker took place in an alley off Guerrero Street on the edge of Sureño territory. Joker made his pitch and Nano made him a counter-offer; three slugs from a throwaway piece that Nano had bought for fifty bucks and a dime bag.

Ten minutes later, Nano breathlessly told the boys at the Sureño clubhouse that he'd heard shots over on Guererro Street and when he'd gotten there, he'd found Joker. Three bangers piled into a car, scooped Joker up and got him to the clinic. He'd already lost a tremendous amount of blood and was barely alive, but they figured what the fuck. Maybe the doctors could work a miracle.

Miracles were in short supply that night. For all intents, Joker was dead the moment the third shot severed his spine; officially, he died in the Mission Street Clinic less than an hour later.

Nano was in the clear. At least he thought he was, until he found out that someone else was in the alley that night: Sad Boy (Ernesto Juarez). Sad Boy was only fourteen-years-old and he followed Ruben around like an eager puppy, trying to gain his favor.

Sad Boy had shadowed Joker to the meeting in the alley. He'd heard the whole conversation and he'd witnessed Nano pump a few shots into Joker's gut. Sad Boy freaked. He had no idea what to do, or who he could trust, so instead of heading to the clubhouse, he took off running, and kept on going until he couldn't run any further.

The next day, the Sureños held a raucous wake for Joker, and Sad Boy's absence was noted. One of the bangers said he saw Sad Boy trailing after Joker last night. The Sureños surmised that Sad Boy must've seen whoever shot Joker and then went into hiding because he was afraid of getting clipped himself.

Payaso wanted Sad Boy found, like now. The sooner he knew which one of the Norteño cocksuckers shot his cousin Joker, the sooner he could take his revenge.

Nano had a big problem. If he didn't find Sad Boy first, he was good as dead, so he started the rumor that Sad Boy hopped a Greyhound to the

Central Valley. Nano hoped to throw the others off while he feverishly worked his contacts.

Nano caught a break when he got word that Sad Boy was crashing in a condemned apartment building out at Hunter's Point. The question was, could Nano get to Sad Boy before Payaso?

Eddy stopped his narrative as Miguel tossed a ballistics report onto the table. "Sad Boy was shot with a Remington R51 semi-auto. Three 9mm parabellums."

"And this is significant why?" asked Pete.

"The model came out five, six years ago. It looked cool, but was a total piece of shit and Remington did a recall. You don't see many on the streets anymore."

Eddy chimed in, "Nano's been packing one for a few years. Always playing with it, doing quick-draw shit. He calls it *el martillo*... the hammer."

"We'd need to get hold of his gun to match the ballistics...," Ron said, "but it's a pretty fucking compelling story."

Pete stared at Eddy for a long beat, then asked the obvious question, "If Nano kept his plans a secret, how'd *you* find out about all of this?"

Eddy looked over at Miguel, and got a nod in return. Clearly, Miguel had asked the same question.

"I found Sad Boy first. I've got a friend who's a fucking wiz with computers and he tracked down Sad Boy's cell." Eddy shook his head. "Everyone in the gangs uses disposables, but Sad Boy had all his pictures and music and shit on his phone and just wouldn't give it up. Stupid fourteen-year-old. Anyway, Sad Boy told me what he'd seen. Begged for my help. I told him to stay low for another day or two to give me time to figure things out."

Miguel jumped in, "Eddy reached out to me, but I was in the middle of another case. In the meantime, Sad Boy got antsy, and then got careless. He was spotted, word got back to Nano, and Nano took it from there."

"Once I knew that Nano killed Joker," Eddy said, "it wasn't hard to piece the rest of it together."

"We don't have a lot to go on except what Eddy heard from Sad Boy," said Ron. "But if we can get a match from Nano's gun, we'd have enough to hold him while we collect more evidence."

Pete agreed. If this was true, then they'd not only solve two open murder cases, they'd also stop a potential gang war.

"Let's go pick up that piece of crap and squeeze him," said Pete.

Ron winced. "You've gotta work on your metaphors, partner."

66

Kelly did what she could to regain a degree of normalcy. She thought if she got back into her old patterns and habits, she'd have a chance, albeit remote, of reclaiming her life. The life she had before her father died; the life before she found out about his secret; the life before she became a murderer.

The week had started off on a curious note; when Kelly arrived at the clinic, she'd smelled the faint tang of gasoline near the back door. The area had been hosed down with water, which made no sense. Also, there were a few splatters of red liquid on the wall. The patterns reminded her of crime-scene photos she'd seen in one of her med school classes. She imagined some kind of gang activity had occurred, but the pieces of the puzzle didn't form a cohesive picture.

There was a steady stream of patients at the clinic, which kept her busy and her mind off other issues. The goodwill that Nathan had earned the day before evaporated when he left a message saying he needed some personal days, leaving them shorthanded again. Fortunately, Vik's brother Krishan was able to take on more responsibility and handled a full share of the workload. Like Vik, Krishan proved to be an excellent doctor blessed with natural charisma. He also had movie-star good looks, which made him an instant favorite with the female patients.

That night, Kelly took Pete to dinner at Boulevard, an upscale restaurant not far from her condo. She needed a change from 44 Degrees, and didn't want to run into a dozen people she knew. She'd reserved a quiet table in the back, where they could talk.

The food was fantastic and the service was attentive without being intrusive. Kelly and Pete spent an hour chatting about nothing specific, both waiting for the real conversation to begin.

Kelly finally broke the ice when she casually asked about the Moretti investigation. She was shocked when he said that the case was still active.

"I thought you said his death was self-inflicted," she remarked.

"I still believe that, but there are a lot of loose ends."

Kelly was suddenly on guard. "Loose ends?"

"Evidence at his house indicated he had company. Someone may have been with him when he died, but we can't be sure because we're having trouble narrowing down the time frame."

"What kind of evidence?" she asked, hoping she sounded only vaguely interested.

"Prints, clothing fibers, and synthetic hair from a black wig. There were also semen stains on the couch. The lab is running tests on the semen to determine how long it had been there."

"Okay, that's disgusting."

Pete managed a smile. "You asked."

"So, he brought home a woman wearing a cheap wig, might've had sex with her, then he shot up?"

"That's the popular theory. If we could find the mystery woman, it would answer a lot of questions."

The mystery woman. Benedetto was right. She'd been incredibly careless.

"Moretti had been at a club that night called The Patch," Pete continued. "We obtained security footage of him with a woman with black hair, but the lighting in the place is too dark to make out her face. We asked the bartenders and some of the regulars, but no one knew her or could provide much of a description. Probably a tourist."

Security footage. Damn it. "She sounds like a dead end."

"I agree, and so does the brass. As far as the DA's office is concerned, we should consider the Moretti case closed and I should spend my time working on the stack of case files on my desk."

Kelly smiled. "Sound career advice."

Pete shrugged. "Probably. I'm just having a hard time getting past the timing of discovering that Moretti killed your father, and then him conveniently dying a few hours later. There's also the question of motive. Why would a drug dealer like Moretti kill your father, unless it was an accident?"

Kelly willed herself to stay calm. She reached for her wine glass with a surprisingly steady hand.

Pete continued, "I've got a few more leads to run down before I'm ready to close the book forever. Moretti has a cousin somewhere across the Bay that I want to talk to. We're trying to locate him. I'm sure he doesn't know anything, but…" Pete stopped when he saw a strange look come over Kelly's face.

"Sorry," he said. "I didn't mean to ramble on. I'm even boring myself here."

He'd completely misinterpreted Kelly's reaction. It wasn't boredom. It was fear. Nevertheless, he changed the subject.

"There is some good news. We think we found the person who killed that Sureño kid who was dropped off at the clinic last week."

Her heart sank. "Please tell me Oscar Sanchez had nothing to do with it. That poor family is going through a lot right now."

"He was number one on our hit list, but it turned out to be an inside job. A smartass Sureño named Nano was making a power play and got sloppy, then covered his tracks by killing two of his own guys."

Kelly slowly shook her head. "It's a sad state when 'good news' is some gang banger killing two of his own."

Pete got defensive. "I didn't mean it like that. It's just…"

She laid her hand atop his. "I know. And I agree. It's better that than a full-scale gang war. Will the killing ever stop?"

"Not a chance. There are too many people out there with bad intentions."

Kelly wondered how Pete would feel if he knew he was sitting across from one.

67

Over dessert, Pete had asked if Kelly wanted to come back to his place. She declined with a kiss on his cheek, explaining she was exhausted (which was an understatement), and he didn't push it. The fact was, he was running on fumes himself.

That changed when he got a call from Ron. They'd found Nano Rojas. Rather, what was left of him.

Twenty minutes later, Pete was striding through the Hunter's Point Shipyards. Ron stood outside the police tape, smoking a cigar and trying to stay warm.

"We've gotta stop meeting like this," Pete said, as he stepped up.

"Hopefully, this will put an end to it. It certainly put an end to fucking Nano Rojas."

"Why here?"

"I believe it falls under the category of poetic justice. He was strangled with his Dallas Cowboys knit scarf, then shot in the head."

"If you had to wager a guess…"

"Blue or Red? I'd lay a week's salary that Payaso got wind of Nano's plans and didn't feel like relinquishing the corner office or the key to the executive washroom. I'm sure Miguel's CI will be able to fill in the blanks, but if I'm right, this should relieve some of the steam from the pressure cooker."

"Got another one of those?" Pete asked. Ron happily handed over a cigar, smiling like a proud first-time father.

68

The first call Kelly received in the morning was from Diego's attending physician at St Francis. Dr Guadagni explained in concise but laborious medical terms why Diego Sanchez was going under the knife this afternoon to have his leg amputated from the knee down. Between the damage from the gunshot, the infections and the fact that his foot and calf were completely insensate, there was no saving the leg.

Kelly was devastated, knowing how traumatic this was going to be for Diego. His childhood would be drastically different; at least at first. All because of a stray bullet fired by another underage boy who had no business carrying a firearm. And for what? This wasn't about territory or drug sales. Not really. It was about an age-old feud between two warring factions that was being fought in the streets and prisons between young men who were born into it. Most of them had no choice. They were either Sureño or Norteño. Mexican Mafia or *Nuestra Familia*. Blue or Red.

She wanted to be the one to break the news to Diego, but Dr Guadagni said he'd already informed the boy and his mother. In his words, "they seemed to take it well." Diego was a tough kid, and it was drummed into him at an early age to never show his emotions, but Kelly highly doubted that behind the façade he took the information "well".

She dressed quickly and headed for the hospital.

Kelly arrived to find Alma Sanchez in the waiting area. The two embraced, holding each other tight, feeding off each other's concern for the youth who was lying in his hospital bed, scared to death, his eyes red from crying, fearing that his life may as well be over.

Alma had been through many traumas in her life, but this was her youngest. Her shining star. She suddenly felt weak in the knees and Kelly eased her over to a chair. They sat together, holding hands, as Kelly apologized for Diego's condition. Alma quickly dismissed that notion. "What do you mean? You didn't pull the trigger."

"No, but maybe we didn't flush out his wound well enough. Maybe we overlooked something."

"Don't talk this way," Alma said, her hand on Kelly's cheek. "You saved his life."

It was the first time Kelly pondered whether her father's work may have suffered as a result of his highly stressful extracurricular life. When you treat a patient, you have to give all of yourself. Complete focus and total concentration. Even if it was a procedure he'd performed a thousand times, a doctor couldn't allow himself (or herself) to function on autopilot. If her father had been in the midst of developing a strategy on how to kill Angelo Moretti, how could he have been in the right mindset when it came to trying to save a life?

But Alma was right. They'd done everything they could. If there was any fault to be had, it was with Diego himself, who'd refused to go to the hospital. Refused out of some deeply rooted loyalty to a gang of drug dealers and killers.

Kelly asked if it would be okay for her to see Diego alone. Just for a few minutes. Alma smiled. She was going to suggest the same thing.

When Kelly opened his door, Diego looked away, embarrassed by the tears on his cheeks. She lingered for a moment, stalling for time, then entered wearing a look of understanding and concern.

"Hi," he said softly. Hooked up to an IV drip, a multi-use monitor that constantly beeped, and buried in sheets and blankets, Diego looked even younger than his ten years. The first thing Kelly did was cross over and turn off the sound on the monitor. The silence made the room somewhat less clinical.

"Is it okay to do that? Is the nurse gonna be pissed?" Diego asked.

Kelly shook her head. "They can read all your vitals at the nurses' station. They just keep the sound on to annoy the patients."

Diego looked confused. "I'm kidding," Kelly added. He didn't react. Kelly wondered how long it would take for Diego to rediscover his infectious smile.

She pulled up a chair and reached out for Diego's hand, but he didn't offer it.

"I spoke to the doctor. He said he told you about the operation they're going to be doing."

Diego nodded. He was trying hard to stem the tears, but was losing the fight.

"It's okay to cry," Kelly said softly.

All he needed was permission. The tears flowed freely. Kelly opened her arms. Diego leaned in and she enveloped him in her embrace. He wept like a little boy.

Just like he should.

After a few minutes, Diego pulled away. He was ashamed. "I'm sorry."

"For what? There's absolutely nothing to be sorry about."

"Spider says I need to be strong."

"You do. You are. But that doesn't mean you can't be human. Human's cry. It's natural and it's healthy for you to let it out."

"Spider says it makes me a *puto*."

"Diego, I'm a doctor. I went to school for many years and learned all kinds of things about the human body. Crying absolutely does *not* make you a *puto*."

Hearing Dr Kelly say it made him smile. At least for an instant.

"Do they *have* to cut off my leg?"

"I'm afraid so. The bottom part is badly damaged. They tried to treat it with medicine, but it didn't help. The infection will spread if they don't operate today. Do you understand that?"

Diego thought for a moment, then nodded. "Is it like cancer or something?"

"It's like that, but fortunately it's not cancer. Once they remove the damaged area, all of the infection will be gone and you'll be completely healthy."

"How do I do stuff? Like play soccer or baseball or... anything?"

"Remember when we talked about prosthetics?"

He nodded. "Metal legs. I don't want a metal leg."

"They come in all kinds of material. I'll come back later and show you some videos of people who have prosthetic legs. It's pretty cool the stuff they can do."

"Okay." Even at age ten, Diego was resolved to his fate. Kids in the gang culture grew up quickly. "Are you gonna be there when they operate on me?"

"Absolutely. Someone has to make sure that they don't operate on the wrong leg."

Diego was momentarily stunned at the thought, and then slowly broke into a tiny smile. "That was a joke, too, right?"

Kelly nodded. "Just not a very good one."

Diego shrugged. "It was okay."

Kelly marveled at his strength. Diego was going to turn out fine if he could somehow stay out of the gang.

Unfortunately, that die had already been cast.

69

The following morning, Kelly spent time with Jessica, leafing through the pictures in their old photo album. They'd done this at least a hundred times before, but it was the first time they'd looked at it since their father's death, and now the photos took on different meanings and evoked more emotional memories.

Kelly stopped at one photograph of her and Jess taken just a week before everything went sideways. Back when they were carefree and had no idea of the tragedies that awaited them. They were holding the tennis rackets their father had given them as end-of-the-school-year gifts. Rackets that would never be used. Kelly removed the photo from the album and slowly ran her fingers over the images. It was the last photo taken of Jessica before she ended up in this bed. Kelly held back her tears as the anger built up inside of her, fueling her resolve. A homicidal monster had destroyed two lives and turned two others upside down. She wasn't going to allow that to happen again.

Pete had sworn to keep digging until he had all the answers. It wouldn't take him long to find Angelo Moretti, and there was no way to know what information Angelo had and could be coerced to share.

The decision she'd been putting off was made. No questions asked and no turning back. She had an obligation to her sister and she was dead set on not letting Jessica down, again.

On her way out of the building, Kelly dropped off a certified check with Ms Spiro, squaring up Jessica's account, then made a phone call to Benedetto.

When she returned to the clinic, there was a small envelope on her desk that had been delivered by a messenger. Other than Kelly's name and address, there were no markings on the envelope. She knew who'd sent it.

She slit it open and pulled out a thumb drive which contained an updated report about Angelo Moretti and a copy of his medical records.

Kelly was about to take another step along her journey.

70

Over the next few days, Kelly was extremely diligent about her preparation, which included late-afternoon excursions to East Oakland to scout the area. If she was going to do this, she was going to do it right, or at least to the best of her ability.

She took Benedetto's words to heart and questioned every aspect of her plan, looking for holes and things that could come back to haunt her. Were there security cameras? Could she gain access without leaving any traces? Did she have a backup plan in the event things took an unexpected turn?

No plan was foolproof. She couldn't account for every unimaginable roadblock that fate may decide to toss in her way, but Kelly wanted to believe that this time around fate would be on her side.

Her first challenge was to camouflage the hit. Her father had become an expert at this, so she took a page from his playbook and found what she needed in Angelo's medical records. In the past two years he'd been treated twice at Express Care in Oakland for anaphylaxis. Turns out he was allergic to shellfish. Extremely allergic. Why he'd eaten it twice in as many years was a mystery, but not one that mattered. He'd been prescribed an EpiPen and had refilled the prescription at CVS six months ago.

The information from Benedetto included Angelo's cell phone records. Fortunately, he was a creature of habit. Every Tuesday and Saturday night he had food delivered from the Golden Palace. Kelly, posing as Angelo's girlfriend, called the restaurant on Tuesday to confirm the order, and the cranky woman who answered said it was the same thing as always. Spicy garlic chicken and a double order of rice to be delivered at 7pm.

Kelly could work with that.

Using Google maps, she found an apartment complex that fit her specifications. It was situated along the route from the restaurant to Angelo's house, and it had four units in the back.

Evidence that fate was smiling upon her came in the form of a house directly across the street from Angelo's that had been on the market for six months. It was a foreclosure, which meant it was empty. Houses in that neighborhood rarely sold and frequently became crash pads for squatters, so Kelly did a few drive-bys and peered in the windows. It was rundown as hell and there was no indication that anyone lived there. Too crappy for homeless drifters meant it was perfect for her.

During her forays to Oakland, she spent time tailing the teenager who delivered food from the restaurant. He was the only delivery person they had, which made it convenient. He drove an old Tercel, and when he brought the orders up to the front doors he never locked his car. Why would he? Maybe he hoped that someone would steal his junker, which was highly unlikely. Even in this neighborhood, car thieves had pride.

The last step in preparation was to make concentrated shrimp stock. She could've bought it at an Asian grocery, but there was no reason to expose herself like that. She bought two pounds of shell-on shrimp, along with dozens of other groceries that she really didn't need, then boiled the shrimp for a few hours to reduce the liquid and increase its intensity.

By Saturday, she was ready to put her plan into action. She hadn't slept the night before, her head throbbed and the very thought of food revolted her. It was as if every fiber in Kelly's body was screaming at her to bail out. That wasn't going to happen. She'd sworn she wouldn't second-guess her decision, and she didn't. She was past right-versus-wrong. If she allowed any doubt to creep in, it would throw off her concentration, and she needed every ounce of focus if this was going to work.

4pm. Kelly parked her car in a pay lot several blocks from Angelo's house. There were no security cameras on the lot. She was dressed in well-worn drab clothing, a beat-up backpack slung over her shoulder. Her hair was tucked up into a baseball cap that was pulled low over her eyes. She could've been a college student or a barista on her way to work.

4:30pm. Kelly nonchalantly approached the back door of the foreclosed house. A large, grizzled dog tied up in the yard next door barked ferociously, but no one seemed to care. She knocked on the door three times. There was no response, which was exactly what she'd hoped for. Glancing back over her shoulder, Kelly slipped her father's electric lock pick out of her pack and inserted it into the lock. Her hands were badly shaking and it took a few tries to get the prong in straight. After a moment, the tumblers lined up and the lock gave way.

She opened the door a crack and peered around the filthy kitchen. An overwhelming stench wafted out that caused Kelly to gag. It was the sour odor of rotten food and the reek of death. She feared she might be entering the final resting place of some unlucky soul. She hoped the smell was emanating from a rodent trapped inside the walls, but she didn't plan on searching the house to find out one way or the other. The neighbor's dog must've gotten the scent as well, because it launched into a frenzy.

Kelly quickly slipped inside and closed the door behind her.

5:30pm. She had set up a high-powered riflescope on a collapsible tripod and watched Angelo's house. She'd wrapped a thin scarf around her nose and mouth to filter out the stink, but it didn't help. The fumes made her eyes water.

Kelly checked her watch. Every day at this time, Angelo made a pilgrimage to an empty lot around the corner where he met his drug runner and picked up the daily take. Right on cue, the door opened and Angelo exited, casually cruising down the cracked pavement, unsuccessfully trying to look intimidating. Angelo Moretti may be a burnout, but the guy was methodical as hell.

She had to act fast. She eased out the back door, and, to her relief, the neighbor's dog was gone. She walked around the side of the house, treading in the shadows.

Crossing the street without being seen was crucial. She couldn't risk the possibility, regardless of how remote, of being identified at a later date. As she looked out from the shadows, her heart was beating hard and her hands were slick with sweat.

Fortunately, the street was empty. Loud rap music blasted out of a nearby open garage, and Kelly could make out some muffled conversation, interspersed with laughter, but didn't see a soul.

She crossed the street, slowing down her gait so as to not attract attention. She had no more than ten minutes to get into the house, do what she needed to do, and get out.

Even if everything went perfectly, she'd be cutting it close.

The rear door to Angelo's house was shielded from the neighbors by a semi-enclosed porch with rippled Plexiglas panels that had yellowed from years in the sun. Kelly slipped on a pair of latex surgical gloves, quickly picked the lock and entered.

The house was a sty, but Kelly didn't have the time or inclination to explore. She had one very specific task, and the clock was ticking. Loudly.

It took her two minutes to search the bathroom, and she came up empty. She spent another few minutes rifling through his nightstands, to no avail. Her pulse was racing and perspiration was dripping into her eyes when she finally found his EpiPen in the kitchen. Who the hell keeps an EpiPen in the kitchen? She made the switch and bolted for the backdoor. As it was closing, she heard the front door open.

Calming her nerves as best she could, Kelly walked up the street a few houses before crossing over to the other side. She made it back to her stakeout without incident.

When she was safely inside the house, she began to shake. This was lunacy! If Angelo had come home just a minute earlier... thirty seconds earlier... she would have been exposed, and possibly shot. Kelly took a bottle of water from her pack and guzzled it down, then forced herself to take several long, deep breaths. She had to slow everything down and be ready for what lie ahead. There were more risks to be taken and she needed steady nerves to pull them off.

6:30pm. Kelly pulled out a disposable cell phone and placed a call to the Golden Palace. She ordered food to be delivered to the apartment building she'd scouted and was told it would be there in thirty minutes. She started the stopwatch on her phone and headed out.

7:00pm. The darkened doorstep across from the apartment building proved an ideal place to wait for the delivery. A few minutes later, the Tercel pulled up at the curb and the teenager hopped out, a bag of food in hand. He trudged up the walkway to the apartment building, and after checking the numbers, headed for the units at the rear of the complex.

Kelly briskly walked across the street and opened the car door like she owned it. A few young kids were riding bikes down the block, but that couldn't be helped.

There were three bags of food in the passenger seat. One of them was marked "Moretti". Her good fortune was holding. Kelly opened the bag, removed the carton of garlic chicken, and pulled a syringe out of her pocket. She quickly emptied the contents of the syringe into the chicken, anticipating that the strong spices and heavy garlic would mask the shrimp flavor.

The chicken was back in the bag, the bag back in the car and the car door closed before the teenager came around the corner, talking on his cell to someone at the restaurant, explaining that the address was wrong.

By the time he was back in his car, Kelly was on her way back to her stakeout position. The rest of the plan was in the hands of the gods… or, to be more exact, the hands of a pimply faced teenager and a spaced-out crack addict.

7:45pm. The riflescope sat a few inches back from a slit in the filthy curtains. Kelly watched as the teen delivered Angelo's food. She watched as the teen muttered what looked like "asshole" under his breath. That almost brought a smile to her face, but she was much too tense to find any humor in the moment.

Angelo's blinds were tilted open just enough for Kelly to observe him as he shoveled the chicken into his mouth, and then realize something was dreadfully wrong. She tracked him as he desperately lunged into the kitchen, ripped open a few cabinets and finally found the EpiPen.

She watched with no emotion as he jabbed the empty auto-injector into his thigh, over and over, followed by his face turning red from lack of oxygen.

She sat witness to him stumbling back into the living room, where he ripped the blinds off the window, smashed his face up against the glass and mouthed the word "help".

Kelly flinched for a moment when Angelo looked directly at her. It was reminiscent of the stare she got from his cousin Tommy when she'd spied on him from across a street. But that was a different street, a different time – and Kelly was a very different person.

As Angelo collapsed to the floor, Kelly closed the drapes. She'd wondered how she'd feel when this was all over. Relieved? Fulfilled? Remorseful?

She was surprised to find that she felt nothing.

71

Kelly spent Sunday in Golden Gate Park by herself. She ignored phone calls from Pete, Alexa and Benedetto, as she sat beside Stow Lake, eating a light lunch and watching a father and his daughter maneuver a pedal boat around a family of ducks.

She took a leisurely walk to the bandstand and listened to a rousing rendition of Aaron Copland's *Appalachian Spring*, before heading off to the Steinhart Aquarium, where she'd spent countless hours as a child. Kelly wandered around the cool dark building, letting her mind travel back to the wonderful memories of visiting the aquarium with her family. She successfully blocked out any negative thoughts and basked in the distant glow of happier times.

She was hungry by the time she left the park, so on the way home she stopped at Molinari in North Beach and picked up a variety of salads and a bottle of Prosecco. She'd felt her phone vibrate a few more times over the course of the day, and when she arrived home, she didn't bother checking the messages. She didn't want to break the serene mood of a lovely day.

Kelly set Spotify to "Acoustic Covers", laid out her feast, poured her wine and hoped against hope that the events of the past twenty-four hours would fade into the dark recesses of her mind. But she knew different. Regardless of how idyllic her day was, the memories of killing the Moretti cousins would stay with her forever.

That night, she went to see Diego. It had been five days since his operation and she'd already visited twice. Despite what Alma had said, Kelly still harbored guilt about Diego's infection and felt that the least she could do is swing by and bring him something to brighten his mood. Tonight it would be chocolate-dipped biscotti.

When she arrived, Diego was alone in his room, his eyes red and swollen. This time he didn't look away. In fact, he stared at Kelly like she was an apparition. "Dr Kelly?" His voice cracked.

"What's wrong?" she asked, as she crossed the room. "Where's your mother?"

"She had to work tonight."

"Is everything all right? Are you having any pain?"

Diego shook his head. "The nurse put medicine into my tube," he said, indicating his IV line. "I feel okay."

Kelly pulled up the chair and handed Diego the small white bag that held the Italian cookies. "I brought you this."

He accepted the offering without much enthusiasm. "Thanks." He placed the unopened bag on the table next to his bed. Clearly, something was troubling him.

"I spoke to the doctor, and he said you get to go home in a few days."

Diego nodded; a moment later, his eyes welled up. "I don't want to go home."

Kelly was perplexed. "Why?"

He sniffed, wiped his eyes. He needed to be strong. He needed to tell her. It was the only way.

"I don't want to be in the gang."

Kelly felt a stabbing pang in her heart. She knew this was incredibly difficult for him, and the real test would come when Oscar and the others started to apply pressure.

"Spider… he says I can still be in, even with one leg, but…" He just shook his head, the tears falling freely.

"Diego, you don't need to be in the gang if you don't want."

Diego's face reflected his inner turmoil. Why did he tell her? Dr Kelly was nice and smart, but she didn't understand. She couldn't know what things were like in the streets.

"I can speak to your brother if you want."

"He won't listen."

"I can be very persuasive."

Diego was intelligent for his age, but his blank look told her that he had no idea what that meant.

"I'm good at getting people to do what I want."

"Not Spider. He's… *terco*."

"Stubborn." Kelly smiled. "So am I."

Diego silently stared at Kelly for a moment. He had more to tell her and he was weighing the upside versus the consequences. For a boy of ten in a family full of gangsters, the opposite ends of this spectrum were extreme and potentially dangerous. Like, really, really dangerous.

Diego looked over at the closed door, then back at Kelly. He made his decision. "There's some stuff I gotta tell you before you talk to Spider."

She'd never seen him so serious. In fact, she couldn't recall ever seeing anyone so serious in her life.

72

Monday morning begged the question: would Kelly be able to return to work and face her staff like nothing had happened? Could she focus on her patients? How had her father been able to hide his alter ego so successfully and for so long?

Her first order of business was to call Dr Knudsen at St Francis and tell him that she'd decided to pass on his offer. She thanked him again for the opportunity, but she owed it to her father, and to herself, to give the clinic her full attention and see if she could make a go of it. He wished her the best of luck and told her to keep in touch. He also offered to put her in contact with the hospital's facilities manager so she could stay informed as to when they were replacing/updating their medical equipment (and looking to sell or donate their older equipment). Kelly hung up with a beaming smile on her face and a tear in her eye.

Once the front doors opened, the stream of patients was non-stop. It helped immensely to stay busy and not have time for her mind to wander places where she didn't want to go.

Shortly before lunch, she treated an elderly Asian man who complained of an excruciating pain in his lower abdomen. After taking x-rays, Kelly returned to the medical bay, where he was calmly waiting.

"Mr Wong. I found the problem." She affixed the x-ray up to the light box and there in his abdomen was the distinct outline of a key.

"Why didn't you tell me you swallowed a key?"

Mr Wong answered straight-faced, "It is undignified."

"And yet there it is in your small intestine. I'd ask how it got there, but the question is not how, it's why?"

"My wife wanted to take the car. I forbade it, but she insisted. She is small, but wiry and strong-willed. She is also a terrible driver." He shrugged. "What else could I do?"

The curtains parted and Annie leaned in. "Excuse me, Doctor. Dr Curtis is here to see you when you get a chance."

"I'll be right out." She turned back to Mr Wong. "You'll probably pass this in a day or two without any complications. I'd suggest taking a stool softener to loosen things up."

Mr Wong nodded. "Thank you, Doctor."

"I'd also suggest selling the car."

Kelly didn't look forward to dealing with Nathan. She was still angry that he'd abruptly abandoned them a week ago, but she softened somewhat when she saw the bandage over his swollen nose and his arm in a cast. "What happened to you?"

Nathan nodded toward the office. "Can we talk in private?"

Nathan closed the door behind him. Kelly motioned for him to take a seat, but he elected to stand. "First off, I'm sorry I left you in the lurch. I had some issues to deal with."

Kelly's response was edged with frost. "Nathan, I'm sorry for whatever happened to you, but I need someone that I can rely upon…"

"I know. I'm not here to ask for my job back. In fact, I'm moving away."

Kelly's iciness gave way to concern. "Is everything all right?"

Nathan allowed himself a smile. "That depends on your perspective. In the past week I came to realize that I didn't want to be a doctor. I only went to med school because my father pushed me to do something *important* with my life. I didn't have the balls to follow my heart."

"What changed? Does it have something to do with this?" she said, indicating his injuries.

"Indirectly. I came to tell you about what happened last week, and about how lucky you are to have a neighborhood full of people who appreciate you more than you know."

Kelly listened with rapt attention as Nathan recounted the events of the night when his father's men tried to burn down the clinic, and how Oscar not only stopped them, but also got Nathan to the hospital. He left out the part about how the Norteños beat the hell out of Burr and Junior.

When Nathan was done, Kelly was speechless. Here was a man who'd risked his life to save the very clinic that she'd essentially fired him from. "Nathan, I don't know how to thank you."

"You don't have to thank me for doing the right thing. I should've stood up to my father a long time ago."

"What happens now?"

"With me, or my father?"

"Both, I guess."

"I could go to the police and tell them everything. My father might be charged with attempted arson, among other things. Of course, his lawyers would work their magic and dear old Dad would get off with a slap on the wrist. But if it were made public, it would put a serious crimp in his business. Maybe even destroy him." Nathan smiled. "For the first time in my life, I have the bastard over a barrel. I like that feeling, a lot, so I'm just going to sit tight and see how things go. Meanwhile, I've raided my trust account and rented an apartment in Florence for a month."

Kelly smiled. "That sounds amazing."

"It'll give me time to get away from all of this and rethink my life, as well as my relationship with an abusive, overbearing asshole of a father. I never got to know your father very well, but I always envied your relationship with him. The love and trust were clear to see."

Kelly opened her mouth to respond, but then realized she didn't know what to say.

Kelly walked Nathan out and wished him the best of luck. She thanked him again for his part in saving the clinic. He said if she felt like getting away from it all for a while, his apartment in Florence had two bedrooms. She could even bring along her boyfriend. Kelly gave him a quick peck on the cheek and urged him not to abandon his future in medicine. He had a tremendous amount to offer and it would be a shame to cast it aside out of spite.

It had been an unexpectedly good day. Between her conversations with Dr Knudsen and Nathan, and the satisfaction she got from treating her patients, Kelly was feeling hopeful for the future. Perhaps it *would* be possible for her to compartmentalize the abnormal events of the past few weeks and consider them outliers. What happened with the Morettis was a complete and total aberration. It didn't define her and shouldn't weigh her down as she moved forward with her life.

Kelly believed she had the strength and discipline to focus on what was important and block out the rest. Jessica, the clinic, her relationship with Pete... that was her future (although the latter was going to be tricky). There was no reason for her to look back.

It was with those encouraging thoughts that she strolled through the night, headed for a rendezvous with Pete. If he got tied up at the station like he normally did, she'd grab a seat at the bar. Maybe Alexa would be there and they could share a glass of wine. If not, she'd treat herself to a glass of that top-shelf bourbon. She was looking forward to spending time with Pete, talking about anything other than his cases. She didn't want to hear any more updates on the Tommy Moretti case, and she definitely didn't want to know if the death of Tommy's cousin in Oakland set off any bells within the SFPD. All she wanted to do was have a wonderful dinner and maybe even talk about where the two of them could go on a holiday.

Kelly was fantasizing about a rental apartment in Florence. How great would it be to step out of your building and look up at the Duomo, or leisurely window-shop on the Ponte Vecchio? Her thoughts of Italy were so captivating that she never heard the person come up behind her.

The last thing she remembered was the intense pain of being clubbed in the back of the head.

73

Pete sat alone in the booth at 44 Degrees and checked his phone for the third time to make sure the sound was on. Still no message from Kelly. It wasn't like her. She'd call if she were running late. Since the death of her father, she'd been more distant, which was understandable. However, in the past week things had begun to get back to normal, or so Pete thought.

He was staring at the single remaining ice cube floating in his scotch when someone slipped into the seat across from him. He jerked his head up, expecting to see Kelly, and was surprised to find Alexa, a glass of wine in her hand. "Did my girl stand you up?"

Pete shrugged. "She probably got hung up at the clinic."

"Probably." Alexa took a sip of wine, then dived in. "Mind if I ask you a personal question?"

"Guess it depends how personal."

Alexa smiled. "Do you have something to hide, Inspector?"

"Doesn't everyone?" He took a drink, set down his glass and nodded. "What's up?"

"Is everything going okay with you and Kelly?"

"As far as I know. Why? What's she said?" Pete suddenly felt like he was back in high school.

"That's just it. She hasn't said anything. The past month has been really hard on Kelly and I worry about her, but she's not letting me in."

"I know how you feel. It's like she's built a wall to protect herself."

"Exactly! She's still mourning her father, but there's something more intense going on... gnawing at her from the inside. I tried to get her to open up, but whenever we get to a place where I think she's going to confide in me, she closes down."

"So, what are we supposed to do?"

"I don't know. Give her time, I guess. Unless you have a better idea."

Pete wrapped his fingers around his glass and swirled his drink, staring into the amber liquid, looking for answers. He slowly brought it up to his mouth and took a long drink, letting the blended malt smooth out his edges.

Alexa knew men, and Pete was clearly conflicted about something. So she was right! Pete and Kelly *were* having problems, but Pete was too macho to admit it and Kelly was too proud to ask for advice.

Pete broke the silence. "I'm not sure if it's a good idea or not, but I'm going to ask her to marry me."

Alexa almost spewed twenty dollars of Chardonnay across the table. "Tonight?"

He nodded. "That was the plan, anyway."

"Have you two talked about it before?"

"I've mentioned it a few times, but Kelly's never been ready to make that kind of commitment."

"What makes you think *now's* a good time? With everything we've just talked about, this could make her implode."

"It could, or it could be exactly what she needs. Reinforce the fact that I'm there to support her through whatever she's dealing with."

Alexa drank the remainder of her wine, set down her glass and ran her finger around the edge, producing a slight vibrating hum.

"Come on, Alexa. What do you think?"

"I think her head's pretty messed up right now, and that's a big question to lay on her. Having said that, you should do whatever's in your heart. Just don't hurt my girl."

"I'd never do anything to hurt Kelly."

74

Not everyone shared that sentiment.

When Kelly regained consciousness, the first thing she noticed was that she was tied to a heavy wooden chair in a large, dimly lit, musty room. The second thing she noticed was the throbbing ache in the back of her skull. She had no idea how long she'd been out or where she was. She also had no idea who attacked her or why.

She was literally and figuratively in the dark.

Tommy and Angelo were obviously out of the picture, but who else knew about her? Why would someone knock her out and imprison her in some abandoned building? The only thing she knew for certain was that this didn't bode well for her.

Her mouth was gagged with a cloth that tasted of dirt and oil. Her hands were lashed to the arms of the chair and she struggled with her wrists to test the bindings. There was a small amount of play, but not enough to wriggle her hands out from the coarse rope. Her feet were tied to the chair legs and raised slightly off the ground so she couldn't touch the grease-stained pavement with her toes. She tried rocking the chair back and forth, to no avail.

The fact that her confinement closely mirrored the way she had bound Tommy Moretti wasn't lost on her.

This didn't bode well for her at all.

Her eyes strained to take in her surroundings and she caught sight of her cell phone, or what was left of it, on the floor nearby. It looked like it had been through a wood-chipper.

Stray car parts were strewn about. A dented bumper was propped up against one wall. Over in the corner, a broken axle stuck out of a rusted brake drum. An engine block sat on a heavy wooden workbench next to a tool chest that was covered in grime and dust. It was either a defunct repair shop or the set of a low-budget horror film.

Who the hell brought her here... and why?

One of those questions was answered when a man stepped to the penumbra of the shadows. His approach was slow and tentative, as if he didn't want to risk revealing himself. She took this as a positive sign. If she never saw his face she wouldn't be able to identify him, which meant she had a chance of getting out of there alive.

That all changed a moment later when he awkwardly moved forward and the weak overhead bulb partially illuminated his face.

There was something familiar about him, but she couldn't place him. She saw so many people every day at the clinic that after a while their faces blurred into one. There was nothing distinctive about him. Average build, average height, dark brown hair. Nothing that would make him stand out in a crowd. That was, until he took another step forward and she saw that half of his face was shiny, like melted wax. But it wasn't wax… it was layers of scarring.

Kelly was stunned.

She'd been taken prisoner by the Hollow Man!

Pete left another message on Kelly's cell, reminding her that he was at the restaurant and asked her to call him when she was finished at the clinic.

He put down his phone and picked up the fresh drink in front of him. Alexa had invited him to join her and a friend for dinner, but Pete declined. Alexa felt bad about leaving him to twist himself into knots with his conflicted thoughts, but agreed with his assessment that he'd be lousy company.

The question was, how long could he just sit there? It wasn't the waiting that bothered him. It was the uncertainty of the situation.

As each minute passed he grew antsier, and his thoughts grew darker. There was no reason to believe anything was wrong, but Pete was a cop, and because of that he tended to look at life with a jaded point of view.

He would finish this drink and then head over to the clinic. He knew he'd arrive to find Kelly patching up a patient, a look of fatigued satisfaction on her face. She'd apologize for being late and he'd say "no problem". They'd lock up and head back to the restaurant, or maybe pick up some take-out and go to her condo.

That scenario brought a smile to his lips. He pushed the darker thoughts to the farthest corner of his mind and allowed himself to imagine a wonderful evening ahead. If everything went well, maybe he *would* propose to Kelly tonight.

Yes, it was going to be a fantastic night.

75

The night was rapidly going from bad to worse.

Kelly had no idea how long he stood there, staring. She'd never paid much attention to him when he came into the clinic ranting about how her father had removed his heart. Most of the time Ramona dealt with him, appeasing him the best she could, before sending him on his way. Kelly had only spoken to him once, trying to calm him down, but he had been too far gone for her to penetrate his deep-seated hallucinatory bluster.

Kelly remembered his eyes being wild and unfocused. Now those eyes were clear and penetrating and filled with pain. Kelly had seen the signs many times before; the stiff way he moved, the manner in which he tilted his head, the tightly pursed lips. This was a man who was physically suffering, but had the fortitude to forego medication and tamp down the pain as best he could. It was like watching a junkie going cold turkey.

"Do you know who I am?" he asked in a voice that sounded like tires rolling over a gravel road. It was clearly agonizing for him to speak and equally agonizing to listen to.

Kelly nodded.

"Who I *really* am?" he asked.

Kelly slowly turned her head from side to side as she made muffled sounds behind the gag.

The man inched closer. He walked with a slight limp and his shoulders were bunched up around his neck. He wouldn't give the outside world the satisfaction of seeing his anguish.

He reached out and Kelly noticed he was missing two fingers on his left hand. The skin was leathery and tight from scar tissue and his dexterity was limited. She wondered how he'd tied the ropes around her hands and feet, but it didn't matter. Nothing mattered except getting out of here alive.

She shivered as his hands brushed her face. For a moment she feared he was going to strangle her, but then she felt her gag being loosened. Before he removed the rag from her mouth, he cautioned her, "Scream, and I kill you." He didn't ask if she understood or would comply. It wasn't a question or request. It was a simple fact, and Kelly believed him. She vigorously nodded, and the filthy rag was yanked out of her throat.

She gasped, drawing fresh air into her lungs. Even though the garage was an incubator for dust mites and countless varieties of mold, she'd never tasted sweeter oxygen.

"You recognize me from the clinic," he stated.

Kelly measured her words carefully, knowing that any wrong comment might set him off. "You seem better now."

He swallowed and winced in pain. The words came out slowly. "Not better. Just not drugged."

"Certain pain medications can have drastic side effects; hallucinations, paranoia, confusion, memory loss…"

"That's why I stopped. I needed to focus. To know the truth."

"The truth?" she asked, treading on thinning ice.

"About who killed my father."

Kelly's heart sank. She didn't know who the Hollow Man's father was, but this turn in the conversation meant the ice beneath her feet was cracking.

"Your father? I didn't have anything…"

He shook his head. "Not you." He swallowed again, his features scrunching up in agony. "Gideon."

The blood rushed out of Kelly's face. She'd foolishly believed that her father's identity was known only by Tommy and Angelo Moretti. If word had spread, it meant she was in mortal danger.

The man stared at her. He was looking for a reaction, and he'd gotten one. He slowly nodded, then turned and disappeared back into the shadows, leaving behind a terrified Kelly, whose only questions now were how much longer would she live and how painful was her death going to be?

Pete finished his drink, checked his phone (still no messages) and stood up to leave. He glanced over at Alexa's table and saw that she was dining with an attractive, slightly older woman who exuded an air of authority and prosperity. Pete immediately recognized her: Deanna Frost, an ambitious, camera-friendly criminal defense attorney who'd represented the defendant in Pete's first homicide case.

The press had dubbed it "The Honeymoon Horror". Marcus Washington and Julie Stein had gotten married at the San Francisco courthouse on a beautiful summer day in August. They spent their wedding night at The Painted Lady, a quaint B&B housed in a refurbished Victorian in the heart of the Mission.

The next day, guests complained of a pungent odor coming from the Garden Suite. When the newlyweds didn't respond to the persistent knocking of the housekeeper, the manager used her passkey to enter the suite. She froze at the sight before her, then turned and projectile-vomited across the brand new carpet runner in the hallway.

The young mixed-race couple had been bludgeoned to death, their heads turned to bloody pulp.

The shocking nature of the case instantly made it international fodder. Locally, the case took on additional importance because Julie Stein worked for the President of the Board of Supervisors.

Pete and Ron were assigned the case, and a prime suspect quickly rose to the forefront. Leonard Bach was a proud member of the Aryan Brotherhood, and lived with his mother just two doors down from the hotel. Bach had recently completed a six-year stint at Corcoran for felony assault against three African-American men. Prison officials were unified in their assessment that any attempts to rehabilitate Bach were futile. It would only be a matter of time before he was back in the system.

The police recovered a short-handled, three-pound sledge from the dumpster in the alley next to Mrs Bach's house. There were no prints on the handle, but the blood and hair on the hammer were a match for the victims.

Leonard Bach was scooped up for questioning before he could pull a disappearing act.

Ron and Pete grilled him for hours. Bach had no specific motive for the murders, other than the blood oath he took to cleanse America by carrying out violent acts against minorities. Racially mixed marriages were at the top of the AB's list of unnatural acts that needed to be punished.

Bach had no alibi, except the word of his fifty-eight-year-old alcoholic mother, who claimed to have heard Len downstairs in his room all night, chanting along to H8Machine and Blood Red Eagle.

The police definitely liked Bach for the crime. He had *means* (the murder weapon was readily available at any hardware store); *motive* (his undying commitment to his fraternity of hatred); and *opportunity* (the murder took place less than a hundred feet from his house).

There was also the fact that Bach had worked a few days for a local contractor who did renovations in the Garden Suite at The Painted Lady. The owner of the B&B had given the contractor a key so his crew could come and go through the suite's exterior door without bothering the manager or the guests. It would have been easy for Bach to get hold of the key and make a copy for himself, which would allow him direct access to the room where the murders took place.

The only problem with the case against Bach was the police had no hard evidence that placed him at the scene that night, or linked him to the murder weapon. Despite pressure from City Hall for an arrest, and the entire Homicide detail knowing in their collective gut that Bach was guilty, the DA wouldn't prosecute without something more tangible.

The SFPD doubled their efforts and launched a massive search to find the store that sold Bach the murder weapon. It was a long shot at best, but one worth taking. Police and Inspectors canvassed everything from big box outlets to specialty hardware stores. Over a hundred and fifty three-pound sledgehammers were sold citywide in the last month, but no cashiers remembered making a sale to Leonard Bach.

No one, until Dwayne Murphy picked Bach out of a six-pack. Dwayne and his son Ja'von ran a small builders' supply store in the Oceanview neighborhood. They carried the brand and model of the sledge that was used to commit the murders, and Dwayne swore he remembered selling one to Bach. "It's not often that a man with a swastika tattoo on his neck shops in a store owned by African-Americans. When he does, it's a memorable occasion."

There was no record of the purchase, so all they had was Dwayne Murphy's word. Ron and Pete knew their evidentiary case was less than solid, but hoped the DA's office would get on board. If they decided to prosecute, the case most likely wouldn't go to trial for six months, and during that time Ron and Pete could dig deeper to hopefully find more solid evidence.

Based upon the sheer preponderance of evidence, Bach was arrested and charged with a double homicide. His case was fast-tracked and a short three months later he sat in a courtroom, dressed in a conservative gray suit and a shirt collar that covered most of his neck tattoos. Bracketing him at the defense table was a team of high-profile, high-priced lawyers who were being paid by a political action group called Southern Pride, which didn't hide the fact that they were a White Nationalist organization.

The case drew comparisons to the O.J. Simpson trial, except in reverse. Bach's defense was spearheaded by Deanna Frost. Tenacious, brilliant and extremely photogenic, she was the perfect choice to convince a jury that her client was a victim of police profiling based upon his past. Yes, he was a member of the Aryan Brotherhood, and yes, he had committed crimes for which he paid his dues. But, the DA's case was based on smoke and mirrors and lacked any substantive evidence.

She set her sights on what she considered to be two "soft" targets – Dwayne Murphy and Pete Ericson – and went to work.

Bach had testified that he'd never been in Murphy's store, and since it was impossible to prove otherwise, Ms Frost painted Murphy as a "well-meaning small businessman who had mistakenly identified her client as a result of pressure from the SFPD and the general feeling of indignation within the African-American community". While the prosecution countered, Frost's summation was difficult to challenge.

When it came to Inspector Ericson, Deanna took off the gloves. She highlighted the fact that it was the Inspector's first case, and she brought every minute detail of the investigation into question. Ms Frost relished taking a sharp razor to Inspector Ericson, and successfully planted the seed that in his eagerness to solve his first homicide case (and a very public one at that), the Inspector overstepped his bounds in pushing for an arrest. No new evidence had surfaced in the past three months, which in her mind made it all the more obvious that her client was not only innocent, but a shining example of prejudicial bias.

Deanna was a courtroom pro and Pete was a neophyte. After a few questions, it was clear he was no match for her, and once she smelled blood in the water, she relentlessly badgered him until the judge called it a TKO.

The trial ended in a hung jury. The SFPD and the DA's office took a public relations hit and Leonard Bach was free to walk the streets. In fact, he sued the city of San Francisco for false arrest and defamation of character. However, the case was dropped three weeks later when Bach was killed in a shootout between the Nazi Lowriders and the 415 Kumi Nation.

Pete came away from the trial wiser and calloused. He knew what everyone knew, that Leonard Bach committed the murders, but Deanna Frost had played the system and played him. Pete vowed to never be played again. From that point onward, he became a hardliner; he wouldn't quit investigating a case until he was convinced that a suspect was either guilty or innocent. If that meant his record of closing cases would suffer, so be it. He wasn't walking into another courtroom without knowing that his investigatory findings were bulletproof.

This philosophy had served Pete well since then and gave him a reputation among defense attorneys as an extremely tough nut to crack.

Pete wasn't eager to see Deanna Frost again, but the table where she and Alexa were dining sat squarely between him and the door. He thought about sneaking out the back, but he was a decorated member of the San Francisco Police Department... he had his pride. Fuck it.

As Pete passed by their table, Alexa gently grabbed his wrist. Pete feigned surprise. "Did you hear from her?"

Pete shook his head. He didn't want to prolong any part of this. "I'll meet her at the clinic."

Alexa nodded, then motioned to Deanna. "Do you know...?"

"Counselor," Pete said without a hint of a smile.

"Inspector," Deanna responded with an open and friendly face. She carried no animosity, but why would she? "I haven't seen you in court lately."

"My arrests haven't been high profile enough to whet your appetite."

Deanna smiled. "I'm still getting business from the last one."

Pete couldn't help himself. "You mean you're still defending racist murderers who…"

Alexa leapt in before it could get ugly. "So, you two *do* know each other." She turned to Pete. "Good luck with everything."

"Thanks." With that, he turned and calmly walked out the door.

"What the hell happened between you two?" Alexa asked Deanna.

"He was inexperienced, I was on the rise and saw an opportunity for an easy kill. I took it." She took a drink, then, "Is he still single?"

Alexa did a double take. "Are you serious?"

"Why not?"

"Weren't you sitting here a minute ago when that cold front came through?"

Deanna shrugged. "I'm not looking for anything permanent."

"Deanna, I respect the hell out of you, but when it comes to Pete Ericson, you're completely tone deaf. He's in a relationship with my oldest and dearest. In fact, there's an excellent chance they'll be engaged by the end of the night."

Alexa had no way of knowing, but the chances of Kelly and Pete getting engaged at the end of the night were infinitesimal… and getting smaller with each passing second.

76

The Hollow Man reemerged into the light with a knife in his hand. This wasn't something he happened to find lying around on a dust-covered workbench. It was a Strider, a US military-issue weapon with a glistening nine-inch titanium blade that looked like it could slice through steel with the flick of a wrist. Kelly didn't want to imagine what it could do to flesh.

"I can help you," she said. "Get you proper medication. Put you into a program to deal with the pain and…"

He held up the knife menacingly. "We were talking about Gideon," he rasped.

Kelly stared at the blade. She had a frightening image of him suddenly lunging and swiping at her throat, severing her jugular with a single stroke. Her focus on the knife was so intense, she didn't hear him when he asked, "Do you know him?"

Kelly looked up to his face. It reminded her of a doll she'd accidently left near a bonfire on the beach one summer. The next morning she retrieved her doll, only to find that one side of its face had been turned into waxy slag.

The Hollow Man caught her staring and leaned in closer. "It doesn't look human, does it?"

There was no right answer to that question, so Kelly remained silent.

"Do you know Gideon?" he asked again, this time with an undercurrent of threat.

Kelly was at another critical crossroads. She surmised he was aware of Gideon's identity, or she wouldn't be tied to a chair about to die. Sticking with the truth was her only course of action.

"I only found out a few weeks ago… after my father's death."

"Gideon brought pain to my family. To me."

It suddenly dawned on Kelly. "When you said my father removed your heart, you were talking about the emotional pain you suffered."

He nodded. "When I found out he… he was Gideon, and that he'd killed my father…" He shook his head, trying to find the right word. "Revenge. I promised revenge."

"Why do you think my father was responsible?"

"My cousin told me."

Kelly felt like someone had just walked across her grave. She barely had enough strength to utter, "Your cousin?"

The man looked at her silently, prolonging the agony of the moment, then acknowledged what Kelly feared. "Tommy Moretti. Do you know *him*?"

Kelly shook her head. Now was the time to lie. "No."

He tilted his head, weighing her response. "How about my brother? Angelo?"

Kelly had no response. His cousin? His brother? Who the hell was this guy? Angelo didn't have a brother. Not one that was still alive.

The Hollow Man saw the emerging awareness in Kelly's eyes. "I had one week left in Afghanistan. We were sent on patrol." He held up his maimed hands, motioned to his scarred face. "Ambushed. Seven died. The troop left me, thought I died, too. It took three weeks, but I finally made it out."

"Anthony Moretti," Kelly whispered.

He nodded. "So you *do* know me. And you *do* know my brother and my cousin… and that they're both dead."

Kelly shook her head. "No! I have no idea what…"

Anthony sprung forward. Kelly's scream was abruptly cut short when the Strider was pressed up against her throat. She froze, knowing that if she as much as swallowed, the razor that lay across her jugular would slice into her tissue.

"Lies. Tommy told me about you. How he was drawing you in. You killed him, then Angelo."

Kelly didn't dare a response. There was no way out of this. At least death would be quick. Tears ran down her face, falling on Anthony's deformed hand and glistening on his waxy skin.

His face was almost touching hers. "*I* killed your father. I stole the car and ran him over. I was wearing Tommy's jacket, which is how they got onto him, but it was me."

It all made sense now. Unfortunately, it was too late. Kelly had killed the wrong man, which in turn had set the balls in motion. Now she was paying for her actions. Paying for her father's actions.

"Jessica...," she said through the tears. Anthony looked at her, a question in his eyes. "My sister. Please..."

Anthony backed up, drawing the knife away from Kelly's throat. He looked offended. "Revenge. Gideon. You. Then it's over. No more killing."

Kelly nodded, weeping harder. "Thank you."

She'd just thanked this man for *only* killing her. The sheer absurdity of it gave her strength. She stopped crying, closed her eyes and took a deep breath. She wasn't ready to die, but there was no way out of this.

It was her time.

When Kelly opened her eyes, Anthony Moretti was gone.

77

Pete walked the two miles from the restaurant to the clinic. He wanted time to think. As a bonus, he'd see if there were any new murals in Balmy Alley. Ever since he was a child he'd been fascinated by the colorful works of the myriad street artists in the Mission.

Pete was midway through the alley when three bangers stepped out in front of him. They were boasting the scarlet of the Norteños and, as such, felt they owned this territory. In a sense, they did.

It was rare for Pete to be confronted on the street. It was inevitable in an urban area, although most street hoods didn't target men unless they were desperate. Women and older people were much easier prey.

Pete remained calm. He knew that the moment he pulled back his coat to reveal the gold shield clipped to his belt, the would-be muggers would turn and sprint in the other direction.

Not this time.

The three bangers stood their ground, as did Pete. He glanced back over his shoulder to see two more approaching from behind.

Pete held his hands away from his body and announced in a loud, clear voice, "SFPD."

Another Norteño stepped out from a darkened doorway. Pete recognized him as Spider. As he walked toward Pete, his posse slid in behind him.

"Word is you been looking for me, Inspector."

"I was. I wanted to talk to you about the Sureños that were killed."

"Some Scraps got smoked? Don't know anything about that."

"Really? Joker and Sad Boy?"

"Oh, yeah. I heard something about Joker, but I don't know anybody named Sad Boy." He turned to his posse. "Any of you know a *culero* named Sad Boy?" Unsurprisingly, they all shook their heads and muttered "no". Spider turned back to Pete. "Never heard of him."

"It turns out they were both killed by Nano Rojas."

Spider smiled, nodding his head. "Cool. We love it when the sewer rats clean up their own shit. Saves us from having to take out the trash, you know?" The bangers exchanged high-fives.

Pete tried a little fishing expedition. "You know anything about a house over by Garfield Square getting shot up last week? We've got a witness who saw a black Impala drive away from the scene. Isn't that what you drive?"

Spider shook his head. "Behind the times, homes. Used to roll in an Impala, but now I got an '08 Suburban. Gray. Sweet rims. Sometime I'll give you a ride. Lots of room in the back to stretch out."

"Do what you can to quiet things down. I'd hate to see another kid like Diego catch a bullet for no reason."

"You know us. We stay chill, take care of our own business. Not looking for a beef."

"Good. Take care, Spider."

The gang parted, creating a lane for Pete, who continued down the alley. "You take care, Inspector," Spider called after him, parroting his words. "And take care of Dr Kelly. There's some bad shit going down out there."

Pete stopped. When he turned back, his face was flushed with anger. "What do you mean by that?" he asked, his voice rising.

Spider shook his head. "Easy. Dr Kelly is *familia*. We look out for her. You should, too."

"Are you talking about the break-in last week?"

"Just sayin' there are some Blancos in the Mission lookin' to stir up shit. Gotta be, what's the word…? 'Vigilant'."

"Thanks for the heads up, Spider. I'll be vigilant."

Pete had no idea what Spider was talking about, but when he turned back around, he hastened his pace, anxious to get to the clinic.

Kelly heard Anthony before she saw him. He was grunting with effort. She tried to remain calm, but the sounds coming from the darkness sent chills down her spine. The suspense of not knowing was worse than knowing. That was, until she smelled the gasoline.

When Kelly finally caught sight of Anthony, she watched in horror as he splashed fuel on the walls and the workbenches. Gas puddled on the concrete floor, reflecting tiny shimmering rainbows of color.

"Don't do this. Not fire," Kelly pleaded.

Anthony went on with his work like he didn't hear a thing.

"Please! You'll burn down the whole block!"

"Fire is very... cleansing."

"You're not like your cousin or your brother. You're not cruel." Kelly's pleading shifted into panic. "You want revenge, fine. Kill me. Use your knife!"

Anthony shook his head. There was an untold sadness about him, as if he really didn't want to do this, but felt compelled to carry out the deed. "Death brings pain. Pain to the dying, but more to the living. Yours will be quick compared to those you leave behind."

Kelly was desperate to keep him talking. She knew Pete had been waiting for her. By now he'd be worried and would go to look for her. She had no idea how he'd find her... *she* didn't even know where she was. But the longer she could put off the inevitable, the greater the chance that someone may come to her aid.

"Anthony. Listen to me. It doesn't have to be like this!"

"Wrong. This is how it ends."

Anthony upended the can and poured the remainder of the gas over his head, drenching himself in fuel. Kelly was stunned.

With gasoline running down his face, he reached into his pocket and took out a Zippo. With the other hand he pulled the Strider out of his belt.

"NO! Anthony, don't do it!"

Anthony had played out this scenario in his mind a dozen times. Nothing was going to stop him.

He flipped open the lighter, thumbed the wheel and a bright yellow flame leapt to life. Kelly screamed louder than she knew was possible, but to no avail.

Anthony dropped the lighter at his feet and an instant later drew the razor-edge across his throat. There was an infinitesimal moment where his eyes met Kelly's, then he collapsed to the floor, engulfed by fire.

Kelly screamed again, this time even louder.

But the result was the same.

There was no one to hear her cry.

78

The clinic was dark, the doors locked. Pete went around the back and saw that Kelly's car was there. She must've walked to the restaurant while he was dealing with Spider and his boys in Balmy Alley.

Pete tried her cell number. It went directly to voicemail. She probably forgot to turn her phone back on after leaving work. He pulled up Alexa's number and tried her. Same result... directly to voicemail. Of course; her phone would be turned off while she was in the restaurant.

Pete thought about calling the restaurant, but he was being paranoid. He imagined Kelly sitting at the table with Alexa and Deanna, having a glass of wine. It brought a smile to his face. The night wasn't exactly going as planned, but he was still confident it would end with Kelly saying "yes".

"NO!" she screamed. "Oh, my God, NO!"

She was in hell. The fire was quickly spreading to the rest of the garage and the stench of burning flesh was searing the inside of her nose.

Kelly might very well die here tonight, but she wasn't going down without a fight. As the smoke rose, she looked around. There had to be a way out of this. She desperately yanked and twisted her hands, trying to free them from the rope bindings, but they held fast.

The smoke got heavier, making it difficult to breathe. She'd probably succumb to smoke inhalation before the flames reached her, but that was little solace. Kelly's eyes watered and her throat was parched. She fought the urge to cough, knowing if she did, she'd suck scorching, noxious air into her lungs.

Maybe she should just give up. Accept the reality that there *was* no way out. No one was coming to her rescue. Why fight it? She'd brought this on and she was getting what she deserved. Wasn't she?

And then she saw Anthony's knife lying on the floor just outside the pyre that fed upon his gas-soaked corpse. She had an idea. It was a longshot, but she had to do something.

Kelly started bucking, trying to rock the chair. If she could manage to make the chair fall sideways at the correct angle, there was a chance, however remote, that she could get hold of the knife, then possibly inch the blade up through the rope. It wasn't a great idea. It wasn't even a good idea, but it was all she had. Especially since the flames were rising higher and the smoke was getting thicker.

She swayed her body back and forth in a controlled rocking motion and the chair legs gradually began to lift off the floor. Kelly felt a tiny sense of hope. She was now confident that she could get the chair to topple over, but would it fall in the right direction?

If it fell away from the knife, she was finished.

The rocking momentum increased. Unfortunately, so did the fire in the garage. Time was running out. Kelly was treading a thin line between increasing the intensity of her efforts and making certain that when the chair gave way to gravity, it fell to her right, in the direction of the knife.

The flames hit a cache of oily rags in the corner and flared up in a fiery ball of intense heat.

Kelly had no choice but to give it all she had. One more body thrust and the chair would tip over toward the knife. As she threw her weight to the right, the chair went along with her and was on the verge of toppling over, when gravity betrayed her. She seemed to hang in midair, leaning over toward the knife, when the chair swung back in the other direction.

"NO!"

Her momentum carried her to her left, and suddenly she was falling. There was nothing she could do as the concrete floor rushed up to meet her. The chair smashed into the floor, leaving Kelly ten feet from the knife. It might as well have been a mile.

It was over.

From this angle, Kelly saw a thin trail of gasoline inches from her face. Once it caught fire, the flames would scream toward her like a blazing freight train.

She instinctively bucked, inching the chair so at the very least her face wouldn't be in line with the rivulet of fuel. A jolt of pain shot up her arm when her hand hit something rough sticking straight up from the floor. She blinked several times to clear her eyes of tears and saw that she'd hit a rusty bolt that was permanently fixed in the concrete. A remainder of some heavy equipment that had been screwed into the floor.

Using every ounce of strength she had left, she began sliding her bound wrist up and down, scraping the rope against the bolt. The screw threads slowly ate away at the rope. It was working! But would she have enough time?

Kelly redoubled her efforts, a newfound hope driving her into a manic state of determination.

The muscles in Kelly's arm and wrist felt like lead and cried out for the brain to send more oxygen. But oxygen was growing scarce as the smoke in the garage got thicker. Kelly could no longer see through the dense cloud of toxic carbon, tar and oil particles. She limited herself to tiny sips of air, hoping she could free her hand before she was overcome.

She was getting seriously light-headed. It would only be another minute before the smoke rendered her unconscious. Kelly used one final burst of adrenaline, feverishly rubbing the rope up and down. Up and down. Up and... then the bolt scraped the skin off the outside of her wrist! Her hand was free!

Kelly operated sheerly out of instinct as she used her free hand to inch herself forward. It took near superhuman strength to drag herself and the heavy chair across the floor until the Strider was finally within reach.

The blade was scalding hot and her hand instantly blistered, but she never even felt the pain. She was too focused on the Herculean effort needed to cut herself free.

The knife was as sharp as she'd imagined, and within moments she had sliced through the ropes. As she struggled to her feet, the trail of gasoline caught fire and the flames raced toward her.

Kelly blindly fled as fire licked at her heels. She stumbled through the smoke, and blessed her luck as she found the door, ripped it open and staggered into the frigid night.

311

The onrush of fresh air fed the hungry fire and a moment later something in the garage exploded. The incendiary blast shattered the front window of the dry cleaner's across the street, set off a cacophony of car alarms, and filled the evening sky with a shower of glowing embers.

By the time the embers floated to the ground, Kelly was halfway down the street, limping away from the scene as quickly as her burned and battered body could take her.

79

When Pete reentered the restaurant, he spotted Alexa and Deanna sipping cappuccinos. Kelly wasn't at the table, nor was she sitting in their usual booth.

According to Alexa, Kelly never showed up. She'd assumed that Pete had met her at the clinic and the two of them had gone to one of their places for the night. Pete tried Kelly's cell once again, and once again she didn't pick up.

He stood in silence, wondering what he should do now. Kelly had been acting strangely the past couple of weeks, and hadn't accounted for her occasional absences. In fact, when pressed, she insisted he didn't have to worry about her, and she didn't need to check in with him every moment of every day. She'd assured him with a smile that she wasn't cheating on him. Sometimes she needed time to herself. She hoped he understood.

He did, but this was different. This was setting off distant alarms. And just then, a fire truck sped past the café, lights flashing and horn blaring. The alarms were no longer distant. Logic told Pete that a fire in the city, even one this close by, had nothing to do with Kelly. But then, why did he have a sinking feeling in the pit of his stomach?

Pete sprinted out the door and ran down the sidewalk, chasing after the fire truck like a Dalmatian.

He arrived at the fire ten minutes later. He badged the uniformed cops who were setting up a perimeter. The lead firefighters were already drenching the burning building with water.

Pete found out the business had been an auto repair shop that closed down last year. Fortunately, the shops on either side stood empty, as did the stores across the street (with the exception of the dry cleaner's, which would need a new plate-glass window).

The fire was still raging, and given the potential of combustible materials, there was the threat of more flare-ups, so no one had access inside the garage. It would be at least an hour before the fire crew could work its way inside to conduct a search. One thing was for certain: there'd be no survivors.

On that depressing note, Pete had no recourse except to wait and pray that the crew didn't find the charred remains of the woman he loved.

Finally, he was given the go-ahead to enter the repair shop. Meanwhile, across town, Kelly was sitting in the corner of her shower, water cascading over her, washing blood, soot and tears down the drain.

After she'd gotten home, she'd stripped off her clothing and inspected her scrapes, cuts, bruises and burns. Once she determined that everything was relatively superficial (except for the angry burn across her right palm where she'd grabbed the searing-hot knife blade), the enormity of what she'd just gone through overwhelmed her. She relived the evening in fast-forward from the moment of waking up in the chair to stumbling out into the night. The images were etched into her brain, especially Anthony lighting himself on fire and slitting his throat.

That would haunt her nightmares for years to come.

Kelly didn't remember walking into the shower, or, for that matter, turning on the water. All she could comprehend right now was that she was alive. Her past was behind her and her future was riddled with uncertainty.

There was enough left of the incinerated corpse to determine it wasn't Kelly. The police forensics lab and the fire department arson investigator would do their best to identify the body and to fill in the blanks as to what happened, but for now Pete had the answer he needed.

He checked his watch. It was past midnight. Time flew when you were having a night from hell. He had so many questions: Where was Kelly? Did she forget their date or did she purposely blow him off? Why was her car at the clinic? Why wasn't she answering her phone?

As Pete watched the fire crew put out the last of the hot spots in the garage, he couldn't shake the thought that destiny had cruelly delivered him to this spot to reveal a physical manifestation of his relationship with Kelly. It was at times hot, at times smoldering, and perhaps now, in ashes.

Pete checked his phone one last time. No calls.

He shook his head at his audacity to think that it was a good time to ask her to marry him. He hoped that giving her something to look forward to would strengthen their relationship and help Kelly weather her emotional storm, but upon further reflection, it was more likely to drive her away. What she needed was time. She'd let him know when she was ready to take the next step.

The best thing he could do was to tie up all the loose ends of the David Harper and Tommy Moretti cases. Hopefully, that would put Kelly's mind at ease.

Pete had no idea that in diligently carrying out his investigations, he wouldn't be putting Kelly's mind at ease.

Far from it.

80

Kelly suffered through another sleepless night. Her body begged for rest, but her mind never got out of overdrive, recounting over and over every moment in that garage. Her temptation to down a few Valium was overruled by her need to be clear-headed. She hadn't begun to process the things she'd learned last night from Anthony Moretti and what the ramifications might be. How many other people knew Gideon's identity? Had Benedetto gotten out the word that the hit on Angelo was done by Gideon? If so, would that misdirect be effective in signaling that Gideon was alive and well?

She needed to meet with Benedetto one last time. She'd been led to believe there were no more loose ends, and that belief almost got her killed. Where was Benedetto getting his information and why didn't he know about Anthony? Or worse yet, if he did know, why hadn't he told her?

Kelly made two calls from her house phone: one to Benedetto to set up a meeting, and the other to Vik to let him know she'd be late (again). Both men were amenable and said they'd be happy to accommodate her.

She had one more call to make, but she didn't know what to say to Pete about last night, or, for that matter, about anything. He'd be worried about her, which seemed to be a constant theme these days. In this instance, he'd have reason to, given the fact that she didn't show up or even call him last night.

Kelly reluctantly dialed his number, and her shoulders untensed when she got his voicemail. "Pete, it's Kelly. I'm so sorry about last night. I was headed to the restaurant when I suddenly got really nauseous. I thought I was going to die." She paused, wishing she hadn't said that. "I caught a taxi home and spent the night in the bathroom. I'll spare you the details. Anyway, sorry again that I didn't call. Let's talk later."

She hung up and stared at the phone. It was getting easier and easier to lie.

An hour and a half later, Kelly was seated across from Benedetto, greedily finishing a flaky palmier from Arsicault Bakery and a double cappuccino. She craved the sugar and caffeine, and after second helpings of both, she was finally able to quell the frayed electrical connections inside her brain.

As always, Benedetto was the model of calm. She'd told him on the phone that she urgently needed to speak to him, but it was apparent she had to get her thoughts in order first. Hence, the nourishment. Once Kelly's eyes were clear and her hands stopped shaking, he bade her to tell her tale.

It took a full thirty minutes for Kelly to recap the night, beginning with waking up in the garage to breaking down in her shower. Benedetto stopped her a few times to ask questions ("What were his exact words when he referred to your father?" and "Did you leave anything behind that could place you at the scene?").

Benedetto assured her he'd get an update on the status of the fire, including the forensics and arson reports. This gave Kelly the opportunity to question the veracity of the intelligence he was gathering.

"Your information has been sketchy, and it almost got me killed... twice. You said that Tommy Moretti killed my father, which turned out to be wrong. You said that Anthony Moretti had died overseas. If I'd have known he was alive, I could've taken some kind of precautions," she said with an edge of anger and exasperation. "As it was, I took revenge on... murdered, the wrong man and then was almost cremated!"

Benedetto took a sip of water, then gently placed his glass down. "I understand your frustration. It's frustrating for me as well. Let me say a few things. The information we collect from the street is often embellished by sources that are looking to make a buck or garner favors. Over the years, I've gotten quite adept at weeding out the bullshit and getting to the truth. In the case of Tommy Moretti, I had several reliable sources tell me that he was taking credit for the death of your father. Either he was trying to protect Anthony, or, more likely, he was looking to bolster his street cred in the right circles. When you combine that with the police findings, I felt rather certain that he was driving the car that struck your father.

"You feel bad that you killed Tommy, but as you yourself discovered, he was onto you and Jessica, and was planning on killing you both. So while you didn't gain vengeance from his death, you accomplished your primary objective, which was to protect yourself and your sister.

"As far as Anthony's concerned, I have no explanation. The United States Army listed him as killed in action. There was no record of him resurfacing anywhere in the country. He had no driver's license, no credit cards, had never applied for a job or rented an apartment. He was invisible. I realize that's no excuse, but I hope you can understand how he escaped our attention. He simply no longer existed."

"Except," Kelly said, "to kill my father and then try to kill me."

Benedetto nodded. "There are a lot of dangerous people out there, and most of them are under the radar, walking around in daylight, working at your local shops, eating at McDonalds, taking their children to soccer practice. Even the ones who do have driver's licenses and credit cards and jobs and houses, have secret lives, some of them incredibly dark. Try as we might, no one can know when a person is going to snap, buy a rifle and shoot up a school or a movie theatre. Similarly, no one could predict that the brain-addled homeless man who came into your clinic ranting about your father cutting out his organs was actually the KIA son of a mob boss looking for revenge."

Kelly's anger abated. Benedetto was right. There were a lot of evil people hiding in plain sight. She was one of them. "I hope Anthony was telling the truth when he said 'this is how it ends', and that the vendetta is over," she said.

"All I can tell you is that Arthur Moretti only had two sons, and Tommy was his only nephew. I highly doubt anyone else in the organization was aware of Tommy's hypothesis that Gideon was your father, because Tommy wanted that reward money for himself. Also, we've planted the information that Angelo Moretti's death was a Gideon hit, so that should put an end to any speculation to the contrary. There is one other thing."

Kelly took a deep breath and slowly exhaled. Despite herself, she even felt a small twinge of a smile. "Of course there is."

"A week ago, two men attempted to set fire to your clinic."

"I know all about it." For once, she was ahead of Benedetto. "Nathan Curtis risked his life to save the building."

Benedetto nodded. "I mention this because you never know who your enemies are, and who's watching your back."

Kelly sat quietly, taking it all in. The incident at the clinic had nothing to do with Gideon, or the Moretti family. It was purely a case of greed and malicious business.

There was no question that society was plagued by countless evil people.

The question was, what, if anything, was she going to do about it?

81

Kelly had gotten word to Oscar (she couldn't bring herself to refer to him as Spider) that she needed to see him. A twelve-year-old boy dressed in low-slung blue jeans, an oversized red T-shirt and a red bandana waited for her outside the clinic and gave her a time and place. She noticed that the boy hadn't even started shaving yet.

Oscar was in Clarion Alley, leaning up against a mural of a heart decorated with a banner that read "we're all in this together". Oscar had a flair for the dramatic, as well as armed bangers on either end of the alley to ensure his safety.

Kelly began by thanking him for protecting the clinic and for taking Nathan to the hospital. Oscar nodded and repeated to her what he'd said to Pete. That she was *familia*. Which provided her with a perfect segue.

"Diego comes home tomorrow," she said. "He's going to need time to recover and adjust to his new way of life. It's not going to be easy."

"Why are you telling *me* this?"

"Because you're the closest thing he has to a father. You need to protect him."

"I always do," Oscar said, his ire starting to rise. "No one messes with my bro."

"Except when he's working as a lookout and catches a stray bullet."
Oscar shrugged. "The price of wearing the colors."

"That's what I wanted to talk to you about. Let Diego go."

"Go? Go where?"

"Don't force him into the gang."

Oscar scoffed. "Force him? It's who he is."

Kelly shook her head. "It doesn't have to be."

"You're talking crazy. Diego loves the gang. He's proud to be a Norteño! Just like me, and our brothers."

"You're wrong. I spoke to him. He wants out."

"Bullshit! You been filling his head with this fucking *chorradas*?"

"No. He asked me to talk to you."

Oscar shook his head in disbelief. "Why didn't he tell me himself?"

"He's afraid to. He looks up to you and he doesn't want you to be disappointed in him."

"So he acts like a *chavala* and begs you to do his dirty work?"

"See what I mean? That reaction? That's why he's afraid to talk to you."

Oscar was getting increasingly angry with Kelly's attitude. "Dr Kelly, you've been very good to my family, but this is none of your fucking business."

Kelly felt herself getting flushed. It was time to lay her cards on the table. "Diego told me about Joker and Sad Boy."

Oscar's face went slack. There was no way his brother would've betrayed his trust.

Unless he was desperate.

Oscar shrugged. "What about them?"

Kelly glanced at both ends of the alley to make sure they were still out of earshot of anyone else.

"You found out that Joker was the one who shot Diego, so you killed him. What you didn't know was that Sad Boy was hiding in the alley and saw the whole thing. When you heard about that, you killed him as well."

"That's bullshit, and you know it. I even spoke to your boyfriend. He told me those Scraps were killed by someone in their own gang."

"That's bullshit, and *you* know it. Your brother Rodrigo in Pleasant Valley Prison, made a deal with an inmate named Chico Romero. Chico convinced his brother Eddy to lie to the police about how Nano was the gunman. In return, you paid off Eddy in firearms to be smuggled across the border to Mexico.

"Eddy leaked the same lie to Payaso, who'd been looking for a reason to take out Nano. In the end, it worked out well for everyone, except the three dead Sureños."

Oscar knew this could've only come from Diego. No one else knew the whole story. His own blood sold him out, and for what? So he could go his own way? How was he planning on getting by if he didn't have the gang? What fucking good was a one-legged Mexican anyway?

"So, you got this fairytale. What do you plan to do with it?"

"Nothing, as long as you respect Diego's wishes."

Oscar seemed to ponder this for a moment, then responded in kind. "You know, I got a story, too. It's about this *guera* who came to me for heroin. *Puro*, and strong as a horse. The next day I hear about this dealer who ODed on heroin. My heroin. I'm thinking it could be an accident, but this woman, she was messed up. Like someone had been beating on her or something. And one other thing, she knows her way around a needle because she's a doctor."

Kelly's blood was racing. Even though they were outdoors, it was hard to breathe.

"I could be wrong, but I think she may have killed this motherfucker on purpose. I don't know. And, of course, I'd never say anything to anyone, because I know how the game is played."

He leaned in close and uttered, "*Comprende?*"

Kelly nodded.

"I'm glad we understand each other, Dr Kelly. You have a good night, okay?"

She watched as Oscar headed down the alley. Her heart was beating fast and her head was spinning. The only coherent thought she could latch onto was that she'd just broken her promise to Alexa.

She had made a deal with the devil after all.

82

Pete was at his desk when Ron arrived with a forensics report from the fire. Since no actual murder took place, it wasn't their case, but Homicide was part of the Personal Crimes Division, which also handled arson. Since Pete was the first inspector on the scene, he became a tangential part of the investigation.

"Don't we have enough cases of our own?" Ron asked, as he tossed the report onto Pete's desk. "We don't have time for this arson bullshit."

"There's nothing for us to do. Bibble is keeping me in the loop out of courtesy."

"Courtesy, my ass. Bibble is an overweight, lazy dickwad who wants to spread the blame when he screws this up. Congratulations for stepping directly into his shit, partner. And by the way, forensics didn't come up with squat."

Pete smiled. "So you read their report?"

Ron shrugged. "I was en route to the crapper when Bibble handed it to me."

Pete scanned the initial findings, which were meager at best. Most of the analyses were pending, as particle testing took time. The bottom line was: the accelerant was gasoline, the igniter appeared to be a common Zippo lighter (with no inscriptions) and there was one fatality. The officer who wrote the report didn't want to officially speculate on the cause of death without further evidence, but there was a Post-it note attached to the back page that read, "Victim appears to have slit his throat with a Strider knife that was found at the scene."

"Slit his own throat?" Pete uttered.

Ron nodded. "This motherfucker definitely didn't want to leave anything to chance."

"Why would someone set themselves on fire if they were just going to cut their jugular?"

"When are you going to listen to what I've been saying? There's no logic behind stupid! If you could get inside this moron's head, you'd find a vast, empty space. Maybe cluttered with a few dumbass thoughts about life and death. Maybe some vague memories about being abused as a child. Don't try to figure it out. Just chalk it up to 'stupid is as stupid does' and move the fuck on."

"Did I ever tell you how inspiring you are to work with?"

"I can see it in your eyes every day," Ron grinned. "It's the only thing that keeps me from cashing in my twenty-year chip and moving to Palm Springs."

"What the hell would you do in Palm Springs? You don't play golf, you don't like the heat, and you're not particularly fond of old people."

"I can get a condo for like 250Gs and then cruise for wealthy, naïve widows. Find myself a sugar momma with a new set of tits."

"I hope the three of you will be very happy." Pete gestured back to the report. "Says here the victim used a Strider. That's a serious military-issue blade. Maybe he was in the service."

"Or maybe he bought it at a surplus store. Or stole it from some homeless guy. I'm telling you, if you spend more than the time it takes for one good bowel movement on this case, you're not the brilliant Inspector I brag about to all my friends."

"What friends?"

"See, that's just hurtful. No need for that kind of stuff." The phone on his desk rang and he answered. After a moment of listening and grunting a few affirmative responses, he hung up. "That was one of many friends, who happens to work for the Oakland police department."

"Oakland?"

"It's a little city on the other side of the bay."

"Thanks. Why'd he call?"

"First of all, it was a she. Tight little Hispanic chick with an amazing ass. Unfortunately, she loves her husband, who used to play linebacker at San Jose State."

"What'd she have to say?"

Ron tapped a file on his desk. "Your favorite case? Tommy Moretti?"

Pete sat up straighter. "Yeah? Is this about his cousin?"

Ron nodded. "Angelo Moretti. This boy genius was highly allergic to shellfish, so what'd he do? Chowed down on some Chinese takeout that had shrimp in it. Throat closed up and he asphyxiated himself. Chalk up one more for this year's Darwin Awards."

"Tommy dies of an overdose, and a week later, his cousin dies from an allergic reaction."

"Sometimes the world is a beautiful place and shitty things happen to shitty people."

Pete grabbed the Moretti binder and flipped through it until he found what he was looking for. "Angelo's father Arthur died a few months ago from a heart attack caused by faulty electrical wiring."

"That family was born under a bad sign."

"Either that or…"

"Or what? Someone is running around knocking off people and making it look like accidents or suicide?"

"You know about those rumors…," Pete began.

Ron stopped him cold. "The mysterious underworld hit man? I don't want to hear about it. It's an urban myth, like the fuckin' Yeti. Everyone claims to 'know somebody who knows somebody who knows who he is', but it's total bullshit. To even mention it is beneath you. If the other guys heard you talking about it you'd embarrass us both. Now, can we do something productive? Like go to lunch? I'll drive, you buy."

Ron grabbed his coat from the back of his chair and headed out.

Pete shrugged on his jacket and grabbed up his phone. He'd listened to Kelly's message four or five times, wondering why she was lying. After spending years interrogating perps and witnesses, he had a very refined bullshit-detector. The question was not only why she lied, but what part of the message, if any, was the truth?

He considered returning her call, but that might lead to a confrontation, which would only serve to inflame an already fragile co-existence. Besides, he had other things on his mind and didn't want to be distracted from trying to figure out if/how the Moretti deaths fit together.

He knew if he could connect the dots there would be a revelatory payoff in the end.

83
(David's Journal)

This won't be an ordinary entry because the circumstances of this contract were anything but ordinary.

The target was a young woman named Hope Miller. A stunning brunette who was a senior at Kentucky Wesleyan University in Owensboro, Kentucky. KWU is a Methodist college with less than eight hundred students.

Hope was raised in Edgewood, Kentucky; one of the wealthiest cities in the state. Her father, Calvin Miller, owned a large commercial real estate company and sat on the Governor's council of economic growth. Her mother was the "lay leader" at the local Methodist Church, "serving as a role model of Christian faith in daily life" (according to Google). Hope was an only child and was doted on by her parents. She wanted for nothing and her success in life was destined. Head cheerleader, student body president, prom queen... they were all a given.

She chose Kentucky Wesleyan, partly due to her mother's urging and partly because she cherished the idea of being an orca in a tiny pond. It didn't take long for Hope to establish herself as one of the shining stars on campus, favored by her professors and longed for by all the males in school.

It turned out that Hope wasn't quite what she appeared to be; she had a deep-seated yearning to break out of the small-town, pampered-rich-girl persona. She craved a walk on the wild side, and soon found a like-minded partner in Larson Hobbes.

I didn't need to look far to find background information about Hobbes. His story dominated the news last year, after he shot and killed twenty-three students (and two teachers) at a Daviess County middle school. He spared the state the cost of a lengthy incarceration when he used his final bullet on himself.

Unlike many mass murderers, Hobbes didn't post nihilistic diatribes on social media or leave behind notebooks packed with satanic drawings, swastikas, or horrific "to do" lists. Authorities never found a reason why Larson Hobbes targeted that specific school. They did the usual round of exhaustive interviews with Hobbes' friends (of which there were very few), former teachers, his grandmother (who raised him) and, of course, Hope Miller.

The news outlets loved her. Beautiful, wealthy, from a solid Christian family. Her tale of getting caught up in Larson Hobbes' web was straight out of a paperback romance novel. According to her, Larson exuded an irresistible magnetism and she fell victim to his outré charm (the press fell all over themselves equating him with Charles Manson).

Hope swore she knew absolutely nothing about Hobbes' plans to go on a killing spree. After hours of questioning, the police affirmed her story. She was an innocent who had no information and no involvement in the incident. If anything, she was a victim as well, and she received hundreds of sympathetic letters of encouragement (and several dozen marriage proposals).

The 'Middle School Massacre' soon faded from the news cycle, as did Hope Miller. She was finally able to get back to a somewhat normal life at KWU.

When Benedetto contacted me with this contract, I was intrigued. I vaguely remembered the name Hope Miller, and certainly recalled her face, because she reminded me of Jess. Same hair, same slim build and same winning smile. That was one of the reasons my initial reaction was to pass on this job. There was no way I could bring myself to do harm to my daughter's doppelganger.

That was until I found out what Hope Miller had done... or worse, what she was about to do.

A phone rang. Kelly was shaken by the sound and momentarily confused, and then realized she hadn't programmed her old ring tone into her new cell phone. She glanced down at the screen and saw Pete's handsome, chiseled face. She felt a twinge of irritation at being disturbed while she was in the middle of reading her father's journal, but she shook that off.

She still hadn't spoken to Pete and he deserved better. But not right now. She let the call go to voicemail, then got up to refresh her wine glass.

After an uneventful day at the clinic, she'd come straight home, pulled together a meal of leftovers, and sat down to do something she'd put off... to read the remainder of her father's journal.

The entry about Hope Miller was his penultimate entry. Despite everything she'd been through in the past few weeks, she continued to have an extremely difficult time wrapping her head around the revelation of her father's past. Even after killing two people herself, none of it seemed real.

She owed it to her father to finish reading what he'd left behind. After all, it was meant for her. Even though the tales of death sickened her, there was an undeniable fascination to the stories.

Kelly had decided that after she'd read this last entry, she'd destroy the journal. She couldn't run the risk that these admissions of guilt could end up in the wrong hands, which were anyone's other than hers.

Pete was still at the station. Not because he had anything meaningful to do, but because at nine-thirty on a Tuesday night he had no place else to go. He'd finished his shift an hour earlier, and the thought of going out to dinner alone was too depressing. He knew if he went home he'd distractedly watch TV, finish off the bottle of Cutty Sark that still had a good four inches left, and stare at his cell phone.

Instead, he sat at his desk, drank a cup of scalded coffee and absent-mindedly picked at a stale egg sandwich from the vending machine. He couldn't bring himself to look at the Moretti binder one more time, and the David Harper murder book had revealed nothing new after a dozen reads.

He contemplated his current situation. An Inspector on the rise, he was well liked by his commanding officers, his closure record put him in the top ten percent across the city, and, most importantly, he hadn't made any enemies in the department. Getting on the bad side of the brass was the quickest route to a transfer to the outer precincts, which was only one step removed from becoming a citizen and working private security at Oracle Park.

The personal side of his life was much more complicated. He didn't know where he stood with Kelly. They'd always enjoyed an open and honest exchange of ideas and dealt with relationship issues by discussing them. There was never any rancor or sulking. They never parted angrily. They'd talked long into the night about a future together, but never made any specific plans. Pete had always assumed they'd settle down together.

He no longer made such assumptions.

He grabbed the Moretti binder, more out of habit than desire. This case was going to taunt him until he was satisfied he'd answered all the nagging questions. Who was the mysterious brunette? Was Tommy alone when he ODed? Was the overdose a suicide, an accident, or had it been administered by someone else? And the big question was, did Moretti's death have anything to do with the deaths of the rest of his family and/or the murder of David Harper?

As he flipped open the binder, his phone rang. He smiled, assuming it was Kelly, but instead the call screen announced that it was Victoria from the forensics lab. Strange. Pete didn't have any cases that were waiting on forensics.

Victoria explained that Inspector Yee had suggested she follow up with his contact at the Oakland PD regarding the death of Angelo Moretti, in the event that something out of the ordinary arose.

She did, and it had.

They'd run tests on Angelo's last meal of spicy garlic chicken. The results showed a very high concentration of shrimp stock in the food. Oakland PD followed up with the restaurant, and the manager adamantly stated that they never used shrimp stock when preparing non-shellfish dishes. Which meant that either someone in the kitchen accidently screwed up...

"Or someone intentionally put it into the food," Pete said. "And the only reason to do that would be to trigger an allergic reaction."

Victoria agreed "One other thing. Angelo attempted to inject himself with an EpiPen, but it was out of serum. Chances are he'd already used it once and forgot to replace it, but if you want to go all conspiracy theory, someone replaced his EpiPen with one that was empty."

"In which case, we're looking at a homicide," Pete said.

He thanked Victoria for the update, and leaned back in his chair. First thing in the morning he'd take a drive to Oakland and personally check in with the officer in charge of the investigation.

Now, he was going home to take on that bottle of Cutty.

84
(David's Journal)

Benedetto presented me with evidence that strongly indicated Hope was behind the Middle School Massacre. While she obviously wasn't the one who pulled the trigger, she'd driven Larson Hobbes to commit the deed. Charles Manson <u>was</u> embodied in their relationship, but in the form of Hope Miller.

She'd kept a notebook (a scan of which Benedetto had obtained), allegedly written in her hand, outlining the details of the shooting; a roadmap for Hobbes to follow. After the killings, Hope celebrated in prose the deaths of twenty-five people. The notebook was rife with years of built-up anger and hatred. If the notebook was authentic, Hope Miller was a bad seed. A female Damian Thorn. A shiny apple on the outside, rotten to the core on the inside.

That wasn't the worst of it. In the notebook she bragged about her newest "recruit" (her word, not mine). Travis Balinger fit the mold of Larson Hobbes: low IQ, low esteem, and malleable as warm clay. She listed three potential targets: two elementary schools and a daycare facility. The question was, "why?"

Benedetto's tech wiz dug deep to find the reason, but came up empty. Hope never had a bad day in her life. No humiliating experiences. No grudges against teachers. So again, why target schools? And why young children? The answer lay amidst the increasingly incoherent ramblings in the notebook. The younger the victim, the greater the social outrage and the societal pain.

I asked the obvious questions: who found the notebook? Why wasn't it turned over to the police? Had it been authenticated? Benedetto provided the answers: Hope's roommate found it, copied it and returned it. The roommate was a rawboned girl named Claire Hemphill, who hailed from a rural town in eastern Kentucky. She was a devout Christian who always had a smile on her face and a bible passage on her lips. She and Hope made an odd pair, but maybe that's why they got along so well.

When Claire found the notebook, it scared her half to death. After she copied it, she immediately took leave from school and showed the notebook to her parents. They in turn gave it to a local reporter who'd written several stories about the original Middle School Massacre. The reporter made a digital copy of the notebook, then presented the hard copy to his editor. And that's where the story essentially died.

From what Benedetto could piece together, the editor had a private conversation with the Lt. Governor. If this notebook was authentic, it would send tremors throughout the state, because Cal Miller had a lot of influence around the Capitol, not to mention having made very generous contributions to the Governor's re-election campaign. The Lt. Governor allegedly contacted the local FBI field office, and they deemed the notebook a fake, written by Ms Hemphill in a perverse attempt to take the haughty Hope Miller down a few pegs. (Despite this conclusion, the Lt. Governor covered his backside by personally contacting the targeted schools mentioned in the notebook and advising them to beef up their security.)

The notebook was officially discredited and after that, no one in law enforcement or the media would touch it. It was destined to be filed along with countless other sensitive documents that 'never existed'.

The reporter, however, had other ideas. Since he'd covered the tragic shooting, he was familiar with the parents of the victims. One father had been extremely outspoken regarding the dearth of answers in the aftermath of the massacre. The reporter took the digitized notebook to him.

The father believed in the notebook's authenticity. He knew he wasn't going to get any traction with the press, so he took matters into his own hands. He happened to work for a large liquor distributer, and a few of the upper management types had "connections", so he went to them for help.

Phone calls were made, contacts were established, and the father was finally put in touch with a person who "knew of a guy". The request arrived on Benedetto's desk, along with a digital copy of the notebook. If the things in the notebook were true, there was no telling when Travis

Balinger might be walking into an elementary school with an AK47 and creating more terrifying headlines.

I agreed to fly to Kentucky to observe Hope Miller for a few days. I trusted my instincts. If she showed no signs whatsoever of psychopathic tendencies, I'd come home. If, on the other hand, I felt she was the epitome of evil that the notebook indicated, I'd take the contract.

I spent a week in Owensboro. After observing Hope for two days and getting a sense of her schedule and rhythms, I stepped up my surveillance. She went for a sixty-minute run every morning at 5am through a densely wooded area that bordered the University. On day three, I entered her room and hid a tiny video camera in a light fixture.

Another few days went by. I watched and listened, but Hope showed no hints of being unbalanced. In fact, I was impressed by how diligently she studied and how generous she was with her time and money. She was quick to pay for things ranging from pizzas for her study group to a few cases of beer for an upcoming coed softball game.

I may have been biased, because seeing her in real time I was again struck by how much she reminded me of Jessica. I had to push those thoughts out of my mind and evaluate Hope for herself, but I found it difficult not to give her the benefit of the doubt.

By day seven I was ready to come home. Hope may have been a murderous puppeteer, but nothing I saw convinced me of that. I declined the job. If I was wrong, it would be the biggest mistake of my life. But if I was right, and Hope was being set up by Claire Hemphill, then I wouldn't be able to live with myself if I killed this intelligent young woman who had such a wonderful future ahead of her.

Kelly's heart was pumping fast. She feared she knew where this was going. If her suspicions were right, she couldn't begin to imagine how it affected her father. How he could go on and pretend that nothing happened. She had to keep reading…

Benedetto took my decision in stride, completely understanding my reasoning. He had no emotional investment in the contracts. He appeared to get no satisfaction from the results. I believe he saw it as some kind of civic duty or public service.

Weeks went by and all was quiet. I read the news every day from Kentucky, and there were no incidents. I'd made the right decision about Hope, and thought about how close I came to snuffing out the life of someone else's daughter.

Then one morning I got a call from Benedetto to turn on CNN. They were reporting on a deadly shooting at an elementary school in western Kentucky. Eighteen children were dead and seven were injured. The shooter took his own life before the police could do it for him. I was stunned. It wasn't one of the schools on the list from the notebook, but it had all the earmarks of the Middle School Massacre. What had I done? Or rather, what could I have stopped?

Later that day the shooter's identity was shared with the public: Khalid Nozari. It was immediately labeled an act of terrorism and the cry for revenge echoed from Frankfort, Kentucky, to Washington, DC. The fact that Nozari was American-born and had no ties with any terrorist groups didn't matter. People didn't care about the facts. They needed an enemy, and here was one that was tailor-made.

The perfect scapegoat.

Hope Miller had chosen well. I know it was her doing. My theory is that she got word, maybe from her father, that someone was trying to frame her with a ridiculous account that she was behind the Middle School Massacre. Hope laughed it off, but in reality what she'd done was shift gears. Travis Balinger was now a liability, and the schools on her list were too hot to attack. So Hope picked up a new recruit, a Muslim no less, and accomplished her goal: a public outrage, the likes of which almost equaled that of 911.

It turned out I wasn't the only one who came to the conclusion that this tragedy was the work of Hope Miller. Two days later, while on her morning run, she was shot and killed. There were no witnesses and the assailant was never caught. Her death made big news in Kentucky, but the rest of the country didn't have the time or interest to mourn the murder of a college coed. They were too busy focusing on the escalating rhetoric coming out of Washington about how America wouldn't sit by idly while terrorists came onto our soil and slaughtered our children. There was even talk about bombing strategic targets in the Middle East.

And all of this could have been avoided.

I'm only one man, and I know I'm not responsible for the actions of anyone else, certainly not for the heinous acts carried out by psychopathic serial killers. Having said that, I can't help but feel the yoke of judgment and inaction.

When I killed Clarence Musselwhite, I felt as if a huge burden was lifted off my shoulders. The burden to avenge the death of my wife and the injury to my daughter, not to mention the pain and suffering Kelly and I endured. There was a strange dark elation that came along with Musselwhite's final breath.

The seventeen people I have killed since then brought me no sense of joy. They were abhorrent individuals who had done terrible things to innocent people and they deserved death, but the vengeance was for others to celebrate. I firmly believe that over the course of my work as Gideon, I've saved lives and spared future victims from heinous acts of cruelty.

The case of Hope Miller was unique. It was the first time I had the opportunity to stop a mass murder. If I had killed Hope, would Khalid Nozari have ended up shooting those children? Perhaps, but it's highly unlikely. If someone would've killed Hitler before he rose to power, would another anti-Semitic dictator have risen to power and killed six million Jews? Perhaps, but it's highly unlikely.

What I take away from this experience is that what I do DOES matter. I'll continue to be extremely selective about my targets, but I've come to the conclusion that I have an important, if not critical, role in the grand scale of things. I haven't developed a God Complex and I'm not suggesting that I'm any more significant than the other seven and a half billion people on this earth, but I truly believe that in today's society, with its crumbling morals and rising conflicts, Gideon is needed more than ever.

Kelly closed the journal, tears running down her face. Was her father a killer or a hero? Can someone be both? Is it possible to consider murder pro-social?

She had read her father's journal cover to cover and now held it in her hands, staring at it, wondering. Should she shred it, should she keep it locked away, or, perhaps, should she use it to record future exploits of Gideon?

Would she take that next step?

EPILOGUE

Two weeks had passed and the painful after-effects of the events that followed David Harper's death were finally beginning to ease up. Kelly had no illusions about her life ever returning to what it had been, but she was hopeful time would heal at least some of the emotional wounds.

The clinic was still struggling, but the influx of money from Benedetto helped tremendously, as did the fact that Dr Krishan Danabalan was working for minimal wages (although Kelly did convince him to accept a slight increase in salary). Also, Dr Knudsen made good on his promise to put Kelly in touch with the hospital's facilities manager and St Francis had already donated three "slightly used" multi-parameter vital sign monitors to the clinic. They were a much-needed upgrade, and the price couldn't have been better.

As the final patient of the night was leaving, Alma and Diego entered. Diego looked uncomfortable on his temporary prosthetic, but his face brightened when the staff gave him a warm and boisterous welcome.

Kelly emerged from her father's office and broke into a smile.

"Diego. How're you feeling?" Kelly asked.

"Okay," he said shyly.

"He is doing very good," Alma said. "The doctors say they are happy with his progress."

"That's great news," Kelly said.

Diego shrugged. "My knee hurts all the time."

His mother chided him, "You'll get used to it."

Diego didn't want to 'get used to it'. He hated it. He hated being a cripple. He hated being different. Kelly read his face and knew what might brighten his outlook.

"I just remembered. We have something here that belongs to you."

Diego was puzzled. "Me?"

"I'm pretty sure," Kelly said. A moment later, Annie came out with a long flat box wrapped in gift paper.

Diego had no idea what it was, but that didn't matter. What ten-year-old didn't love presents?

Annie laid the box on one of the beds and Diego looked at his mother for permission. Alma shrugged. "Dr Kelly says it's for you. Open it, *mijo*."

Diego ripped off the paper and prised open the box. When he peeked in, his eyes lit up, then started to tear up.

"*Que es?*" Alma asked.

Diego pulled out a high-tech prosthetic with a carbon steel blade on the bottom.

"A blade! It's so cool!" Diego squealed with delight. He turned to Kelly. "It's just like the one you showed me in that video!"

Alma looked at Kelly with wonder. "It's too much. We can't..."

Kelly took hold of Alma's hand and smiled. "The doctors and nurses here wanted to do something for Diego. It's our pleasure."

"You've already done so much for us."

"The doctors at St Francis did the real work."

Alma shook her head. "They nursed him to health, but you saved his life."

"I only...," Kelly began, before Alma cut her off with, "I know what goes on in my family, doctor."

Kelly blanched. She wondered exactly how much Alma knew.

Alma drew Kelly into a hug. "We are *all* one big family, you know? And family needs to watch out for each other, *mija*."

Kelly decided not to try wading through that cryptic statement. If Oscar had told his mother about their agreement, Kelly was in serious jeopardy. But she highly doubted he'd confess his multiple sins to his mother.

Alma turned to her son. "*Diego, no tienes algo para Dr Kelly?*"

Diego stopped marveling at his new blade and pulled a folded piece of paper out of his pocket, which he handed to Kelly.

She opened it to find a pencil sketch of her face. It was incredibly lifelike. On the bottom of the page, 'Thank you' was scrawled in incongruously bad handwriting.

"Diego, this is beautiful." She meant every word, and he knew it. Diego blushed and looked away.

Alma beamed. "I told you. This one has a future."

Kelly smiled. "I think you're right."

It had been two weeks since the fire in the auto repair shop. In that time Pete had seen Kelly twice; once for lunch and once for drinks. Both times were very cordial. He still didn't know if their relationship was off or on, primarily because neither did she.

After their last "date", they agreed to spend a day together the following weekend. Lunch in the park, followed by dinner some place nice in the city, maybe one of the trendy new restaurants springing up in the Mission. Pete took that as a good sign. He loved Kelly and thought she felt the same, but the events in the past month had taken a major toll and created a chasm between them that was proving difficult to cross.

The case binders on his desk were accumulating a layer of dust. The search for Tommy Moretti's "mysterious brunette" proved fruitless, and by now the trail was ice cold. The Harper case had become an afterthought within the department, since their official position was that it had been solved. Pete had vowed to himself, and to his partner, that if nothing new turned up in the next few days, he'd move the binders into storage.

The police in Oakland had also come up dry on the Angelo Moretti case. They'd interviewed the employees at the restaurant, the ex-delivery boy, and any neighbors who would talk to them (none had seen anything suspicious). The facts pointed to Angelo being poisoned, but there were no suspects and no one really cared if the case went unsolved. Angelo Moretti was nothing but dogshit on the bottom of an old shoe. He wouldn't be missed, and was quickly being forgotten.

Pete was at his desk, Googling local restaurant reviews, when he got the call. It was Bibble in Arson. "The lab ran the DNA on the briquette in the garage," he said in between bites of something crunchy. "Guy had no criminal record, but some over-achieving Poindexter in Forensics cross-checked the results with military records because of the Strider knife and everything."

"And?" Pete was starting to get anxious. Somewhere in his well-trained gut he sensed something was about to turn his world on end.

"The pile of ash was a guy named Anthony Moretti."

"Anthony *Moretti*?" Pete wasn't expecting *that*.

"Yeah. The Army made the lab double-check because they'd listed him as killed in action a couple of years ago. Got caught in an ambush in Afghanistan. Fucking Army. Keep worse records than us. Anyway, the guy must've been suffering from PTSD or some such shit to set himself on fire like that."

"You're sure the last name is Moretti?" Pete was still reeling.

"Yeah. I'll send the file over."

Pete sat back in his chair, letting the incredulity of the moment spin around in his brain. Another Moretti, another strange death. Even though this one was *clearly* suicide, it was one too many coincidences.

This threw doubt on everything. The Harper Case, Tommy Moretti and Angelo Moretti. They were connected somehow. They had to be.

And Pete wasn't going to stop until he figured out how.

Early the next morning, Kelly drove out to Colma.

She was finally ready to have a long talk with her father.

CPSIA information can be obtained
at www.ICGtesting.com
Printed in the USA
LVHW091626160121
\76650LV00004BA/41